SECRET TEDDY SOCIETY

BREAKING THE CODE

By

J.S. GILMORE

For permission requests, write to the publisher.
JSG Inc. 1044 Mann's Hill Road, Littleton, NH 03561

ISBN - 978-0-9848772-6-3

Library of Congress registered 2012

Acknowledgments

The support from family and friends is almost a given when one branches out on their own, but sometimes support can come from complete strangers that believe in what you're doing. This has been the case for the Secret Teddy Society.

I would like to thank everyone that has helped make this book a reality through their gracious acts of support and generosity: Kirsti Jespersen, Wilber Van Scoik, Bill Agresta, Hugh Hendrix, Win & Elaine Dermody, Jonathan Lane, Joe Pasquarelli, Danielle Bennett, Razi Rashid, Ms. Mulyono and Amanda the doodler. Your gestures of support have been truly humbling.

To my family for their unwavering support and constant encouragement. The light of day was merely a gleam that flickered through the window curtain while my family lived just outside the office door. Breakfast, lunch and dinner felt more like visiting hours, but their understanding and help was, and is, immeasurable.

My mom and dad helped make sense of it all; life, and how it worked (and didn't, sometimes) Encouragement, reassurance, help and support were never questioned; the answer was always 'yes.' This book is a reflection of my family and the love and loyalty that comes with it. The love you give is always returned. Sometimes words can't express all that you feel, so I will simply say, Thank you.

Contents

SECRET TEDDY SOCIETY
Breaking the Code

PROLOGUE

THE BEGINNING

The incarnation of the first teddy bear came from the unified love and acceptance of a nation in 1902. While on a hunting trip in Alabama, the President of the United States, Theodore "Teddy" Roosevelt, refused to shoot a cornered and injured black bear. The word of his compassion spread rapidly across the land. There was a popular cartoon depicting the President with a cute black bear on a leash. Magazines and newspapers flooded the country with the popular characters, generating more affection for the story. A toy maker created a stuffed bear that he called Teddy's Bear and presented it to Theodore Roosevelt. This action, unassuming as it was, created an event that neither science nor logic could explain — life from love. The overwhelming collective love of a nation gave birth to the phenomenon that did not stop at the first stuffed bear called Teddy. The toy bear went into production to fill the insatiable demand. There were all types of stuffed toy bears, different sizes, shapes and colors, but one thing made them all the same, their name. The name was the identity. The identity was the compassion. The compassion was the love and the love became life. Life became — the Teddy Bear. As a human hugged and loved their bear, awareness was born. Human contact was key. Now aware of their human families, it took many years before the first teddy took its first breath. Breathing brought movement and sensation. As time went on more bears were learning this ability and began teaching other bears how to "wake". Stories of teddy bear movement were legend but the tales never ended well for neither bear nor human. This unexplainable existence created such turmoil in the human world that teddies instinctively stopped moving. It was for the best of both worlds. The Teddy Code was created and a Teddy Council formed for protection to both humans and teddies alike. The Code would be the fabric of coexistence between the two cultures. There were documented events of such interactions between teddies and humans but those documents have since gone missing, erased from history. The stories are still around, but they are — just legend.

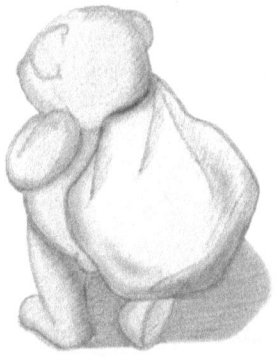

BALLINGER'S SECRET

Nothing like this had happened before, not in the history of the Secret Teddy Society. D needed to get word to the Council immediately, and he must do so without being seen.

He was breathing heavily as he ran through the streets of the old Georgetown neighborhood. Because there was no moon, it made the night darker than usual. It was difficult to avoid the illumination of street lamps when taking the faster more direct route. The best strategy was to stick to the shadows and hide in bushes. Nevertheless, D's intelligence was urgent; he could not afford to take all the obvious precautions. The discovery he had made was far too important; time was of the essence.

A large blue satchel bounced on D's shoulders as he skipped over curbs and splashed through puddles. The auburn colored teddy slowed to catch his breath. "Wait up!" Lyle shouted, lagging farther and farther behind.

Lyle was an Insider teddy who had just left his family — something that was all but unheard of in the teddy world. The little brown bear with his stubby little legs and a red ribbon tied around his neck knew they needed to hurry, but surely, a rest wasn't too much to ask. "Can't we stop for a minute?" Lyle called out.

D reluctantly ducked into the hedges and set the blue satchel down. When Lyle caught up, he was exhausted. He bent over with his paws on his thighs. "Thanks for stopping," he gasped. "I don't know how you do it; how you can run so fast with that heavy bag flopping around on your shoulders."

He had enough on his mind. D had just performed an unauthorized Teddy Nightmare on a human named Louis Longley, a powerful Washington politician, and what he had uncovered was so disturbing that he was having a hard time comprehending its implications. He didn't need anything else to go wrong tonight and having an Insider slowing him down was getting on his nerves.

D's raspy voice was tinged with exhaustion, "If you're going to tag along then you need to keep up. And take that red ribbon off your neck, it's very seeable."

Lyle quickly reached for his neck and placed a paw on the ribbon as if he were protecting it. "But this was Marie's. She gave it to me. She's gone now and this is all I have. I can't take it off."

There wasn't time to argue. D needed to set a few things straight. "You're outside now. This is my world. When my family no longer needed me, I joined the Rough Riders. It is the purpose of the Rough Riders to maintain a teddy communications network and look after Insiders like you. That's what we do. And right now, I have — we have — extraordinary information that needs to get to the Council immediately — if not sooner. They must know what Senator Longley is doing. But — we won't be able to deliver that information if we get caught because someone sees that red thing around your neck, so take it off! Hold it in your paw or something, I don't care."

Lyle reluctantly pulled the tie end, and it fell from his neck into his paws. He was crestfallen. He felt as if he had somehow betrayed Marie. He looked sadly at the ribbon, then, rolled it up in his paw clenching it tightly as if life itself depended on it. Lyle was not going to lose it.

He didn't mean to sound callous, but D didn't have time to be delicate. "Let's get moving. It's just around the corner."

D hoisted the blue satchel over his shoulder and gave Lyle a sympathetic look. It wasn't much, but it did help. D understood how hard it was for Lyle to leave his family. Typically, a teddy takes on the characteristics of his human and their milieu without particular consideration. It just happens. However, in Lyle's case, he made a personal decision to leave because he could feel himself changing into something he didn't like, something that Louis Longley and his bear Ballinger had become. They were driven by power and greed, character traits that sometimes accompany easy success, especially in the world of politics.

Once Louis Longley set his sights on the Presidency of the United States, nothing stood in his way of fulfilling his ambition. His oldest friend was Ballinger, a grizzled, dark brown, bristly haired, teddy who sat in Louis' private office at home and watched the political machinations of self-serving greed. Teddies learn by mimicry, by watching and copying, and Ballinger had learned from the best — or was it the worst?

Needing to continue to the Council, D turned to step away from the bushes and onto the unlit sidewalk when Lyle quietly asked, "Was that your friend — the one in there?" He tilted his head toward the blue satchel over D's shoulder. D paused for a moment, holding his emotions in check, before he answered: "His name was Audie. He was my best friend . . . and the best Rough Rider there ever was." D cleared his throat, his voice filled with fury, something that is uncharacteristic of a teddy, and roared, "Why was Longley destroying good teddies? How could a human do such awful things? I don't get it." It was too much to comprehend. D wanted his friend back.

The last time D and Audie spoke, Audie mentioned having a lead on the bears that had gone missing, important bears. He had revealed Louis Longley's name. After that, Audie disappeared. D had mentioned the coincidence to Bullock, the STS Chief Marshal, but was told to keep out it.

Angry and frustrated, D found out where this Longley person lived and secretly performed a Teddy Nightmare to get some answers. D got his answers and more. He found the missing teddies; they were in Longley's closet torn to pieces and stacked in a pile. D was devastated at the sight of his best friend, Audie, lying on top. In addition, as if that weren't enough, he discovered that Ballinger, a Teddy Council bear, belonged to Louis Longley. This knowledge changed everything. This had to be more than a coincidence. D had to inform Chief Marshal, Bullock, of his suspicions. Perhaps he might even have an opportunity to inform Theodore himself about the Ballinger-Longley connection.

D stared blindly at the ground. He couldn't shake the feeling that something big was about to happen, something that would shake the teddy world to its very foundation. He turned to Lyle and asked, "How well do you know Ballinger?"

"Ballinger? You can't know Ballinger. Not really," Lyle replied. "He's always in the office. I didn't see him much. Why?"

"Nothing. Never mind," replied D, sorry that he had spoken aloud.

"You think Ballinger knows what's going on?"

"Forget it. Never mind. Forget I asked."

"I don't really know him. Marie placed me on the bed every day while Ballinger sat in Louis' office."

"I said drop it."

"*No you didn't*. You said '*forget it*,'" exploded Lyle in frustration. "Well, guess what? I can't forget it. Maybe you can, but I can't. I said some terrible things to Ballinger before I left. I don't think he'll forget that. If he ever caught up to me, what do you think he'd do? And, if you think he might be involved in what Louis was doing then he's a very dangerous teddy." Lyle paused thoughtfully. "I got out because I didn't want to become like him. Yeah, I broke the Code. So, what now? I know you have to report it, that's your duty. But I broke the Code to save myself. What about me? What about the one? If the one doesn't matter then how can the many? Like you, I have no human connection. My human is dead. Marie *was* my family not Louis — and *certainly* not Ballinger." Lyle unleashed a burden of pain and loneliness he'd carried for the last year. Marie had been everything to him, his *raison d'etre*. However, when she died in a tragic automobile accident, Lyle's only relationship was with Louis and Ballinger and that dark and gloomy house.

The bears stood silently appraising each other, coming to terms with what they had to do. D broke the silence, "We need to get going." Lyle nodded in agreement, and they left the safety of the hedges.

At Council headquarters, D and Lyle stood outside the large pristine grounds of Hallow Oaks Manor, a historic home and museum in the Georgetown neighborhood of Washington D.C. A brick wall, overgrown with ivy, surrounded the gardened property. An old wooden guardhouse that was no longer in use stood near a seldom used side walkway entrance. Inside the guardhouse, under loose floorboards, was a secret passage leading directly into the basement and the Teddy Council. The passageway was peculiar in that it didn't appear to be designed for human travel. It was much too small.

D was nervous, a rare emotion for him, but he wasn't at all sure how the news of the night's proceedings would be received. And what about Lyle? What was he to do about him? He looked at Lyle with consternation. If he brought him with him to the Council, it would be flaunting a disregard for the Code. It was a serious dilemma for D. It is always dangerous to leave an Insider outside. Insiders don't know how to protect themselves alone outside in the dark with humans roaming about.

"I have no choice. You have to stay out here," D said, looking around for cover for Lyle. D pushed the satchel as far into the ivy as possible and pulled a few limbs and leaves around it. With their backs to the wall and buried in the ivy, they were invisible to humans who weren't paying attention.

"Just keep tucked in here and don't move. You'll be fine."

Lyle could feel his body begin to shake in trepidation at the thought of being left alone outside.

"You won't be long, right?"

D had no idea how long it would take to explain to Bullock and Theodore that he had found Louis Longley, a well-known politician, was the human involved in destroying prominent teddies that had gone missing, and that he belonged to Ballinger, a powerful Council bear that may or may not be involved as well. Never mind the fact that he also broke the Code.

Two minutes, tops, thought D sarcastically to himself. "I don't know. Just sit tight," he replied. "You know what to do if something happens, right?"

"NO!" panicked Lyle. "What's going to happen? What? What do I do?"

"Nothing. Nothing's going to happen," said D in his most reassuring voice. He regretted that he had said anything. "I'll be back before you know it."

Lyle's eyes zipped back and forth between the ivy leaves keeping a close watch for anything that might be dangerous. He had no idea what to look for since he had never been outside of the house before.

What's that? Is that danger?

He watched carefully as a car passed. Huh, they really can't see me, can they? With that thought, Lyle was becoming more comfortable.

D slipped into the old guardhouse, pulled up a loose board and disappeared into the passageway.

It was impossible to enter the Council without being discovered due to the acute hearing that teddies possess and, of course, the loud creaky hinges of the secret entrance doorway.

As D entered, Bullock was there to greet him. He was a large tan bear with black pads on his paws, a bullish nose and a dark brown kerchief tied around his neck. He had a few tatty spots on his body that he enjoyed talking about, when given the chance.

"What's going on? You're out kinda late," Bullock observed.

"Sorry for the intrusion but there's something I need to tell you," D said, his eyes searching the room not knowing if anyone else was there. His urgency was obvious by the tone in his voice.

"Okay, shoot," said Bullock.

D took a deep breath then began to relate the evening's business.

Bullock listened to what D had to say. It was not an adventure pleasing to Bullock. It was also something difficult to believe. When D finished telling his side of what happened, Bullock lowered his eyes and raised a paw to his forehead.

"Hmm." Bullock was overwhelmed with implication. This was like nothing he'd dealt with before, a direct attack towards a Council bear. Bullock would have to consider the facts, not the insinuation. "Let me get this straight. You did a nightmare on a human — without consent. You found shredded bodies in his closet — and the human was Senator Longley — who belongs to Ballinger, a Council bear? Did I get that right?" Bullock was offended at the thought of such a thing. "What's more, you think Ballinger had something to do with all this? Am I missing something? Did I leave anything out?"

The way Bullock put it all together made D uncomfortable. Maybe things didn't happen exactly the way he remembered. Had he forgotten anything — anything important? It certainly didn't look good from Bullock's point of view.

It was hard to read the Chief Marshall's face but there was definitely annoyance in his voice. "What do you think I should do?" he continued angrily. "Do you think I should wake Theodore to tell him what you just told me? Son, you've got nothin'. I can't do anything with this. You can't prove that Ballinger had anything to do with Longley's actions. A human's gonna do what a human's gonna do and a teddy can't do much about it. You've put me in a very awkward position. You make an accusation like this and I can't just ignore it. Hell, son, and then there's you! What were you thinking going into that house on your own? I'm not even going to ask if you had help. I don't want to know." Bullock paced back and forth. What do you do in a situation like this? Nothing! What could he do?

D stood still while Bullock admonished him for bringing accusation against another teddy, but not just any teddy — a Council member.

D's face changed at the sight of Theodore entering the room. He had never met the first teddy before and was more nervous than he'd ever felt. Bullock noticed D's eyes staring over his shoulder and turned to see, Theodore, the head of the Council approaching. His worn yellowish brown fur expressed a quiet wisdom. Every step fell with control and confidence as he approached. D felt a sense of nobility from the old bear but all that displayed was modesty.

"Is there a problem here?" Theodore asked calmly. His relaxed voice cut the tension in the mood.

"No. No problem. He was just leaving," replied Bullock, nudging D towards the door. Bullock didn't want to bother Theodore with such nonsense.

Theodore reached out and put his paw on D's shoulder. "I'd like see you privately for a moment."

Bullock didn't say a word as Theodore led D to his private quarters to talk. The door closed behind them. It was a modest but comfortable room with a small soft bed and a table with two chairs pulled away as if waiting for company. A few black and white pictures of President Theodore Roosevelt decorated the walls and one badly faded picture of what appeared to be a teddy bear. Clean was the first impression that struck D. No dirt or dust in the room anywhere.

"I didn't mean to cause any problems Mr. Theodore, sir." D glanced nervously about the room.

"Please don't call me that," snipped Theodore.

"Sir?"

"Call me Teddy. Everyone calls me Theodore but actually, I don't care for it. That was my person's name, not mine. I really don't remember when or how it happened, but everyone started calling me Theodore. And that's not my name. I stopped correcting bears years ago. My name is Teddy. I was the first one, of course . . . maybe . . . I think so anyway. But it doesn't really matter. I guess everyone thinks Theodore sounds more dignified. Anyway, I know who you are, and I know you're a good bear. I also know you're one of the best we have out there. I'm told you're doing a great job."

D was flattered that Theodore knew who he was but more importantly, that he was held in high regard by the number one bear.

Theodore continued, "I heard what you said to Bully. He didn't take it very well, I hear." Theodore chuckled. "He means well, but sometimes he just —"

D was taken by surprise. He had no idea what to think or what to say.

"Uh, no sir. It was all my —" D stammered.

"Listen," chimed Theodore, "I've heard a lot of things recently and I am aware of the bears that are missing. Something's going on and I have my suspicions. But what I need right now is someone I can trust."

This was strange for D to hear because teddies took great pride in their integrity.

"Sir?"

"I have a request and I need you to keep this between us. Tonight you've shown that you are willing to go beyond the Code to do what you think is right. I understand that things are not always black and white. Sometimes things don't fit into round holes or square holes. Sometimes we need to make our own holes to make things fit. Do you get what I'm saying, son?"

D would have nodded his head at anything Theodore said at that point. That he was not in trouble was all he seemed capable of grasping.

"Yes sir."

"What I'm going to ask is not something to take lightly."

Theodore began to explain his surreptitious task, and as the weight of his words began to sink in, D realized just how big this was; it was really, really big! It was something D had always wished for, a genuine adventure. An enormous sense of pride formed when he realized that he was the only bear standing there. Theodore trusted him and him only. Self-sacrifice and duty went hand in hand in the appeal. D would not be looked upon as a hero during the mission. In fact, it would be quite the contrary. The big picture was what was important. Family, loyalty, truth, and code were all that mattered in the teddy world, and D would do whatever was required to demonstrate it.

Theodore handed the audacious auburn bear a folded piece of paper and continued.

"I need you to go to the 82nd Division and talk to Cappy. He's in charge. Give him that note and he'll set you up. You're going to be the new Outsider in the Glenmore neighborhood. Once you're settled in I need you to find Ike."

Something didn't sound right suddenly. "Excuse me, sir, but did you say Ike, as in the old communications —"

"Yes," Theodore inserted abruptly.

"But — sir, I thought he was missing."

Theodore didn't want to go into detail; that would have to wait.

"He still is, as far as you're concerned. Do you understand?"

D understood perfectly. He knew about working in gray areas — that some things needed to be kept in the dark. It was for the best. Moreover, after everything that had just happened it was more prudent than ever. There was only one response for D to give.

"Yes sir."

Theodore gave a slight nod before continuing. "When you find Ike, tell him what happened here and listen to everything he tells you. It's going to take some time because he won't trust you at first. He probably won't come to the window when you call, but stay with it. Earn his trust. We need him." Theodore knew he had the right bear for the task. He slapped D on the shoulder and gave a quizzical look. "I don't need to tell you how important this is — and I don't need to remind you that this is strictly confidential, right?"

D stared him straight in the eyes and never said a word. Theodore smiled and said, "You're a good bear." With that, he reached for the door. D looked closely at Theodore and noticed the frayed stitching behind his ear. It blended with his fur and was hard to see, but his age was evident, his wisdom overpowering.

This was the first teddy bear, thought D. It made him proud to be one himself.

"I'll do my best, Teddy, sir."

"Teddy's fine. You can drop the sir. And good luck."

His back straightened from the call to duty and trust that was put upon him by the most important bear in the teddy world. The problem was that no other teddy would know about his sacrifice, not now anyway. D walked rigidly past Bullock, giving a polite nod, heading for the exit. Bullock watched the proud auburn bear enter the tunnel with the sound of the noisy hinge closing behind him. He turned to Theodore with a questioned look.

"What was that all about?" he asked.

"He has been punished and sent to another outpost," replied Theodore quickly. Trying to avoid further questioning from Bullock, Theodore turned to go back to his room.

"That's it?" called out Bullock with confusion laced in his voice. "You sent him away? What about his accusations, you know — Ballinger."

Theodore stopped and didn't turn around.

"Yes. That's it . . . He thought he was doing the right thing, and I know I did the same," replied Theodore firmly and left.

Theodore and Bullock had been best friends for over a hundred years, yet this would be the first time Bullock ever questioned his action.

"Where'd you send the boy?" asked Bullock.

The door to Theodore's room closed with no reply.

That was difficult for Theodore because he had never kept anything from Bullock before. It wasn't that he couldn't trust his oldest and dearest friend but knowing the innate nature of a teddy was truth and honesty, something Bullock defended fiercely, might make it hard for Bully to refrain from giving the mission away if asked. If Bullock had knowledge of what had been set in motion, it would mean lying to others, even to Ballinger. Lying was learned behavior, and Bullock had never learned about such things. Theodore couldn't take a chance to find out if Bullock could dissemble effectively or not. The less he knew the better.

Climbing out of the tunnel in the old guardhouse, D cautiously approached the spot where he'd left the nervous inside bear and whispered, "Lyle." There was no answer. "Lyle," he intoned a little louder. D could see his furry feet sticking out from the ivy. They appeared to be pushing back farther into the wall, if that were possible. Vines and leaves rustled as Lyle tried to stay hidden.

Finally, D reached out and grabbed Lyle by the arm. "Why didn't you answer me?" he scolded.

Lyle jumped. "I didn't know it was you."

A silly expression formed on D's face. "Do you think a stranger would call out your name?"

Lyle was embarrassed. He looked everywhere except at D.

"I don't know. I just —"

"Forget about it," chirped D with a grin. "Come on. We've got a long trip ahead of us." Thus began their journey, the adventure of a teddy lifetime.

"Where are we going?" Lyle asked.

"I can't tell you."

"Oh — okay."

D picked up his satchel and they started walking. He was prepared for the next round of questions from Lyle, anticipating such queries as — why can't you tell me, what happened inside, or, did you meet him? The usual questions that follow mysterious and secretive behavior, but there were none. Not one. Every step was a quiet one. D's prepared response was like a trap set to be sprung. It sat in his mouth just waiting. No question came. D was starting to like Lyle. This was how it would be. They were now friends.

The next evening, Ballinger showed up at the old guardhouse and sat quietly inside for a moment to collect his thoughts before entering the secret passage. Ballinger had all day to figure out his next move and what he would say. What he didn't know was if anyone had reported the incident yet. If so, what would they think? After all, there was no evidence of his involvement. For all anyone knew it was all Louis Longley. He was the one with the problem. A teddy can't control a human. Nevertheless, if Ballinger had knowledge of what was going on, then it was up to him to report the crime. However, if there was no report, indicating that Ballinger was aware of destroyed teddies in Louis Longley's closet, then there was no problem. Exposing a shameful incident, this close to the heart of the teddy world, would be an embarrassment for Ballinger as well as the Council. They would need to keep this as quiet as possible.

Ballinger lifted the floorboard and wiggled down into the tunnel. His walk was confident though his mind was not. He remained unsure of what he was walking into. He opened the passageway door to the Council to find Bullock sitting at a large table in the middle of the room. It was almost as if he were waiting for someone.

"Hey, Bull," said Ballinger in a serious tone. "Something happened last night that I need to tell you about."

"Yes. I heard about it," replied Bullock in the same serious tone.

"You did? So you know someone did a Nightmare at my house last night?"

"Yep."

"What are you going to do about it?"

"To tell you the truth — it's already been handled."

"Really?" Ballinger stood waiting for an answer. "And?"

"Theodore took care of it."

A wave of concern washed over him. "He did? Oh." Ballinger began to worry about how he appeared. Was he too eager? Did he ask the right questions for someone who wasn't supposed to know anything? Did he seem nervous? "Good." Ballinger tried to appear relaxed but found it difficult. "So what happened?"

Bullock stood up from his chair and slowly walked to Ballinger. "He punished him; sent him away."

"He did? Excellent! This kind of thing cannot be tolerated," said Ballinger noticing Bullock's demeanor as he stepped closer. Bullock was an intimidating bear although Ballinger never thought he was very smart. "So, where did he go?"

"Dunno," he replied simply with a stern look about him. Bullock was now standing face-to-face with Ballinger. "So, Louis has been killing teddies? *Your* human — killing teddies.

Looks like we've got a bigger problem than a bear doing an unauthorized Nightmare."

Bullock had just said something very interesting. There was a question that Ballinger wanted badly to know the answer to: was this an authorized Nightmare? Did the Council send someone because they knew what was going on? The answer was no, Bullock had just said it himself. That was good news for Ballinger. His role now became more defined. He could think of himself as the victim.

"I didn't know what he was doing!" insisted Ballinger. "How could I have known? If I had known about it I would have said something — done something."

Bullock glared at him, his thoughts jumbled. Nothing this sinister had happened before, not this close to the Council. But there was something that Bullock noticed as they spoke; Ballinger never asked who did the Nightmare. That should have been the first question. Bullock let out a sigh. "We got a serious problem, and it's up to you to clean it up. Unless you want us to go in there," charged Bullock.

"What can I do? I don't control him," Ballinger answered.

"I don't know. You're in charge of the Rough Riders, do another Nightmare and set him straight. Heck, send in a *Kage Kuma if you have to. But this needs to stop and it needs to be kept quiet. If this gets out . . . I don't need to tell you, do I?"

Ballinger felt more confident now that Bullock wanted him to take care of it. The situation was looking better. The last thing Ballinger wanted was the Council to get involved. For Bullock to recommend using the Kage Kumas meant he was dead serious. The Council has kept their existence a secret from the rest of the teddy world. Rumors had surfaced of an elite band of mysterious and highly trained bears that were only used under extreme conditions to protect the teddy world, but then again, they were just rumors.

"I'll take care of it. I don't know how yet, but I'll do what I have to," said Ballinger.

* **Kage Kuma** – [ka-gae koo-ma] Translation: Shadow Bear

BREAKING THE CODE

Over two months had passed since D performed the Teddy Nightmare on Louis Longley and things appeared to be back to normal. There were no more reports of missing teddies and the Longley matter seemed to be under control. However, appearances can be deceiving.

Ballinger was more intent than ever in taking over the Council. He needed to discredit Theodore, show the teddy world that he was incompetent as a leader. Ballinger hated the way Theodore treated the Teddy Code, as if it was more of a guideline than a rule. Ballinger felt the Code was the Code and breaking it needed severe consequence. Bullock may be the Chief Marshal but Theodore was ultimately responsible.

Ballinger had recently been informed about two young bears that had broken the Code in front of a human male. Normally this would not concern the bear in charge of communication and the Teddy Network but he had been trying to find something to demonstrate Theodore's weakness, his lack of leadership. This might be what Ballinger was looking for. The report also stated that another moving violation occurred at the same address over eight months ago.

This was exactly what Ballinger wanted to hear. A clear case of reckless behavior that had been neglected by Theodore and Bullock. Ballinger would use these two bears as his proof of Theodore's ineptitude.

**

The house at 2300 Glenmore Drive was pretty much like every other house in the neighborhood except for two small things.

"You almost done?" whispered Bobby Bear, holding up a slightly worn and matted paw to his mouth so that his voice carried. An average height bear with a stocky build, light brown fur and a buff colored muzzle, Bobby Bear had one colorful characteristic, his red pads on his front two paws. He stood near Waldo, who was a bit smaller bear, with pure white fur, a round black nose and one ear that curled down.

"Gimmie a second," said Waldo, "just a little . . . more . . . time." Waldo was so focused on his task that he didn't realize his tongue was sticking out. A pair of swim goggles sat pushed up on his head as he grappled with a few tools that he borrowed from the garage to help build his creation. Turning the screwdriver one last time, "There! — It's finished."

"What is it?" asked Bobby Bear, staring at a cardboard box lying on its side with the flaps opened. A toddler's activity desk was placed inside as a control center with a large yellow plastic key (ready for turning), several sliding knobs, and one big red button.

"*Ugh!*" Waldo rolled his eyes with a look of annoyance. "It's a time machine, of course, can't you see that?"

"Yeah — now I see it. Wow, that's nice. So, you're a time traveler?"

"Not yet, but I'm gonna be."

"What'cha gonna do with it?"

"I'm going back in time to find something," replied Waldo, stepping into his new time traveling device.

"Find what?"

"*Something I lost,*" he said with impatience, "and I have to travel back to the last place I had it."

Not sensing the frustration, Bobby Bear curiously asked, "What did you lose?"

Waldo pretended not to hear as he positioned a small footstool, as the seat, at the controls. He could feel his friend staring at him and waited for the inevitable question once again.

"What did you lose?"

"It's a piece of paper, *okay?* I lost a piece of paper that says something and I need it," said Waldo, feeling irritated. "Now stand back so you don't get caught in the time wave."

He pulled down his goggles and Bobby Bear took two steps back. The countdown began, "3 – 2 – 1," and just as Waldo hit the big red button, he glanced down and saw something on the ground that looked familiar. "Oh, here it is," he said proudly. "I found it. See, I told you the time machine would help me find it."

"Wow, it didn't even look like you went anywhere."

"That's because it happens so fast that you can't see it."

"You're right. I didn't see it. So, what does it say?"

Waldo heard the question but acted a bit coy as if he didn't know what he was talking about. "What?"

"The paper, *the paper,* what does it say?"

"Nothing, nothing at all," he replied, turning his back.

"*What*?!" cried Bobby Bear. "You went back in time to find

a piece of paper with nothing on it?"

"No," he said with a hint of silliness. "It says something, of course."

"What? What does it say? Tell me what it says! I want to know what it says! Are you going to tell me what it says?" Bobby Bear began peering intently over Waldo's shoulder to get a glimpse of what he was hiding.

"*ALL RIGHT!*" shouted Waldo sharply, and then, lowered his voice. "All right — I'll tell you."

Not wanting him to know what was really on the paper, he thought up something quickly.

"It's a secret message," said Waldo, as this was the first thing to pop into his head.

"You mean something like a secret agent would get?" asked Bobby Bear.

Inspiration flashed in Waldo's eyes. "*Exactly!*" he answered quickly. *A secret agent, that's it,* he thought. And with a quiet yet serious tone he said, "Yep, I'm a secret agent *and you can't tell anyone.*"

"Why?"

Waldo threw up his hands dramatically and said, "Jeeze Louise, Bobby Bear, the key word in Secret Agent is *SECRET.* So if you blab to everyone that I'm a Secret Agent then it's not really a *secret* anymore is it?"

That sounded quite logical. "I guess not."

Waldo leaned closer, looked left, then right, and dropped his voice. "Can you keep a secret?" he asked, hoping this would distract Bobby Bear from the paper.

"You mean like the STS?"

"*Yes,* just like that," replied Waldo swiftly.

Bobby Bear was referring, of course, to the Secret Teddy

Society that all teddy bears belong to. It stated that teddies were not allowed to come to life in front of people, and that getting caught was breaking the Teddy Code, which was exactly what happened to Bobby Bear and Waldo.

The bears had been best friends since the beginning, which is the start of a teddies life. Each bear has their own beginning but Bobby Bear and Waldo's life began almost simultaneously from the love and human contact of a seven-year-old girl, named Bobbie. She was a confident little girl that never had a problem telling the truth, which became a strong trait in the bears that she unwittingly brought to life. Naturally creative, Bobbie's imagination fueled her adventurous side. She was a bit small for her age and extremely athletic. She could run like the wind and often challenged anyone for a race around the house. Her baby blond hair began turning a soft light brown with every passing month. Bobbie had a hard time making up her mind about some things, and when it came to naming the bears, nothing seemed good enough. Out of the blue, her dad called the smaller white bear Waldo, as if that had always been his name. She loved the name and thought it fit him perfectly. The other bear remained nameless and was referred to as Bobbie's Bear. The progression was obvious. Bobby Bear it became. Putting a "Y" at the end of his name made it a boy's name, at least that's what Bobbie figured.

From the day the two bears were brought home, from Hot Ticket, a trendy large department store, they had been side by side. Though Bobby Bear liked to be a good bear, Waldo, on the other hand, liked to be adventurous, this sometimes got him into trouble.

Being a teddy bear could be a bit humdrum at times especially when left alone for long periods. Every bear had their own temptations to break STS code, but few did. Some, however, couldn't help themselves.

For Bobby Bear and Waldo, their troubles began last week when James, the father of the house, was trying to write his first book. His daughter, Bobbie, always felt bad leaving for school because her daddy was left home alone while Mommy was at work.

One day, before school, Bobbie strolled into her daddy's office carrying Bobby Bear and Waldo. She walked to the desk and placed the bears on top near the pencil holder.

"Why are you putting them there?" asked James.

She gave him a concerned look and said, "They're here to keep you company so you won't be alone."

She turned to Waldo and said those three little words that he hears every morning before she leaves for school: "You be good." And with that, she felt better, smiled at her daddy, and left. James was moved by her thoughtfulness, and only briefly wondered why she said that to Waldo and not Bobby Bear.

He smiled and turned to the bears sitting on his desk. They stared back with blank expressions. *Maybe I should write a book about Teddy Bears*, he thought, *No, that's silly.*

He would stick to something more adult, more important, something with big life issues or focusing on the human condition. James believed in karma, life mysteries and things that couldn't be scientifically proven or denied. This was what he wanted to write about, however, coming up with something fresh or, more importantly, interesting would be his challenge.

Trying to type at his old computer, his fingers hit the keys clumsily, and he had no idea how to make them go faster. Embarrassed by his lack of skill, James decided to go "old school," and pulled out his trusty pen and paper. He knew that the more he practiced the better he would get at typing, but there was also a sort of charm that went with writing by hand, it made him feel nostalgic.

James tried to find time to write in between his daily chores while the family was away, but he mostly liked to work late at night when everyone was asleep and the house was quiet. He would occasionally nod off sitting at his desk. One night, when he fell asleep, he was awakened by something, a vague disturbance that was not exactly a noise, it was subtler . . . or maybe it was nothing at all. Sleepily, he looked around, stretched his stiff back and then stood up from his chair. Still quite sleepy, he wandered into the kitchen. He stopped at the doorway and blinked, not sure he could believe his eyes. He saw the refrigerator door was wide open and a very odd furry creature stood in front of it. Startled as he was, he stepped back out of sight to collect his thoughts. *Am I dreaming?* When he cautiously peeked around the corner again, James noticed the furry creature was having trouble standing. It was wobbling. *What do I do?* The top half was white and the bottom half was light brown. It was not very tall. James couldn't imagine what it was. It didn't look like a squirrel or a raccoon. On the other hand, it didn't appear terribly threatening, either. Indeed, it seemed somewhat familiar. He decided to confront the beast. As he tiptoed up behind it, in his bare feet, he heard what sounded like two people arguing.

"Stop moving around," said the creature, "you're going to make me fall."

"Hurry up, I'm getting tired," a different voice said. "Can you reach it?"

"I've almost got it," the creature said to itself in a tone that sounded like a ghostly whisper.

Unaware that James was standing just behind him, the fuzzy critter leaned farther into the fridge.

James' heart raced as he thought to himself, *Okay, you can do this*. He reached out his trembling hands, grabbed the beast by the shoulders, and spun it around. To his surprise, the creature separated in two. With the top part in his hands, the bottom half took off running.

He was now face to face with half a wooly something that he suddenly recognized as Waldo, one of the teddy bears that his daughter put on his desk. Apparently, he was standing on Bobby Bear's shoulders to reach the milk.

This has to be a dream.

Holding the small white bear, outstretched with both hands, he stared at Waldo who was holding a carton of milk. The frightened little bear stared back.

Waldo found himself in a situation that he'd never been in before. In fact, this was the one situation that all teddies fear the most. He couldn't think of what to do or what to say. What could a teddy bear possible say at a moment like this? His mind was spinning like a roulette wheel that eventually comes to a stop, and when it did, something tumbled out of his mouth.

"I found the milk."

His heart dropped as he realized what he had just done. He and Bobby Bear had gone against the first rule of the STS — No Teddy Bear is allowed to move or speak in front of a human. He had no idea what to do next.

When his mouth opened again he heard himself say, "Can I pour you a glass of milk? It's not getting any colder you know."

Waldo couldn't believe what he was saying. It was his worst habit. Whenever Waldo got scared or nervous he'd just start talking and couldn't seem to stop.

"Why don't you get three glasses while you're up, 'cause I'm thirsty, are you thirsty? I know I am, how 'bout you?"

Waldo felt like he was hovering above his body, and had completely lost control of his own voice. He couldn't shut up.

"Where's the one that was with you — the one that ran off?" James asked, convinced this was a dream. "Was that Bobby Bear?"

"Yeah, that was him. He's probably back on the desk. It's kind of what we're supposed to do," he answered, knowing there was no pretending — not now.

Waldo still held the milk as James carried him into the office. There, in his usual spot, was Bobby Bear, up on the desk, right next to the empty spot were Waldo usually sat. Bobby Bear remained still and lifeless when James said, "Bobby Bear, you don't have to pretend anymore, I know you can hear me."

He did not answer and did not move. James looked at Waldo for some help. Waldo simply shrugged his shoulders.

"What do you think I should do?" asked James. Waldo stared at Bobby Bear for a moment, his face filled with thought. Turning back to James, he opened his mouth and answered, "I dunno. He's not supposed to move ya' know."

James was sure Waldo would tell him some secret word or phrase or something that would make Bobby Bear come to life.

He gave it some thought, then, said something almost any father would say in this situation. "Bobby Bear, you answer me right now or you and Waldo are in big trouble." James didn't realize that he had just stumbled upon Bobby Bear's weakness. Since he does not like to get into trouble, Bobby Bear broke down.

"I knew it! *I knew it!* I knew you'd get us into trouble Waldo," stammered a very nervous and scared Bobby Bear. "I knew it! We're in trouble aren't we?"

"No," said James. "I just said that to —"

"What's it going to be: Pistols at twenty paces? The Rack? The Dungeon?" Bobby Bear's eyes widened in fear. "Wait, I know: the naughty chair! *Not* the naughty chair, PLEASE not the naughty —"

"Bobby Bear!" James interrupted. "You're not in trouble."

The nervous young bear stopped mid-sentence with his mouth wide open. A pleasant look of surprise crossed his face. Then, he noticed Waldo still holding the milk. "You got it after all," he said and began smacking his lips together.

Both bears felt so relieved they avoided trouble, that neither one remembered the most important rule they just broke from the Secret Teddy Society.

James was well aware that he was dreaming, but one thing did trouble him. This was the first time, to his recollection, that he noticed he was dreaming. Normally dreams made perfect sense in their nonsensical way. He never questioned why his house never looked like his house, in his dreams. This was different. His house *was* his house. Everything was exactly as it should be: the pencil cup, the outdated computer, the old clock on the wall, everything. But since there was no real logical reason why or how these teddy bears were moving and talking, James decided to ask why he'd never seen them move before.

Waldo simply began to explain the Secret Teddy Society,

and how all Teddy Bears were bound by the Teddy Code. "Once you break the Code, the Teddy Council decides what happens to you," he said.

Bobby Bear had forgotten all about the Council and looked at Waldo with fear in his eyes. The look on his face made Waldo curious, "What? What is it?"

Bobby Bear could only eke out two words in a scared breath, "The Council." Waldo's face turned downward and James felt the unexplained sense of doom from the bears.

"Is it that bad?" James asked, glancing from one scared bear to the other.

Waldo nodded slowly while Bobby Bear stared blankly at the floor.

"So, you're telling me that you just broke the Code — the Teddy Code?"

Waldo nodded somberly. His troubled face was obvious.

"Come on. How bad could it be?" James couldn't imagine how a council of teddy bears could be that intimidating. Besides, they were in *his* house, what could they possibly do?

"Fluffy," Bobby Bear whispered. Waldo nodded again and began to tell the story that would explain their fears.

"Do you remember Big Red Fluffy bear?" he asked. James searched his memory and recalled a bear he bought for Debra when they were dating about 15 years ago. James was a songwriter recording an album when he found a big red fluffy bear in a quaint gift shop across the street from the studio. It was impossible not to smile when you saw him. Fluffy bear's name did describe him well except the word 'big' wasn't really a description of his size but rather his belly. It was round, it was big, and he was, in fact, fluffy. And with fur that was dark red, naming him was the easy part.

"Yeah," replied James cautiously. "What about him?"

"He was our teacher."

"Teacher?"

"Older bears teach the younger bears about life and breathing and stuff like that."

"Whoa, whoa, wait a minute," James cut in. "Breathing?"

Waldo rolled his eyes and felt he had to explain a bit more about the teddy world so James would understand the gravity of their situation.

"When a teddy is born, they can't move yet."

"Wait — born?" interjected James, trying desperately to understand what he was hearing. He knew that as soon as he woke up he would forget everything, but it was all so detailed, so — real.

Dramatically, Waldo took a deep breath and stared at James. "Yes. That's when the love from human contact brings awareness to a bear for the first time. Born," explained Waldo. "Anyway," he continued, "they're aware of things around them but they don't know how to move or even that they can move. They're just aware of stuff. It's like being numb. That's when older bears come along and teach the younger ones how to take their first breath and how to move."

James was mesmerized at the intricacies of new life to a teddy.

"What's it like? You know, taking your first breath. Do you remember?" asked James mysteriously, completely unaware of anything but Waldo speaking.

Waldo closed his eyes, took several breathes, and recalled the exact words of Fluffy bear, an ability that Waldo never gave much thought about: "Imagine yourself like a balloon filling with air. Picture the balloon growing bigger. Then, let the air out of the balloon. This is you. You're the balloon. When you fill the balloon in your mind, you fill your body. Do this over and over. Suddenly, you'll take your first breath. Once that happens, your head will start spinning. You might start gasping for air. Just relax., It's normal. It's a feeling like you've never had. Now comes the fun part. Once you're relaxed — take a deep breath — hold it — then let it go. Clear your mind and think only of your breath. Do it again and again, each time picturing yourself floating like a feather. You'll begin to feel a tingle in your belly and your head will feel funny, light almost. Everything will feel different, more — alive, more sensitive, more aware. You'll see things, you'll feel things that you've never seen or felt before. Things will be blurry at first and then comes the colors. You'll love the colors. And when you're ready, turning it off is simple — pop the balloon. Let the air out and let it go flat. You'll feel your body go numb and still. It may sound easy but you'll need to practice a lot before you can do it naturally. But it *will* come."

Waldo slowly opened his eyes and James couldn't say a word. There was nothing to say. They looked at each other in a brief silence before Waldo continued, "Anyway, he taught us lots of things. He was a good friend."

James batted his eyes a few times snapping his trance. "Was? What do you mean was?" asked James.

"That's what I'm trying to tell you. He's gone. He was caught moving. He's been gone for a while now. That's the thing. People don't always notice when things are missing, even their own teddies," said Waldo with a disgusted tone. "You didn't even know he was gone." Waldo shook his head sadly. "How do you not know this?"

James was beginning to feel bad that he hadn't noticed the

missing bear. He wasn't aware that he had to keep track of a teddies whereabouts, but this conversation would change everything.

"Okay, so if he was caught — then who caught him?" asked James, knowing that if something like that happened he surely would have known about it. You don't keep a thing like that quiet.

"We didn't see it because Bobbie had put us in the playroom earlier, plus it was during the day. But it was a repairman that you let work in the house while no one was home." Waldo's voice had a pinch of irritation. "You know you shouldn't do that — let a stranger in the house. Even a kid knows that."

James thought for a second and remembered a refrigerator repairman that was in the house while they had a family emergency. He recalled not having any choice in the matter because Bobbie had fallen and cut herself badly and needed to go to the hospital.

"Wait a second. That's the day we took Bobbie to the doctors for stitches. My hands were tied. The repair guy was here and we had to leave in a hurry."

"Yeah, well, that's a pretty good excuse — I guess," Waldo said reluctantly.

"When we got home the door was unlocked and the repairman was gone. He didn't even fix the darn thing. They told us that he ran out of the house scared and wouldn't return. They sent someone else to finish the job." James' face brightened suddenly. "I do remember the repair company asking if we had a small pet bear in the house. I had no idea what they were talking about. So you're saying *that* was Big Red Fluffy bear?"

Waldo simply nodded. His eyes kept tilting towards the milk and wondered if it would be too forward to ask for a small nip. Bobbie Bear had a distant look on his face as his thoughts were clearly elsewhere.

"Was Fluffy bear in the fridge as well? Is that where he got caught?" asked James as he began to see a common thread between the two events. Waldo once again nodded mechanically as his eyes were now fixed on the carton of milk that sat seductively on the desk almost beckoning the small white bear. James followed his stare straight to the carton. Small beads of sweat dripped down her sides like a sultry moist milk maiden. Waldo appeared so focused on the creamy drink that it didn't take Sherlock Holmes to deduce what he was gazing at.

"Milk?" James blurted with a chuckle. "You like milk?" James laughed at the thought. "Fluffy was the one that got you hooked on milk?" His laughter was starting to annoy Waldo.

"Have you *tasted* milk?" voiced Waldo emphatically, his eyes piercing with passion.

The word 'milk' was being thrown around loosely, capturing the attention of Bobby Bear. They both glared at James.

"Wait a minute. Are you mad at me?" James didn't want to ruin what was turning out to be the best dream of his life.

They weren't mad at James. In fact, they loved him almost as much as Bobbie, but they didn't really know how to act in such a situation. This was uncharted waters to them, or any teddy bear for that matter. Teddies don't get to talk to humans and Waldo was enjoying this as much as James.

Jumping up quickly, James dashed to the kitchen, grabbed a few small glasses and darted back to the office.

This was the moment when teddies would do what comes naturally after breaking the Code; stop moving, go lifeless and let the human think he imagined the whole thing. This was their opportunity. James left the scene. Just go blank. The instinct may have been there but something happened, something neither Bobby Bear nor Waldo could have foreseen. It was simple yet complicated at the same time. Their education of the Code was unfinished, due to their teacher, Big Red Fluffy bear, being taken away. The Teddy Code made it clear that moving in front of a human was wrong. The two young bears assumed there was a good reason why teddies don't move in front of humans, but James was, after all, family. This was a gray area. Once caught by someone, can you keep moving in front of that someone? They knew they were already in trouble, so what was the point in pretending now? Getting caught in the act while holding the milk was more than enough proof of their existence. The secret was out. Since they were in trouble anyway, why not make the most of it? Waldo had so many questions of his own, besides, they hadn't gotten to the milk yet, and it was sitting there, looking as good as ever. This was the adventure of adventures for Waldo and Bobby Bear. They would get the chance to do what no other teddies could — live in another world. Waldo figured, since it was James that caught them moving, then that's how it would remain, only him. That sounded fair. It might not be what the Council had in mind but that would be how Bobby Bear and Waldo would interpret it. The justification of their action was greatly influenced by adventure, excitement and desire. They would pay the price for it later.

Returning to the desk, James reached for the carton of milk and poured three cups. The bears sat still with vacant expressions as James thought that his dream had ended. He stood silently, barely breathing, as he slowly leaned closer. His shoulders drooped and the excitement left his face. *It's over*, he thought.

A soft whispered voice quietly asked, "Are those for us?" Bobby Bear batted his eyes hoping the answer was yes.

"They sure are," replied James with a relieved smile. "So, you're not mad?"

Waldo looked away as he searched for the best words to describe something he couldn't really explain. "Not mad, just — a little upset, I guess. I don't know!" Waldo didn't want to use that word. He thought it was too strong, but that's how he was feeling. Being the first time talking with a human, Waldo didn't want to get angry. "You still shouldn't have let someone in the house that you don't know. Fluffy would still be here." Waldo couldn't help it, that's how he was feeling — it just came out. Such relief. He didn't mean to say it, but he couldn't stop himself. Bobby Bear instantly froze. His eyes wide and his mouth open as milk dripped from the corners. He was alarmed that Waldo would say such a thing. Staring nervously at James, Bobby Bear waited for his reaction.

"So let me get this straight. You're mad at me, or 'upset', for letting someone in the house while we were out? Right?" asked James as he tried to box Waldo into a situational corner. Waldo looked sternly and nodded as milk foamed around his mouth. "Okay, so a teddy, who's not supposed to move, gets caught moving and it's my fault. You're blaming me for *him* breaking *your* code? Right?"

Waldo's face changed to a confused look and answered, "Well, if you put it like that, sure, it's sounds completely different."

"Yeah, but that's the only way *to* put it! You can't blame me for something that he did wrong. Just because he was caught doesn't make it my fault."

A thought popped into Waldo's head. "Wait a minute. The Code doesn't say we're not allowed to move. It says we're not allowed to move in front of humans. So if the repair dude wasn't here, then Fluffy wouldn't have gotten caught."

James began to grin as he realized just how crazy this conversation was. Waldo was actually proud of himself for making such an astute observation. Infected by the smile that emerged from James' face, Waldo found a similar one slowly brewing on his. The two were now smiling at each other.

Waldo was experiencing something very different. He was feeling more passionate than normal. It was fun interacting with James.

Curious about the teddy world and where Fluffy bear went, James asked, "You said he was taken away. What happens? Who takes you away?"

"Thugs," snipped Bobby Bear sharply.

"Did you say thugs?"

They both nodded.

"They take you to the Council so they can decide what happens to you," explained Waldo. Hearing the word thug, James pictured a vicious teddy with a matching demeanor.

"Are they big and bad bears?" asked James lightheartedly.

"No. They could be anyone. They're usually just other teddies that have done something wrong and have to do something good to be allowed full teddy rights again."

"So you really don't know what happened to Fluffy?"

Waldo paused to take a sip of milk then stared into James' eyes. "All we know is that the Council took him away — and we never saw him again." An eerie silence filled the room. James was starting to understand the concern of the bear's. Their true fear was the unknowing. If they knew what happened to Fluffy bear then they would have something to prepare for, but the waiting for an unknown castigation meant their imaginations might torment them worse than the punishment.

The mood was awkward and James thought he should say something. "So — what about Sparky? Does Bobbie's stuffed cat Sparky belong to the STS?"

"*Pffh*, no. That's just silly," chuckled Waldo. "It's only Teddies." He gave Bobby Bear a knowing look and they both laughed. "They probably have their own thing, something kitty something, probably, I don't know. I've never seen it move before. It just sits there."

James couldn't believe what he was hearing, and yet, the proof was right in front of him. He saw real life in the Teddies' eyes.

Waldo had the most beautiful brown eyes; they looked so real. They practically jumped out from his white fur. A lively greenish blue filled Bobby Bear's eyes that James seemed to remember only being small black beads before.

The darkness that was once outside was replaced with light as morning had come and James suddenly realized, for once and for all, that this was no dream. Bobby Bear and Waldo appeared to be enjoying the conversation. After all, they'd never talked to a human before. They're not allowed to, it's in the Code. Bobby Bear and Waldo had the best night of their lives, but it didn't take long to realize that it was *because* they broke the Code. James was family yet they also belong to the Secret Teddy Society. This created a real dilemma.

I can't believe I am sitting here talking to Teddy Bears, thought James.

Knowing this was as unbelievable as unbelievable gets, James pinched himself — just to be sure.

"Ow!" he chirped.

Waldo and Bobby Bear stared at him strangely. James leaned forward. The bears did the same. He slowly raised his hand and pointed his finger into Waldo's tummy, and gently pushed in and out. A reluctant smile appeared on Waldo's face as the tickle grew.

"Can I ask you what you're doing?" asked Waldo as he tried hard not to laugh.

James sat back in his chair, let out an incredulous laugh, and shook his head. "I gotta tell ya', I don't believe it. I really don't believe you guys are sitting here talking to me right now."

Bobby Bear turned to his best friend and shrugged his shoulders. The two young teddies had heard stories about others breaking the Code but they didn't imagine anything like this. What was so bad? Why the fuss? It was great. James seemed like he was enjoying himself. No harm no foul. Why the secrecy?

Inspiration flashed and a serious look swept James' face. "Can I ask you a question?" They both simply nodded. "Can I write about it?"

Waldo's eye twitched with uncertainty. "About what?"

"You — and Bobby Bear, of course, you know — this! You guys. Moving?"

Bobby Bear was unclear of what he would write about exactly. "You want to tell stories about us?" he asked politely.

Excitedly James said, "Yeah! Just what you guys were telling me about. You know, you're adventures around the house, learning about life. Do you know how much people would love this stuff?" His enthusiasm was infectious as Waldo and Bobby Bear loved the idea that humans would be interested in a teddy bear's life. The normal life of a teddy is boring really. However, if James wanted to write about it, they couldn't see the harm.

Waldo had one small request. "Could I be a Secret Agent?"

James laughed, picked him up playfully, and spun his swivel chair around in circles. "Yes! Absolutely. I wouldn't have it any other way. This is gonna be great." James was relieved to have something to write about. It might not have been the subject matter he wanted, but it just landed in his lap. It would practically write itself.

Life was gone in a flash. James heard a noise come from the kitchen and the smell of coffee wafted through the office.

The family was awake and getting ready for work and school. His wife, Debra, appeared in the office doorway suddenly. She didn't know whether to smile or shake her head at his silliness.

"You've been up all night?" she asked as James' office chair came to a stop while he was holding a small white teddy bear up in the air.

He quickly glanced up at Waldo and slowly lowered his arms. He turned to Bobby Bear, who sat very still and very quiet. James noticed their eyes were not the same. The color was gone, replaced with the small black beads. He put Waldo back in his spot, next to Bobby Bear.

"Yeah, I'm still trying to think of something to write about," he answered, knowing he couldn't say what really happened last night. She would never believe him. He was having a hard time believing it himself.

"So, you had company last night?" she asked in all seriousness. James couldn't understand how she could have possibly known about his night. He stared back in disbelief as his mind searched desperately for words to explain, but how did she know?

"And you're the one that's been drinking the milk so fast?" she added.

James turned to see what had so obviously tipped her off. Three small empty glasses and a warm carton of milk were blatant clues to his unexplainable night.

He began putting words together, giving enormous thought to each one. He needed time to think. "I — was —"

His wife was used to his antics and inane humor but was slightly annoyed that he spent all night playing with teddy bears. "You know what? Don't even start. You'll just say something completely stupid." She gave a slight grin, because it was actually cute, telling James that he wasn't in trouble. Debra turned to go back to the kitchen. "You'll be picking up more milk at the store, ya' know?" she said teasingly as she left.

"Sure, no problem. I'll get more milk while I'm out," he replied in relief. He quietly chuckled and turned to the bears that sat lifeless on his desk. Storylines of action, adventure and drama were all bouncing around his head about a secret world of teddy bears. He couldn't wait. James grabbed a pen and began writing his first book.

One week later, Waldo held the piece of paper that he found with his time machine as he told Bobby Bear he was a Secret Agent. Bobby Bear fell right into character and became the evil villain "Dr. Meany."

"You will give me the paper now, Secret Agent Waldo."

Clinching his hand tightly, Waldo answered, "You're going to have to torture me, Mr. Meany."

"That's DOCTOR Meany, and that's exactly what I had in mind."

"What are you going to do to me?" asked Waldo with a slight quiver of fear in his voice.

"It's the water torture for you."

Waldo wasn't expecting to hear that, and while this might be just a game, he was starting to get nervous. They walked down the dark hall of mystery to the torture chamber, also known as the bathroom. Pointing to the shower, the evil Dr. Meany said, "Get in, Agent Waldo."

"I don't care what you do, you'll never get the secret paper," said Waldo dramatically, trying to hide his fear because no teddy likes to get wet.

"We shall see about that. Not even you can stand the water torture."

Waldo stepped into the shower, reminding himself that it was just pretend, until Bobby Bear reached for the handle.

"STOP!" cried Waldo. "All right, all right, I'll give it to you."

Dr. Meany looked deep into Agent Waldo's eyes and said, "We're *way* past that now, Agent Waldo. Where's the fun in that?" The sinister scowl on the evil doctor's face made Waldo's fur a bit prickly.

He turned the shower handle and Waldo's eyes got big as the water landed on his fur.

"WET! WET! BOBBY BEAR, IT'S WET!" Waldo jumped out of the shower, dropped the paper and grabbed a towel.

As Bobby Bear laughed, he noticed the paper on the floor.

It was Bobbie's homework. Waldo had taken it from her room because he wanted to learn just like her. He thought Bobby Bear would laugh if he found out, so he kept it a secret.

Waldo forgot about the paper while he was trying to dry off.

"You know you're not supposed to do this," said Bobby Bear.

"Part of the Teddy Code says, *'No object shall be moved from its place so that a human will notice.'* If Bobbie comes home from school and cannot find her homework, we will be in trouble *again*. Haven't we been in enough trouble?"

Peering over the top of the towel, he answered, "Relax, she won't miss it."

Bobby Bear picked up the paper, slapped it against the wall, and flattened out the wrinkles. He went to the door and peeked down the hall. "Okay, the coast is clear," he said in a low raspy voice.

Waldo dropped the towel, squinted his eyes, and said in his usual playful way, "Cover me! I'll draw their fire while you slip behind enemy lines and plant the phony document."

"This is serious, Waldo," said Bobby Bear sternly. "This has to be put back before Bobbie gets home from school."

Waldo knew it was serious but did not want to show that he was worried or admit he did something wrong. Just then, they heard the front door. The bears would normally hear the family car before it reached the driveway, but they were too distracted.

They turned to each other. "She's home!" they both said at the same time.

Trapped in the bathroom with her homework, they needed to do something quickly. Bobbie's bedroom was across the hall. They needed to replace her homework and get back to the desk before anyone noticed. "We're home!" yelled Bobbie as she ran through the door with Debra close behind. She threw her backpack on the floor and ran into the office, as she does every day, to hear about Bobby Bear and Waldo's daily adventures.

Bobbie sat in her daddy's office staring at his desk and noticed something missing. No Bobby Bear and no Waldo. "Daddy," she called out, "where are the bears?"

Back in the bathroom, the two teddies had to act fast. "Now's our chance," whispered Bobby Bear. They both ran across the hall into Bobbie's bedroom. "There it is. That's the book the paper was under," said Waldo, pointing to the desk.

James was in the kitchen when he heard Bobbie ask about the bears. *Oh-no*, he thought. *What are they up to now?*

Bobby Bear heard footsteps approaching. He grabbed Waldo and jumped under her bed. Peering out from the dark, they noticed something in the middle of the floor.

"The paper," Waldo squeaked. Somehow, the paper was dropped in all the excitement. "What do we do?"

Bobbie appeared in the doorway. She stopped for a moment as if something was wrong. Bobby Bear put his finger to his lips. "Shhh," he whispered.

From down the hall, her mother called out, "Can you please come back and pick up your backpack off the floor."

Bobbie rolled her eyes realizing that she forgot something. "Jeeze Louise!" she muttered and disappeared from the doorway.

"She's gone," Bobby Bear said quietly. Knowing he didn't have much time, he wiggled out from under the bed, grabbed the homework off the floor, scampered up the chair at the desk, and slipped the paper under the book. "There, it's back," he said, feeling like he just lit the fuse of a bomb and needed to get as far away as they could, fast. "Let's go!"

Waldo crawled out from under the bed and peeked out the door. "All-clear."

They darted down the hall. The bears heard the patter of feet coming from all directions and turned into the first door they came to, diving into a basket full of clothes, in the laundry room. Waldo looked up just in time to see James walk past the door.

"Psst."

James stopped and came back into the room, thinking he heard something. He stood quietly for a second.

"PSST!"

His eyes went straight to the laundry basket. A fuzzy white face looked up at him from under the dirty clothes. "Is that you, Waldo?"

"Yes," he answered in a hushed and worried voice.

"Where's Bobby Bear?"

"Right here," the scared brown bear answered, pulling a shirt from his face.

"What are you two doing in there?"

Bobby Bear began talking about the Time Machine and the piece of paper that Waldo took, while Waldo interrupted with tales of the water torture and Doctor Meany.

James was trying to make sense of everything when he said, "Okay, let's get you guys back to the desk." He plucked them from out of the basket and carried them to the office. As he turned the corner, there was Bobbie standing right in front of him.

"What are you doing with Bobby Bear and Waldo?" she asked.

Thinking fast, James decided to improvise. *Why not tell her the truth? She'd never believe it, anyway.* So, he did. He simply repeated what they just told him. When he was done telling the story of the Time machine and Doctor Meany, she looked at Waldo and said, "I thought you'd be good company for Daddy." She smiled, took the bears from him and placed them gently on the desk where they belonged. She gave him a big hug and said, "You tell the funniest stories. I can't wait for the next one."

She skipped off to do her homework, which was back where it belonged as well. "I can't wait either, Pumpkin," he said looking at the bears, sitting very still and very quiet.

A SLIP OF THE TONGUE

Every morning Bobbie would walk into her daddy's office for a hug goodbye. Then she would look at Waldo and say those three little words (that reminded him of what he needed to be reminded of), "You be good."

She'd lean close to his face and give him the look. She may have done it playfully but she was serious and Waldo knew it.

Even though Bobby Bear and Waldo sat on James' desk, their person was still Bobbie. After all, she was the one that brought them to life.

Ever since she got Waldo and Bobby Bear two years ago, she would pretend that Waldo was the adventurous one, while Bobby Bear followed close behind questioning if what they were doing would get them into trouble.

The bears loved Bobbie because she treated them as if they were people. They had so much fun with Bobbie on her adventures that they would make up their own when she was away. Waldo wanted to be just like her: creative, funny and, of course, adventurous.

As soon as Bobbie and Debra walked out the door for work and school, Waldo jumped down from the desk and peered out the window to watch them leave. As the car pulled away, he found himself thinking about the Teddy Council. He remembered the night they were caught getting into the refrigerator. All they wanted was the milk. Oh, that smooth and creamy drink, it was their weakness. James was right when he asked if Fluffy bear was the one that got them hooked on milk. Fluffy had a drinking problem.

Big Red Fluffy bear was the one responsible for teaching the two young bears about teddy life and the ways of the Code. Bobby Bear and Waldo would marvel at the way Fluffy walked about the house while the family was asleep. They would soon find out why he wandered so. One evening, over eight months ago, Fluffy invited the two bears to join him in the kitchen. It was self-serving actually. Fluffy had a difficult time reaching the milk by himself and enlisted Bobby Bear and Waldo to help him with his small yet fatal addiction. Fluffy was their teacher and therefore had the trust of the adolescent bears. Curiously, following him to the refrigerator, Fluffy pulled the door open and pointed to the chilled carton of milk.

"You see that?" he asked. "That's milk; the tastiest thing in the whole world." Fluffy gave a slight chuckle. Intensity beamed in Fluffy's eyes confirming what he said. Milk was the only thing in focus as he gazed at the creamy cold drink. He turned and said, "Okay, you two, come here." Grabbing Bobby Bear firmly by the arm, he positioned him at the foot of the open fridge. Another faint giggle slipped from Fluffy's mouth.

Bobby Bear turned, giving a peculiar look. "Is this supposed to be funny?"

"No."

"Why'd you laugh?"

"Did I? Huh. Dunno." Fluffy's face was hiding something.

"'Cause to be honest; I'm kinda nervous right now."

Fluffy was embarrassed about his troublesome tick. Anxious moments brought on a slight case of the nervous giggles, most of the time he wasn't aware he was doing it. He didn't like it but he couldn't control it. "I didn't laugh and I don't think this is funny. Let's hurry up shall we?" snapped Fluffy. He then turned to Waldo. "Now you, climb up on his shoulders and grab that carton." Without question or hesitation, Waldo saw the whole escapade as an adventure and quickly grabbed onto Bobby Bear and maneuvered up his body. Using the shelving in the fridge to balance himself, Waldo slowly stood on his friend's shoulders. The milk was just at the tip of his paws.

"I can't quite reach it," whispered Waldo.

Bobby Bear was fairly sure that what they were doing was not in the Code. Maybe this was part of the lesson, he thought, trying to rationalize the moment.

Waldo stretched his body and straightened his toes to reach the milk. There was a sense of accomplishment and satisfaction when he grabbed onto the cold carton of milk. The look on Fluffy bear's face was all Waldo needed to see. Fluffy took the carton from Waldo. Scampering down the backside of his best friend, Waldo lost his grip and hit the floor. Feeling embarrassed but not wanting to show it, he sprang to his feet with a smile. "So, what do you do with it?" asked Waldo quickly, trying to divert his clumsiness. That was the most ridiculous question Fluffy had ever heard. "You drink it!" he answered defiantly. With that, Fluffy popped open the folded flap and tilted his head back slowly as not to spill the delicious drink. There was a glaze over Fluffy bear's eyes as he swallowed.

"Can I try?" asked Waldo curiously.

Fluffy regained his focus and slowly handed the carton to Waldo.

"Okay. Just take it slowly and don't spill anything. Remember, we have to leave everything so that a human can't tell," said Fluffy.

Waldo grabbed the carton and tipped it to his mouth. The first drop was all it took. Life would have a whole new meaning after that. How could anything so cold be so good? Bobby Bear had a twinge in his stomach that told him something was wrong. It would often happen when Waldo was about to do something stupid. He should have listened to his stomach. Waldo handed the carton to his best friend and muttered a few unknown words. The pressure to try the drink was more than Bobby Bear could stand. Before he knew what he was doing, the carton was pouring creamy drink into his mouth. That was it. The forbidden fruit had been tasted. The bears were hooked. It would be their undoing.

Back in the moment, Waldo was at the window thinking about the Council. They broke the first rule of the Teddy Code and the two young bears were going to be punished, but when — and how?

He imagined a dark cell and being tied to a chair while spiders crawled over him. He hated spiders. He wasn't very fond of snakes either and could feel something slither at his feet. Panic set in and his mouth popped open to scream but all that was heard was a pitiful squeak for help. A voice returned from the distance. "Waldo! It's me!"

The darkness was everywhere. "I can't see you," shouted Waldo.

"I'm right here. *I'm right here,*" the voice answered, drawing closer.

"Where are you? I can't see you. There's spiders, lots of spiders and don't step on the snakes," Waldo yelled urgently to the voice in the distance. He could feel things dancing on his fur.

Suddenly, the voice was right next to him. "Spiders — that's just silly. Waldo, just open your eyes."

He did as the voice asked only to find his best friend in front of him. "What are you talking about?" asked Bobby Bear. He had no idea why Waldo was so upset. "What's this about snakes?"

Waldo glanced around and found himself at the window with the curtain brushing against him and the drawstring wrapped around his feet. He looked at Bobby Bear, his eyes wide, his breath short, and paws twitching nervously. "The Council," he said faintly.

"What about the Council?"

Waldo remembered why he was at the window. "Nothing — come on. We need to do something."

He grabbed his friend by the arm and off they went to Bobbie's room.

"Why are we here?"

Waldo didn't answer. He was focused on Elvis, a large good-looking bear with soft shaggy light gray fur, who sits in the Big People's Chair in the corner of her room. Standing over three feet tall, Elvis was the largest bear in the house. His muzzle was like a Greek god. It was long and slightly sloped downward. He was truly a handsome bear.

Elvis was part of the Teddy Network. Almost every house with a teddy has a Network bear. Any news that happened in the teddy world was passed through them. Waldo hoped that Elvis had some news from the Council about their punishment.

He told Bobby Bear to stand at the door to make sure James was not about, since the other teddies will not move in his presence.

Waldo took a deep breath and approached the handsome bear. "Hey, Elvis, have you heard anything yet?"

Elvis didn't like to move during the day or when humans were awake but he could see the worry on Waldo's face. The large black marbley beads that were Elvis' eyes grew into a vibrant steel gray as he came to life and reluctantly answered.

"I haven't heard anything yet. It may take a little time," said Elvis.

This doesn't help at all, thought Waldo. "So, you don't know anything?"

"No."

Waldo turned towards Bobby Bear and shook his head sadly.

Feeling like he should say *something* else, Elvis added, "I'll let you know as soon as I hear. Okay? There's been a new Outsider keeping me informed, but I haven't seen him since I reported you guys last week."

Waldo gave a forced smile and nodded. The weight on his shoulders was obvious as he walked out of the room, headed toward the office.

***

At Hallow Oaks Manor, Bullock had received word about Bobby Bear and Waldo's violation. More detail would be needed to determine their punishment, but it was clear from what they heard, these bears needed to be brought back to the Council. This was not a glimpse of a bear caught out of the corner of someone's eye, or a child saying that, 'their bear moved.' The report was; two young bears were caught moving and are continuing to move in front of a human, an adult human at that. This was not normal in the teddy world. It was added that the human was writing teddy stories. This typically would not concern the Council since teddy bear stories were quite common. However, what gave cause for further investigation was the type of stories this human was writing. This was a special circumstance. His bears were still moving. Did he have insight into their world from the two mischievous teddies?

Since creating the Council, the Secret Teddy Society had been fairly quiet, until recently. There are the occasional Trust Busters who fall victim to the influences of their humans and violate the teddy trust. However, these two bears were showing a clear disregard for the Teddy Code. *What to do?* pondered Bullock. He couldn't let the situation get out of control. A teddy thug would be dispatched to retrieve the Code breakers and lead them back to the Council.

Bullock had a sense that the teddy world was changing. The amount of teddy incidents over the last several years had been on an increase.

Theodore seemed distant and Ballinger was acting suspiciously. No more prominent bears had been reported missing, but there was uneasiness among certain Council members. The cause for concern was real, at least Bullock thought so. He could feel it.

**

After his disappointing visit to Elvis, Waldo moped back to the office. James was sitting at his desk working on the stories, when Waldo climbed up and sat in his spot. He began tapping the pencils in the pencil cup, back and forth.

"Is something wrong, Waldo?" James asked. The look on his face said "yes" but he answered, "I don't know."

He kept tapping the pencils back and forth.

"What do you mean, you don't know?'"

Waldo slapped the pencils hard. "I don't know if I'm in trouble or not. The Council is going to do something — but I don't know what — or when."

"I know you told me about Big Red Fluffy bear, but you don't really know what happened to him. Maybe it's not as bad as you're thinking. Maybe, 'cause you guys are so young, they'll go easy on you."

Waldo wasn't convinced. "Maybe."

He didn't want to make light of their situation but it was, after all, teddy bears he was talking about. A teddy bear council just didn't sound menacing to James.

Scuffle, scuffle, creek, thud. James heard something from the other room. He looked at Waldo, still sulking and tapping the pencils, and said, "Hold that thought, I'll be right back."

He headed toward the noise, which seemed to be coming from the kitchen. He got to the kitchen doorway and stood quietly watching Bobby Bear push a chair into place in front of the refrigerator, then, climbed up and reached for the milk; all the while mumbling, ". . . Waldo likes his milk cold."

Bobby Bear decided to cheer up his friend by making his favorite snack.

James felt that he could use a little assistance. "Can I help you, buddy?"

At that point, he had climbed almost inside the refrigerator and James couldn't help but smile as all he could see was a furry little bear bottom sticking out of the fridge.

Bobby Bear grunted then replied, "No thanks, he likes it cold."

James chuckled and noticed two glasses on the counter that he got down from the cupboard.

"You can help me down though," he called, his voice sounding suddenly urgent.

James hurried over and plucked him from the fridge then carried both the bear and the treat into the office.

They drank milk while James listened to Waldo vent his concerns. He talked about the Council and the more he talked the more anxious he became. James remembered that he got very chatty when he was nervous, so as Waldo prattled on, James slowly smiled because it was amusing to watch.

Waldo became aware of the grin on James' face.

"What are you smiling at? Do you think this is funny? Do you think being locked in a room full of spiders and snakes is a joke?" he snapped, staring intently at James. "'Cuz this is serious."

James had never been scolded by a teddy bear before and hiding the smile was harder than he thought. Waldo was painting a fairly grim view of the Council and what they might do. True, Waldo told James about Big Red Fluffy bear, but they didn't really know what happened. Maybe nothing happened. Maybe Fluffy was somewhere in the house right now. James would convince himself of anything but the truth. He didn't want them taken away; they were his story, after all. He had finally found something to write about and wasn't going to let a silly council of bears intimidate him.

"I won't let anything happen to you, buddy," said James, trying to comfort the uptight white bear.

Waldo gave a half-hearted smile. "Thanks, but this is the Council we're talking about," he replied. "There's not much you can do, but thanks for saying."

James didn't know how to take his remark. Was he saying that the Council was so powerful that they could take a bear out from under his nose, that there was nothing he could do about it? Even though James had proof of teddy life in front of him, he struggled with the concept of an all-powerful council that could impose its will on a human.

It wasn't long before the sound of the family car was heard pulling into the driveway. Bobby Bear and Waldo know that sound very well.

"Oops, they're home," said James. Peering out the window, he could see Bobbie and Debra sitting in the car.

James took the glasses of milk back to the kitchen, while the bears went to their spot. He returned to the desk and peeked out the window once more to see Bobbie getting out of the car, but something was different. She looked sad, as if she had been crying. Normally, she would grab her backpack and bound into the house, running straight to the desk to hear what the bears had been up to that day, but not today. Something was wrong today. Something happened at school.

The door opened and Debra walked in followed by Bobbie, which was also unusual. James noticed Debra moving her lips without a sound. *She's upset,* she mouthed.

He gave a sympathetic look with an understanding smile, walked over and crouched down and asked, "Rough day, Pumpkin?"

The tears in her eyes said everything as she reached for a hug.

"Is there something I can do?" he inquired softly. He felt her head turn back and forth on his shoulder.

"Do you want to talk about it?" He felt another headshake. "Okay," he said in all seriousness. "What if I tell you what Bobby Bear did today?"

Since she loved the stories so much, she slowly lifted her head. James brushed the tears off her cheek. She nodded. He picked her up and walked to the desk where they sat down in his chair.

Bobby Bear and Waldo sat in their usual spot facing James while he worked, which meant Waldo was looking straight at Bobbie as tears trickled down her face. There was something about Waldo's expression; James couldn't tell exactly what it was but he could sense it.

He told her about Bobby Bear getting into the refrigerator for the milk, which made her smile. He described how his furry bottom was sticking out, wiggling back and forth, as he maneuvered around the fridge. She let out a little giggle.

Suddenly, the problem came bouncing out of her mouth. "Daddy, why are kids so mean?"

James wasn't sure exactly what to say, since he had always wondered that himself and never had a good answer. "Why, was someone mean to you at school today?"

She didn't answer but she didn't have to.

Meanwhile, Waldo could not believe what he just heard.

Someone was mean to her? Who could be mean to her? The sweetest, kindest, most loving person in the whole world and someone was mean to her? Waldo's mind was racing. It was getting harder to remain still as he wanted to know who this big Meany was.

James sighed. "I know kids can be mean sometimes, Pumpkin, and I'd like to say that this will never happen again but —"

"How can I stay away from mean kids?" she interrupted.

"Well . . . you won't always know who's mean. Has your best friend ever said or done anything that you thought was mean?"

She thought for a second and remembered a time when a friend hid her backpack at school and she went without lunch. Her friend said it was just to be funny but she remembered it not being funny at all. She nodded.

"Have Mommy or I ever done anything that you thought was mean?"

Her mind quickly filled with several instances but didn't want to answer since she understood what he was trying to say.

"Pumpkin, all you can do is be the best person you can be. And I think you've already got that down pretty well."

She smiled and turned to Waldo. "Has he been a good bear today?"

He simply said, "Yes, he's been very good."

She picked up both bears and gave them a big hug and a kiss. "Do you mind if I borrow them for a while Daddy?"

"Not at all. They're your bears."

And off the three of them went to her room.

Bobbie placed the bears on her bed and said, "I'll be right back." She turned and ran out of the room only to return with two short pieces of yarn and two small pieces of paper. She began to write, sounding out each word as she made each letter. "Waldo," she said slowly, moving her pen across the first piece of paper. Her pen formed the words "Bobby Bear" on the other. He liked hearing Bobbie say his name while she wrote. She taped each piece of paper to the yarn then loosely tied one of the strands around each bears neck. The bears had never seen their names written before and this was special to Waldo. It made it official, like a badge of honor.

Waldo could see it now: *A council bear stood at the podium and cleared his throat before he read from his cue cards. "For courage above and beyond the call of duty; for putting yourself in great peril to save the lives of others and keep the teddy world safe from evil; I give you this medal with your name showing all who see it that you, Waldo, are officially named Waldo."*

The crowd cheered while the medal was placed around his neck. He smiled so hard that his cheeks made it difficult to see. Teddies reached out to touch him when someone began tugging on his award.

"There," said Bobbie, adjusting the paper around his neck, "Now you have your name tags for Show and Tell tomorrow."

Waldo snapped out of his daydream realizing what he heard.

I'm going to school? he thought. The bears had never left the house before, not since they were born. Waldo was bubbling with excitement and could hardly keep from looking at his best friend. Bobby Bear was so nervous that he could hardly keep from looking back.

"You two are going to school with me tomorrow so I need you on your best behavior," said Bobbie, looking straight at Waldo. "You promise?" she asked, not expecting an answer. Waldo was becoming so used to talking and moving about the house, he almost said "Yes".

Of course, Bobby Bear wasn't really listening at the moment, for he had his own thoughts racing through his mind.

It was going to be a long night for the bears and even Bobbie was nervous since she had never had to speak in front of the class before. Not to mention, being made fun of for her Show and Tell subject by a certain Meany.

The mood changed in an instant as Bobbie vented her frustration. "I don't know if you know this, but people can be mean. It might not be everyone but they're out there. Mean and rotten." Bobbie had a strong dislike for mean people and there was one in her class that was at the top of her list. "Why do they feel the need to say things when you didn't even ask? I didn't ask anyone if they liked what I was bringing for Show and Tell, but they felt the need to *pipe in*. 'Oh, that's stupid. You still play with teddy bears?'" Bobbie worked herself up all over again. "I didn't ask their stupid opinion — but they just had to give it!" Both bears could feel the anger and vexation inside Bobbie and it was bothersome. "I'd like to put a tack on *their* seat to see how they like it," said Bobbie as she remembered when someone had done it to her. She never found out who did it but she had her suspicions. "I'm tired of getting picked on."

Waldo had never heard anything like this from Bobbie before. He never thought about revenge, but if that's what would make Bobbie happy, then, count him in.

She kept both bears with her that night to make sure they got a good night sleep. When Bobbie closed her eyes, Waldo and Bobby Bear both knew that a good night sleep was not to be had.

In the morning, James came to wake Bobbie for school. He would always begin by singing a silly made up song, which, for some reason did not bring a smile to her face, however, Bobby Bear fought the urge to giggle.

> *"If it's dark inside your head,*
> *that's because you're still in bed.*
> *With your eyelids closed at night,*
> *doesn't stop your dreamy sight.*
> *Hear the sunlight, smell the day.*
> *It's a beauty, I must say!*
> *Shake the sleepy, stop the dreamy;*
> *sun is bright and very gleamy.*
> *Come on, open up your eyes,*
> *see for yourself, it's no surprise.*
> *By the way, I have to say, have you had a —"*

"Stop singing Daddy, that's not even a real song," she said in her morning groggy voice, not wanting to open her eyes. Bobbie was not a morning person.

"Come on, Pumpkin. It's time to get up."

She slowly rolled over and said, "I don't want to go to school today."

"But you were looking forward to Show and Tell; I know Bobby Bear and Waldo were looking forward to it," he said.

Realizing that the bears would be with her, she felt more at ease. "Okay, I'll get up."

James started to sing, *"She's getting up. She's getting up. She's getting up, up, up, up, up."*

"Daddy," she scolded with a laser like stare.

He stopped singing and asked, "Is it that I'm annoying you or that I can't sing?"

She simply replied, "Yes."

A grin slipped out. "Well, your breakfast is ready, Pumpkin."

James went to get the morning paper that was normally tossed onto the front lawn, but for several weeks now, the paper hasn't always been there. He checked everywhere; the porch, the hedges, even the neighbor's yards. Nothing. Some days it was there and some days it wasn't. He called the paper to see if his subscription ran out or they changed how they delivered, but still nothing.

"Did anyone grab the paper this morning?" he called out to anyone.

Debra was busy with breakfast dishes when she answered, "No. I haven't seen it for a few days."

Not wanting to deal with it any longer, he relented and took his coffee to the office.

After breakfast, Bobbie collected her backpack and the bears, while Mommy waited at the door. She went to the office to say goodbye. James leaned forward and gave her a kiss, then he looked straight at Waldo and said what Bobbie would normally say at this time, "You be good." But James was serious and Waldo knew it.

Bobbie smiled, turned and walked to the front door. With every step, Bobby Bear was getting more nervous. With every step, Waldo was getting more excited.

"Goodbye, Daddy," she yelled as they left.

Side by side, the bears were squeezed together in Bobbie's arms, as she walked into the brisk morning air. They could feel their bodies stiffen as the cold breeze brushed through their fur.

Waldo could see Debra's shiny red car. He had heard it many times pull in and out of the driveway, but this time would be different. This time he would be a passenger.

Ding, ding, ding, ding went the car door when Debra opened it. Bobby Bear saw Waldo out of the corner of his eye and his friend had a look of excitement glued on his face. Bobbie climbed into her seat in the back. Debra took the bears and placed them in the front seat next to her.

"*Mommy*," Bobbie said in a reminding tone.

Debra reached up, grabbed the seat belt, and buckled both bears in safely.

"Did you snug it tight?" Bobbie asked.

Debra gave a slight tug on the belt and said, "They're snug as a bug."

Waldo felt so excited; he wanted to look around but knew he couldn't; that he had to remain perfectly still. Bobby Bear, on the other hand, was so scared; he wanted to close his eyes but knew he shouldn't.

The car backed into the street, coming to a slow stop, Debra shifted into drive and the car began moving forward. As the car accelerated, Waldo could feel the sense of speed from the tires pulling the car across the road. The tops of trees and telephone poles moved faster and faster past the window as the sound of the engine roared louder. Waldo felt like he was riding in a rocket.

Waldo's imagination took off: *Houston, we have a go. Everything looks good. Flipping to ultra-big super rocket power – nnnnnnow.*

The car zoomed straight ahead. Waldo loved watching objects fly past the window in a blur. The engine began to slow.

Houston, we have a problem. Losing power. Losing power!

The car came to a stop at a traffic light and the engine purred softly.

I don't know what's wrong. I seem to be floating . . . There appears to be no power and no thrust. Repeat there is no . . .

Just then, the light changed and once again, Waldo's body flattened against the seat as the car sped forward.

Control, everything's back to normal. Power has returned – repeat, power has returned.

The road up ahead was in some need of repair, making the car bounce erratically.

There seems to be space bumps but everything looks good. I don't know how much more of this the ship can take though.

They approached the school and Debra weaved through the long parking area. The car swerved left and right forcing the bears side to side in their seat.

Houston, I'm out of control. Repeat, out of control. It doesn't look like I'm gonna make it back. Tell everyone that . . ."

The car came to a stop right out front of Roosevelt Elementary as it does every morning.

"We're here," said Debra.

Bobbie let herself out of her car seat and was all ready when Debra opened the door.

"Don't forget your backpack," she reminded her, then opened the passenger door and unbuckled the bears. She grabbed them by the arms and handed them to Bobbie then leaned over and gave her a kiss.

"Have a good day and I'll be right here when you get out."

Bobbie held the bears close and turned to go to class.

Kids came from every direction all headed to one door. The bears had never seen this many people before. Bobby Bear could also feel Bobbie's nerves as she squeezed him even tighter than usual. He didn't mind. He understood being nervous. He felt it, too.

Waldo was amazed at all the kids and suddenly found himself wondering which one was the big Meany, the kid who'd upset Bobbie. He studied each person that came into view. Somehow, he felt he would know the big Meany when he saw him. None of the kids he saw appeared particularly mean. As they walked the crowded hallway, kids bumped into each other as if they were doing it on purpose. Bobby Bear felt unnerved. It would be so easy for one of the other kids to bump him straight out of Bobbie's arms.

"Are those your stupid bears, Bobbie?" a snide girly voice called from behind.

That's him, thought Waldo. *That's the big Meany, but that's not a him voice, that's a her voice.* Waldo hadn't considered the idea that the big Meany could be a girl.

He wanted to turn around but the Teddy Code would not allow it.

Bobbie didn't respond and continued walking to class.

Bump, nudge. Bobby Bear was in a state of panic. *Tighter, please hold tighter*, he kept thinking over and over.

Suddenly, a big shove from behind made Bobbie lurch forward. Trying not to fall, she put her hands out. Now loose, the two teddy bears went sailing to the ground. Waldo tumbled into the crowd, landing on his back, staring straight up. Bobby Bear came to rest face down on the walkway. Footsteps brushed dangerously past his head until he felt a dull jab in his side and skidded across the ground as someone stumbled over him. This was the worst thing that had ever happened to Bobby Bear his whole life. He wanted to scamper away to safety, but he couldn't move. It was torture. At this point, all he wanted to do was go home.

Waldo watched as kids stepped over him while he lay motionless on the ground. Faces looked down at him, some smiling, some laughing and some with concern. Waldo thought anxiously, *Where's Bobbie? Where's Bobby Bear?*

A face leaned over; a familiar face, her eyes filled with tears. It was his favorite person, Bobbie. She gently picked up her little white bear and said, "I'm sorry, Waldo. I'm sorry." She found Bobby Bear still lying face down and scooped him up, too. She was clearly upset but did not want to cry. Tears threatened to spill.

"It's okay, Bobby Bear, she's a big Meany." Her voice trembled as she brushed a smudge of dirt from his face.

He remembered what she said earlier. *She's right, kids are mean*, he thought, concentrating on just staying still.

A friend hurried over to help her collect her things.

"Are you all right, Bobbie?" asked Kristi. Tall and skinny with long brown hair, you could always see Kristi with her Hello Kitty lunch box and matching hair clips. Kristi cared about everyone with an exception or two. It was Kristi's question toward fact or fiction that Bobbie found alluring.

Kristi always seemed to find something good in everyone but that got disguised in her cautious and skeptical demeanor.

"Thanks. I'm okay," said Bobbie.

"Who did it? Was it Tiffany?"

Bobbie didn't answer. Waldo almost turned his head when he heard the name of the big Meany. Bobbie, meanwhile, was too choked up to talk about it. She didn't even want to do Show and Tell.

She found herself in class, where she hung up her backpack on the wall and maneuvered around the room towards her seat. Waldo was hoping to get a glimpse of this Tiffany person, but he didn't know what she looked like. He only heard her voice — a mean sinister voice that he wouldn't ever forget.

How will I know her? he wondered.

A loud bell rang and the kids moved to their seats like they were actors in a well-rehearsed play. Bobbie found her desk and sat down, still holding her bears. After what happened, she was not about to put them down.

A grown-up walked in the door.

This is not a kid, thought Waldo. *This must be the teacher.*

"Good morning. Does everyone remember what today is?"

"YES, MRS. LARKIN," the class answered in unison.

Bobbie tilted her head down and whispered to the bears. "That's my teacher. We like her."

Mrs. Larkin was tall with dark brown skin and black hair, which she usually wore up in a bun. But that's not the first thing you noticed about the charming second-grade teacher. There are smiles, and then there are smiles. Mrs. Larkin had the latter. She also had a rather funny sounding laugh, but it suited her perfectly.

She took roll, calling out each student's name one by one. Waldo listened intently until the teacher called out one name.

"Tiffany?"

A voice from behind answered, "Here."

Waldo's ears were working at their best and he now knew where she was. He still couldn't see her face, since he couldn't turn around, but his imagination was already hard at work piecing together what she might look like. He imagined she'd be tremendously ugly, with beams of evil shooting from her black lifeless eyes. A defining scar down her cheek was classic for someone so evil, Waldo was sure of that.

"I see many of you have brought some interesting things for Show and Tell," said Mrs. Larkin. "Why don't we get started? Let's see here, Alli Anderson goes first today. Please come to the front of the class, and try to speak loudly so everyone can hear you."

She glanced around nervously as she walked to the front of the class. Alli held what appeared to be an old gray stuffed sock with a tail.

"This is Chimpsee, I got him when I was a baby. My daddy bought him when he was in China . . ."

Waldo was trying to listen but his mind kept wandering back to Tiffany. If only he could turn around, he'd see for sure what he imagined. He envisioned a bully with a cruel face and a cold heart that left an icy wind as she walked, her peg leg scraping scornfully across the floor. He pictured her with black matted hair, with chewed off fingernails from her pointed teeth, and her body so large that she could squash Bobbie like a bug just by sitting on her.

Oh, what I would like to do to you, he thought. *It's got to be something that would make her feel like she made Bobbie feel, something that would embarrass her in front of the whole class. It's got to be good, but what?* His mind ran though a few scenario's. *If I could get some glue, somewhere, and put it on her seat, somehow, then she would sit on it and be stuck to her seat forever. Ha! Stuck forever, that's a good one.*

As Waldo was busy plotting, Bobby Bear was listening to the kids doing their Show and Tell.

Next up was Danielle Braswell, who could always make Bobbie smile because she was unpredictable with what she would do or say.

"Danielle, do you have something for Show and Tell today?" asked the teacher.

"Yes, ma'am," she replied and proceeded to the front of the class holding only her lunch box.

"This is my Show and Tell," she said and held up a small red metal box with a plastic white handle. "I know some of you are thinking that this is just a lunch box. True, but this is no ordinary box. This is a box of mystery — a box of wonder and magic," she said in a theatrical voice.

"That's just a lunch box," sniped Cody Evens. You could always count on him for a dose of reality.

"Lunch box, you say?" said Danielle, unfazed by the verbal jab from Cody. "Yes, but like no other. This box is a doorway to the unknown. Yesterday, when I opened this very box, I found a ham sandwich with an apple and potato chips." She lifted the box higher and slowly panned from right to left.

Bobbie started to snicker as the class hung on every word, waiting for what she would say next. Even Mrs. Larkin was smiling. Bobby Bear found himself completely taken in.

A magic lunch box, wow, he thought.

"Now, I have noticed that every day for as long as I can remember, every time I open this very box, somehow, some way, a different meal occupies this space. How does this happen? When does this happen? *Why* does this happen? All very good questions — but only one question *really* matters. What is inside this mystery box — today? Even I do not know."

The class erupted into guesses, and the teacher was as curious about the answer as anyone. Never before had a class been so interested in what Danielle was going to have for lunch.

She lowered the box and turned it towards herself. Slowly opening the lid, she peeked inside. The class was dead quiet. Danielle's eyes widened in surprise as if she'd uncovered the tenth wonder of the world. She spun the box around to the class. "Peanut butter and jelly, Fig Newtons and corn chips!" she exclaimed. The children burst out laughing as Danielle smiled and walked back to her seat.

"Very good, Danielle. That was fun and very creative," said the teacher.

Bobby Bear was most impressed with the magic lunch box and he was beginning to relax, while Waldo was still thinking of the perfect plan for Tiffany. Nothing seemed good enough. He just needed the right plan to let precious Tiffany know the power of the teddy bear.

Suddenly, it hit him; the most brilliant idea, the perfect plan.

That's it. I got it, he thought excitedly. *Why didn't I think of this before?*

Waldo was positive this was just the thing to get back at her, to right the wrong.

"Tiffany Connors, you're next," Mrs. Larkin called out.

Waldo snapped from his daydream plotting and heard the words he was waiting for.

Finally, I get to see the big Meany.

Suddenly, there she was. He didn't see her face but the sweet smell of springtime fresh fabric softener filled the air as she breezed by Bobbie's desk. He loved that smell. Golden hair swung back and forth as she stepped with confidence.

That can't be her, he thought. *Where's the peg leg? There must be a different Tiffany.*

She got to the front of the class and turned. Waldo saw her face and couldn't believe it. He'd seen a face just like it on a doll in the playroom; a pretty face, a perfect face.

How can this be the big Meany? How can I tell? he wondered. *I need to be sure?*

"My Show and Tell is my Jewelry box," she said in her very princess way. Waldo could not forget *that* voice; *that* tone.

Yep, that's her. There was no doubt. He also became clear what he had to do. As Tiffany spoke, Waldo plotted.

The plan Waldo had in mind was a technique used by teddies around the world in severe cases of teddy bear abuse by humans. It involves the Teddy Network, Teddy Thugs, usually, the bear that was abused, and an elaborate scheme tailored to the individual. The plan takes place when the person is alone and normally asleep. This select group of bears would gather around the human that has done harm to a teddy and create a "Teddy Nightmare." It is very dangerous, and different results occur, but it is usually successful. The goal of a Nightmare is to bring conscious thought of remorse while the person thinks they're still asleep. It works well because it forces them to question their cruelty to teddies as if it were their self-conscience talking. However, different dangers can occur depending on the individual. This is why teamwork is essential.

While Tiffany was giving her Show and Tell report, Waldo was delighted in his plan.

Tiffany leered at Bobbie, while she was talking, and said, "This necklace was bought at Tiffany's and is very expensive. My Mommy said that I was named after the famous store because I'm special just like their — tongue."

Tongue? Waldo thought that was odd. Tiffany had stopped cold and was staring directly at him.

Why is she looking at me like that? he wondered. He was suddenly aware of what he was doing. His tongue was sticking out. It was an awful habit. His intense concentration seemed to almost push it out of his mouth. The moment of heated thought brought him to the edge of awake. He pulled it in before anyone else noticed. Since the whole class was focused on Tiffany, no one else could see Waldo's face.

She stood motionless and speechless. Her mind was a jumbled mess. She had lost her thought and completely forgot what she was supposed to say next. All Tiffany was aware of was a teddy bear had just stuck out his tongue at her. She looked around the class to see if anyone else had seen it, but every face was directed at her.

What was that? she wondered as confused as one could be. A few kids started to laugh; then more joined in. She quickly remembered where she was.

Mrs. Larkin noticed Tiffany's awkwardness. "Is that it — Tiffany? Are you finished?"

Every word that she had learned since she was born seemed to vanish. "Um, uh," she mumbled. Her head nodded slowly as she glanced about the room. She walked in a daze back to her seat, staring at Waldo as she passed. He sat still while facing straight ahead. Inside, he was laughing. She'd gotten exactly what she deserved and he hadn't even had to call in the Teddy Thugs.

The other children kept laughing and some were whispering to each other as Tiffany shuffled by. Her face burned bright red in embarrassment.

Suddenly, an alarm sounded in the class, interrupting the laughter. Bobby Bear had never heard a sound like that before and nearly jumped out of Bobbie's arms. Mrs. Larkin stood up and said, "Okay, class, it's a fire drill. Please line up and proceed down the hall to the playground."

Bobbie stood up and got in line while still holding her bears.

"Leave everything in the room, everyone," said Mrs. Larkin.

Bobby Bear nearly cried out. *Don't leave me alone in here! Not with this horrible noise! No!*

Bobbie seemed to almost hear Bobby Bear's thoughts because she hesitated. She didn't want to leave her bears, but she couldn't disobey the teacher. She went back to her desk and placed the bears in her seat, then hurried back to get in line. Tiffany was the last one to get up from her desk. Walking down the aisle slowly until she was next to Bobbie's seat, Tiffany stopped as if she had dropped something. She knelt down to look Waldo straight in the eyes and whispered, "I know you can hear me and I know what I saw. I thought Bobbie was crazy when she said you were alive . . . I didn't believe her but . . . I just want to say, I'm sorry."

Mrs. Larkin was standing in the doorway and called out, "Come on, Tiffany. The whole class is waiting on you."

"I'm coming."

She turned back to Waldo. "I just wanted to say that — I believe."

Both bears remained still as Tiffany stared. "I guess I gotta get going. So . . ." She stood up and walked out of the room.

Hearing the footsteps fade in the distance, Bobby Bear looked at Waldo. "What did you do?" he asked, completely confused about Tiffany's comment. Waldo gave a crooked half-smile and replied, "Nothing, well . . . nothing really."

"What do you mean, nothing really?"

"I may have stuck out my tongue or something when she was standing up there."

Waldo was bracing for the worst. Here comes the lecture, the yelling, the insults; he knew how this worked.

"So — now she knows, *too*?" exclaimed Bobby Bear.

"Don't get mad!"

"Mad? Why would I be mad? She's a kid. No one's gonna believe her, anyway." Bobby Bear wore a big smile. "She got laughed at by the whole class. Now *she* knows what it's like." He slapped Waldo on the shoulder. "You did it! You got her back!"

Waldo was confused for a second. "Oh — yeah, I did!"

"Sticking your tongue out; so *simple*, and no other teddies around to see, either. Was that your plan?" Bobby Bear asked. "'Cause that was brilliant, *just brilliant*."

Waldo didn't want to admit it was an accident. "Well, not quite. I thought about using the Teddy Nightmare plan actually."

Absolute amazement appeared on Bobby Bear's face. "I would have *never* thought of that. *That* would have been *great.*"

Once again, Waldo did not get the response he was expecting. Bobby Bear would often surprise him by not getting upset when he told the truth about things. This made him feel good. He also couldn't believe that something so simple would change someone like Tiffany.

She apologized to me. I didn't see that coming, he said to himself. *Maybe that was enough.*

Before long, they could hear the sound of kids laughing and scuffling from outside. The fire drill was over and the children were finding their way back to their seats.

Bobbie got to her desk to find the bears sitting right where she left them. She wanted to ask if they were all right but didn't want to say it out loud. She picked them up and Bobby Bear was just glad to be back in her arms.

Before she could sit down, Mrs. Larkin said, "Bobbie, since you're still up, why don't you go ahead and do your Show and Tell."

She didn't really want to do it anymore for fear of Tiffany shouting something mean. Besides, no one else brought a teddy bear for Show and Tell, she would stand out like a sore thumb. Just then, a hand reached out to gently pet Waldo on his head. "This one's my favorite," said Tiffany with a smile, then continued on to her seat.

Shocked did not even begin to describe Bobbie's reaction. Completely baffled, Bobbie stood motionless when the teacher asked, "Bobbie, are you ready?"

She looked down at her bears and regained her confidence knowing she wouldn't be alone. Then she walked to the front of the class and turned facing everyone.

"This is my Show and Tell," she said and held up her two teddy bears. "This one is Bobby Bear and this one is Waldo."

At that moment she decided she was not going to talk about the teddy world and how her dad said they come alive. Making fun of her would be one thing but making fun of daddy was something else.

"My mommy and daddy got them for me when I was little. I put them on my daddy's desk to keep him company while he works at home," she said. "He likes them so much that he's writing stories about them."

If she wasn't going to talk about the teddy world then what would she talk about? What else do you say about teddy bears that you won't get laughed at for? The room was quiet. Bobbie decided she should head back to her desk when Mrs. Larkin noticed someone raising their hand. "Yes, Tiffany, you have a question?"

"Is it true they come alive?"

Tiffany wanted to hear the truth from Bobbie. Actually, after what she saw, she *needed* to hear the truth.

It was as if someone pressed a pause button, as the class appeared frozen waiting for a response.

Bobbie didn't know what to say except to answer in the only way she knew how.

"Yes," she replied quietly. Her eyes went straight to the floor. The can of worms had been opened and there was nowhere to hide. Frozen solid, she waited for the teacher to say, 'Thank you Bobbie,' or 'Good job', something that would allow her to slink back to her seat.

Before Tiffany could ask another question, a different voice came from across the room.

"How do you know?"

Bobbie noticed that no one was laughing. They actually seemed interested. Maybe it's because she'd never been known as a liar or someone who exaggerates a story. Whatever the reason, the expression on their faces gave Bobbie permission to continue.

"Um . . . my daddy caught them getting into the refrigerator one night."

A few giggles were heard but not because they didn't believe but were picturing the scene.

"Why were they in the refrigerator?" another kid asked.

Bobbie slowly smiled and said, "They were after the milk. They really love milk."

The class laughed and Bobbie started to relax.

"You can see them move?" asked Britney Manning.

"No, I can't, because I wasn't the one that caught them moving, my daddy did."

"How do you know your daddy isn't lying?" asked Britney in a skeptical tone.

Bobbie thought for only a second. "Because he's my daddy," she said as a matter of fact. That was something that most every kid would understand. Even Britney couldn't argue with that.

"Which one is *your* favorite?" Tiffany asked with genuine interest.

Bobbie wasn't ready for that question. She simply answered, "I don't have a favorite. I love 'em both." She smiled.

"What are they like?"

Bobbie didn't really think about it, she just opened her mouth and the words came out. "Well, teddies are supposed to be like the people that love them the most. They learn things from you. Like, Waldo is adventurous and Bobby Bear is more worried about doing the right thing."

As soon as she said that, she knew they were just like her. It took her saying it out loud to understand it.

Bobby Bear had that twinge in his stomach, something was wrong. Bobbie was telling the class about the Secret Teddy Society. But then again, everyone was being nice to her, and even Tiffany was friendly.

The more questions that were asked the more she told them about the teddy world and how it worked. She had an answer for every question. By the time she finished, the whole class believed. Even Mrs. Larkin was impressed with the detail of her story and imagination of the teddy world.

"So, your dad is writing about their adventures?" asked the teacher.

"Yes."

"Do you think he could come and read some of his stories to the class?"

"I guess so. I can ask him."

Mrs. Larkin told her that she did a fantastic job and everyone clapped as she took her seat.

Bobby Bear and Waldo listened to the teacher, for the next several hours, talk about spelling and how she learned things when she was little.

Waldo could feel Tiffany staring at him as if waiting for him to move or do something. But he wasn't going to do it. He'd broken enough rules for one day.

When the bell rang, signaling the end of the day, Bobbie grabbed her backpack and headed for the door. Her Mommy was waiting out front as usual.

"How was Show and Tell today?" asked Debra.

A smile appeared on Bobbie's face as she held up her two bears and said, "They were *great* today."

Debra took the bears from her so she could strap them into the front seat. Bobbie climbed into her seat in back.

While Debra was busy putting the seatbelt around the bears, Tiffany appeared next to the car.

"Hi, Bobbie."

"Hi."

Debra pretended to take a little longer buckling in the bears.

"I wanted to say I'm sorry," said Tiffany.

Bobbie was unsure of what to do or why she was even saying it.

"For what?"

"For the mean things I said. For everything."

Debra finished snugging the bears in and closed the passenger door.

"Hello, who are you?" Debra asked in a friendly voice.

"I'm Tiffany. I'm in Bobbie's class."

Debra had heard all about Tiffany and some of the things she had done to Bobbie but she kept a smile on her face.

"It's nice to meet you, Tiffany."

"It's nice to meet you, too. I guess I should be going. My mom is waiting. Goodbye, Bobbie. Bye, Waldo," she said as she ran off.

Debra reached in and buckled Bobbie into her seat. "What was that all about?"

The confused little girl was still wondering that herself. "I don't really know."

On the way home, Bobbie could not stop thinking about what Tiffany said.

Something's not right. Why did she talk to Waldo? she wondered.

She couldn't wait to get home so she could have her daddy ask Waldo what happened.

The car pulled into the driveway and Bobbie was kicking her feet. "Let's go, let's go."

Debra ran around the car to let her out. "I think we made it in time," she said, catching her breath.

Bobbie stared at her strangely. "In time for what?"

Debra smiled and said, *"Before you explode."*

"That's just silly," said Bobbie with a grin. Grabbing her bears and her backpack, she ran straight to her daddy's office. "Hi, Daddy," she said very excited.

"Hey, Pumpkin: why the hurry?"

"I need you to talk to Waldo and Bobby Bear for me. Something happened at school today and I need to know because I wasn't there and Waldo was there, and she said something to him and I think he did something or said something that made her change and I don't know what, and —"

"Hey, hey, slow down," he said abruptly. "Just start at the beginning."

She drew in a deep breath and then told him about her day, at least everything that she was aware of. ". . . So I need you to talk to Waldo and find out what happened, 'cause I think she knows. I know she didn't believe me when I said it. That means something happened. *Oh, yeah*, she said she liked Waldo the best. *Why Waldo*, and not Bobby Bear, he's the sweetest." She looked at her small white bear and apologized, "Sorry, Waldo."

Waldo couldn't get too mad at the comment; he knew it was true.

"Will you talk to him?" she asked in a pleading voice.

"Of course, but I can't promise they'll tell me, okay?"

She gently placed them on the desk then remembered her teacher's request. "Oh, and Mrs. Larkin wants you to come to school and read your stories to the class." She turned and took off down the hall. "Thanks, Daddy," she called out as she ran.

James could only smile at the bears while they sat in their spot. He whispered, "You boys have had quite a day."

After Bobbie and Debra had gone to bed, James was in the office working on the stories. He was curious himself, to hear about what had happened at school. He got up and checked to see if everyone was asleep. Before asking about their day he thought a tasty treat would help soften the mood, so he went to the kitchen and prepared their favorite snack.

When James returned to the desk, Waldo saw what was in his hand. This told him the coast was clear.

"Ah, my favorite. What's the occasion?" asked Waldo.

James set the glasses down and poured the milk. He then handed one to Waldo and one to Bobby Bear.

"It's a big day for you guys, your first day at school and all," he said in a cheerful voice. James decided to keep the mood light and breezy so Waldo wouldn't think he was in trouble for anything he might have done.

Waldo nodded as he drank. Bobby Bear had the classic milk mustache as he took another sip.

"So was it fun? Tell me what happened," asked James in a playful yet curious tone.

Bobby Bear was afraid of that question when Waldo wiped his mouth and said, "Fill-er' up," pushing his glass closer.

James grabbed the milk and started to pour. "Another glass, Waldo? Wow, you must have had an exciting day." James was trying to think of anything he could say to get some answers. He pushed the glass back and Waldo took a sip.

"Yeah, it sure was," he replied, still gulping and catching his breath from drinking so fast.

"Did anything exciting happen?" asked James, hoping this would start him talking.

Waldo's eyes got big. "Oh, yeah, it sure did. I got to see the big Meany. You remember when Bobbie was so upset? Well, I know who did it. I know who made her cry," Waldo said. He filled James in on everything that happened and was just about to tell the best part.

" . . . next thing I know, she's not saying a word and just staring right at me," Waldo said, when he was suddenly kicked.

"Hey! Why'd you do that?" he cried, rubbing his leg.

Bobby Bear leaned over and whispered in his ear. Waldo sat up straight and looked at James as something was apparently wrong. Bobby Bear quietly pushed his glass over for a refill. James poured another glass and pushed it back, feeling the tension in the room. Bobby Bear picked it up and took a long slow sip as he peered over the top of the glass.

"Hey, what's wrong?" asked James. He was confused. Everything seemed to be going so well.

Waldo shook his head, stood up, and walked to the edge of the desk to look him straight in the eyes. He reached out, put one paw on each side of his face, and pulled James close. Now, face-to-face, Waldo whispered, "I can't say this out loud because no other teddies should know what happened."

James was on the edge of his seat and all he could think about was how great a story this was going to make.

"You're in the office. No other teddies are around," said James quietly.

"Teddies can hear much better than humans. Wait . . . did you hear that?" Waldo whispered.

"No," replied James softly.

"I did. That's what I'm talking about. We can hear things, lots of things, quiet things. We can hear things you can't," Waldo explained.

"Can you whisper it to me?" he asked in his quietest voice.

Waldo looked left, then right, then into his eyes. "Okay, but you can't tell the others, especially Elvis," Waldo whispered with a serious look on his face.

The Council cannot find out that Tiffany saw him move. Even though, a child seeing a teddy move is a minor violation in the Teddy Code, it is one more violation that would make Waldo's punishment worse.

Waldo was already a "Trust Buster" because he broke the Code. He just doesn't want to be labeled a "Bad Bear." A "Bad Bear" is one that does bad things all the time, and on purpose, without thinking about other bears or the Code, only himself.

"I won't say anything to another teddy, I promise," said James.

With that, Waldo told him about sticking his tongue out at Tiffany. James couldn't help but chuckle. Waldo laughed with him as he remembered her dumbfounded expression.

"So, the whole class laughed at her because you simply stuck out your tongue?" Waldo was unsure if he was mad or not, so he slowly nodded his head, yes. His eyes were carefully trained on James'.

"That would have been fun to see."

Waldo, yet again, did not get the response he feared. He thought for sure James would have been mad.

After telling him about everything that happened at school, Waldo felt tired and wanted to rest a while.

"It's been a long day," Waldo said in his sleepy voice.

James agreed and decided he should get to bed as well, as they would talk more tomorrow. They all said goodnight.

Later, as Bobbie slept, a voice pierced through the windowpane. "Hey, Elvis," called Dakota. He was the new Rough Rider in the neighborhood taking over for Patches, who had been sent to another district.

"Hey, Koty."

"I was nearby and thought I would mention that I heard the Council is sending a thug for the boys."

Elvis was saddened by the news, but knew it was coming. "Thanks, buddy. Anything else?"

"Nope. I'll keep you posted when I can. G'night."

"Night," replied Elvis. He watched Dakota disappear from the window. It was hard being a Network bear. It meant having to report all teddy activity that violated the Code. It was never personal and Elvis didn't like it, but it was part of the job. If the Code was broken, it was reported.

SOMEONE'S COMING

Bobbie doesn't like being late for anything and couldn't seem to remember what put her behind schedule. All she was concerned about was the morning bell. It was about to ring and she was not in the classroom. The halls were empty and the school was quiet as time was running out. *I can't be late. Please, don't make me late*, she secretly pleaded to herself as her trodden feet echoed off the walls. The bell rang at the moment she slipped through the door. She hurried to her seat while Mrs. Larkin began writing on the blackboard. No one was paying attention to her or the teacher while she wrote "TEST TODAY," in big letters.

Bobbie anxiously read the words. She hated pop quizzes.

Brushing the chalk dust from her hands, Mrs. Larkin turned and said, "Okay, class, write a page-long essay about Show and Tell. And — you may begin."

The class was busy writing while she stared at her blank piece of paper, wondering how to even start. Her pencil hovered above the page waiting for the words to flow, but there were none.

"Bobbie? Is something wrong?" Mrs. Larkin asked her, noticing that she wasn't writing.

"I'm not sure what to write," Bobbie whispered, afraid the rest of the class would make fun of her.

"Do you remember Show and Tell?" asked Mrs. Larkin.

"Yes."

"Then simply write about someone's Show and Tell. Maybe Tiffany's jewelry box?"

Tiffany? Bobbie heard the teacher but that couldn't be right. *I should write about Tiffany?*

Suddenly, the golden haired girl appeared next to her desk.

"Yes. Tiffany," she said, pointing to herself as if she heard what Bobbie was thinking. Flaunting her paper, she continued to the teacher's desk and placed it in front of Mrs. Larkin.

How'd she do it that fast? Bobbie wondered.

When Tiffany turned to walk back to her desk, Bobbie noticed what looked like large ears sticking out from under her golden hair, furry white ears. Also, on her feet, instead of shoes, she wore fuzzy white bear slippers.

Why is she wearing slippers in class?

No one else seemed to notice.

Tiffany stopped next to Bobbie's seat. "Don't forget to mention my expensive necklace." She lifted it from her neck proudly.

Bobbie glanced up at her, confused. She didn't like Tiffany because she had been so mean, but then there was the apology. What about that, was it sincere? Had Tiffany changed?

"Why are you wearing bedtime slippers to school?" Bobbie asked, pointing at her feet.

Tiffany giggled. "Slippers? *Slippers*! That's just silly, these aren't slippers."

She lifted her pant leg and Bobbie saw nothing but white fur going up as far as she could see.

Tiffany began laughing and the whole class joined in. Bobbie quickly realized that everyone had bear feet and ears. The class was turning into teddy bears in front of her eyes as they began to sing:

"Don't you want to be, a teddy bear like me?
Wake up, wake up and see, the fun that it can be."

Bobbie screamed and opened her eyes to find her daddy standing next to her bed.

"Good morning, Pumpkin," he said with a smile. "Did my singing scare you?"

For a brief moment, Bobbie was not sure where she was. She stared at her daddy then glanced at his feet. There was a distressed look about her.

"What are you looking for?" he asked.

"Bear feet," she replied almost breathless.

"Nope, I got my slippers on." He kicked one foot up on the bed in a playful manner. "See, no bare feet, just my slippers." James didn't understand what she was really talking about but she didn't correct him. "Hey, are you ok?" he asked.

She threw her head back down on her pillow. "I had a bad dream."

James sat down on the edge of the bed. "Do you want to tell me about it?"

Bobbie could tell what was bothering her. Normally dreams don't make a lot of sense but she seemed to understand this one.

"It was about school and what happened yesterday," she replied.

Suddenly her eyes got big with excitement and in a hushed voice she asked, "Did you talk to Bobby Bear and Waldo?"

His face lit up. "Yes — and boy have I . . ." James stopped cold as he remembered what Waldo asked him. Trying to be casual, he peeked over at Elvis who was sitting in the Big People's Chair.

James promised he wouldn't say anything in front of other teddies, especially Elvis.

He gave Bobbie a look and motioned with his eyes out the door. She didn't understand until he moved his lips, silently saying 'Elvis.'

Like filling in the last piece of a puzzle, she finally got the picture and quickly said, "Is breakfast ready? I'm hungry. Are you hungry, Daddy? I know I am. Let's eat." She sprung out of bed as if it were Christmas morning, pulling up the covers in a half attempt to make her bed. "Do you wanna eat? Let's go eat. We should go eat . . . You comin', Daddy?" She walked briskly towards the kitchen.

James needed a private place to tell Bobbie about what happened at school.

Where can we go that no teddy can hear? he pondered. Then, he glanced out the window and saw the SUV parked in the driveway. *The car. Perfect!*

Debra was busy making breakfast, when James asked if he could take Bobbie to school. Debra gladly agreed. She wouldn't mind getting to work a little early.

James wasn't trying to keep secrets from his wife but he knew that unless he could prove the teddy world existed it would only put a strain on their relationship. Telling a child seemed harmless. Who would believe them? But if they treated their bears better because they believed, then what was the harm?

What James never considered was what would realistic and rational adults think of his claims?

Bobbie sat down at the table and stared intently to her daddy, her eyes squinting like she was trying to see into his mind.

"Hey, Pumpkin, guess who's driving you to school today?" said James in a lighthearted tone.

"Um, hmm, let's see — Waldo?" she guessed with a smile.

"*No*, go on, guess again."

"*Daddy*, I know it's you," she said, tiring of the game quickly. She wanted information not games.

After breakfast, she grabbed her backpack and ran into his office to say goodbye to Bobby Bear and Waldo before going to school.

Running out the front door, she yelled, "Hurry up, Daddy, let's go." She couldn't wait to hear the news. Debra glanced up, surprised. Bobbie wasn't usually in such a hurry to get to school.

Bobbie climbed onto her seat and James buckled her in. He got in the car and started it up. Before he pulled out of the driveway, he looked back at Bobbie and said, "Okay, this is what Waldo told me."

He backed out into the street and headed towards school.

"Well, first, Waldo told me he finally got to see the big Meany — that's what he calls Tiffany. She was nothing like he imagined, apparently."

"What did he imagine?" she asked.

"He thought she would have this cruel face and icy wind, I think. He said she smelled more like springtime fresh fabric softener with golden hair," said James with a bit of a question in his voice.

When Bobbie heard this description, she knew her father could not have known those details without someone telling him, since he hadn't met any of her classmates. If she ever had any doubt about Bobby Bear and Waldo coming to life, as he said, it all went out the window right then.

As James continued, Bobbie listened with a new trust.

"What's this about a magic lunch box? I'm not sure exactly what he was talking about."

Bobbie laughed. "That was just Danielle being funny. She's always doing stuff like that."

"It turns out that Bobby Bear was fascinated with a box that could produce food anytime you want it," he said with a grin.

Finally, James got to the part where Waldo told him about Tiffany's Show and Tell.

"Waldo said he wasn't really listening to Tiffany because he was busy thinking about his plan to get even with her."

"Even for what?" she asked.

"For making you cry," he answered. "Remember, a couple of days ago, you came home from school crying and asked why kids are so mean? That got Waldo so upset that he wanted to find out who the 'big Meany' was."

Bobbie didn't know that Waldo felt that way and could feel her eyes welling up.

"He really said that?"

"Yes he did. He really loves you a lot. They both do."

The car zoomed along, getting closer to school.

"So, did something happen with Tiffany?" she asked.

"*Oh, yeah*, so, Waldo said that he had just thought of the perfect plan to get even with Tiffany and, I guess, in his excitement, he stuck his tongue out at her."

Bobbie burst out laughing because she could only imagine what Tiffany saw.

"I remember that because Tiffany was talking and suddenly she said 'tongue' and no one knew what she was talking about," Bobbie said in between giggles. "She just stood there staring at me, but now I know it was Waldo she was staring at." She laughed even harder. "So, she saw him move. She didn't say anything about it. I wonder why?" she asked herself out loud.

"Maybe she knew no one would believe her," James answered. "And maybe kids would laugh at her, like she did to you."

Bobbie thought about that and understood how someone like Tiffany, that makes fun of others, could not stand to have anyone make fun of her. She would have to prove what she saw before she could say anything.

"*That's* why she apologized to me, because she knows," said Bobbie, now understanding. James nodded.

"Waldo told me that she apologized to him, too. He said it was for pushing you, and dropping them on the ground," he said.

Bobbie could not get over the details her daddy described, plus it was nice to know how Waldo felt about her. This made her think even more about how she treated the bears.

They pulled up in front of the school and James let her out of her seat. He knelt down to look in her eyes. "Now you know there are two others that love you the way Mommy and I do," he told her.

She smiled and leaned forward for a hug.

James whispered, "Just be the best person you can be, Pumpkin, and everything else will take care of itself."

Bobbie grabbed her backpack and headed off to class.

"Someone will be right here when you get out." He stood there for a moment and watched her disappear into the crowd of kids, walking happily to class. He couldn't help but wonder why it was that the older you get the less you smile when going to class.

***

At the Council, Bullock was having a hard time deciding what to do about the two young bears that were continually breaking the Code by moving in front of James. A teddy thug was already on his way to escort Bobby Bear and Waldo back to the Council, but this, however, was new ground for Bullock. Normally a bear would simply stop moving, no matter how extreme the act. Humans have caught teddies moving in the past but no one ever believed the human that talked about it. The story never ended well for the humans. Insane, crazy, nutcase and liar were some of the words used to describe these people. They would often lose their jobs or families because of what they witnessed. Lives were ruined because of an animated teddy. This was merely one of the reasons why teddies don't move in front of humans.

Bullock discussed the problem with Quincy, another Council member, for how to handle such a precedent. With nothing to base their punishment, Bullock reluctantly went to Theodore to get his thoughts on the matter.

Theodore would not normally be involved in the punishment process of a teddy; it was the Chief Marshall's job, which was Bullock. This, however, was puzzling. If they took two teddies away from a family that had their bears out in the open, they would surely be missed. This in itself would break the Teddy Code. The answer seemed to involve James somehow. The Council needed more information about him. Who is he? How much did he know? What was he doing or saying about the teddy world? Once Theodore heard which district and neighborhood this took place, he took an interest in the case.

***

James had a few errands to run after dropping Bobbie off at school, one of which was to visit a friend that owned the Village Bookstore. James took the first two chapters of his book and made them into a short story to get some feedback from the local community. Since he had never written before he felt real critiques would help his writing. He had printed a few copies to place in the "Local Writers" section. It was a very popular hangout among readers in search of something new, so James figured this was the perfect place to start.

The house had been quiet for several hours when Bobby Bear and Waldo decided it was a good time to find out if there was any news from the Teddy Council.

Waldo scampered down the hallway to Bobbie's room, with his best friend close behind, to ask Elvis the usual question and get the usual answer.

Waldo stood in front of the Big People's Chair. "Hey, Elvis. Any word yet from the Council?"

By now, Waldo was so distracted with his new life, out in the open, in front of James at least, that he seemed to forget just how dire their situation was. Waldo had a slight carefree demeanor about him until he heard Elvis' reply.

"Yes."

Waldo wasn't expecting that. He was hoping the Council might just forget about the whole thing. You know, let them continue running around the house with a freedom that no other teddy was allowed to have. Apparently, that was just wishful thinking.

He swallowed hard, and his voice cracked out the question, "Is it — bad? Are we going away?"

Elvis glanced over to Bobby Bear standing in the doorway, as he normally does, to make sure no one was around, and saw the concern on his troubled face.

"I don't know. Someone's coming. That's all I know."

Waldo was stunned; his mind flooded with thoughts of what was going to happen and who was coming for them:

Two small black bears wearing black masks tiptoed through the house, like a shadow on the wall, while Waldo and Bobby Bear slept. They were "Kage Kumas" or "Shadow Bears" and few teddies had ever seen them. It was rumored they worked exclusively for the Council doing the most dangerous of deeds in order to keep the teddy world a secret.

James had fallen asleep at his desk, as usual, and unaware of the intruders in the house. Trained in sneakiness, these bears were here for one reason: bring Bobby Bear and Waldo to justice. The Council cannot have these two bears running around the house blabbing to James about how the teddy world works. An example must be set for the others. The Code must be followed, or else.

The office was quiet except the tick and the tock from an old style clock, which helped cover the perfectly timed footsteps of the silent guests. Slipping past James was the easy part. As these two stealth teddies approached their targets, asleep on the desk, Bobby Bear and Waldo were completely unaware.

The Kage Kumas positioned themselves next to the unsuspecting bears. One gave a silent hand signal and they both reached out swiftly, covering the mouths of the two sleeping teddies. Bobby Bear was so startled that he kicked the pencil cup. Before so much as a rattle was heard, a paw reached for the loose pencils, muting the sound that would have woken James. Waldo had never seen a bear move that fast before. He knew they were in trouble.

James stirred in his chair while a breathless moment of absolute still locked the bears in place. The way the Kage Kumas stood, all you could see were Bobby Bear and Waldo sitting in their usual spot, their black fur blended in the shadow cast from the desk lamp, they were virtually invisible.

James resumed his loud, heavy breathing and when one of the dark bears put his paw to his mouth, Bobby Bear and Waldo understood they were to make no sound — or else. The other Kage reached for the light bulb in the lamp, giving it a twist. The room went black. Bobby Bear felt a slight breeze when he noticed the shadow next to him was gone. A knock at the door broke the monotonous sound of the clock.

James woke to a dark office and reached for the lamp, turning the switch with a click, click, but no light came on.

(Knock knock) Someone was at the front door.

James got to his feet, still feeling a bit groggy and stumbled towards the sound. Pushing his chair aside, he felt his way out of the office.

Little did he know, this was the Kage's plan to escape.

Kage number one, still on the desk with Bobby Bear and Waldo, quickly motioned the two bears to follow him. They jumped to the floor, as quiet as a feather landing on a pillow, and followed step for step behind James. Waldo thought about shouting for help but he knew it would do no good; the Kages would stop him cold. And then there was the Council. If he or Bobby Bear resisted it would only make things worse. What about the other rumor — Kage attacks on humans. What if they turned on James? — What if something went terribly wrong? Bobby Bear and Waldo would never forgive themselves if James got hurt because of them.

Getting to the front door, James peered out the side window and didn't see anyone. He flipped on the porch light but nothing happened.

(Knock! Knock!) The sound startled James. He quickly looked out the window again but still there was no one there. Feeling a bit nervous he reached for the knob and slowly opened the front door. It cracked open and James cautiously stuck his head out, darting his eyes left and right.

Four bears were standing near his feet, against the wall, hidden by the dark. Crowded in the corner, they waited for the door to open to make their escape. Two of the bears were very nervous and very scared and didn't want to go outside. Waldo wished he could find a way to alert James quietly. He would help them. He could save them.

Bobby Bear's paw tightened on Waldo's wrist. Bobby Bear shook his head slowly from side to side, his eyes wide in terror. Even James might not be able to stop the Kages. And he definitely couldn't stop the Council.

Waldo felt resigned to his destiny.

"Hello?" said James, peering from the small crack. No one answered. He inched the door open a bit more and put one foot out

onto the front porch. With one hand, he flipped the light switch several times in hopes the light would magically fix itself. It didn't. From where James stood, he could see the porch light and noticed the cover off with the bulb removed. Pushing the door open, he stepped outside to fix the lamp. The bears were waiting for this moment. While James was busy putting the porch light back together, the covert team with Bobby Bear and Waldo slipped into the night.

The family car pulled into the driveway, snapping Waldo out of his nightmarish daydream, and the two bears raced to the desk. He could feel his heart racing. He was scared — very scared. Even though Kage Kumas were kept from the teddy world, the rumors of their existence were taken seriously. If the legend was true, Waldo wouldn't have a chance. No human, not even James could help no matter what he promised. If the Council came for them, they'd have no choice but to go.

Back in their place, the bears heard the door open and a voice called out. "Boys, I'm home. I hope you haven't gotten into too much trouble," said James, almost hoping to see that they had. He walked into the office and saw them sitting in their place.

"Hey, guys, what are you doing up there on this beautiful day?" He was in a good mood. "I have a fun idea. Let's go for a drive."

What? A drive? Bobby Bear thought anxiously, remembering the trip to school.

Something about seeing James' face made Waldo's fears subside. An adventure was always welcome, as long as it didn't involve Kage Kumas or the Council. He jumped up eagerly. "Can I look out the window?"

"Absolutely."

Waldo hurried to the edge of the desk. Hopping up and down, he threw his paws in the air waiting for James to pick him up. Bobby Bear was in no hurry to go anywhere, but James scooped him up, too.

He headed out the door.

"Oh, man! Oh, man!" Waldo murmured with excitement.

Oh man, oh man, thought a very worried Bobby Bear.

James opened the car door and placed both bears in the front seat and began to buckle them in.

Mrs. Mallory, out for her daily walk, was passing by as James fussed with the seatbelt.

"Hey, hey, hey, I won't be able to see," complained Waldo.

"Sorry — force of habit."

Bobby Bear, actually, was hoping to be buckled in because it makes him feel snug and safe. He didn't like the car moving so fast.

Mrs. Mallory noticed James was talking but couldn't see to whom.

James closed the passenger door and turned around to find her standing next to the car.

"*Oh* — Mrs. Mallory, didn't see you there. How are you today?"

Her dyed frizzy black hair was her trademark and could be recognized from several houses away. Most of the neighbors tried avoiding her because of her sense of curiosity. You could often find her at the wrong place at the right time. She loved old crime dramas and fancied herself a bit of a detective. Mrs. Mallory loved to gossip about what was happening in other people's lives. She secretively told James about John Michaels, that lived next door, and how he was an ex-government spy or something. Her modus operandi was to bake cookies and show up unannounced. Once in the doorway the frizzy haired gossip would practically invite herself in. While at Mr. Michaels' house she noticed a sizable gray teddy bear on a sofa in the front parlor wearing a white scarf with the name Ike stitched in black. She also saw a signed picture of the President on a bookcase with a personal message, "The dirty jobs that no one sees. Thank you." James always liked John because he kept his nose out of everyone's business. From time to time, he would catch a glimpse of John smiling at his silly behavior when he played in the front lawn with Bobbie.

Mrs. Mallory didn't seem to hear James, as she was too busy trying to figure out why two small furry heads were sitting in the front seat. She would lean to the left, as James would step to the right. She stepped to the right, while he leaned to the left. This dance would last only for a minute.

"*Well*, have a good day," he said sharply, dismissing her, as he hurried around the car.

He got in and turned the key, the motor came to life. "Where do you boys want to go?" he asked. Bobby Bear and Waldo were aware of Mrs. Mallory standing just outside the car and didn't answer and didn't move.

"That's all right — I have an idea," he said and backed out of the driveway while his nosey neighbor stretched her neck as far as a neck could go. A very interesting look was on her face as they passed. That only made James smile. Let her tell *this* around the neighborhood, James chuckled to himself.

As the car headed down the road Bobby Bear was nervous and really wanted to buckle up. He wanted Waldo safe too and began to pull the seatbelt across both of them.

"Hey, what are you doing?" asked Waldo.

"You should be safe. I want to be safe," commanded Bobby Bear.

"No. I don't want it."

Bobby Bear was not going to listen and tried to buckle the belt.

"Hey, cut it out."

"You should wear your seat belt."

"I won't be able to see."

"Right, and no one else will be able to see you, either," Bobby Bear pointed out. After all, there were people out there in the cars on the road. What would they make of a fuzzy bear waving at them? But, Waldo wasn't in the frame of mind to listen to reason.

Bobby Bear once again tried to buckle up, but this time he was sneaky. Waldo felt the belt slowly slide across his fur.

"Stop it! — Will you tell him to stop it?" cried Waldo to James, hoping he would understand.

"Actually — you should be wearing it," confessed James.

"Yeah, but I can't see," Waldo said sadly as he folded his arms and began to sulk.

James was a sucker for the pout. "All right, you can take a look."

Waldo quickly stood up in the seat and peered out the window while Bobby Bear remained seated.

"Wow!" he said with wonder in his voice, "I can't even run this fast." Waldo loved the feeling of the car speeding as it went. "How fast are we going? — What's that?" asked Waldo pointing at everything he saw, not waiting to hear an answer. The barrage of questions went on for several miles until Waldo shrieked, "WHAT'S THAT?"

James noticed instantly what he was asking about this time.

He was staring at the fun park: bright colors, rides, music in the air and lots of people everywhere.

"Bobby Bear, you've got to see this!" he yelled. Waldo was so excited James could see him shaking. "Get up here — you've got to see this!" Waldo was bouncing on the seat.

They stopped at a traffic light that was right in front of the fun park. Waldo couldn't take his eyes off the spinning rides and the beautiful colors of wonder. A car pulled up beside them blocking his view. This broke the spell that had a firm grip.

Waldo was now staring at the driver of the car next to them. A lady with golden sun drenched hair and big glasses sat unaware of being watched. Waldo reached down and grabbed Bobby Bear by the arm. "Come on, come on, you need to see this."

Bobby Bear slowly stood up and looked out the window.

"Waldo! That's another person! What are you doing!?" Bobby Bear shouted in alarm.

As they stood at the window the lady next to them glanced over and saw what appeared to be two teddy bears looking back at her. Instantly, both bears froze.

A child holding up her bears to have fun with passing cars perhaps, she wondered.

The two bears were motionless staring out the window until the golden haired lady did something that neither bear expected. She playfully stuck out her tongue.

Something came over Waldo as he was caught up in the moment and couldn't seem to stop his tongue from slipping out of his mouth.

Bobby Bear could not believe what Waldo had done and without even thinking, he reached over and struck Waldo on the shoulder. "Why did you do that?" scolded Bobby Bear. Just then the light changed and James stepped on the gas pedal. The car that was next to them didn't move. The last thing Waldo saw was the expression on the golden haired lady's face as they pulled away. Waldo laughed and tumbled back in his seat. Bobby Bear gave him a stern look.

"Waldo! You're going to get us into more trouble!"

"No, I'm not," Waldo said confidently.

"Whoa!" said Bobby Bear, staring magically out the window at the fun park. "What's that?"

Waldo stood up next to him and said, "See? I told you. I told you."

They both felt the car slow down and turned into the parking lot.

"What are you doing?" Bobby Bear asked.

James said nothing, but sent the bears a mysterious smile.

The car weaved back and forth as the bears clung to the door trying to stay on their feet. James turned the wheel fast and the car came to a quick stop in front of Sir-Licks-A lot, an ice cream stand at the fun park.

"Okay, you guys stay still and I'll be right back."

He opened the door and stepped out of the car. Music filled the air and the smells (oh, the smells!) Bobby Bear and Waldo had never smelled anything like that before.

Stay still? Stay still? How can I stay still? thought Waldo, hearing all the fun that was about.

They crouched as low as they could while still able to see out the window. The bears watched James walk up to a small colorful building and stand behind two other people. James turned his head to the car and saw two faces peeking through the glass. He was pushing his hand down signaling them to get out of sight. Bobby Bear thought he was waving and began waving back. James just rolled his eyes and glanced around to make sure no one noticed the animated teddy bears.

Someone spoke to James from inside the colorful building, which snapped his attention. He approached a small window and took two items from the person behind the counter then headed back towards the car.

"What's he got?" Waldo asked.

They quickly sat down in their seat while James got in and handed them two small ice cream cones. The two teddies were very happy as he gave them a gift, but neither one understood what to do.

A silent moment passed before James said, "Well? Go ahead, give it a try."

The bears looked at each other in confusion. Before James could explain, Bobby Bear felt the cold and wet drip on his paw.

"What's this?" Bobby Bear asked in a bit of a panic.

James chuckled and said, "Give it a lick before it melts."

Bobby Bear stared at the drip then slowly stuck out his tongue, lightly touching the creamy drop. His eyes widened and his face lit up. It was as if everything he'd ever wanted instantly appeared, as the deliciousness melted in his mouth. Waldo licked his creamy cone and suddenly words escaped him. Nothing could begin to describe the feelings he was having at that moment. He closed his eyes and devoured the ice cream. Sounds came from his tongue that it never made before, and Bobby Bear had as much ice cream on his paws as he had in his mouth.

James sat and watched these two small bears make a complete mess out of themselves and the car. He could only smile as the noises of pure teddy happiness were surrounded by music and laughter from outside.

When the ice cream was all gone Waldo slowly opened his eyes and gazed at James.

"What — was — that?" he asked, still catching his breath.

Bobby Bear was now licking the drips from his paws.

"That, Waldo, was a tasty treat called ice cream. It's frozen milk with a lot of sugar." Knowing how much Waldo loves milk, especially cold milk, he thought it would be fun to see how they liked it.

"So what'd you think?" James asked.

Waldo smiled, sat back in the seat and closed his eyes. "Wow — That was — That was . . ." Waldo could not finish the sentence because he didn't know how.

What? What was that? I don't know what that was. It was . . . I don't know. I just don't know, thought Waldo, feeling befuddled.

James started up the car and headed for home. All the way back, Waldo could still taste the ice cream in his mouth. Bobby Bear didn't stop licking until every spot was clean.

When they got home, James went straight to work on the stories while the bears seemed lost in a dream. A whole new world opened up to Waldo that day. At that moment Waldo could almost justify being a Trust Buster. If he and Bobby Bear hadn't broken the Code and been caught by James, they might not have ever tasted ice cream, the best thing in the whole wide world. Right then — it all seemed worth it.

A THUG IN THE HOUSE

Bobby Bear and Waldo's predicament had taken a serious turn, now that a teddy thug was on his way. However, Waldo was also plagued with something else: desire. He couldn't stop thinking about ice cream. It made his stomach flutter at the thought. He wanted it. Problem; it was in the freezer, *and* it was on the top shelf. Needing to distract his mind from worry and the Council, Waldo focused on the puzzle at hand, how to get to the ice cream? Waldo wasn't trying to be naughty or bad, and it's not as if it were stealing. He was, after all, family. This was just Waldo not wanting to bother James. There was no need to put him out when he could simply get it himself. That's all. It was part of the game. Waldo was growing up — mentally, anyway. Teddy Bears don't physically grow but they do mature, and Waldo liked turning everything into an adventure. His adventures were becoming more complex.

"I need something to stand on — something to make me taller," he murmured to himself. The only thing he could think of was the Time Machine seat, which normally belonged in Bobbie's closet. It was actually a small footstool for Bobbie to reach things. Waldo couldn't ask for help from his best friend; he already knew what the answer would be. Shaking his head to himself, "He can be such a goody-two-shoes," he muttered quietly.

Waldo had begun digging around in Bobbie's closet when he pulled back a small mound of clothes piled in the back corner. He screamed and fell backwards.

Bobby Bear heard the cry and came to his rescue. He rushed into the room to find Waldo sitting on the floor staring at the pile of toys and clothes in the closet. "Waldo, what's wrong?"

He slowly pointed and stuttered, "Fluff, Fluff . . ."

Bobby Bear cautiously leaned over to look. "Is something in there?"

Waldo stood up, walked into the closet and gently pulled back the clothes. Bobby Bear couldn't believe his eyes. Stuffed way in the back, hidden by a normal child's mess, was Big Red Fluffy bear.

"Is that you, Fluffy?" Bobby Bear asked. Fluffy nodded. "I thought the Council took you away."

"They did," he answered while slowly crawling out from the closet.

"They let you come back? What happened? How'd they let you come back?" asked a *very* interested Waldo who then reached out and poked him to make sure he was real. He received an annoyed glared.

"Yes, it's me, and they let me come back — but I'm on probation."

Waldo didn't know what that word meant. All he cared about was Big Red Fluffy bear was back, and that was nothing but good news for them. He gave Fluffy a big hug. "You don't know how glad I am to see you."

Bobby Bear felt the same way. Fluffy was glad to see them too, he missed being with his family.

Waldo began to think that things weren't as bad as he thought after seeing their lost friend.

"What happened? What was it like? Was it bad?" he asked anxiously.

Big Red Fluffy bear looked at the floor and said, "I can't talk about it. I'm sorry. I just can't."

Waldo went right back to worrying again.

"But everything's all right now, right?" asked Bobby Bear hopefully.

Fluffy could only think of one thing to say, "Yes, everything's fine." Fluffy wasn't sure that it was the truth, but any other answer would have only complicated things.

Waldo glanced back into the closet and spotted the stool. "There you are," he exclaimed. The ice cream would have to wait. This was huge.

"So, do you live in the closet now?" Bobby Bear asked politely.

"Yeah, at least until someone finds me and thinks I've been misplaced all this time."

"What really happened that day? You know — when you were . . ." Waldo asked, not sure if Fluffy would talk about it.

"You mean the day I was caught?"

Bobby Bear and Waldo both nodded and waited for the story.

"Well, it was morning and I heard the usual breakfast noises in the kitchen. I was thinking how good a glass of milk would taste." Bobby Bear and Waldo looked at each other and smiled.

They too suffered from the lure of milk. "I heard a voice that I didn't recognize saying something about 'having it fixed in no time.' After a moment, I heard everyone leave; the car pulled away, then nothing. I figured the house was empty. I checked the hall and didn't see anyone. I listened for a while and didn't hear anyone, so I went to the kitchen and straight for the fridge. I opened the door and started for the milk when suddenly a man came from out of nowhere and grabbed the door from me. I looked up and saw a strange man. He hadn't noticed me yet. I had to do something. I should have just fallen down, but I wasn't thinking. I just took off. I ran straight to Bobbie's closet. He must have seen me run away 'cause he came looking for me. He had a big belt that jingled as he walked. I heard him come into the room. He kept saying, 'That couldn't be what I saw, that just couldn't be.'" Fluffy let out a nervous giggle trying to imitate his voice. It wasn't funny at the time but Fluffy's annoying habit flared as he revisited the scariest moment of his life. "Then — it got quiet. I knew I was in trouble — I just broke the Code, ya' know? I was only hoping it would be a minor violation. And right when I thought he was gone — *Bam!*" Bobby Bear and Waldo flinched. The story was mesmerizing. Fluffy continued, "He pulled back the clothes and saw me. I almost jumped. Remember the balloon thing I taught you? I tried letting the air out as fast as possible, to go limp, ya' know? I'm not sure I made it. He reached in and picked me up. I didn't move, of course, but I sure was scared. He just stared at me. He looked in my eyes for what seemed forever. He said, 'I saw your eyes. Those aren't the same. I must be out of my mind. There's no way you just ran from the kitchen. Can you hear me?' he said. He looked me all over, trying to find something — I guess. I'm not sure

107

what happened next, but I landed on the floor and he was gone. Something scared him and he never came back."

Bobby Bear and Waldo hung on every word as Fluffy described his moment of breaking the Teddy Code because it sounded exactly like what happened to them. They were hoping for even the smallest of information on how the Council allowed him back with his family.

"So he must have told someone what he saw," Bobby Bear asked.

"He did," answered Fluffy. "He told his wife everything, and apparently she has a teddy that's part of the Network. That's how the Council found out."

Big Red Fluffy bear headed back towards the closet when Waldo said, "Wait a second, you never told us how —"

"We'll talk more, later," said Fluffy. "You two better get back to your spot. They're home." He turned and disappeared into the closet.

Just then, they heard the family car pulling into the driveway. They rushed back to the office, where James was working, and scampered up on the desk.

"Hey, guys, is it that time already?" he asked, then peeked out the window and saw the car in the driveway. He noticed Bobbie hurrying to get out of her seat.

The bears returned to their spots.

Right on cue, Bobbie came bounding in the door, followed by Debra, threw her backpack in the corner and rushed over to the desk.

"How was school today, Pumpkin?" James asked.

Bobbie jumped up and down. "I'm having a sleepover," she said excitedly then turned to the bears. "It's a teddy sleepover and you guys get to make new friends."

Bobby Bear was always happy making friends while Waldo was uncomfortable meeting new bears and was not sure how fun that would be.

"That sounds great. When is this going to happen?" James asked.

"Saturday," she answered. "Did anything fun happen today?"

James started to smile and said, "We went for a drive today." He continued to tell her about the car ride and their first experience with ice cream, which made her laugh.

When James was finished telling her about their adventure she remembered what Mrs. Larkin asked of her.

"Oh, Daddy, you're supposed to read to the class tomorrow."

"Really? Do I have to?" he kidded.

She glared at him with a serious face and didn't say a word. She gave him *the look*.

"Okay, I'll do it," he said, trying not to smile. "Jeeze Louise!"

Later, after Debra and Bobbie had gone to bed and the house was silent, James worked on his stories while the two bears were in their spot, very still and very quiet. Bobby Bear kept nodding off, but Waldo wasn't sleepy; he had something on his mind.

The only sound in the room was a tick, followed by a tock, over and over again. Suddenly, "Supergreatiestfantaculicious!" Waldo blurted, breaking the monotonous silence. James jumped and knocked over his mug onto the floor. His heart racing as he glared at Waldo who was looking back innocently with his big brown eyes.

Debra called out in a startled sleepy voice from the big bedroom, "What was that?"

James began picking up the broken pieces. "Oh, nothing," he called out. "I dropped my mug. Sorry about the noise." He took the broken mug to the kitchen and returned to the desk. "Waldo, what was that about?" he scolded as quietly as he could. He didn't mean to startle James but something had been bothering him all day and he finally found what he was looking for.

"The ice cream," Waldo answered.

"What about the ice cream?"

"You asked me what I thought about the ice cream," Waldo said, as if the question had just been asked.

"That was hours ago."

"I know, but I couldn't think of the right word and it just hit me."

The thought of not knowing how to describe such a delicious treat, the likes that he had never tasted before, did not sit well. The word that had escaped him all day seemed to magically pop into his head. Waldo sat back as if an enormous burden had been lifted from his shoulders. "Supergreatiestfantaculicious," he said quietly, closing his eyes and dreaming of that icy cone of wonder. James could only smile and felt this was the perfect time to go to bed. "Goodnight Waldo. Goodnight Bobby Bear," he whispered.

He got up to leave and heard a soft voice return. "Nighty night," Waldo said with a sweet sleepy breath. Bobby Bear was already asleep. He turned out the lights and headed down the hall.

As the sound of sleep echoed in the house, Big Red Fluffy bear emerged from the closet in Bobbie's room and walked to the Big People's Chair.

"Hey, Elvis," he whispered.

Elvis looked at Fluffy, who was now standing in front of him. "Hey, Red."

"You know why I'm here don'tcha?" asked Fluffy bear.

"Yeah."

"Are you disappointed in me?" Fluffy asked apologetically.

"I figure you're here because you have to," Elvis replied.

"They told me that if I bring them back, I would be allowed full teddy rights again. I have to do this so I can come home," he explained sadly. "I don't want to take them away but I have to. They broke the Code, too, you know," said Fluffy, trying to justify his task.

"I know they did," he answered, "and you have to do what you have to do, just don't mislead 'em. They're expecting someone to come and get 'em. Right now, they're pretty scared and I think they would rather it be someone they know than someone they don't. It won't be as bad as you think. Just be honest and they'll understand. That's part of our Code, too." He wanted to reassure Fluffy.

"It's hard because they're my friends; I've known them since their beginning. I don't want to come back and not have them here. What do I do?" Fluffy already knew what the answer was.

"Just be honest with 'em, be their friend and everything will work out." Elvis always did have a way of putting things. "When are you taking them?" he asked.

"I don't know yet," replied Fluffy. "They want me to find out more about James. So I don't know when I should tell them that I'm the one. I don't want 'em to tell James that I'm here, but I know the longer I go without telling 'em the harder it'll be."

"Listen, just stick to the Code and everything will be fine. There's a reason we have it. It works," Elvis said reassuringly.

Fluffy knew he was right — he was always right.

"I sure have missed talking with you," said Fluffy who then paused. "I needed that. You're always just so — cool."

Elvis leaned back in his chair. "Thank ya', thank ya' vury much," he said and they both laughed quietly.

This made Fluffy feel a little better, but he still had a job to do, a job he didn't want to do. They both said goodnight and Big Red Fluffy bear headed back to the closet, stopping briefly to watch Bobbie while she slept. "I missed you, too," he said in a voice that not even he could hear before returning to the pile of clothes.

***

At the Longley mansion, Louis was asleep while Ballinger was wide-awake with concerns about the direction of the Council. Ballinger was in charge of communication and the Teddy Network, which allowed him to keep close tabs on the whereabouts of most teddies and their movements. His irritation only grew with the failed attempts to locate Lyle and D. He regarded the Network as his personal possession and took great pride in being able to find a bear anywhere within a week. But it had been over two months and still nothing.

A new concern had developed. Ballinger was already aware of Bobby Bear and Waldo. He also heard that James was writing teddy stories, but what he didn't know was that James was writing about the teddy world in great detail. The latest report came in from the 82nd Division, citing, the bears continued movement, but the more troublesome information was about James' books at the Village Bookstore titled <u>Secret Teddy Society</u>.

This was an outrage. What was being done about this? Ballinger fumed. Furthermore, he was informed that Bullock and Theodore were having a hard time deciding how to deal with such an unusual case. This infuriated Ballinger enormously. Black and white it was. Exposing the truth about the teddy world and the clear disregard for the Code was a slap in the face to Ballinger. Harsh and severe punishment needed to be taken immediately. Ballinger would not stand idly by while Bullock and Theodore fumbled over their own feet. The security of the Secret Teddy Society was at stake and Ballinger would take his own steps to ensure it. Theodore was taking this too lightly. He had lost his grip over the teddy world and someone needed to point that out. Maybe a change in leadership was required. Maybe soon.

Ballinger took it upon himself to send a message to the Local Company leader, where the incident occurred. Measures needed to be taken. There was a thug already in the house; he would take care of it. The stories could not be made public.

One bear would prove to be an important ally to Ballinger in the teddy world, Tiger. He was the most feared and dangerous teddy in the Kage Kuma division. These top-secret bears were never seen by normal teddies or acknowledged by the Council. Some things were best kept secret due to the nature of their actions. When extreme situations arose that went against ethical behavior, the Kage Kuma team was dispatched to deal with such unpleasantness. Keeping them hidden from the teddy world was essential because they worked outside the Code — way outside. But their actions would be justified by keeping teddies safe.

Ballinger had summoned Tiger to discuss his assignment of discreetly tracking down Lyle and D without the Council's knowledge. D had exposed Ballinger's secret to the Council and he wanted retribution. Ballinger also needed Lyle back home. When Louis found Lyle missing, his behavior became so erratic that he tore the house apart. His trust issues flared at his personal staff and accused them of stealing his beloved keepsake.

Ballinger paced angrily in Louis' office as he spoke to Tiger.

"I've had you looking for those two for well over two months now. You're telling me you can't find one former Rough Rider and a little mama's bear with a red bow?"

Tiger stood silently while he was chastised. Ballinger was merely venting. He was more frustrated that Bullock wouldn't tell him where Theodore had banished the intrepid auburn bear. The target of his ire changed, revealing his true contempt. "We wouldn't be having this discussion if he'd simply tell me where he was."

Ballinger was fueled by mimicry. He'd seen Louis rant many times about his troubles. For whatever reason, it did seem to help.

"Does anyone else see what I see — an old bear that has lost his touch? Theodore. Ha! Really! He can't even handle a couple of stuff nosed bears. This is getting ridiculous," raged Ballinger. "I'll tell you what *I* would do." Ballinger suddenly stopped. His beady eyes shifted side to side in a daze as a thought materialized. "Better yet," he said, turning his eyes to Tiger, "you! I need you to do something. This will be between us. Do you understand?"

Tiger nodded obediently and mechanically asked, "What about the other thing?"

Ballinger swiped his paw. "Forget about them. We can deal with them later. But this . . . this needs to be dealt with, and not *softly* by Theodore." The mind of Ballinger began formulating his move. This was his chance. Two young code breakers could be spun into so much more. It would include Tiger and his clandestine exploits.

Tiger stood close to three feet tall and used to be a soft creamy white teddy with unusually small ears. His off-white pelt was stained black in a ritual of the Kage. His eyes were small and also black as they sat buried in his short fur to where you could hardly see them. This made him appear even more menacing. Emotionless and cold was Tiger since becoming a Kage, an attribute that served him well when called upon for duty. Tiger had a secret — a dark secret. It was rumored that he had done something so horrific in his past that no one would speak of it. Whatever happened to Tiger, it changed him. Some say he changed in more ways than one. Ballinger found him fascinating as well as extremely valuable.

The Council bear explained how Bobby Bear and Waldo were caught moving and how they continue to move in front of James. But he knew that two young bears breaking the Teddy Code were not enough to demand the use of the highly secretive Kage Kumas. Something dire would need to be at stake. For Ballinger to get Tiger's attention he would need to paint James as the villain trying to expose and ruin the teddy world. That Bobby Bear and Waldo were traitors to the Secret Teddy Society, seduced by the wicked ways of the human world. Each time he mentioned James, Tiger would twitch his right eye. A slight red flare came with each twitch. Tiger's eyes began to glow. Anger, pure rage, was building in Tiger at the image Ballinger had created of James. Something was happening, yet Ballinger wasn't afraid. In fact, this change brought about a sinister leer to his pointed face. Tiger was just the bear for the task.

"Now I'm not going to tell you how to do your job — you do what you think you have to, but just make sure these two traitors don't make it back to the Council."

"And for the human?"

Ballinger grinned. "I'll leave that completely up to you."

Louis Longley would have been pleased with his bear. Ballinger was now taking action, a step in the right direction for the protection of the teddy world and his pursuit for power. Theodore was yesterday. Ballinger is today. The world was changing and the Council needed to change with it.

*****

As morning began, seemingly without Bobbie, as usual, James tried every day to wake her with a smile, but this would prove to be a difficult task. When he was a small child his daddy would sing to him, and so he figured that's just how a dad was supposed to wake their children.

He sang quietly:

> *"I can see the sunlight peeking through the pane,*
> *but if you look directly at it you will go insane.*
> *The sun is trying hard to say,*
> *get out of bed and start your day.*
> *The time has come to go to school,*
> *I sing this song because it's cool —"*

"*Daddy!*" a sleepy voice rang out abruptly. "It's not cool to sing *that* song." She rolled over and looked at him. He noticed a slight smile on her face, although, she would never admit to liking his songs.

"Hey, I guess we'll be classmates today!" said James. Bobbie forgot that he was coming to her class to read.

"Are you bringing Bobby Bear and Waldo?" she asked as she got out of bed. He hadn't thought about it. He didn't know if it would be a good idea since Bobby Bear didn't enjoy going to school the last time.

"Do you think I should?" he asked while he straightened her pillows and she pulled up the blankets to make the bed.

"Sure. Everyone loved them before. Besides, I think Waldo would like to see Tiffany again," she said with a smirk.

After breakfast, Bobbie grabbed her backpack and headed for the door. James gathered the bears and off they went. They were going back to school, and this time Waldo had to be on his best behavior.

James parked the car in the school parking lot and they joined the migration of students that happens every weekday at this time. A mass of kids funneled together through two large doors of Roosevelt Elementary on their way to another day of learning, which some took more seriously than others. Walking the hallway to class, the bears remembered the last time they were here.

Right there is where we fell, Waldo remembered.

Bobby Bear refused to think about that day.

"Hey, Bobbie," said a voice from behind. Waldo knows that voice. Tiffany walked up to meet her.

"Is this your dad?" she asked while wearing her friendliest face. "You're going to read to us today?"

"Do you want me to read to you?"

"Of course, I like Bobby Bear and Waldo."

She reached out to pet Waldo, who couldn't move while she rubbed her icy hand on his furry head. *Stop it! Stop touching me!* he wanted to shout. Despite the fact that Tiffany had apologized, Waldo still didn't trust her.

They arrived at the classroom and Mrs. Larkin was at her desk when she saw Bobbie and James enter. "Good morning and welcome to our classroom," she said with a bright smile.

"This is my daddy."

"Yes, we've met," replied Mrs. Larkin. "I'm glad you were able to do this. Your daughter delighted us with her 'Show and Tell,' and when she mentioned you were writing stories about them I thought the class would love to hear more adventures."

"Bobbie didn't tell me that I had a choice," he joked.

"Well, we're not ready just yet, so, if you would like to sit down, we have a few things to do first," said the teacher.

As James walked with Bobbie to her desk he remembered being in this very classroom when he was little. Everything came flooding back just walking through the door. They reached his daughter's desk and she sat down; then James headed to the back of the class to find a seat for himself. As he walked down the row of students he suddenly felt like he was wearing a clown costume because all eyes were staring at him as if they were expecting something funny to happen. But then again, a grown man carrying two teddy bears was pretty funny all by itself. There, in the corner, stood an empty desk. The closer James got — the smaller it looked. He paused, trying to decide if he would fit. The whole class watched him as he studied the situation.

The bell rang and everyone settled down as Mrs. Larkin began roll call. James made his move. He crouched and began sliding into the small opening. His knees pressed on the desktop while the rest of him squeezed into the seat. The teacher watched, giving an awkward smile as he squirmed back and forth for a better fit.

While Mrs. Larkin spoke to the class, James wedged himself firmly in the desk, holding two bears, remembering his days of grade school. The smell of the classroom brought back memories. But what smell was it? The pencils; the wooden desks; the dusty chalk erasers, it was all of it. He placed his hand under the desk expecting to find gum that he put there over twenty years ago. The faces have changed but the classroom was exactly the same. As much as James didn't care for school when he was young, he did enjoy being in the classroom now.

"I used to sit in this class when I was little," he whispered in Bobby Bear's ear. "I'd get such butterflies every day before class."

Bobby Bear liked the idea of getting butterflies before class. He imagined them flying around, landing on his head and tickling his ears.

James got lost in time for a minute or two, when Mrs. Larkin brought him back to the present. "We have someone here today that is going to read to us. He's writing about the adventures of two bears, Bobby Bear and Waldo, that you all met during Show and Tell. So right now I would like to ask Bobbie's dad to come up and read."

The class turned and watched him struggle, removing himself from the tiny desk. Hearing quiet chuckles and snickers, he walked to the front of the class and introduced himself.

"I know you've already met Bobby Bear and Waldo," he said as he held up the bears. He turned and placed them on the teacher's desk facing the class. "Today, I thought I would start at the beginning," he said and began to read.

The class listened with care. Even Mrs. Larkin seemed enthralled. He read for what only seemed like several minutes when it had been half an hour, and the class was still paying attention. He finished the story and set the pages on his lap. *This is great*, he thought. *They really listened.*

He sat for a moment in brief silence when someone started clapping. Sitting in the corner wearing a satisfied smile was the teacher, who seemed to enjoy the story more than the kids. The rest of the class joined in.

Waldo had never experienced applause before, not directed at him anyway. He liked it, a lot. Bobby Bear was fairly sure that telling stories about the teddy world was not good.

James was just about to get up when the teacher asked if anyone had questions about the story. He was not expecting to have to answer questions. Since James was actually writing from real events, he wasn't sure he'd know how to respond to real questions.

Initially, no one raised their hand as he looked around the room. A small voice came from the corner, "Do they sleep?" The voice belonged to Mrs. Larkin.

Feeling a little uncomfortable, James tried to answer. He was confident that adults would never believe his story, no matter how much detail about a secret teddy world, but if children were going home telling their parents that a strange man had two teddy bears that moved, that could be a potential problem. He had no choice but to answer.

"Yes, they do, but they don't need to close their eyes when they sleep," said James, having a hard time looking at her.

"The story seemed *very* detailed. Did this really happen or are these just stories you make up?" she asked.

James didn't know what the teacher was trying to do. Did she want to hear the truth or did she want to hear that these were just made up stories? He realized that if he told the truth, that they're real, no one would believe him. But, if he said he made them up, then he'd be lying. This put him in a troubled spot.

Actually, Mrs. Larkin had a secret reason why she was so interested. Many people, other than James, have experienced strange teddy phenomena.

The children's faces stared at him waiting to hear what they already believed, and the teacher waited for an answer.

There was only one thing for him to do. He took a breath and started to say, "It's —".

Suddenly, the Principal, Mr. Tosh, poked his head in the classroom door. "Excuse me, Mrs. Larkin. I have a new student joining your class today," he said in a very gentle voice. He walked into the classroom holding a scared little girl by the hand. Her face appeared red from the tears she'd been wiping away.

"This is Tory Demuress; I think I said that right." He was hoping for a smile; there wasn't one.

Mrs. Larkin knelt down and took her hand from Mr. Tosh. "I'm so glad you can join us. We have a seat just for you," said Mrs. Larkin with a soothing smile. They walked slowly to the back of the classroom as Tory kept her head low. The teacher took her backpack and sat Tory in the desk that James had recently occupied. She seemed to fit just fine.

Bobby Bear and Waldo took note of the sad girl.

Watching a child cry is one of the saddest things for a teddy bear. They are especially good at comforting sad children, which was Bobby Bear's first instinct. Bobbie, too, noticed the girl. Everyone knows what it's like to start in a new school with strange kids staring at them.

Bobbie made up her mind to do something. She got up, walked to the teacher's desk and grabbed a tissue from the box (that the teacher always kept handy) and took it to the new girl.

Bobbie held out the tissue, while the whole class watched. Tory timidly reached for it and gave a look that didn't need any words. Bobbie went back to her seat, as the mood in the room completely change.

An act of sincerity and kindness — James was so proud of his little girl he could have easily cried, but not in front of the bears they wouldn't understand.

James felt this was a good time to leave, so he gathered up the bears from the teacher's desk. "I won't take up any more of the class's time," he said. "Thanks for letting me read today." He smiled and waved at Bobbie. Mrs. Larkin stopped him at the door.

"I would like to thank you for taking the time to read your stories," she said. "And about that last question, I already know the answer." She gave a wink and reached out her hand.

This left James even more confused than before. Did she *know*? Or was she just kidding around? He couldn't tell.

"You're very welcome. You have a wonderful class," he said and reached to shake her hand.

"If I could arrange it, would you come back and read some more?" she asked.

"I'd love to, just let me know when," James said. He was not sure what he had gotten himself into but the words just came out. *I'd love to?* he thought. *Oh, man.*

Mrs. Larkin noticed Taylor Bingham raising his hand vigorously. A quiet portly little boy, Taylor was often picked on by other kids for just about everything he did.

"Yes, you have a question?" asked the teacher.

"Can we say goodbye to the bears?" asked Taylor bravely, bracing himself for the laughter and teasing from the class.

"I think that would be very nice," replied the teacher.

Taylor stood, expecting snickers and laughter, but to his surprise, no one laughed. In fact, several other students got up as well and walked to meet James and the bears. Tory, however, remained steadfastly in her seat.

Bobbie approached her daddy.

"Hey, Pumpkin, how'd I do?" he asked her.

She threw her arms around his waist. "You did great," she said with a big smile. "And you guys did great, too," she added, directed at the bears. James and Bobbie both happened to notice Tory alone at the back of the room. He looked at his daughter. She gave him a sweet smile and slowly left his side to go make a new friend.

What the heck did I do right? he asked himself. He watched Bobbie reach out and shake Tory's hand.

As James walked towards the door, hands reached out to pat, rub, scratch and tickle the bears as they passed. Bobby Bear was very nervous at first but was surprised at how gentle the kids were. Waldo thought this was the best thing ever.

Since teddy's feed off of human contact, Waldo had never felt more alive.

All the way home, Waldo was feeling very special, he never had so much attention before and couldn't stop thinking about the rush of all those hands on him and the smiles sent his way. Waldo saw how much people enjoyed the story, his story. This was, after all, about him and how he broke the Teddy Code. A rebellious feeling began to fester. Meanwhile, Bobby Bear was busy worrying, as he usually did. This time he worried that James may have gone too far. He'd told a lot of teddy secrets today. He didn't think any good could come of it.

"I think that went very well. It sure seemed like everyone enjoyed the stories," James expressed.

Bobby Bear never even heard James because his thoughts were a mile away.

"Ladies and gentlemen of the jury — you've heard testimony of the accused, Mr. Bobby Bear. He says that he did nothing wrong. He says that he is a good bear and deserves a second chance. Well, I say NO! I say throw him in the darkest cell and throw away the key. Look at his face. He clearly possesses the face of a 'Bad Bear.' Do you want a 'Bad Bear' in our society? I know I don't." Bobby Bear nervously glanced at the jury and noticed a familiar face. It was James looking very disappointed. Bobby Bear only wants to be a good bear and knows that none of this would have happened if James hadn't written his stories.

Next to him, Waldo was having a very different daydream. *"Ladies and gentlemen: you've heard the stories, and yes, they're all true. The daring and dangerous adventures that only he could survive — The man of mystery — The man of wonder — The one that we all know, and love: The cute — the loveable — WALDO!"*

Applause filled the air. Surrounded by adoring fans, a rhythmic chant slowly builds from the crowd. "Waldo, Waldo, Waldo, Waldo..."

James heard Waldo chanting his own name in a dreamy voice. This made him smile as he kept his eyes on the road. Since he can't resist a good chant, he joined in, "Waldo, Waldo, Waldo..."

James was having so much fun that he decided a treat was in order. Bobby Bear snapped out of his daydream with a scowl.

Hearing his name over and over again, Waldo suddenly realized James was singing while bouncing back and forth in time. A smile formed as he watched James acting silly.

Feeling the mood change, James became aware of his own voice. Something was missing. No one else was chanting and the fun was gone.

Bobby Bear just glared at James. He was beginning to get angry at James for giving away the teddy secrets. Waldo, however, had a pleasant smile on his face. "Are you all right, Bobby Bear?" asked James and started to turn the wheel.

Before Bobby Bear could grunt, Waldo cried out, "Supergreatiestfantaculicious!" and began jumping up and down shaking his paws. "Oh, my gosh! Oh, my gosh!"

James pulled into the fun park parking lot to get some ice cream at the colorful Sir Licks-A-Lot stand.

Bobby Bear had completely lost his anger as if it somehow fell out of his head. Both bears were standing at the window when James told them to "Keep low."

He pulled into the same spot as before, turned off the car and said, "I just thought you boys were so good today that an icy treat was called for."

Bobby Bear and Waldo could not have agreed more, the look on their faces told James he was right. "Stay low — I'll be right back."

He got out of the car and went to get in line. As he waited to place his order, the bears watched other people getting their cones. Waldo noticed something different about one cone, covered with tiny lumpy colors. This was no ordinary ice cream. His eyes fixed on this magnificent treat. James glanced back at the car and happened to notice Waldo's fascination. James smiled to himself.

Just then, someone came close to the car and the bears sat down quickly in their seat. A moment passed when suddenly the car door opened.

"I think you'll like these," James said as he got in. The bears didn't move for a moment.

"It's okay, no one's near." The bears saw what he was holding as total amazement filled their faces.

"What is that?" asked Waldo in a curious voice.

James handed them the ice cream cones.

"Sprinkles," he answered. "They're . . . hmm, I'm not exactly sure what they are. They're like little colorful candies on top of ice cream."

Just when Waldo didn't think something so good could get any better; they put candy on it.

Bobby Bear didn't know where to begin. *Do I start at the top — maybe the bottom — how 'bout the middle?* He studied the situation. It wasn't long before he felt it dripping on his paws and he knew right where to begin.

The Network was abuzz about a book titled <u>Secret Teddy Society</u> that was having an effect in the local community.

James appeared to be convincing some people that the Secret Teddy Society was real. How would this affect the teddy world? One report of teddy abuse had already been received due to the stories. It was someone from Bobbie's class. Would there be more? Dakota had just delivered an urgent message to Elvis regarding an added assignment for Fluffy bear.

Normally, most teddy activity occurs at night when people are asleep, but this was important, and Elvis needed to get word to Fluffy *now*. He went to the closet but Fluffy was gone. He called out in a strong whisper, "Hey, Red!" Elvis heard the slightest of sound coming from the hallway and dashed frantically for his chair; fearing he was about to be the next victim of breaking the Teddy Code. He couldn't help but feel how ironic the situation was, as he never had difficulty getting into his chair before. With every grasp he took his paws felt useless. The sound was coming closer and time was running out when Elvis managed to get into the chair and assume his lifeless position. That's when he noticed Fluffy ambled through the door.

As relieved as he was to see Fluffy, it was anger that took over. "Where've you been?" asked Elvis with irritation stuck to every word.

Fluffy was very surprised to see the family Network bear talk during the day.

"In the office," he replied with his eyes fixed nervously on Elvis'.

Elvis stared back. The moment was tense when he remembered Fluffy had a job to do. A job he didn't want to do.

"I have some news. Word is out about the stories. It looks like he plans on letting others read 'em. They don't want that to happen and something needs to be done."

Fluffy stood there for a moment before he realized what Elvis was saying. "And they want me to do it?" Fluffy asked hoping to hear anything other than yes.

"It's part of your assignment, so I guess so," Elvis answered more calmly.

Fluffy's face dropped. "This is from the Council?"

"No. This came from L.Co."

Fluffy didn't understand how this was a Local Company matter. "I don't get it. These are just stories. Right? Why are they making the call?"

"I don't know. I agree — it doesn't sound right, but — I'll help as much as I can," he added, hoping this would make Fluffy feel better.

Elvis sighed. He couldn't read Fluffy very well. It was hard for Elvis to adapt to this family. Even though he had been in the house for over two years, he used to belong to another.

There was a little girl that brought him to life, for his beginning. She was a sweet girl who never left her bed. She had a laugh that Elvis still hears in his sleep. They were always together. They mostly played "Spaceship." It was because the machines and tubes next to the bed helped create the scene. Katie was sick. Elvis didn't understand at first until he spent more time in a chair by the window than in the bed with Katie. She began sleeping longer and their playtime grew shorter. Katie would sometimes sleep for a whole day until one morning she never woke up. Elvis sat in his chair and watched the men in blue take her while she slept. Elvis was never the same after that. His person was gone.

Elvis had a hard time sleeping in Bobbie's room because it was too quiet. He didn't like the quiet; it gave him time to think.

Elvis often thought about loyalty. His, to Katie, and his now, to his new family. The teddy world gets a little complicated when it comes to loyalty because of human relationships and the Teddy Code. The Code always comes first, but the love for humans and their families can be quite strong at times and this was one of those times. This family had the respect for everything living and non-living and that is tops in the teddy world.

"Did they say what they wanted me to do?" Fluffy asked in a sad, beleaguered voice.

"No, they didn't. I guess whatever you can do," replied Elvis.

This was not what Big Red Fluffy bear wanted to hear. *I gotta stop him from writing stories,* he thought, *how do I do that?*

They heard the car pulling into the drive and Elvis climbed back in the Big People's Chair while Fluffy headed back to the closet.

Elvis sat feeling terrible about leaving Fluffy that way. He would try to think of a way to help.

BEWARE THE BEAR

Teddies don't normally get to meet many other bears because of the Code. Being born into a human family is what life is all about for a teddy bear. Belonging was primary and instinctive. Other teddies in the same household become part of your family, but outside is another world.

Roaming from house to house to spread news in the teddy world was the duty of the Rough Riders or "Outsiders", as inside bears called them. It was not usual for a teddy to sneak out of the house just for fun; the risk of being caught was too great. The Code was to be maintained at all times and the Council took breaking the trust of the Code seriously.

The social aspect of a teddy was primarily up to their person or family. For example, people can be found riding the highways on their motorcycles with their bears securely strapped to the back. Grandparents take to the countryside in their campers while teddy bears sit comfortably on the dashboard. Some have even taken their teddies skydiving as well as other extreme sports. Teddies are in fact, everywhere, but a teddy meeting other teddies is short on opportunities.

One of the best ways for one teddy to meet another is when kids get together for a sleepover. This puts bears close together while children sleep.

Each teddy comes with their own special abilities, just like humans; but there are several characteristics that all teddies possess. Hearing for a teddy is much like a dog or cat — very sensitive. However, it is the frequencies that set teddies apart from the rest of the listening world. They have the capability of hearing and speaking in a wave spectrum that humans can't. The Teddy Tone is their natural voice and they use it while in the company of people. They do have the capability of speaking in other sound spectrums that they discover on their own and the human frequency becomes the second tone they learn.

Because their mouths move when they talk, regardless of what tone they're using, a teddy needs to be very careful when communicating with other bears.

On Friday afternoon, Bobbie bounded home from school with one thing on her mind: the sleepover.

She slammed the door open, threw her backpack in the corner, and ran to the desk. This time she didn't ask about any new adventures because she knew one was on its way.

"Hey, Bobby Bear, Waldo. Do you remember what tomorrow is?" she asked, pausing, almost waiting for them to answer.

"Oh, come on — you remember, it's the SLEEPOVER! But not just any sleepover, it's a teddy sleepover so you can meet new friends."

Debra came through the door and saw the backpack in the corner. "Bobbie, can you please put your pack where it belongs," Debra called out sharply.

"Jeeze Louise, I keep forgetting."

Bobbie always forgets. She doesn't mean to, but she does. It's not as if it's hard to put away her backpack or anything. *Why do I keep forgetting?* she reprimanded herself.

Meanwhile, Bobby Bear and Waldo, now reminded of tomorrow's activities, began to imagine what it would be like:

"Hi. I'm Princess Cutieton, What's your name?" she said in a soft sweet voice.

"Sir Waldo," he replied.

"Did you say, Sir Waldo? Are you from England?"

"No, no. But I have done things for the British Secret Service that is quite hush, hush," said Waldo in a lowered voice, tapping his nose.

Waldo loved it when Bobbie and James slipped into their British accents. They would do it for hours. Bobby Bear and Waldo practiced their accents whenever they could, but they had a hard time keeping it serious. He knew all about James Bond and the life of a spy. Action, adventure, covert missions and foreign lands of mystery all tugged at Waldo's sense of intrigue.

"So you're a secret agent?" she asked. Waldo gave a confident but coy smile with a slight nod. "Have you been on any secret missions?" she discretely inquired.

"Mm, yes, indeed," his English accent emerged as he puffed out his chest and stiffened his jaw. "There is one adventure I can tell you about. I was in the deepest, darkest part of the Mousentrappenese jungle looking for the stolen crown of the Empire."

"You? Why you? Surely the Queen has other secret agents."

"True. But no one was coming out alive. That's when they always call me."

Princess Cutieton's eyes flared in admiration as Waldo continued, "They dropped me from a plane in the dead of night. My parachute was caught in the trees and I had to cut myself free, landing hard on the ground. I took the same path as the other spies before me and it didn't take long before I discovered the headquarters of the sinister mastermind Doctor Meany. He lived in a huge palace buried deep in the forest. Slipping in and finding the stolen crown was the easy part. It was getting out that was a bit tricky. Once I had gotten past the poison arrows, venomous snakes and trap doors, I thought the hard part was over. I was wrong. The jungle turned out to be a bit of a sticky wicket. It was dark and I had somehow lost my direction when I suddenly found myself surrounded by evil monkeys," he said raising one eyebrow.

"Oh, my, that's the worst kind of monkey," she added.

He flared his eyes and began gently stroking his chin. "Mm, indeed," Waldo agreed.

"What on earth did you do?"

"Well, I noticed that these were no ordinary evil monkeys. These were the dangerous and deadly Long haired, snake tooth, twizzle tailed, fire breathing, jumping monkeys."

Princess Cutieton let out a frightful gasp as Waldo continued. "Luckily, I happen to speak a little 'Twizzle'. So I said, 'you-twizzle me-twizzle we-twizzle okee-twizzle-dee.' They looked at me as I looked at them. Then slowly they gathered around, closer and closer. I began to think my Twizzle was a little rusty when suddenly they picked me up and took me to their camp for a celebration."

"My, that sounds absolutely fantastic," she said as impressed as one could be.

"Mm, yes, indeed," said Waldo also impressed.

That was fun. His imagination was taking his mind away from his problems. Meeting new bears made him nervous but now he was feeling more confident with his tales of adventure, but his ego threw him a curve ball. The story dipped into his actual dilemma.

Princess Cutieton was completely in awe when her eyes widened and stared at Waldo with sudden recognition.

"Wait a minute. Are you THE WALDO? The one that broke the Code?" The way she asked was not of blame or shame but real interest.

Waldo's imagination and conscience collided revealing his true concern about the sleepover. He tried to act as if it didn't bother him, he even tried to act rebellious, but it was, after all, his conscience. Waldo was fighting with himself.

"Oh, yes, Now I know who you are. Everyone knows who you are. You're the daring bear who broke the Teddy Code," she said. *"I imagine you have some real dangerous adventures."*

"Yeah, I've done some things that are dangerous," replied Waldo as his accent faded. He gave an arrogant grin while recalling his troubled past. *"I broke into the great cold metal box to get my paws on the secret white liquid that has untold powers."* The taste of milk began fueling his imagination. *"I've made humans go insane with one look,"* remembering the expression on Tiffany's face while his mind rambled on. His voice soaked in an over confident bluster. *"Humans applaud when I enter a room."*

Waldo, for one slight moment, felt the rush of his defiance the more his daydream meandered. Rebellion began tearing at the goodness within. He started rationalizing something that was completely his fault into something that he felt wasn't a big deal. Why couldn't he be considered brave for breaking the Code? Besides, it's not like it was the end of the world. He did, after all, get to experience milk and ice cream, something that almost made it all worth it. He had been the center of human attention. Waldo was walking on shaky moral ground and he knew it. This was not the quality of a teddy and definitely not what a good bear should be.

"Oh, my. That doesn't sound good at all," she said with *uncertainty as Waldo's conscience spoke a little louder. "You must be terribly worried."*

"Worried? Me? Phf — nah," said Waldo, *trying to convince himself.* It wouldn't work. Waldo *was* worried.

Bobby Bear sat nervously as he imagined quite a different scene:

From across the room, he saw a very cute girl bear. She was the softest light brown color he had ever seen. She wore a pink bow on one ear and a pink heart on her left chest. The pretty girl bear made eye contact with Bobby Bear, who quickly looked away. Out of the corner of his eye, he saw her approach.

"I noticed you from across the room and thought I would say hello; do you live here?" she asked.

"Yes, I — I do," stammered Bobby Bear, *still not able to look her in the eye.*

"What's your name?" she asked.

"Um, Um, uh, B-B-Bobby, Bobby . . . uh . . . Bobby . . ." He *couldn't seem to remember his name. "I mean, Bobby Bear. Yeah, Bobby Bear, that's right."*

"Are you sure?" she said with a giggle.

He nodded slowly; fairly sure he was right about his name.

"Well, Bobby Bear, are you normally like this?"

He shook his head no.

"Let's see, are you nervous or just shy?"

He shrugged his shoulders.

Another bear approached and asked, "Who's this?"

"He said his name is Bobby Bear but he doesn't talk much," the first bear answered.

Suddenly surrounded by strange teddies, they gathered closer and closer. All he could hear was the question, 'What's your name?' repeated over and over. Bobby Bear didn't like this dream anymore.

The daydreaming was interrupted.

"I have to go pick up my room before the sleepover," Bobbie said, returning to the desk.

The anxious brown bear didn't need any more proof that the sleepover was a bad idea. If he's going to have trouble with his own name then what chance does he have at making new friends? It would just be embarrassing.

Waldo, on the other hand, was beginning to look forward to it. How could he miss with his twizzle tail jumping monkey adventure? But then again, what if he was confronted about his offense. What if they asked questions or shunned him. Learning about friendship from Bobbie further entrenched their innate loyalty, and trust from the teddy world, but making new friends for a teddy would be just like any other human. A bear can appear one way but turn out to be something else once you got to know them. This would be a constant learning process for all humans and teddies while meeting new acquaintances. Some are leery at first while others are openly trusting, but there is a phrase that warns: "You don't really know anyone." The two young bears have heard James say this to Bobbie many times.

The phone rang as Debra was preparing dinner. As usual her hands were wet and she had to reach for a towel. "Every time," she sputtered while quickly grabbing the phone before the answering machine picked up. "Hello?"

It was an old friend from high school. "Hey, Deb, it's Sandy. I just heard about the book that your husband wrote."

"Oh, really? How'd you hear about it?"

"Do you remember Dorothy McReynolds? Well, she was talking to Stacy, who said she heard from Laura, that she found it at the Village Bookstore. Laura said while she was buying hers that several other people bought one."

"Wow! That's great."

"I also heard that James talks to the bears when no one's around. Is that true?"

Debra became agitated. "Now where'd you hear that?"

"Dorothy was talking with Stacy and mentioned that her mother knows Mrs. Mallory. You know, that witchy haired lady that knows everything. Well, she said that she heard James talking to the bears. Apparently, he didn't know she was there. She says that he believes his own story."

It was getting hard to stay polite when such rumors were being spread around. "Well, I'll tell you what Mrs. Mallory can do —" Debra stopped before she said too much.

Sandy interjected, "Hey, don't get me wrong. I think it's adorable."

That's not what Debra was thinking. It was embarrassing. Sure, James has fun, in his own way, but painting him as a nutcase was hard for Debra to hear.

Bobbie was picking up her bedroom when her dad appeared in the doorway. "Hey, Pumpkin, there's someone at the door for you."

"For me?" she asked excitedly, dropping some dirty clothes and running to the front door. There stood Tiffany.

"Hi, Bobbie."

"Hi," she replied, surprised to see her, especially alone.

"I know we haven't been the best of friends," Tiffany admitted in a voice that Bobbie had never heard before. It was nice and sweet, almost.

"I didn't think we were friends at all," chirped Bobbie innocently.

"I wanted to change that and give you my special necklace to say we're friends."

Tiffany handed her a shiny silver necklace with a small diamond placed beautifully inside a heart shaped flower. Completely baffled and confused Bobbie said the first thing that came to mind when someone hands her a gift.

"Thank you," she responded cautiously, still unsure about why she was here. "But, it's so fancy!"

"It is," Tiffany agreed.

"I'm not sure my daddy will let me keep it."

"Sure he will." Tiffany glanced around the room as she stood just outside the front door. "Hey, I have an idea," said Tiffany. "Why don't you come for a sleepover tomorrow night, and you can bring your bear — Waldo." In fact, the golden haired girl had been informed about Bobbie's little get-together.

Kristi had been talking with Tiffany earlier that day and incidentally mentioned Bobbie's sleepover plans. Tiffany seemed very interested.

After what happened at Show and Tell, she wanted to know a lot more about Bobbie and her bears, and she didn't want other kids finding out before she did.

Bobbie simply told her the truth. "I can't because I'm having a sleepover too. Sorry," she said in her kindest voice. "I really need to finish cleaning my room."

Before Tiffany could invite herself to the sleepover Bobbie thanked her once again and went back inside. Tiffany didn't understand what just happened as she watched the door close in her face. Rejection was not something Tiffany was used to. It didn't make any sense. She used her kindest voice. She smiled her sweetest smile; she even gave away her favorite necklace. Nothing worked the way it normally would. Confusion evaporated in a second as anger took over. She stood at the door for a moment seething, then turned and walked home, a few houses down the street.

Bobbie still had no idea what she was up to. *Maybe I should've asked her over,* she thought while admiring the beautiful pendant. After placing the necklace on her desk, she went back to cleaning her room and quickly forgot about inviting Tiffany.

The next morning, James was ready to wake Bobbie with a new song. He was just about to start singing when he entered the bedroom to find her already awake and ready for breakfast.

"Are you feeling all right?" he asked, only half kidding, as he truly was surprised to see her out of bed.

"*Daddy,* I feel fine," she answered in a scolding tone.

"Are Bobby Bear and Waldo up yet?" she asked, darting past him, headed towards the office.

"Oh, I suppose so. I haven't checked on them yet. Why?"

139

She stopped in her tracks and gave a look that even he knew exactly what she was saying without saying a word.

In a long drawn out voice, James said, "Oh, that's *right* . . . the sleepover."

She snapped out of her look and dashed down the hall to check on the bears.

Entering the office, she found them in their usual spot. "It's time for breakfast," she said, picking them up to join her in the kitchen.

Debra was taking the Saturday morning to sleep in. She suffered from daily headaches that doctors had no answers for, and the only time she was pain free was when she slept. It didn't normally slow her down, but some days were worse than others.

Bobbie sat down at the counter and placed both bears in the stool next to her. She noticed her mother wasn't around.

"Is Mommy still sleeping?" she asked with concern.

"Yeah. She didn't sleep well," answered James. He noticed her worried face and decided a distraction was in order. "So, what's it going to be, Bronco Bobbie?" he asked in his best western accent. He popped a toothpick in his mouth and flung a dishtowel over his shoulder to add to the character.

Bobbie was always good about playing along with her daddy when he suddenly said something funny.

"I'll have what ther' havin'," she said, pointing at the bears sitting next to her.

James' face turned serious as if she said something horrible.

"Are you *sure*? Are you really sure you want what ther' havin'?" he said dramatically.

Her eyes squinted and her lip sneered, she replied, "Yup. I'm sure! And don't make me say it twice."

It was all he could do to stay in character. He could feel a laugh bubbling in his throat so he swallowed hard to keep it down, which added to the effect.

"All right, but don't say I didn't warn ya'," he said, then slid a bowl down the counter that stopped right in front of her. He nervously reached into the cupboard and pulled out a box of cereal as he tried to keep his hands from shaking.

"What's that?" she asked, seeing the tremble in his hand.

"I ain't quite sure what it is. Some folks call it 'The Stuff.' They say, it's ground up grubs and bugs and dirt that only a Bronco like you is tough enough to eat," he said.

Bobbie smacked her lips together; "Mm, sounds tasty."

Meanwhile, Wild Waldo imagined himself sitting in an old western saloon waiting for his grub.

"I haven't seen you in these parts before stranger, you new in town?" asked Milly, a friendly little waitress bear.

"Just passin' through Ma'am, thought I'd stop in for some fixins," he said in a gravelly weathered voice.

"What'll it be?" she asked.

"I'll have the roughin'est, toughen'est meal ya' got."

"Oh, you want . . . 'The Stuff,'" she said knowing what he was talking about.

Wild Waldo slammed both paws on the counter. "That's right. Give me 'The Stuff'."

Waldo snapped out of his daydream as he noticed James pouring milk into a bowl in front of Bobbie. Needless to say, this grabbed the attention of Bobby Bear as well.

"Thank you, partner," said Bobbie in her cowboy voice. She took several bites while Bobby Bear and Waldo were dreaming of a breakfast with milk. James stood back in disbelief that she's actually eating 'The Stuff.'

"Mm, this is good."

James stared in amazement as she took another bite. Bobbie noticed his face and became instantly annoyed.

"Ya' gotta a problem, pal?" she barked out loud with milk dripping from her chin.

"N, n, no — I just ain't never seen nobody eat it before — and — and live."

"Well, git use to it mister — 'cuz I'll be back ev'r mornin' for more o'the same."

Both Bobbie and her daddy dissolved into giggles. It was a good morning.

After breakfast, Bobbie took the bears back to the playroom to get ready for the big day.

Bobbie took friendship seriously. When she asked her daddy 'why kids were so mean', she couldn't understand how one day someone was your friend and the next day they weren't. It was difficult to keep track of who was your friend and who wasn't. Bobbie became protective and fiercely loyal to those that were the same.

One by one they arrived. Kristi and her bear, Travis, showed up with Kimmie and her bear, Peekaboo. Then Tory had a cute little teddy called Smiley, poking out of her backpack, while Zella brought a tattered looking bear named Zeek. The last to show was Danielle and her bear Squiggles. She may be late but she's always on time because nothing starts without her.

The sleepover was an important event for Bobbie. It would be the first time she had anyone stay the night. She didn't have to decide which of her friends to invite to because all of her friends were coming. Some were loud, and some were quiet, but they all loved having fun, and they all loved teddy bears. They were all so different in personality, but one thing bound them together, their loyalty to each other. Tory was the new girl in town, but Bobbie saw a quality in her that she recognized; one that escaped most people — kindness.

The girls gathered in the playroom where Bobbie had a table set up for a tea party. The girls introduced the bears to each other and started to giggle as Danielle asked Squiggles, "What does a bear wear when he doesn't have any clothes?"

She used a funny squeaky voice to answer for Squiggles. "Um, I don't know."

"Bear skin," she said with a chuckle.

Bobby Bear and Waldo love a good joke, but were trying hard to understand that one. The puns went over their heads.

The girls played tea party and dress up, when Zella found a floppy hat in the playroom closet. It was too small for her, so she put it on Zeek. This made everyone laugh and soon the girls began putting clothes on all the bears.

Waldo could only sit still while Bobbie slipped a pair of shiny white dance shoes on his feet. He didn't have to imagine how ridiculous he looked because he could see what Kimmie was doing to Peekaboo. A tiny pink skirt with polka dots and a feathery pink boa wrapped around her neck. Sure, it looked good on her, but she's a girl.

The laughter was loud enough to make James poke his head into the room to see what all the fuss was about. He immediately noticed Waldo, which brought an instant smile to his face. Since Waldo was facing the door he could see James. Trying to ease the moment he asked, "What's Waldo getting dressed for?"

Bobbie giggled and said, "He's getting ready for dance class."

James smiled and gave Waldo the thumbs up. "You look good, buddy."

This did not make Waldo feel any better.

Dance class, he thought. *I don't want to go to dance class. I want to be an international bear of mystery!*

Bobbie had a pile of her old clothes in the playroom closet for just such an occasion, and Danielle wasted no time in dressing Squiggles in some swim shorts and glasses.

"Ready for the beach," she said as she set him on the table for all to see. Squiggles thought the shorts felt kind of funny on his fur. He didn't mind the thought of going to the beach; sticking his toes in the sand and such, but he hated the idea of getting wet.

Waldo saw Squiggles and felt a little jealous because he thought the glasses looked pretty cool.

Zella, known best for being creative, thought Zeek should be a sports bear and found a small football t-shirt that said Lil' Gator. The shirt was a little big, which Zella quickly stuffed with paper for the shoulder pads. This made him appear lumpy, but he sure did look like a football player. Bobbie ran out of the room and returned with a toy helmet that fit rather well. Zeek had no idea what he looked like, but Bobby Bear was most impressed.

It wasn't long before all the bears were dressed and Bobbie went to the stereo to turn on some music. She placed Waldo on the table and started moving him around as if he were dancing. This made him feel foolish in front of the others. Dancing alone was one thing but in front of strange new bears was something completely different. It was hard for him to be too mad because some of the dance moves were actually pretty good. After one particular move, Waldo thought to himself, *I might have to remember that one.*

Debra called from the kitchen, "Dinner."

The girls ran to eat, leaving the bears alone in the playroom.

While the kids were gone Waldo wanted to say something but was afraid to.

The urge to get up and meet each other was strong, but humans were awake and just down the hall. It was too risky. There were too many sounds coming from the kitchen, which made it hard to tell if someone were coming or not. They needed the house to be quiet and the humans to be asleep before anyone felt comfortable moving about. They could use the Teddy Tone to talk but no one wanted to be the first to say anything. There was a silence in the room as usual, but this was different, it was an awkward silence. Like going to a school dance where no one wanted to be the first person out on the dance floor, it was going to take someone else to talk first, but until then, the silence only got louder, and everyone heard it.

After dinner, the kids returned and began to chat about school. Kristi knew just about everything that went on and loved to tell anyone who wanted to hear, and even those who didn't. Her topic of choice for the night was Tiffany and what happened at Show and Tell.

"I heard that she saw something so scary that it made her forget what she was doing," said Kristi mysteriously.

"In class? What could be that scary in class?" replied Kimmie, knowing how silly that was.

"She wouldn't say. I guess it was too scary."

Bobbie found herself saying something even she didn't expect. "I know what really happened." This caught everyone's attention. "My daddy told me that Waldo did something."

More interested than ever, a soft voice was heard, "What did he do?" asked Tory, which was unusual since she was so shy.

Bobbie, not sure if the girls are going to believe her, hesitantly answered, "He stuck out his tongue."

The girls giggled and turned to Waldo sitting in his chair, still wearing the white dancing shoes. He didn't know if he should feel proud or embarrassed of what he'd done. Either way, he had to keep reminding himself to stay still. The human contact was affecting Waldo and clouding his judgment. He also didn't want the other bears to find out about what he did to Tiffany. This was his conundrum: human love or teddy secrets? It would test his loyalty — but to whom?

"How does your dad know he did that?" asked Kristi.

Bobbie could tell that everyone else was thinking the same thing.

"Waldo told him," she replied.

"So, what you said at Show and Tell is really true?" Kristi asked with doubt in her voice. "Do you have proof?"

Just then, James stuck his head in the door. "Does anyone want a treat?" he asked, swinging a tray out from behind his back with a bunch of bowls on top. The girls noticed the bowls were filled with ice cream topped with hot fudge.

"Yeah," they all yelled at once.

He placed the tray on the table and the bowls were quickly snapped up. Waldo saw what was in the bowls but didn't recognize the oozy brown mess.

I know that's ice cream, but what's that dark stuff? he wondered. *That doesn't look very good.*

As James turned to leave, a question came from Kristi. "Is it true that Waldo only talks to you?"

He knew it was only a matter of time before someone asked that question. He smiled, and glanced at Waldo. "Yep, it's all true," he answered quickly. Bobbie felt a sense of pride, as her daddy didn't even flinch when he heard the question.

"How do we know it's true?" she asked, trying not to sound like she didn't believe, which was quite impossible.

The girls looked at Kristi as if she said something very bad, then looked back at James for the answer. The girls sat quietly waiting.

"So . . . it's proof you want, huh?" James thought for a second. "Tell you what, I want you to write or draw something on a piece of paper. I'll leave the room and you show it to Waldo — *only* Waldo, not anyone else until after," he said. "Then I'll come back and get him. We'll go somewhere private so he can tell me what's on the paper. Ok? Sound fair?" Kristi thought that sounded fine. The other girls agreed.

Bobbie grabbed a piece of paper and a pencil and handed it to Kristi. James left the room while Kristi went to the corner, making sure no one could see.

As the doubting girl wrote on the paper, Waldo had another dilemma. He was now aware of what was about to happen, so were the other teddies in the room. Once Kristi was finished drawing, she was going to show him something that he would or wouldn't reveal to James as proof of teddy life. This was a real pickle. Even though bears appear lifeless it doesn't mean that they aren't aware. If Waldo revealed the truth to James — then the other bears would hear. What then?

What else could happen? How much more trouble could this cause?

A couple of minutes passed when Kristi walked up to Waldo and slid the paper in front of his eyes. Even though his mind was deep in troubled thought, Waldo saw what was on the paper. He didn't like it — but he saw it. After a few seconds Kristi folded up the paper several times and put it in her pocket. Bobbie leaned out the door and called to her daddy, "Okay, you can come back now."

James grabbed Waldo and took him to the office. As they walked the hall, Waldo realized how much he loved being held by James; he loved being held by Bobbie. He loved his people and didn't want James looking like a fool in front of Bobbie's friends. The little white bear made a bold yet easy decision. James closed the door to the office behind him then placed Waldo on the desk.

"Hey, buddy, were you having fun?" James grinned.

Waldo leaned back and lifted his feet in the air. "*These* are not fun," he said, showing the shiny white shoes. James reached over and took the shoes off his feet. Waldo wiggled his toes, feeling free of the dancing shoes.

"Have you had a chance to meet the other bears yet?"

Waldo picked up one of the shoes to inspect it a little closer. "No — not yet. They're too busy putting silly clothes on us," he answered, as he looked the shoe all over. "Who can dance in these things anyway?"

James almost forgot why they were alone in his office. "So, what did Kristi put on the paper?"

Waldo slapped the shoe down and gave a crooked smile. "She was trying to be a smarty pants," he said in a sassy tone.

"What do you mean?"

Waldo looked around the desk and found some paper and a pen then started to draw. James watched the lines begin to take shape as he moved the pen every which way. Waldo's tongue slowly slipped out as he focused on his work. He finished and slid the paper to James.

"Well, let's see. That sort of looks like a bear wearing shoes and dressed in a . . . uh . . . um, a tutu?" he said unsure. James was impressed that Waldo could draw as well as he did. "This is what Kristi showed you?" he asked. Waldo nodded. "Okay, let's go have some fun." Waldo liked that idea, but then noticed James pick up the piece of paper he drew on.

"*Hey*, no, you can't take that. You can't show that," Waldo insisted.

James looked at the paper and didn't need to ask. He opened a drawer on his desk and pushed it way in the back.

"Sorry, buddy, I'll toss it out."

Waldo smiled. James picked him up and headed for the door. Suddenly, James stopped, giving Waldo a serious stare.

"Hang on a second," said James as concerned thoughts poured into his head. "We can't do this." Waldo was puzzled as James continued, "I can't do this. What are we doing? Proving you exist to a couple of kids? Why? Waldo — why didn't you say something? We shouldn't be doing any of this! I don't need to prove anything to them. This will surely get you into more trouble with the Council. I can't have that."

Waldo gazed expressionless at James. For the first time everything was clear to Waldo. James showed real concern about a teddy and not himself. There was only one place that Waldo belonged — home with Bobbie, Debra and James. Nothing else mattered to Waldo anymore, not what other bears thought, not even the Council. Besides, Fluffy had taught

Waldo about a rule in the Code that fit the moment: A good bear always follows his heart. Waldo was a good bear; he knew he was.

The look in Waldo's eyes relaxed. "Can I tell you something?"

James didn't say anything he simply nodded.

"I love being here," said Waldo. "This is a great family, and that's why it's okay. It's okay to tell a couple of kids that the teddy world is real. Do you think anyone is actually going to believe them? One thing will happen though; they'll believe. And that's the way it used to be. I'm in trouble, sure, but I'm not going to stop loving being a part of this family because I did something wrong. I don't want to hurt the teddy world, but some old guy telling a few children what someone drew on a piece of paper is hardly proof of a teddy world."

"But what about the other bears in the room?" James asked.

"Eh, they're probably just a bunch of blabber mouths anyway."

James heard incredible wisdom from a young teddy bear. He was right. James was so moved, his stomach tickled with butterflies. A smile erupted on James' face that quickly disappeared. "Wait. Old guy? What do you mean 'old guy'? I'm not *that* old."

Waldo was unaware of the smile on his own face when James realized how funny that was.

"We'll talk about this later," said James playfully. "Let's go have some fun."

Waldo was actually looking forward to be lovingly scolded by James later. Waldo hoped there would be a later.

The girls stopped what they were doing and watched James pull out a chair to sit down. He placed Waldo in the middle of the table facing Kristi. No one said anything as he slowly looked around the table at each girl.

"Waldo and I had a little chat, and, of course, he told me what you put on the paper," he said, staring straight at Kristi, who felt confident that James was going to have to tell the truth about Bobby Bear and Waldo, that it was all made up.

"It was a picture," he said, pausing to notice Kristi's face. She remained still. "It looks like a, like a . . ." He stumbled a few times to see the reaction as he blurted out, ". . . like a bear wearing dancing shoes and a tutu."

Everyone quickly turned to Kristi to see if he was right. The expression on her face confirmed it. Kristi reached into her pocket, pulled out the paper and slowly unfolded it. The girls leaned over the table to see.

Kristi stared at James with confusion, then to Waldo.

"B-but, but how?" she stammered.

The other girls knew how, because they already believed, it just took a little longer for it to sink in to Kristi that Waldo actually told him.

The teddies in the room were as shocked as Kristi, except Bobby Bear, who expected that to happen. This was something that none of the other bears had experienced before, a teddy so blatantly defying the Code. Zeek and Travis were Network bears, bound by the Teddy Code to report what they heard. Apparently, Waldo didn't care what rules he broke, or care about the Secret Teddy Society. Elvis, in Bobbie's bedroom, easily heard what was going on and found his loyalties in question as well.

When James saw the paper, he wasn't surprised that Waldo knew what was on it; he was amazed that the picture Waldo made was *exactly* like the one that Kristi drew.

Kristi wanted an answer to a question that James couldn't fully explain.

"Why don't they move in front of us?" she asked.

James couldn't tell Kristi the real reason. In fact, he didn't really know himself. Actually, Waldo didn't fully understand why teddies aren't allowed to move in front of humans either. It never occurred to Waldo to ask. It's in the Code, there's no reason to question. Waldo did tell James this much: if you want to know everything about the teddy world, then you probably need to talk to a Council bear like Theodore, the first teddy.

James had to say something, but his answer probably wasn't going to satisfy Kristi.

"I don't know why they won't move," James hated to admit. "I know it's complicated, but maybe it's because people just wouldn't understand how. It's not scientific. People don't tend to believe things they can't prove with science."

Kristi and the other girls listened as James tried his best to explain the unexplainable.

"I know this seems crazy, but all you need to do is love your teddy bears and they'll love you back. It's really that simple. It's the same thing for humans, too," he said.

James smiled and stood up, patted Waldo on the head, and looked at Bobbie as he left the girls to play. She could not have been more proud of Waldo and her daddy at that moment, the smile on her face told him so.

The girls all reached out to pet Waldo, which he really liked. Kristi was the first to pet him, then she turned to her bear, Travis, and pulled him close for a hug. The other girls did the same. (The teddy world just got a little stronger)

After that, the feel of the sleepover had changed, and the girls were now more aware of including their bears in just about everything.

Something happened at that moment. Suddenly, the other bears felt differently. It was hard to explain. No one could say exactly what it was, but there was something. Somehow, the feeling of love and belonging was kicked up a notch or three. The bears clearly felt it. The girls hugged a little tighter and began including them in their normal conversations. It was nice, very nice. Thoughts emerged from Squiggles. He wondered if Waldo was the reason for the sudden change. Maybe believing in the teddy world was enough. Besides, the girls never actually heard Waldo speak or anything, and he never moved. Everything came through James. And, in fact, none of the bears could prove that Waldo did anything in front of James, anyway. Perhaps it was some sort of magic trick for the girls. Either way, things felt better than ever for all the bears, and to think it was because of Bobby Bear and Waldo breaking the Code. This was a quandary for Zeek and Travis. Maybe they shouldn't say anything at all.

Everyone went to Bobbie's bedroom to settle down for the night. Gathered on the floor in their sleeping bags, the mood was right for a ghost story.

"You want to hear something scary?" asked Zella. The girl's faces filled with excitement and squeezed their bears tight. Zella was always making up stories to tell and songs to sing, so she thought up a story on the spot. Bobbie ran to the door and turned off the light, leaving a soft shadowy glow from a nightlight near her desk. Zella's voice was calm and breathy.

"One day a girl named Sarah found a teddy bear at the park. She looked around and didn't see anyone. The bear was sitting on a mound of dirt all by itself. She picked up the bear and took it home.

"That night she was listening to her mommy talking about a little girl that was missing from the area. No one knew where she was, or what happened to her — she was gone — along with her teddy bear," Zella said in a mysterious voice.

The mood was getting darker as Zella stared into everyone's eyes. The bears were listening with care since the story seemed to be about a lonely lost teddy. When Zella looked at Waldo she could feel something, as if he was really paying attention. At that moment, she seemed lost in her own story, and continued even more dramatically.

"Sarah thought about the bear she found at the park. *Is this the little girl's bear?* she wondered. *How can I be sure it's hers?*

"Later that night, after she had fallen asleep, she suddenly opened her eyes to find a strange girl standing next to her bed covered in dirt.

"'Who are you?' asked Sarah.

"The strange girl leaned closer and said, 'I'm the girl that was killed in the park.'

"Sarah was now face to face with a *ghost*. 'You mean you're dead?'

"The girl nodded her head, yes.

"'Why are you here?'

"'I've come to warn you about something you have,' said the girl covered in dirt.

"Sarah had forgotten about the bear until the girl pointed to the teddy bear at the foot of the bed.

"'Beware the bear. The Were-bear,' she said. 'Beware the bear.'"

Bobby Bear found himself not wanting to hear any more of the story. He had never heard of a Were-bear and didn't like the sound of it. He tried not to listen but he wanted to know if they were dangerous or not.

Zella continued her story:

"'What about the bear. Is that your bear?' asked Sarah.

"'Yes, he *was* my bear until the moon gets full — then, he becomes a *Were-Bear*.'

"'You mean *he* killed you?' Sarah was starting to get very scared.

"'The mound of dirt where you found him, that's where my body is,' said the ghost.

"Sarah screamed and her mommy runs into the room, turning on the light. 'What's wrong, what's wrong?' she cried."

The girls hugged their teddies even tighter and Zella's voice got louder as she continued:

"Sarah said the little girl that was missing was just in her room. She said it was a teddy bear that killed her and buried her in the park.

"Her mommy said she just had a nightmare, but Sarah knew better. Her mommy turned out the lights. She tried to go back to sleep, but she kept looking at the teddy at the foot of the bed. She could feel him staring back. Finally, she *jumped up, grabbed the bear* and *threw him in the closet* and closed the door. As Sarah climbed back into bed she looked out the window and saw it was — a full moon.

"*Boom!*

"She heard a thud at the closet door.

"*Boom-Boom!* The thud got louder. *BOOM-BOOM-BOOM!*"

The girls flinched with each 'boom' as Zella's story became more convincing as she spoke.

"All Sarah could do was pull the covers up over her head. 'Beware the Bear,' Sarah heard in her head over and over.

"The next morning Sarah's mom was making breakfast and listening to the news about finding the little girl buried in the park. She went to tell Sarah that she was right about the little girl . . . and when she opened her bedroom door, Sarah was *gone*. All they found was the teddy bear sitting on her bed where Sarah used to sleep.

"So the next time the moon is full, make sure your cuddly little teddy bear is not . . . *A WERE-BEAR*," she yelled, pulling Zeek up and pushed him into their faces.

Everyone jumped then started laughing.

Bobby Bear about wet himself and couldn't, for the life of him, understand what was so funny.

No one could tell if Zella just made up that story, or if it was real. The teddies didn't need any proof; it sounded very real and now they know about Were-bears.

The girls talked for a while longer before falling asleep. The bears sat and stared at each other as the sound of sleep filled the room.

Finally, Peekaboo spoke up. "Has anyone else heard about a Were-bear?" she asked hesitantly in the teddy tone. You could feel the mood lighten.

"No, and I don't like the sound of it either," replied Bobby Bear, most relieved that someone broke the tension.

"Can you imagine a teddy so bad that it kills people? I mean, that goes against everything in the Code, *everything*," said Peekaboo, feeling quite upset.

Waldo's nerves were starting to bother him and he could feel his insides start to jitter. "Yeah, they sound really, really — bad," Waldo said as his mind went blank and that was all that came out.

"I've heard of a Were-bear," said Travis.

None of the bears knew if they should really believe Zella about Were-bears, but since another teddy said they exist then it must be true.

"You have?" asked Bobby Bear, beginning to get concerned.

"Yep, and they're the most scary bears of all," replied Travis.

Everyone wanted to know more, except Zeek — he seemed disinterested. He would glance about the room as if trying to avoid eye contact.

"Where do they come from?" asked Smiley with a skeptical tone. Smiley, like Tory, was quite smart and a little shy.

Travis didn't actually know where they came from; he'd only heard of the legend. He did like the attention, something he'd learned from Kristi, and now he had to think of an answer quickly. "They come from another country far away," said Travis, which he thought was true. Still, he didn't want to push his luck. Travis hoped that was the last question.

The room was silent for only a second when the one word that Travis did not want to hear came floating by.

"Where?" asked Smiley, staring and waiting for a reply.

He was in a spot, and either had to answer, or confess that he doesn't really know where they come from.

"Werebearlonia," just slipped out of his mouth. Travis knew at that moment that he should have kept his mouth shut.

"You mean WereBologna," said Smiley and started to laugh. Everyone joined in as the mood completely changed to relief.

Bobby Bear and Peekaboo still wanted to know where Werebearlonia was and how could you tell if someone was a Were-bear. Not wanting to appear foolish they kept quiet, but looked to each other for comfort, as they were the only bears not laughing.

"*Okay*, so I don't really know where they come from, but I *have* heard about 'em. They're big and mean with large teeth and claws. Maybe I haven't seen one, but that doesn't mean they don't exist," confessed Travis. "It's the moonlight — something about the moonlight that makes them change — that's what I heard — a Rough Rider told me."

In an instant the bears realized that they were right back where they began, not knowing if Zella was making it up or if she was privy to a deadly teddy secret.

One thing good about the Were-bear talk was that no one brought up Bobby Bear and Waldo's transgression. It seemed that there were more dangerous things to talk about than two bears that broke the Teddy Code.

Bobby Bear walked over to Peekaboo and sat down as Travis started discussing other ways of how one could turn into a Were-bear. Waldo saw his best friend talking and laughing with Peekaboo, which made him a little jealous.

"Hey, Zeek, you belong to Zella. Do you know if she's telling the truth about Were-bears?" asked Squiggles.

"This is the first time I've heard her mention anything about 'em. I'm not sure how a human would even know of such a thing; but to be honest, I have heard of the legend of a Were-bear. It's kept secret like the Kage Kumas. Teddies don't spread rumors of horrible creatures that act in such savage ways. Besides, it is just a legend. No one's actually seen one, not that I know of, anyway."

"Yeah, but — I've heard about the Kage Kumas. I've never heard about these Were-bear creatures," said Squiggles.

"True. But Kage Kumas are teddies that protect us from evil, not the other way around. They're a popular legend, but Were-bears — they're pure evil, and do things that no teddy bear would ever dream of doing," replied Zeek. "Insiders don't know what Outsiders know. I only hear some of these things because Network bears talk to Rough Riders. They tell me things that are going on in the teddy world. There are some things you just don't talk about — and Were-bears is one of those things."

"Travis knew about 'em'"

"Because he's a Network bear."

"Oh, yeah," said Squiggles. "Let me ask you something — do you believe it?"

Zeek leaned back a little too far and fell over. This made Zella stir a bit and the bears froze in their spots. After a moment she began breathing loudly, which told the bears that she's asleep. Zeek took a calming breath and answered, "I don't know if I believe it. I know one thing; I don't wanna believe it."

Waldo got the nerve to go over to Smiley. He didn't know why he was so nervous but he was. "Hi, I'm Waldo," he said, trying to sound confident.

"I know who you are. I've heard about you and your friend, Bobby Bear," she replied.

Waldo couldn't tell if this was a good thing or not.

"You mean, like — um — what do you mean exactly?" he asked.

"You're a Trust Buster. I've heard all about it," explained Smiley. "Tory came home from school one day and told me.

She tells me everything since she doesn't really talk to anyone else too much," said Smiley in an accepting way. "You seem to be taking it very well."

"What? Taking what well?" asked Waldo curiously, still trying to shake the jitters.

"Breaking the Code. Aren't you worried about what's gonna happen?"

"Yeah, well, the Council has someone coming for Bobby Bear and me — and I'm pretty sure they're taking us away," Waldo said, looking anywhere but at her.

"Did you actually hear that?" she asked.

"Yeah . . . well . . . no. That's kind of the problem. I haven't heard anything about anything. I only know that someone's coming for us. That's it," he said, not wanting to think about it right then.

Smiley began to talk. She went on about how fascinating their situation was — and the feeling that happened when James told Kristi what was on the paper — how the girls cared more about their bears suddenly. That started her explaining the possibility of a bigger picture. Waldo wasn't really listening; he kept saying, "Oh, really, that's interesting," every time she paused, until, she said something that caught his attention: "What if you were meant to get caught?"

Waldo's mind froze. "What?" He didn't understand what she could have possibly meant by that.

"I mean, what if you and Bobby Bear were supposed to get caught so that the stories could be written about you?" she said as inspiration took over. She was imagining the whole story unfolding as she spoke. "Because *I* felt it — I really felt it — and everyone else did too. It was there. You might have done something good."

"Wait! Wait! You mean like I did a good thing? You *are* talking about breaking the Code, right?" Waldo asked. He would welcome any positive take on his negative position.

"Yeah," she answered innocently. "Listen for a second. I know you got caught, but what I don't know is why you keep moving. There must be a good reason, and from the looks of it, it's because of him. You must have something pretty special going on here to continually break the Code — I can only imagine. I also imagine that you're going to be in some serious trouble when the Council catches up to you."

Waldo became frustrated at hearing about his predicament from a stranger and interrupted. "Yeah, I think we all know I'm in deep trouble. Is there a point to all this?"

Smiley stopped and gave a reassuring look. "Yes. What I'm trying to say is that, whatever that was back there, earlier, with Kristi, was something that hasn't happened for a very long time. That was special. If your stories help a few others the way it did us, then yes, I'm thinking maybe it was a good thing. I can't speak for you, but I know Danielle hasn't hugged or talked to me like that in a long time. She believes. You know a lot of people are scared of some legends, but what if this legend gave something else?"

There was a feeling that hit Waldo — hope. Would others see it the same way? Is there any wiggle room in the Code for such a situation? Or is breaking the Code simply breaking the Code? Waldo gazed wishfully at Smiley and liked how she put everything. It was as if she got it. The relationship between a teddy and their family *was* special, and gaining the trust of your family was what this seemed to be about. Waldo and James had that. Suddenly, Waldo felt strong. Sure, he was going to be punished — and he knew it. He was ready for it. After all, Fluffy returned and he and Bobby Bear will too.

Zeek overheard her explanation and even though he quietly agreed — that's not what came out. Truth came out. "I'll tell you what I think. I think you're in big trouble. I think that when they send the thugs to get you — that you're going straight to the Camp. It ain't what it sounds like, because it sure as heck ain't camping. If you haven't heard of it before that's because Insiders don't find out until they get there. And anyone that *has* been there — won't talk about it. It's where Bad Bears go. And you, Mr. Waldo, have been bad."

The room fell quiet as the other bears were now looking at the rebellious white teddy. The mood wasn't going away until Waldo responded. Everyone waited.

Backed into a corner, Waldo felt the need to defend himself. "I don't know if it was a 'good thing'," he belted as he looked at Smiley, "and I don't know about any camp or what the Council's going to do — but what I do know is that I got to do things that none of you have ever done. I've had conversations with a human. I got a chance to live in a way that I never imagined — and I loved it. I know I'm in trouble, and yes — I'm scared." Waldo couldn't stop himself as he was truly nervous about his destiny. He started to ramble on as usual. "But I didn't do it as a Bad Bear, I did it because I didn't know why it was wrong. It actually felt right. Bobby Bear and I wanted to have fun and James wanted to write stories. It was great. But I guess everything comes with a price. I never stopped to think about what I was doing might really hurt the teddy world. I don't want that! I don't want to leave my family; *I do know that.*

Smiley was concerned and felt sorry for Waldo. "Please, don't get upset."

Waldo calmed down and took a few long breaths. "I'm sorry but I'm really worried about what's going to happen. I'm sorry I was loud," he said in a sincere voice.

Smiley relaxed. "I understand. I didn't mean to say anything wrong. I just meant that sometimes when you think the worst is going to happen — it doesn't happen at all. Actually, sometimes something good happens — that's all." She smiled.

Suddenly, everything seemed to disappear: no humans, no other teddies, no nothing, just her and that smile, that big bright smile.

Wow, he thought, as her face seemed to light up the room. *What is that?* A feeling stirred in the pit of his stomach that he'd never had before. Waldo stared at her for what seemed like hours.

"Are you all right?" a soft voice echoed in his head. Waldo's mind was in a fog when he heard the voice repeat, "Waldo, are you okay?" Smiley gave an anxious stare as he was clearly dazed.

"Yes, definitely," he answered robotically, not really knowing what he was agreeing to.

"Okay — if you're sure. I'm going to get some rest," said Smiley.

Waldo simply watched as she snuggled into Kimmie's arms. The other bears did the same and soon everyone was asleep.

Somewhere in the middle of the night a strong whisper provoked the beginning of a dream: "Waldo . . . WALDO!"

He tried to open his eyes but sleep wouldn't let go, he was just too tired. "Oh, who is it?"

"It's Zeek. Come on. Get up."

"Why? I'm tired."

"No time for that. Come on. I need your help." He was very insistent and began pulling on Waldo's arm. The tired little white bear opened his eyes and saw Zeek standing over him in an agitated state. He appeared to be different somehow. Waldo knew it was him — but maybe it wasn't.

"What — what is it?" Zeek pulled harder. Waldo gave a relenting sigh. "Okay, I'm coming. Jeeze Louise." The tired little bear sat up and noticed that everyone else was still asleep. Dark lumps were scattered on the bedroom floor wrapped like mummies in their sleeping bags. It seemed like more lumps than before.

Zeek leaned in so close that their noses touched. "Come on, buddy. I need some help. You're not going to believe this," he whispered and turned towards an open window.

Waldo got up to follow and asked, "What are you doing?" He tried to keep his voice down so he wouldn't wake anyone — especially Elvis.

"You'll see," replied Zeek strangely.

That's when Waldo noticed the most obvious thing; the Big People's Chair — it was empty; Elvis was gone. The window was found wide open with no one watching.

"Hey, Zeek! Where's Elvis?" asked Waldo, his head turning violently left and right in search of the family Network bear.

Zeek didn't answer. He moved into the open window. "Come on, buddy. We need to hurry," said Zeek and leapt to the ground.

Waldo didn't have time to think. He quickly followed and jumped out the window. He tried to talk to Zeek but it was all he could do to keep up. Zeek dashed from bush to bush through the neighborhood. Waldo ran as fast as he could and finally caught up to Zeek in a small clearing.

Waldo asked politely, "Where are you taking me?" He began looking around nervously expecting Elvis to catch them at any moment. As Waldo's eyes searched for the handsome bear, he instantly recognized the scene. Swing sets, park benches and trees; he has seen this place before.

"The park? You brought me to the park!"

Zeek didn't respond but kept his eyes on a big wooden box in the field sitting all by itself. "Come on," said Zeek, walking cautiously towards the crate.

As they got closer, Waldo noticed small holes all around the large container as if something was alive inside. "What's going on here?" Waldo asked firmly. "And Why wasn't Elvis in his chair?"

Zeek reached out and put both paws on the box and stared back at Waldo. "I got him," he said very mysteriously, then leaned his ear against the wall to listen.

"Who?" asked Waldo tensely and took a step back. Zeek turned his head quickly with an obvious glare as if Waldo should've known who.

"The one that's caused all the problems; the one that can make everything better," said Zeek. He turned back to the crate like an old friend. "Beware the bear," he said softly while caressing the box. This was all very strange but Waldo was too frightened to notice that nothing was as it seemed — except one oddity did catch Waldo's eye.

"Hey, Zeek, what happened to your arm? Is that what it looks like?" Waldo asked with his nerves tingling.

Trying to hide his arm Zeek replied, "It's nothing. It's just a little bite that's all."

Waldo heard movement inside the box and jumped back. "Something's in there! *What's in there?*" he screeched. Waldo quickly realized what had to be in the box. "Is that Elvis? Is Elvis in there? You've got ELVIS! *Why do you have Elvis in a crate?*"

"Waldo? Is that you?" said a familiar voice from inside. Waldo knows that voice, but that's not the one that he was expecting.

"Bobby Bear? Is that you?" Waldo ran up to peek in one of the holes. "Hey, you've got Bobby Bear in there!" he yelled, trying desperately to see inside, but it was too dark.

"That may sound like him . . . *but it's not . . . Beware the bear*," boomed Zeek, becoming more excited.

"Waldo, let me out of here!" cried Bobby Bear.

Pushing Zeek out of the way, Waldo frantically pulled the front panel of the box open. "Bobby Bear, are you okay?" asked Waldo, his voice unsure. He took a slow step into the dark. Abruptly, Waldo was pushed from behind and fell forward into the crate as the door closed tightly behind him.

"*Hey!* What are you doing?" he screamed. Waldo scampered to his feet to peek out a hole. "Zeek! ZEEK! What's going on? What are you doing?"

Waldo heard heavy breathing but couldn't tell if it was him or something else as he was now trapped inside the crate.

A soft friendly voice came from behind. "Waldo? Is that you?"

The glow from the street lights poked through the air holes leaving pockets of darkness all around. Waldo turned slowly and could only make out a shadow in the corner.

"Yeah, it's me . . . Is that you, B-Buddy?"

The shadow got closer and stepped into a small stream of light. "Yeah," replied the familiar voice of Bobby Bear.

Waldo could now see the face of his best friend. "Boy, am I glad to see you," Waldo said with relief pouring from his mouth. "What's going on? Why are we in here?"

"I don't know," answered Bobby Bear. "I think he's the one. I think he's from the Council. He's here to take us away."

They both leaned against the wall and peeked out the air holes, which were only big enough for an eye. They saw Zeek pacing back and forth mumbling, "Beware the bear. Anytime now, anytime now."

Waldo turned to his best friend. "So what happened?" he asked.

"I'm not sure," answered Bobby Bear. "He woke me up and told me that he needed my help. He said it was for everyone's safety and that I was the only one that could do it."

"Do what?"

"I don't know. He told me it was urgent — so I followed him."

"*What are you two talking about in there?*" Zeek yelled.

"Hey, Zeek! Are you the one?" asked Bobby Bear.

Zeek muttered and rolled his paws together like he was waiting for someone. "Beware the bear — anytime now."

The night seemed to turn brighter when the moonlight broke through the trees. Zeek appeared to be in a trance as he stared at the moon and a sinister smile slowly formed on his face. "Beware the bear is here, *is here*," he roared with a crazy laugh. He held up his paws to the moon.

Waldo again saw the wound on Zeek's arm. "Bobby Bear, do you see that?"

"What?"

"His arm, he didn't have that before tonight."

"Yeah, I did that."

"What do you mean; *you* did that?" asked Waldo cautiously.

"Yeah, after I followed him out here, he tried to push me into the crate. Well, I didn't want to go in — so I bit him," explained Bobby Bear.

Waldo's face dropped as he asked, "*YOU* bit him?"

"Yeah. Why?"

An eerie voice whispered from outside, "Are you watching?" Waldo turned to see an eye peering through a hole. It was Zeek, and he was sounding very strange indeed, as he continued, "You'll see — just watch. Just watch and you'll see. *Beware the bear!*" he bellowed.

Waldo was getting scared and angry at the same time and cried out, "*Watch what?*"

Zeek hollered back, "Turn around! Turn around *now*! Beware the bear. *Beware the bear!*"

The moonbeams streamed through the air holes and landed on Bobby Bear. Everywhere the beams touched him he began to change.

Waldo noticed the growing fur on his friend and stepped back so fast he fell down. "What's happening?" screamed Waldo, trying to get as far in the corner as he could.

"What? *What?*" Bobby Bear yelled, wondering why Waldo was cowering in the corner.

"SEE! I told you. *I told you*," said Zeek still peering in the crate. "Beware the bear. Is here — *is here!*" His maniacal laugh only added to the fright.

Waldo couldn't believe what he was seeing. "You're a — a Were-bear?" he yelled at his best friend.

Bobby Bear saw his own fur growing longer where the lunar light touched. He stuck his arm in a moonbeam and watched claws grow from his paw.

"CLAWS? . . . CLAWS?! . . . I'M GROWING CLAWS! TEDDIES DON'T HAVE CLAWS! *Waldo, help me*!"

That was all he needed to hear to remove his fear. Waldo noticed the moonlight. That was the key. Without hesitation, he sprang to his feet, lunged, tackling Bobby Bear into a corner where the light didn't shine. As fast as he started to change he went back to normal.

"What's wrong with me?" asked Bobby Bear in a distressed voice.

"You're a Were-bear," said Waldo, breathing heavy.

"But . . . how?" asked Bobby Bear, checking his fur all over and then stared at his paws.

"I don't know."

"Claws, Waldo? I had claws. Jeeze Louise, teddies don't have claws. What if I —"

"Don't say it!" Waldo snapped angrily. "You didn't and you won't. So just stop it!"

A moment of silence followed, as Waldo was trying to think of what to do next. Bobby Bear thought about what his best friend had just done.

"Hey, Waldo . . ." he said in a kind gentle voice. "Thanks."

"No biggie. Just stay down and out of the moonlight," Waldo replied not wanting him to get all mushy. He then noticed Zeek was no longer peeking through the hole. Waldo stood up to take a look just as someone ran past. "What was that?" he asked in a low voice.

A loud THUD from outside rocked the crate.

"WHAT WAS THAT?" Bobby Bear shrieked, sitting in the corner, shaking nervously. Waldo sat down next to him and they hugged each other. Another THUD, along with what sounded like a growl. The commotion got louder and louder. They could only imagine what was happening outside. Then, as soon as it started, it was over. An eerie howl in the distance echoed in the box. They could only feel each other's embrace while they sat in silence.

Bang! Bang! Bang! The wall shook violently. The box cracked open and a tall dark shadow entered. Bobby Bear could feel Waldo squeeze tighter. The shadow started towards them.

"I lully, Waldo," said Bobby Bear fearing the worst.

"I — I — lully you too," said Waldo reluctantly.

"Isn't that sweet. You two love birds need a little more time?" said the shadow as it stepped into a moonbeam. A smile as bright as the moon was aglow on Waldo's face when he saw Elvis standing in front of them looking like the hero Waldo always knew he was. Realizing that he was still holding Bobby Bear in a big bear hug, he quickly let go and stood up.

"But how'd you know where we were?" asked Waldo.

"You think you can sneak out without me knowing it? Elvis said almost laughing. Waldo was never happier to see anyone than Elvis right then.

"What was all the ruckus out there?" asked Bobby Bear still sitting in the corner.

"I was across the street and thought I saw Zeek standing next to the crate acting strangely. By the time I got here he was gone. I tried to peek inside the box when something, or someone, jumped on me," explained Elvis. "We tussled for a bit then it ran off into the woods. I'm not sure what it was but I think it growled at me."

"Did it bite you?" asked Waldo alarmingly.

"Did it what?"

"BITE you! *Did it bite you?*" he asked again urgently.

Elvis thought for a second and looked himself over, since Waldo was so adamant. "No — I don't think so. Why? What are you getting at?"

"The Were-bear — that was a Were-bear you tussled with," insisted Waldo.

Elvis rolled his eyes. "What are you two talking about? That's crazy talk and *where's* Zeek? I saw you guys follow him out the window."

"That *was* Zeek," cried Waldo. "He's the one that attacked you. I think he's turned into a Were-bear, too." Waldo's eyes darted around urgently to see if Zeek was about.

Bobby Bear sat quietly in the corner as Waldo tried explaining things to Elvis, who was having a hard time believing the story.

"Waldo, there's no such thing as a Were-bear," said Elvis.

Just then, Bobby Bear stood up and thrust his arm into the light of the moon. Waldo and Elvis watched as his fur started to change, and claws grew from his paw. Elvis could not believe his eyes. "You mean . . . you're a . . ." Elvis couldn't bring himself to say it.

Bobby Bear lowered his paw and it returned to normal.

"Yes. He's a Were-bear," said Waldo. "And before you ask, we don't know how. Zeek brought Bobby Bear out here because, somehow, he knew he was a Were-bear. I thought he was the Teddy Thug that's supposed to take us away, but since

Bobby Bear bit him, now he's a Were-bear. I don't really know what's going on. None of this makes any sense."

"Wait a minute, Zeek bit Bobby Bear?" asked a confused Elvis.

"NO! Bobby Bear bit Zeek. So now he's a Were-bear and loose in the park," said Waldo intently. His body flinched and twitched at the slightest of sounds.

A long howl came out of the dark.

"That sounds close," said Elvis, thinking there may be some truth to their story after all. "Let's get you boys home."

"What do we do about Bobby Bear? We can't leave him like this — and he can't go out in the moonlight," said Waldo.

"Here. Use this to cover him up," said Elvis and threw a blanket at him.

"What are you doing with a blanket?" he asked.

"I didn't know if I was going to need it or not — so I brought it."

This didn't really answer his question but Waldo never gave it another thought. He simply tossed it over his friend and they headed back home.

It was hard for Bobby Bear to walk since the blanket was too big. He kept stepping on it and tripping. Every time he stumbled, his feet would stick out from under the blanket and claws would shoot from his toes. Waldo's first instinct was to scold him about being more careful, but he was afraid of making Bobby Bear upset. You just don't know how a Were-bear is going to react to being yelled at. If Waldo was instinctively sure of one thing — it was, never scream at a Were-bear.

They climbed back in through the window and found everyone still asleep. The girls were curled up in their sleeping bags when Waldo noticed the obvious. Zella had her arm wrapped around Sparky, Bobbie's stuffed cat. Zeek was gone. Just as Waldo noticed so did Bobby Bear and Elvis. They all looked at each other and knew a Were-bear was out there somewhere. They found their spot and huddled together next to Bobbie. Elvis climbed up in the Big People's Chair and kept a watchful eye the rest of the night.

Bobby Bear was asleep as soon as he hit the floor. Waldo's mind was still racing. *That did not just happen. There's no way that just happened,* he repeated over and over as he drifted off to sleep.

THE ANTIDOTE

Waldo woke to a familiar voice and an unfamiliar song:

"Peaches have fuzz but they don't have fur,
Bears aren't bare but they wish they were.
Tables can't walk 'cause their legs won't move,
Can you tell a cow's thought? Can you tell a cow's mooed?
If the sun is hot then you should not touch,
If the moon is full then he ate too much.
If you lay there sleeping but your eyes won't shut,
Your eyes are trying to tell you that it's time to get up."

The sound of James singing while the girls giggled would normally make Waldo happy, but he was too busy assessing the situation. He wanted to make sure that no one had fallen prey to the Were-bear that was loose in the neighborhood.

No screaming, that was good, thought Waldo. *Better yet, no one was missing, well, no one except . . .* Waldo instantly thought about Zella, how upset she'll be when she notices her bear is missing. However, Zella wasn't upset, she was smiling and laughing. That's when Waldo noticed who was sitting next to her.

Zeek, he screamed to himself. *But — how — when?*

He wanted to look around for Bobby Bear but couldn't move while the girls were still there. He definitely wanted to talk to Elvis and find out how and when Zeek snuck back in the room.

Whoosh! Waldo was picked up and squeezed next to his best friend in Bobbie's arms.

"Let's go get some breakfast," she said, and joined the rest of the girls as they gathered their bears and headed off to the kitchen.

Bobbie began playfully bumping into Zella as they bounced down the hall. Zella was holding Zeek on the side that faced Waldo, which meant that with every bump they came face to face.

Bounce! Bump! Bounce! Down the hall the girls went giggling and laughing. Waldo, however, didn't feel like laughing or giggling. With each bump, he looked into Zeek's eyes. With every bounce, he could smell Were-bear on his breath. Wincing, each time their heads knocked together, Waldo swore he could hear Zeek's mouth chomp on every bump and bounce. It was just a matter of time before he was bitten and turned into a Were-Bear.

The girls gathered around the breakfast table as Danielle plopped Squiggles down and began moving his arms around. "I'm as hungry as a bear," she said in a gruff voice for Squiggles. The rest of the girls quickly did the same. Soon, all the bears were on the table, bouncing up and down, chanting: "*Hungry as a bear, Hungry as a bear, what we have for breakfast, we really don't care . . .*"

The bears were actually having fun as they were chanting along in their teddy tone; all except one — Waldo. He could not understand how everyone was having such fun when a Were-bear was sitting right across the table. He couldn't take his eyes off Zeek. With every bounce, he stared. With every chant, he glared. Suddenly, he remembered Bobby Bear. *He's a Were-bear, too. My best friend's a Were-bear,* he thought, and couldn't begin to imagine what must be going through *his* mind. He was going to help his friend somehow — some way. Even though Waldo's best friend was a Were-bear, he wasn't afraid of him. Bobby Bear had been Waldo's friend for a long time and he'd never been angry or aggressive before — at least not with Waldo. However, he did bite Zeek last night. That didn't sound like his mild mannered chum. Waldo glanced at his old friend nervously, wondering just how dangerous his seemingly innocent pal really was. Then there was the phrase that James always said: 'You don't really know anyone.'

After breakfast, the girls and their bears went home. James and Debra took Bobbie to get a new glove for T-ball.

The house was empty of humans. Waldo ran straight to Elvis. "How . . . I mean, when did Zeek get back in the house?" asked Waldo anxiously.

In a puzzled tone Elvis answered, "I don't know what you're trying to ask, Waldo."

A blank expression on Elvis' face sent shivers through the little white bear. "Last night! Zeek? You know . . ." Waldo didn't want to say the word out loud, "— the growly thing?" Waldo's eyes were trying to help describe as they flared with his eyebrows raised.

Elvis lightly chuckled. "I'm not getting your meaning."

Frustration swept his body when it became instantly clear. *Zeek did something to Elvis, something that made him forget everything. This is useless*, he thought.

Waldo needed an expert. He needed someone old and wise in the ways of the teddy world. Waldo needed to see George, the one bear that could explain what happened, and more importantly, how to cure Bobby Bear from being a Were-bear.

He bravely went to the big bedroom where Debra and James slept, and there on the bed, resting on a pillow, was the old one, George. He was once the Network Teddy until that job was handed down to Elvis. George was Debra's bear and has been ever since she was a little girl. Every morning Debra makes the bed and gently places him on her pillow like she's done for close to thirty years.

George was an imposing looking bear, standing almost as tall as Elvis, with dark brown fur and a black leathery nose that was cracked and weathered from age. His eyes turn an emerald green when he comes to life; they are quite distracting but very comforting. It more than suits his wisdom filled face.

If anyone knows about Were-bears it would be George. He knew everything — or at least he used to.

Waldo climbed up on the hope chest at the foot of the bed. "Um, George sir?" he said politely.

"Hey, kid. It's good to see you," replied George in his strong aged voice.

"Can I ask you a question?"

"Sure."

"Do you know anything about — Were-bears?" Waldo looked down as he asked.

"Were-bears? What do you want to know?" asked George. He felt a smile coming on but fought the urge because he could see that Waldo was truly worried.

"Well . . . I'm not sure, sir — I guess — how do you stop being one?" Waldo asked plainly. He needed to get to the heart of the problem.

"Who wants to stop being a Were-bear?"

"It's Bobby Bear," he said sadly.

George did happen to know the legend of the Were-bear, but it was quite different and much worse than what Waldo was troubled with. However, if Waldo believed that his friend was a Were-bear, then George needed to be serious to help. Though George stays in the big bedroom, he could still hear Zella telling her ghost story. He also feared Waldo's imagination had gotten the better of him. From what George heard about Were-bears, he was fairly sure that Bobby Bear did not fit the description, nor was Bobby Bear capable of doing such a dastardly deed that would create a Were-bear.

"He's got the curse does he? Oh, that's not good." George shook his head. "Boy, I wish I could help but . . ." He stopped to think for a second, putting his paw to his chin. He was trying to think of a remedy that was fun, yet believable to tell Waldo. George assumed that there wasn't anything he could say that would convince Waldo that his best friend wasn't a Were-bear. He could see it in his eyes. This had to play out. Waldo needed to find a cure, even a make believe one. "Well — I have heard of one thing that can cure him," said George, lowering his voice. "It might be dangerous. Are you sure you wanna do this?"

Waldo's eyes were wide, focused on George. He slowly nodded, understanding that he would do whatever it took to save his friend.

George continued, "Okay, there's a rare nut that has been known to change Were-bears back to normal."

"That's GREAT!" yelped Waldo, feeling a sense of hope. "I knew I came to the right place."

"Whoa, slow down. This is where it gets a little tricky," George said, trying to add a touch of realism, yet having a little fun of his own. "First you have to find the nut, *then* — give it to him so he doesn't know you're giving him the antidote. If *he* knows, then the *curse* knows, and it'll fight the antidote. He *can't* know about it."

"What's an antidote?"

"Oh, right . . . It's something that makes bad things better," George said simply.

"And this nut will make him better?"

"Absolutely."

"Where do I find the nut?" asked Waldo with excitement. He was listening to every syllable of every word that George spoke. He stared at his mouth to make sure he didn't miss a word. Waldo had to get this right. It was the most important thing he's ever had to do.

"In the kitchen you'll see a green glass jar on the counter, right next to the fruit bowl. Lift the lid and take a nut. You'll only need one," said George, still fighting the smile that was struggling to bust out.

"What if he finds out? Then what?"

George gave a grim look. "Then you must give it to him at the moment he starts turning into the Were-bear. At *that* *moment* — the curse is vulnerable."

"How do I do *that*?" asked a very worried Waldo, now aware that it might not be as easy as it sounded.

Just as George was about to tell him, Bobby Bear was in the doorway.

"There you are. What are you doing in here?" asked Bobby Bear with his eyes moving about the room. He had never been in James's bedroom before and looked at everything with care.

"Umm . . . I was just talking with George," said Waldo uneasily, hoping he didn't ask about what.

Luckily, he was more curious about the bedroom than what Waldo was doing.

"Welp, see ya', George," said Wald then jumped down off the bed and grabbed Bobby Bear by the arm. "You hungry? Come on."

"Bye, George," said Bobby Bear as he was dragged out of the room.

"You go back to the desk and I'll get some snacks," said Waldo and disappeared to the kitchen.

"But, I'm not hungry," he called out as Waldo left.

Bobby Bear climbed up on the desk and sat in his spot while the troubled little white bear went searching for the green glass jar.

"Where is it?" Waldo uttered softly.

He shimmied up the stool and onto the counter. Sitting next to the fruit bowl was the green jar just as George said. He lifted the lid and looked inside. "The antidote," he whispered.

He instantly noticed a problem. Some nuts were whole and some were split in half. "What do I do?" he asked aloud. Knowing how bad his friend had the curse — only a whole one would do. He carefully selected one peanut then jumped down and headed for the pantry. His eyes roamed the shelves until he spied a bag of marshmallows. *These are soft and squishy,* he thought. *I can put it in this.* Waldo had never tasted one before so he pulled one out of the bag and took a nibble. His eyes grew. *Whoa, these are super tasty*, he thought while he smacked on the gooey treat.

He took another one and put the bag back in its place. He pushed the peanut inside one marshmallow and headed back to cure his friend.

"I got something you're gonna like," said Waldo with a lilt in his voice. He scampered up on the desk and handed Bobby Bear the fluffy snack.

"What is it?" he asked and began squishing it curiously.

"I don't know, but I think it should be called a tastysquish," said Waldo as he gently pinched it.

Bobby Bear put it to his mouth and took a little nibble.

"NO! You don't eat it like that," said Waldo sharply. "You eat the whole thing."

Waldo took his and stuffed it in his mouth. "wike wis," he mumbled with his mouth full.

Bobby Bear laughed at how silly he sounded then pushed the whole tastysquish into his mouth and began to chew. Waldo watched closely until he saw him swallow. He felt like he had his old friend back.

"How was it?" he asked.

"It was super tasty," answered Bobby Bear. "But I think it has seeds." He held out his paw and revealed the peanut. Waldo became panicky when he realized he didn't swallow the antidote.

"Can I see that?" he asked and reached for the nut in Bobby Bear's paw. "You're supposed to eat this," explained Waldo and handed it back, hoping Bobby Bear would simply pop it in his mouth and swallow.

"It's kinda hard." Bobby Bear studied it for a second. "I don't wanna eat it," he said and pushed it back to Waldo.

Now what do I do?

Waldo was feeling desperate — so, he tried the first idea that popped into his head. "Hey, I think I saw something in your mouth. Open up and let me look."

Bobby Bear thought he was acting a little strange but opened his mouth anyway. Waldo leaned over to look. "Yep, sure enough — you didn't swallow all the tastysquish," he said, then lifted his paw and threw the peanut into Bobby Bear's mouth, who quickly began choking and coughed it up onto the floor.

"What are you doing?" cried Bobby Bear.

Waldo picked up the antidote, lunged at his best friend and tried to force it down his throat. They wrestled around on the desk when the nut slipped out of Waldo's paw, falling behind the desk. He leapt after it — but it was gone.

"*Waldo*! What's gotten into you?" screamed Bobby Bear, clutching his throat.

Waldo had no choice but to tell him that he was trying to help. "I have the antidote."

"The what?"

"The antidote, the Were-bear antidote, *you know*," insisted Waldo. "You can be normal again."

"What are you talking about? What about Were-bears?" asked a perplexed Bobby Bear.

Waldo was peering down behind the desk trying to see where the nut fell.

"George told me about the antidote and how it will make you normal again, but now it's fallen behind the desk so I've got to get another one, Jeeze Louise — I'll be right back." Frustrated and urgent, Waldo hopped down off the desk and headed for the kitchen, leaving his best friend even more confused.

Bobby Bear needed some answers and there was only one place to go. Jumping to the ground, he scampered out the door and down the hall until he got to the kitchen, tiptoeing past so Waldo wouldn't see. Bobby Bear went straight to the big bedroom.

"George? I hate to bother you, but can you tell me what's gotten into Waldo?"

George smiled and told him what Waldo had asked about.

Bobby Bear had a puzzled expression. "Why does he think I'm a Were-bear?"

"I don't know," answered George. "It probably came from the ghost story last night, but somehow he believes it. I think the best thing you can do is play along."

"What do I do?"

"Did you eat the nut?" asked George.

"The nut? I don't know. He's trying to make me eat something and he won't stop," he answered.

George chuckled at the thought. "Okay, here's what you do. Start to change into the Were-bear and then eat the nut. Once you do that, he'll stop," said George.

"But I'm not a . . . How do I . . ." Bobby Bear was more baffled than ever.

"Just roll around on the ground and scream like you're in pain. Just make it up. You'll do fine," George said with a smile.

"Oh, you mean pretend." Bobby Bear quickly understood.

George tapped his nose.

He thanked the wise old bear and took off toward the office. As he passed the kitchen he glanced in and noticed Waldo wasn't there. Just as he got to the office door Waldo walked out, coming face to face. "There you are. You're out of breath. Do you feel all right?" asked Waldo suspiciously.

Bobby Bear felt this was the perfect time. "Actually, I feel kinda funny," he answered.

"What do you mean funny?" asked Waldo, studying him very closely.

"I feel . . . I feel . . . *Ahh!*" screamed Bobby Bear. He grabbed his stomach then doubled over.

"This is it — isn't it?" Waldo asked anxiously.

"What's happening to me?" yelled Bobby Bear, glancing up to see the look on Waldo's face. "Ahhh! Oooh! — Something's happening! SOMETHING'S HAPPENING TO ME!" he shouted. Bobby Bear loves a good pretend game and he was starting to like this one. He dropped to his knees, hunched over, and let out a growl.

Waldo hadn't heard the growling before and became very cautious.

He didn't do that last time. He's getting worse, thought Waldo. There was no time to waste. He knelt down in front of Bobby Bear and stuck the peanut in his mouth.

There, he thought, and sat back on his heels to wait for him to return to normal.

Bobby Bear could feel the nut on his tongue and was afraid that if he ate it — the game would be over, so he spit it out.

Waldo saw the nut fly from his mouth. "NO! Come on! You have to eat it!" he yelled.

It was hard for Bobby Bear to keep from laughing and the only way he could disguise it was to growl even louder.

Waldo was beginning to get scared as he scrambled to find the antidote. He picked it up from the floor and wiped it off.

"Come on, boy — you can do it," said Waldo, who was now wary about getting too close to the bitey end.

Bobby Bear was having so much fun but didn't know how much more he could take before he might start to laugh. He tilted his head back and let out a big howl. Waldo quickly threw the antidote into his mouth. The nut lodged in his throat forcing Bobby Bear to cough.

"SWALLOW IT!" yelled Waldo.

Bobby Bear was actually choking on the peanut and fell over, landing hard on his back. The nut suddenly popped out and landed right in front of Waldo.

"NO!!!" screamed Waldo. He swiftly picked it up and jumped on top of Bobby Bear, stuffing the nut back into his mouth. "NOW EAT IT!" he shouted.

Bobby Bear was no longer having fun, so he ate the nut in hope that Waldo would stop.

Lying on his back, Bobby Bear lay prone with Waldo sitting on his belly, watching very closely. They both waited to see what happened next.

All this commotion had captured the attention of Elvis, Big Red Fluffy bear and George. They watched from the doorway and kept out of sight.

Bobby Bear stared up at Waldo, who was still sitting on his stomach, and Waldo stared back.

A moment of silence passed as they looked at each other.

Bobby Bear softly asked, "Um, Waldo?"

"Yeah."

"Can I ask you something?"

"Sure, buddy. What?"

"Can you . . . um . . . Can you get off me now?" asked Bobby Bear.

"Oh, sure . . . yeah," said Waldo, still reluctant to move. He sat for a moment more, just staring at him to make sure it was really his best friend staring back.

Slowly, Waldo slid off Bobby Bear's belly and helped him to his feet.

"I thought I almost lost you there for a second," said Waldo, still looking his best friend square in the eyes trying to see any sign of the Were-bear. "How do you feel?"

Bobby Bear glanced over Waldo's shoulder and noticed George and the others in the doorway. "I feel . . . great," he said with a subtle wink to George.

They both hugged and Waldo was glad to have his friend back.

Elvis wasn't used to seeing George out during the day and couldn't help but admire him as they strolled down the hall.

Before George disappeared to his room, he stopped to speak to Elvis.

"Hey, thanks for keeping me informed. You're a good bear — and those are two good kids back there," said George in his confident voice. "I know what they're doing is wrong, but they're just kids and they *are* only doing it around James. I'm not making excuses — just sayin'. You're doing a great job. You do as you see fit . . . Goodnight, Elvis."

Elvis didn't say a word as George turned and climbed up on the big bed, returning to his pillow. That was the best thing he could have heard from such a great bear like George.

Elvis could still hear Bobby Bear and Waldo talking and laughing. He noticed Big Red Fluffy bear headed back into Bobbie's room.

"Hey, Red," Elvis called out. Fluffy stopped and lifted his weary head. "Come up with anything yet?"

Fluffy heard the laughter in the distance. "No — nothin' yet," he replied shamefully, then disappeared into the closet.

Elvis worried for Fluffy. The Council was concerned that Big Red Fluffy bear was taking far too long and might not be the bear for the job. If they send someone to take over, then Fluffy will have to leave and not come back. Elvis would like to find a way to help without Fluffy knowing. Elvis could feel the sadness as the laughter continued down the hall.

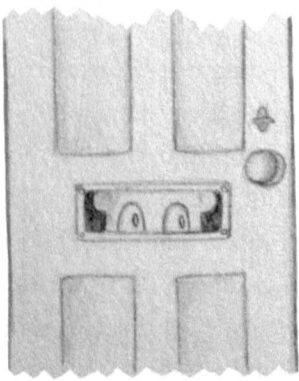

MISTER JERKWEED

James returned from the store and pulled the family SUV in front of the house. He parked along the curb to make room in the driveway to play ball.

"Hey, Pumpkin, let's go try out your new glove," said James.

"Sure," she answered excitedly.

Debra's car needed to be moved into the garage to avoid a hit by a stray baseball. He reached up to the sun visor and pressed the garage door opener. James loved watching the door open because it revealed his personal vehicle, a classic 1968 Camaro sport car. It was beautiful — at least James thought so. He rarely drove it because he never seemed to have the time and the SUV simply had more space for the family.

After moving Debra's car next to his in the garage, he grabbed a piece of red chalk and drew a large home plate on the driveway. The playing field was ready.

Inside, the phone rang, which startled Waldo because he sits next to the one on the desk. Debra picked up the phone in the kitchen. "Hello?"

A polite male voice responded. "Debra? Hey, this is Rick from the bookstore. Is James available?"

"He's actually busy at the moment," answered Debra, holding the phone with her shoulder to her ear as she dried her hands from getting dinner ready. "Can I take a message?"

"Sure. Tell him his book sold out. I don't know if he has any more copies, but he needs to get more. They sold pretty fast, I must say. I bought one myself and read it. It's really good. He's just making this up on his own?"

"Yeah. Why?"

"I knew he wrote songs and such, but I didn't figure him for the literary type. He's put some really good detail in this secret teddy world of his. He must have been planning this for a while. Anyway, if he has any questions, have him give me a call."

Debra was shocked at what she heard. "Yes. Absolutely, I'll tell him. He'll be delighted. Thanks, Rick." Debra hung up the phone with a pleasant smile. She couldn't wait to tell James the good news, but dinner wasn't going to cook itself so she went back to slicing onions. With every slice, Debra could feel her eyes burn. She reached to wash her hands when the phone rang once again.

"Why does it only ring when my hands are wet?" she joked out loud and answered the phone.

"Hello?"

"Hello. This is Mrs. Larkin, your daughter's teacher."

"Yes. How are you?"

"Fine, thank you. I was hoping to speak with your husband regarding his stories."

"He's outside playing ball with Bobbie at the moment. Could I take a message?"

"I hope so. I was asked to see if he would be available to come read his stories again tomorrow around 10:00 am, if possible. I know it's short notice, but I would really appreciate it."

"I'm sure he'd love to," said Debra pleasantly. "I'll make sure he gets the message."

"Thank you so much. So — I can count on him?"

"Most definitely. I don't see any problem."

"That's great. Thanks again. Have a good evening," said Mrs. Larkin.

Debra hung up the phone and was greatly encouraged that people were enjoying the stories. *Maybe he's got something,* she thought.

Since he left the music world, James had no real income aside from a few advertising jingles he wrote from time to time. He hated doing it, but it did pay well. His desire to work at home was all he wanted since he spent so much time on the road while Bobbie was growing up. He didn't want to lose any more time with his family. Debra understood, and didn't mind at first, but the money was getting tight and her headaches were growing worse. The harmony in the house would have its discord.

Outside, James was busy practicing baseball with Bobbie.

"Hey, you want to try and hit a pitch?" he asked with a curious tone.

"*Daddy*, we don't do it like that. It's T-ball, not pitch ball," Bobbie said, almost reprimanding him for his suggestion.

"This is how the big leaguers do it. But if you want to play like a little girl then, okay," he said in his best teasing tone. He was hoping to goad her into trying to hit one. The expression on her face told him it worked. She walked over, picked up the bat, and stood next to home plate.

"Oh, so you're a big leaguer now, huh?" he said and stepped into position.

James had always felt the need to explain things in great detail whenever he taught anything. This made lessons tedious and much longer than they needed to be.

"You see this?" He held up the ball. Bobbie eyes instantly zeroed in on it. "This is the only thing that's important, *the only thing*. Never take your eye off the ball — never," he said as seriously as he could. "When you're catching it — you keep your eye on the ball. When you're hitting it — you keep your eye on the ball. Wherever the ball goes," he waved it around, "your eyes go."

Everywhere he moved the baseball her eyes followed. James had never seen such focus from her before. She was ready. He did his wind up and let it go. *POW!* The bat smacked as she made contact. The ball flew over his head and bounced off into the bushes. James looked back at Bobbie and put his finger to his eye to wipe away an invisible tear. "That's my lil' slugger," he said while sniffling in a pretend cry. "You bring a tear to your daddy's eye." His sense of pride was bubbling.

Bobbie giggled and wanted to try another one. James retrieved the ball and got ready to pitch again.

Rufus, the neighbor's dog, barked playfully next door. The large shaggy brown retriever was quite gentle. His owner, Kurt Steelbash, was strict in discipline. It bothered Kurt that Rufus was so friendly. He wanted a man's dog, not a playful licky dog. Even though there wasn't a fence, Rufus knew he wasn't allowed past the hedges that separated the two properties. He acted as though the shrubs were electrified. Rufus would often sniff along the shrubbery as if he were looking for a weakness in their defenses.

Kurt didn't like James or anyone that allowed himself to act silly in public. He felt this was a sign of weakness, which Kurt suffered from his whole life. Being only five foot six inches tall, Kurt was picked on as a child. He was always shorter for his age but his belly was larger than most. His real name was also part of the problem — Curtis Plomtkin. He would have to live with "Turdy Plump-kid" through his adolescent years. Fights were common for Kurt, although he would normally hit the ground and tuck into a tight ball. He didn't like getting hurt. His answer to the problem took him to the weight room where he spent hours each day working on his body to achieve an intimidating look. Everything about him changed. First, was his name, it was a lightning rod for ridicule. He chose a name that sounded strong. Steel, was his first thought, but that alone was a bit too obvious. So, Steelbash it was. His first name was simply a variation of his old one, Kurt. Clean, simple and rugged. Perfect. The way he walked and talked also changed. He figured Hollywood was the perfect example of how to act. He adopted a Jersey accent and developed a swagger that was last seen on an eighties police drama. Kurt didn't know one bully that got picked on. That's when he switched sides and became the aggressor. It worked perfectly. No one bothered him again. The years of pent-up anger would no longer be kept inside. Kurt had become everything he hated when he was a child. Kurt was a bully. With confidence swelling in his muscular body, he would find ways to antagonize those that showed weakness. James was a perfect target and conveniently lived next door. It started out with little things like tossing beer cans over the hedge and taking James' newspapers before he woke. There was no acknowledgement from James, which only annoyed Kurt more. The constant laughing from the other side of the hedge was infuriating. Things would only get worse.

Bobbie waited for the ball, as James walked back to the pitching spot and began his announcer voice.

"Stepping up to the plate is Bomber Bobbie a rookie from Louisville. She's been hitting everything this year, but struggled a bit with the fastball. Let's see what the pitcher, Rocket McGee, is going to throw. Rocket winds up, the crowd is chanting — 'Bobbie, Bobbie, Bobbie' — here's the pitch," said James.

There was a focus and intensity in her eyes as she watched the ball meet the bat.

BAM! The bat made contact, and the ball soared over his head once again, sailing farther than before.

At that moment, next door, a friend of Kurt's arrived in a large black pickup truck that he parked in front of Kurt's house. Ray was a large man, standing over six feet tall with a flat top haircut and shoulders that looked molded out of hardened steel. His jawbone was so square that it didn't look natural. It was a distracting feature. Ray never talked much because Kurt did all the talking. This would be Kurt's best friend. Ray stood in the driveway and yelled, "You comin'?" The garage door opened and a brand new pickup emerged, which also was black. James couldn't help but glance over the hedge as the big truck stopped long enough for Ray to jump in. Kurt stepped on the gas and the truck screeched in reverse bouncing recklessly into the street. He turned the wheel hard and slammed on the brakes, too late. Kurt had just backed into James' older model SUV that was parked in the street. He jumped out of his truck and walked angrily to the scene. James watched it happen and heard the crunch as it hit.

As Kurt walked, he called out to James, "You'd better hope nothing happened to my truck." Kurt's rear bumper had dented the back hatch of the SUV. The small muscular man quickly checked his own truck. There wasn't a mark on it.

"You're a lucky man. There isn't any damage. What the hell are you doing parking in the street like that? Someone's gonna get hurt because of you," berated Kurt. His face was red as he yelled, but it was masking his embarrassment. Kurt couldn't apologize because Ray was in the truck. Admitting he did something wrong would appear weak in front of his friend; that wasn't going to happen.

James calmly looked at the dent in his car and asked, "Who's going to fix this?"

Kurt had no choice but to become aggressive.

"What?!" hollered Kurt. "You think I'm going to fix that? For all I know that was already there. Look at this thing. What is it — a hundred years old? You shouldn't park in the street, you moron."

James never thought much about his angry neighbor. He was aware that Kurt didn't like him but he didn't know why. He stepped closer to Kurt, his heart was racing, but he kept a cool composure. James was mad. However, he realized it was best to stay calm. He noticed Bobbie watching with concern. He took a breath and lowered his voice, "Look, we've got a problem here," said James plainly. That comment seemed to inflate the right vein on Kurt's forehead as outrage erupted.

"*A Problem?* I don't see a problem, *jerkweed.*" Kurt had a marvelous and colorful vocabulary. Inventive and creative words flew from his mouth often when things didn't go as planned. His voice did carry, which captured the attention of his large friend Ray, who appeared suddenly. Even Bobby Bear and Waldo could hear the venomous words through the window in the office.

Ray gave a threatening stare. "Is there a problem here?"

James glanced up at Ray. "I don't have a problem with you — just Kurt."

"Well, if you gotta problem with Kurt — then you gotta problem with me."

That was something James didn't expect but never missed a beat as his response slipped out naturally, "Then you've got a problem — Ray."

Ray wasn't much of a thinker; he wasn't used to it, not with Kurt around. The problem now belonged to Ray, and he didn't know what to do with it. One thing was for sure; posturing had taken center stage. Everyone was acting tough and no one could back down, not now. Pride had stepped in, which became the real problem. James was familiar with human nature and how a moment like this was volatile. Kurt and Ray were acting this way for each other. The question was: would they act this way alone?

Bobbie began to panic when she heard the angry words from Kurt. Things were out of control. The situation had gone too far and James would try a different approach, later. Right now, his concern was Bobbie.

"I'll tell you what — we'll talk about this some other time, 'cuz I'm in the middle of an important ball game."

James turned and walked up the driveway to Bobbie, who was still standing at home plate holding her bat. Tears filled her eyes. James knelt down. "Pumpkin, it's okay. It was just a little dent — that's all — just an accident." James forced a smile.

Bobbie watched the two men climb into the truck and speed away. Bitterness seethed in her eyes.

"*He wasn't very nice*," she growled. "You know what, Daddy? — He's the *jerkweed*."

James had never heard his daughter use such an expression before. It took him by surprise and he almost laughed. It was wrong, but it was adorable. James mustered a scowl and barked, "Pumpkin!"

He tried to give a threatening look, unfortunately, that stinking smile slipped out instead. He turned quickly but it was too late, she saw it. That one slip-up changed the mood. Bobbie got a funny little smirk that she tried to disguise as anger. James and Bobbie had a common dislike for Kurt. They went back to playing ball and James used the moment as fuel. Bobbie was ready to hit anything at that point. Seeing her daddy laugh and smile made the stench of anger evaporate to a light fragrance of agitation, which disappeared at the next pitch.

Dinner was almost ready. Debra went out front to tell them to wash up. As she stepped out the door, she felt the intensity between the two. They appeared to be having fun — however, there was a serious tone to their demeanor.

"What's going on out here?" she asked in a playful tone.

James assumed she was talking about the incident with Kurt.

"It was just a little accident with our neighbor. He backed into the car. It's nothing. I'll take care of it," James said. He didn't really want to get into the details at the moment.

"Seriously?" she said, not believing James would be that calm about such a thing. She walked tentatively to the car and saw the dent. "He just did this? Just now?" Debra shook her head and muttered a few words that were inappropriate for Bobbie. "He's going to fix it, right?" She wasn't really asking. James knew that.

"Yes. I'll take care of it. There's no need to get upset about it," said James, trying to smooth things over. A distraction was needed. As James searched for a diversion, a small, angry voice rang out. "He's just a *jerkweed*, right, Daddy?"

Debra's anger was now officially diverted. Bobbie had captured her full attention at such harsh words. That wasn't quite what James had in mind, but it did the trick. James quickly ran into damage control. It was his fault, after all. If he hadn't laughed the first time she said it then this wouldn't have happened.

Debra snapped, "Bobbie! We don't say that!"

The puzzled little girl looked to her daddy with confusion. He had to say something, and the only thing he could think of wasn't what Debra wanted to hear. "Mommy's right, Pumpkin — that's *Mister* Jerkweed. You need to be polite when you talk about adults." Even though James kept a straight face, that was all Bobbie needed to hear from her daddy. The glare, however, that James received from Debra, slowly melted as she saw what he had seen earlier from a cute little seven-year-old. Smiles began to emerge on all their faces.

"Hey! You gotta see what I've been teaching Bobbie," James said. He turned to throw the ball.

That sparked Debra's memory. "Speaking of teaching," she said, "Bobbie's teacher called and wants you to read again tomorrow."

James was focused on throwing a good pitch and barely acknowledged.

"Okay, that sounds fine."

Bobby Bear and Waldo had been listening to the arguing from inside. They couldn't see what happened but they knew an unfriendly tone when they heard it. Waldo didn't know what a jerkweed was. It sounded like a plant of some sort. He was sure it was an insult by the way Kurt spoke.

The laughter was back and Waldo realized that no one was in the house. He could slip over to the window to see what the commotion was. As soon as he moved an inch, Bobby Bear reached out and grabbed his arm. "What are you doing?" he said sharply.

"I just wanna take a peek," replied Waldo, almost begging. "Do you hear that? That's fun — that's what that is, and I wanna see, don't you?"

"Yes — I do — but not now. We just can't. Not now," pleaded Bobby Bear, still with a firm grip on his arm.

"Come on. We'll just take a peek and then get right back. Simple," said Waldo.

"You always say things are simple when they're not."

"Just a peek. You know you want to see, too."

The two friends stared at each other, each one tense. Eventually, Bobby Bear relented. He always did. Waldo felt the grip relax and he slipped over to the window with Bobby Bear peering over his shoulder.

"What's he doing?" asked Bobby Bear as they watched James wind up to throw another pitch.

"I don't know."

The ball flew out of James' hand towards Bobbie. She swung the bat with all her might and hit it over his head yet again.

They heard Debra yell something.

"Did you see that?" cried Waldo. *How could James do such a thing?* "He tried to hit her with that ball."

"I most certainly did," answered Bobby Bear alarmingly. "If she didn't have that stick she would've been . . ."

As Bobby Bear was talking, he and Waldo noticed James look towards the window.

"Uh-oh!" they said at the same time. Like a flash, they were back in their spots.

Not so long after that, they all came in for dinner.

"That was very good, Bobbie," said Debra. "I can't believe that was your first time hitting."

They headed to the kitchen, all except James.

"I'll be right there," he said, stopping at the office door. "I just want to make a quick note."

He walked in, sat down and looked at the bears sitting lifelessly in their place. "Okay, I know you guys won't talk now, which is fine, so listen. Are you boys trying to get caught again?" James asked sternly. The bears didn't know if he was expecting an answer. They remained still. "I know you wanted to see what all the commotion was about, but if you get caught again — won't that just make things worse? Maybe you don't think I care about what happens to you, but I do. I know I'm writing stories about the teddy world but these are just stories. No one actually believes it. What you guys are doing is impossible, humans know that — but if you're caught — then what?" he said in a serious yet sympathetic tone. James felt a presence behind him and slowly turned around.

"Am I interrupting?" asked Debra. She was disturbed at what she witnessed.

"Uh . . . no . . . no. Not at all. I was just . . . um . . . practicing for tomorrow. You know — reading."

Debra stepped closer and crouched down to look him in the eyes. In a kind yet worried voice she said, "I know things have been stressful — and I know you're working hard on the book, maybe a little too hard. Why don't you take some time off. Get out of the house. Hey, you know that camping trip you've wanted to take?"

Frustrated, he sighed, "Debra — I'm fine." He glanced at the bears and exhaled. "I know how it looks, believe me, I know. But . . ." James was trying hard to find the right words to tell her that it's all real. However, unless he could show her — there *were* no right words. "Yeah, maybe you're right. That does sound nice. A little time away might be good," he said, hoping that this was what she wanted to hear.

"Well . . . good. And dinner's ready." She leaned over and gave him a kiss.

"I'll be right there."

Her footsteps faded down the hall and he turned back to the bears who remained lifeless on the desk. He closed his eyes, leaned back in his chair and fought the urge to wish that none of this had ever happened. He was suddenly afraid to open his eyes. When he did — the bears were still there, sitting quietly in their spots. He was actually happy. He sat up, gently rubbed their heads, and went off to eat.

The house at 2300 Glenmore Drive was now under surveillance by a Kage Kuma. Tiger's mission was to make sure the traitorous Bobby Bear and Waldo never made it back to the Council. The other part of his assignment was to deal with the villainous human, James. The details of the covert job were vague but Ballinger made it clear that no measure was too severe to secure the teddy world. Tiger could use any method he felt necessary to silence James and deal with the young disloyal teddies.

Tiger would remain patient and reconnoiter before making his move. As the Kage was lying in wait from the boundary bushes, he witnessed an unknown teddy approach the little girl's bedroom window. It was too dark and Tiger was too far away to get a look at the mysterious teddy.

From the Big People's Chair, Elvis heard a familiar call outside. It was Dakota with a message from the Council. He motioned for a meeting at the front door.

Elvis climbed down from his chair to join Dakota at the mail slot. Big Red Fluffy bear noticed Elvis pass by the closet and slipped out quietly to follow.

"Hi, Elvis," said Dakota, peeking through the slot.

"Hey, Koty. What'cha got?"

"Word is that Big Red needs to bring the kids back now, *and* stop James from sending out the book — or they're going to send another to finish the job."

Fluffy bear was tucked just inside the office doorway within earshot of the conversation.

Elvis paused for a second, as this was not news he wanted to hear. "Did they say who they might send?"

"They mentioned Zeek. He's close, he knows the house, and he's on the list."

"Zeek? Hmmm — No need for that. I'll take care of it. Fluffy will get the job done. Thanks for the update."

Elvis turned to head back to his chair. He stopped in the office doorway to look in at Bobby Bear and Waldo asleep on the desk. He thought about the trouble the two bears were in and how something so innocent has affected the teddy world, but more importantly his family. He liked James and Debra and Bobbie. He liked Waldo and Bobby Bear, too.

A raspy whisper broke the quiet. "Hey, Elvis," said Fluffy bear and walked up beside him.

Elvis was aware that Fluffy had followed him down the hall.

"So — you heard?" asked Elvis.

"Yeah — I heard," replied Fluffy. His eyes were focused on the two sleeping bears. "What am I gonna do?"

Elvis put his arm around him. "It'll be fine. Things just have a way of working out," he said while patting him on the shoulder.

The words didn't mean much to Fluffy bear, but the way he said it made him feel it was true.

Elvis walked towards the door. "You coming?" he asked.

"I'll be right there," replied Fluffy softly.

Elvis left the room while the weary bear stood and watched his friends sleep. His mind was distressed.

How is this going to be fine?

The burden was heavy as he turned to leave when a soft voice came from behind, "Fluffy? Is that you?"

Turning back, he could see Waldo crawling quietly to the edge of the desk.

"You should be asleep," said Fluffy kindly.

"What are you doing here?" Waldo whispered, trying not to wake Bobby Bear.

Fluffy wasn't ready to tell him yet, but now was as good a time as any. "Actually . . . I've got something to tell you." Fluffy decided to say it as plainly as he could. "I'm the one."

He was actually glad to say it. He'd been carrying this guilt around, and now he was finally able to unload the weight of the secret.

"What do you mean?" asked Waldo, still a bit groggy.

"I'm the one. The Council — they sent me to bring you back." Fluffy dropped his head waiting for the angry words.

Waldo was shocked and didn't know what to say, yet felt relief that it was Fluffy and not a stranger.

"Why didn't you tell us?"

"I didn't know how," he answered. "I was waiting for the right time — but there never seemed to be a right time."

"So . . . that means you're a . . . thug?" asked Waldo.

Fluffy could only nod in disgrace.

"I just . . . I've never seen one before," said Waldo. "And you're not what I was expecting." An awkward quiet smoldered in the room as Waldo thought for a moment. "So does this mean this is it? Are we leaving?" Waldo asked with sorrow swelling in his big brown eyes.

"Yeah," he answered sadly.

"When do we leave?"

"Tomorrow — maybe."

"Maybe?"

"There's just something I need to do first, and *please* don't ask," Fluffy said in the kindest way he could.

Waldo could see this was hard on him as well, so he nodded his head and morosely crawled back to his spot.

"I'll let you know when it's time," he added. Fluffy said goodnight and went back to the closet. Neither bear would sleep that night.

In the morning, Debra took Bobbie to school while James made a few notes, then selected an adventure for reading and put the rest of the stories in a drawer on the desk.

"Okay, you guys ready?" James asked. The bears didn't answer — they were too nervous. He grabbed the teddies and headed out the door.

As they drove to school, Bobby Bear stood up and looked out the window while Waldo sat in the seat with more on his mind.

James noticed Waldo not acting himself. "You okay, buddy?" Waldo shrugged his shoulders and stared at the floor. "Is something wrong?"

He couldn't hold back. "We have to leave," he said in a scared and worried voice, almost hoping James would have an answer to his problem.

"Leave? You mean someone has come for you?"

"Fluffy . . . Big Red Fluffy bear is the one."

"He's back?" James asked. "Where is he?"

"In Bobbie's closet."

Bobby Bear was hearing this for the first time as well. He knew Fluffy was back, but he didn't know that he was the one. Something's not right. Waldo would never lie, but this was Fluffy bear he was talking about.

"What do you mean?" asked Bobby Bear angrily. "It's *not* Fluffy! *You're wrong!*" He turned and glared out the window, no longer enjoying the view.

James was now seeing the affect it was having on both bears. The playfulness was gone. He was losing sight of the fact that these were teddy bears. He pictured them more as children, and seeing their reaction to the trouble they were in was hard to watch. He wanted to help — but what could he say? What could he do?

"When are you supposed to leave?" asked James, having a hard time focusing on the road.

Waldo shrugged. "Soon, I guess."

The mood in the car changed as worry set in and the engine was the only sound.

Arriving at school, James parked the car and sat in silence for a moment. Bobby Bear blankly stared out the window as James and Waldo looked at each other. So many thoughts ran through his mind, the first one was how could he help. "Is there something I can do?" he asked.

"No — I don't think so — no," answered Waldo. He truly wished there was some way he could say yes.

Bobby Bear was in no mood for story time when all he could think about was the Council:

"So, you're the one responsible for exposing the teddy world to humans," said an elder bear looking down from behind his tall desk. "Do you know what you have done? Do you know the trouble that you've caused? Do you know what we must do?"

Bobby Bear was too scared to answer.

"Are you listening? Are you listening, Bobby Bear?"

Snapping out of his dream, he heard James asking, "Bobby Bear, are you listening?" James was trying to get his attention. Bobby Bear had a blank expression on his face. "Come on. We need to go," said James.

Holding the two bears in his arms, he went to the main office to sign in. As he entered, he couldn't help but notice how quiet the office was — it was too quiet. No one was there. He signed his name in the logbook and saw a lot of signatures for today. *Huh, I wonder what that's all about,* he thought.

"Where is everybody?" he asked out loud to himself. "Hello?" He waited for a moment. Since he knew where he was going, he decided to move on to the classroom. The silence was obvious as he walked the hallway. *This isn't right.*

He stopped just outside Mrs. Larkin's classroom door to check himself — and the bears.

"You guys ready?"

He took a deep breath, knocked twice, and waited for an answer — there wasn't one. He knocked again much harder — still nothing. Slowly he opened the door. The more it opened the emptier it got.

"Where is everyone? This is getting *very* strange."

He stepped back into the hall and looked around. *What do I do?* He noticed a woman walking briskly towards him.

"Uh, pardon me, miss?" he called out. "Can you tell me where I can find Mrs. Larkin?"

The woman noticed the bears in his arms.

"They're in the auditorium waiting for you," said Mrs. Dunn. She stepped closer and reached for his arm to walk him in the opposite direction. James suddenly recognized the lady pulling him down the school corridor; she was his old teacher.

"You're Mrs. Dunn."

She slowed her pace. "Do I know you?" she asked, looking at him again more carefully.

"You were my teacher. I don't even want to mention how long ago."

She stopped, put her hand to her chin, and studied his face.

"I'm James, or Ji —"

"I remember. You used to play piano for the class and sing your songs," she said with a smile. "You haven't changed a bit. You were a good kid. So, now you're a writer?" she asked.

"Well, no. I guess. Sort of." James never thought about calling himself a writer. "It's my first book, and Mrs. Larkin has got me reading it to her class. She's my daughter's teacher."

"Yes, I've heard about the stories. I've also heard that you think they're —"

Not wanting to hear what she was about to say, James quickly interjected, "Do you know why she wants me to read in the auditorium?"

"Actually . . . I think she can answer that best," she said as Mrs. Larkin was seen coming out of the office.

"Thank goodness," said Mrs. Larkin with a relieved sigh. "I wasn't sure you were coming." She walked swiftly towards him. "I called your house and no one answered, so I assumed you were on your way. Thank you so much for doing this." She stopped only for a second to greet him then lead the way towards the auditorium.

"No problem. Glad to do it," he said as they went. "Can I ask why such a big place for a story?"

They stepped a little more slowly while she explained. "It's all quite remarkable, really. You've done something very special and I'm not sure how this all happened so fast," said Mrs. Larkin. "Over the weekend I started getting phone calls from parents wanting to know where they could buy your book — not to mention the bears, and I don't mean three or four parents. Then I got a call from the principal saying Mayor Anderson was asking as well."

"The Mayor?" James' voice cracked.

They stopped just outside the doors to the auditorium.

"One thing led to another . . . and . . . everyone wants 'em. I really didn't know what else to do. This was the only thing I could think of." She reached for the auditorium door and pulled it open revealing the entire student body.

James couldn't believe what he saw. "Are you kidding me?" he asked. "This is because of some stories about a couple of teddy bears?"

"I know. It's amazing. I do have to admit that I helped spread the word a bit. They really are good; and, of course," she said, then lowered her voice, "there is the added mystery about the bears." She gave a wink. James was still unsure of what she meant.

"So, I'm just supposed to go in there and read?" he asked as he peered inside.

"That's why they're here," answered Mrs. Larkin with that smile.

These people are here to see us? thought Waldo. *Wow.*

Bobby Bear didn't know what to think. If there was anything that could take his mind off of Big Red Fluffy bear, this was it.

James was tickled with a dash of nervous when he stepped through the door. He could see the stage as Mr. Tosh, the school Principal, was at the podium speaking to the students:

"The fundraiser will be held on Saturday at noon, here in the auditorium. We hope you can join us for what should be a good time and a good cause. For those who would like to volunteer with setup please see Ms. McCracken.

"We're honored to have Mayor Anderson joining us today at Roosevelt Elementary for this assembly."

Mr. Tosh noticed James entering the building with Mrs. Larkin.

"I see our guest speaker has arrived and we would like to welcome him to the stage. He's going to share some stories he's written about two teddy bears that come to life."

James walked between the folding bleachers that stood against the back wall, and through the rows of chairs set up on the floor, obscuring the lines of the basketball court. Children, teachers and parents filled the seats of the sizable venue. Heads were turned and eyes were focused on James as he made his way onto the stage.

Mr. Tosh said, "Please put your hands together for James and his bears, Bobby Bear and Waldo."

The applause was loud and sudden. Waldo was sure this was all for him as he began imagining himself addressing the crowd:

"Thank you. Thank you, everyone," said Waldo with both paws in the air, "and may I say, I am so happy to be here tonight. This was so unexpected. I really don't know where to begin. I couldn't have done any of this without James and, of course, Bobby Bear." Waldo could hear his name ringing out from the crowd.

Bobby Bear had never seen this many people before and felt uncomfortably nervous. *My paws are so sweaty. Does my breath smell? My fur is a mess. What are we supposed to do?* he wondered.

James walked to the center of the stage and sat down in one of two chairs that were waiting for him. He set the bears in the empty seat next to him and adjusted the microphone.

"Wow! This is a bit of a surprise. When Mrs. Larkin asked me to read to her class today, I didn't know she had this many students," he said with a forced smile.

"I'm going to read the newest adventure called <u>Bobby Bear and Waldo and the Were-bear</u>."

This caught Waldo's attention and he didn't like where this was going. *You can't tell about that,* he wanted to yell out but couldn't.

James continued on with his story to an audience that was completely attentive. As Bobby Bear listened to James tell the tale of the Were-Bear, he began to understand what had gotten into Waldo.

When James finished the story, the room burst into cheers and applause.

After Waldo heard how James described and told the tale — it didn't seem so bad. It actually sounded exciting. He could see how people would like these adventures. This made him feel differently about telling the stories. It wasn't about exposing the teddy world — it was about fun.

"Thank you," said James then stood up to leave.

Mrs. Larkin came walking out on the stage and thanked him for reading. "It was very kind of you to share your stories with us today," she said into the microphone. The audience applauded as they left.

BACKPACK OF LIES

The drive home was long and quiet. James marveled at the fact that he just read to the entire school. Waldo could still hear the applause and imagined himself the cause of it. Bobby Bear, on the other hand, dreaded going home because Fluffy bear was there waiting to take them away.

Not knowing how much time he had with the bears, James headed for the one place that always makes them happy.

"Guess where we are?" he asked as he turned the car into the parking lot of the fun park.

Waldo sprang to his feet and looked out the window.

"Supergreatiestfantaculious!" he cried at the sight of Sir Licks-A-Lot. He turned to Bobby Bear who was now lost in thought, imagining himself in front of the Council.

"The time for play is over," scolded an elder Council bear from behind a long large desk in a room that felt like a basement. It was cold and stark and dimly lit. Other teddies sat alongside the elder bear as he continued. "We must make an example of you. One that tells all other teddies that this type of Trust Busting is not tolerated." Bobby Bear was visibly shaking. He couldn't begin to

imagine the punishment that awaited. "Do you have anything to say in your defense before we pass judgment?" asked the elder bear with a condemning sneer.

Bobby Bear desperately tried to find the right words to explain what happened, when only one word popped out of his mouth: "Waldo?"

The elder bear was silent as he stared thoughtfully at Bobby Bear. He then turned to the other Council members and they began whispering back and forth, occasionally looking up from their huddle.

Bobby Bear nervously watched as he heard a faint word here and there, "...blame... ...trouble... ...Waldo..."

The whispering stopped and they switched their attention back to the frightened brown teddy.

"You make an interesting point. Since Waldo is the reason you're in this terrible trouble, we will let you select your punishment," said the elder bear. "You can have the one with chocolate sprinkles, or the one with rainbow sprinkles."

Bobby Bear was dreadfully confused.

"Which one do you want?" the elder bear asked. A lack of understanding of what the Council bear was saying left a blank expression on his face.

"Which one do you want? Bobby Bear, which one? Pick one."

His paws felt cold and sticky.

"Bobby Bear, which one do you want?" asked James. The dazed teddy became aware of the ice cream dripping on his paws from the cones that James held in his hands. "Do you want the chocolate one or the rainbow?"

He slowly reached out and took one without looking. It didn't matter to him, he wasn't in the mood for ice cream. He gave a look to Waldo that he's never given before. Bobby Bear was mad.

Ice cream melted over his paws while he sat in anger, only taking a lick from time to time. Most of the creamy goodness found its way to his lap and the car seat.

"Hey, buddy — are you okay?" asked Waldo, taking several licks from his cone.

Bobby Bear glared at him, but there were no words that he could use to describe what he was feeling right then. He had never experienced this before, especially towards his best friend. Waldo had gotten them into more trouble — again. This was all *his fault*.

Arriving back home, the car pulled into the driveway and stopped. James unbuckled and noticed the mess that Bobby Bear was sitting in.

"BOBBY BEAR!" he cried. James saw the smolder in his troubled green eyes. "Hey, what's wrong?" he asked, softening his tone. "This isn't like you." He reached over and took the ice cream from him and handed it to Waldo. James hurried around to the passenger side, opened the door, and knelt down beside the distressed bear. He reached for some napkins in the glove box. "Why the face?" Bobby Bear sat still as James wiped his paws and waited for a response.

The house was still under surveillance by Tiger, who remained in the boundary hedges between the houses, buried in dirt and leaves. Daytime for a teddy was most dangerous, even for a Kage Kuma. It was hard to keep concealed and movement was nearly impossible without detection. From his vantage point he could partially see the car that pulled into the driveway. Tiger didn't have to wait long to see the human that was accused of trying to expose and ruin the Secret Teddy Society. He heard James scolding Bobby Bear for something. The villainous picture that Ballinger had painted was true. This human needed to be taken care of. A red wave splashed in his eyes. Anger was building inside of Tiger at the thought of such an evil person. It was getting harder to remain still.

Back at the car, James was still cleaning ice cream from Bobby Bear when Waldo suddenly dropped both ice cream cones and they bounced off the seat onto the floor.

"WALDO! Oh, *come on*," James cried out. He reached over and quickly scooped up the cones, holding them precariously in one hand with the napkins in the other. "What has gotten into you two?" He started wiping faster as ice cream dripped down his arm. "You're making a terrible mess. This isn't like you. Were you not hungry? Are you not feeling well? What's going on?"

James was hoping one of the questions would get an answer. That's when he noticed the life in their eyes had gone. They weren't going to answer. Something was terribly wrong.

A sense began nagging at James. He could feel it; he's noticed this before. A darkness swept the mood.

"What *is* that?" he asked curiously out loud. Still wiping Bobby Bear's paws, James felt an unusually cold chill. He slowly looked down and saw feet standing behind him, a pair of old ladies shoes that he recognized.

He turned around to find Mrs. Mallory standing in his driveway, watching him clean ice cream from two teddy bears while talking to himself — or the bears. She couldn't tell which.

"Oh! *Ha hah*," he laughed uneasily. "Mrs. Mallory, how are you today?"

Her expression was one that he had seen many times in the movies when someone was in shock. It was classic. She stared at James with her mouth slightly agape. No words were spoken. She glanced at the bears who sat lifelessly in the car, covered in ice cream. Her eyes switched back to James with a question that he couldn't answer; not one that she would understand, anyway.

"It's not what it looks like," he said quickly. "Well, actually, I guess it sort of is." He let slip a nervous laugh. "You see, I stopped to get some ice cream for Bobbie, when she gets home from school . . ." Just then, James remembered how early it was. " . . . in about two hours," he added, realizing that his story had a major time flaw and was not very convincing. Ice cream dripped from his elbow while the two stood motionless waiting for anything to break the awkward moment. Her feet instinctively stepped back, one slow step at a time, and she continued on her walk, never taking her eyes from his.

"*Whew* — that was close," he chuckled as he imagined what she must have thought.

At that moment, the big black truck pulled in next door. James refused to look but something happened that he couldn't ignore; an empty beer can hit him in the back. Turning his head, James heard Kurt laugh as he dashed inside while his obsequious friend, Ray, sat in the passenger seat. Ever since Kurt backed into his car, Debra had been bugging him to get the dent fixed. Now was the time. Bobby Bear and Waldo sensed the anger in James. With a decisive look on his face and ice cream running down his arms, he set the cones on the ground and reached up and grabbed the garage door opener that was clipped to the sun visor. Since Ray had assumed Kurt's problem — then he would deal with Ray.

There was a confident and purposeful demeanor James carried as he walked next door. Ray noticed him in the rearview mirror, as he swaggered up the driveway. Ray was caught off guard at the sight of James approaching yet instinctively climbed out of the truck to confront him. He puffed his large chest and stiffened his back as the two were now face-to-face. James had one play and it was based on human nature. Since Kurt wasn't standing next to him, Ray would need to act for himself.

Ray wasn't physically threatened by James, since he was about thirty pounds heavier and three inches taller. However, such brashness created confusion and uneasiness. "What can I do for you?" Ray's rugged voice belted.

There was an obstinate look on James' face as he answered, "I have a solution to your problem." His heart was racing and only hoped that Kurt stayed in the house.

"Let's hear it."

"The two of us drive out to the old Kellogg Mill — I leave the keys under the seat and we go into the abandoned building. The one that comes out — has a ride home — *and* gets to keep the car."

The thought was laughable, but something didn't feel right. His unyielding delivery was unexpected. It was hard to read. Clearly, Ray had the physical advantage. But what was really going on here? Ray's eye twitched as he studied James. The obvious answer was: this was a bluff. But there was no one else around, and Ray didn't really know James. What was he thinking? What was he capable of? Would there be someone else to help James at the mill? Would he bring a gun? Ray needed help but Kurt wasn't there. He couldn't look away; it would show weakness. The first thing to try was to dismiss the suggestion. Show no interest. "That piece of crap?" he said, pointing to the vehicle in James' driveway. "What the hell would I do with that?"

James raised his arm in the direction of his house and pressed the garage door opener. Ray turned to see the large door slowly reveal the beautiful classic sport car.

"No . . . My 68' Camaro."

James' expression never changed.

Ray stared at his dream car. The stakes just got interesting. Ray would love to have that American classic but at what cost? There were too many unknowns. Every ounce of this was bizarre. He turned back to James with trepidation. A question entered Ray's mind: was this worth it? It was just a dent after all. There was an easy answer for all of this. Without any need to think it over, he said, "You know — I'm a metal guy and I could have that dent popped out in no time. You won't even know it was there. How's that sound?"

That was exactly what James wanted to hear, and the relief almost buckled his knees. "That sounds fine," said James, still keeping his firm exterior. "As long as I can't tell it was there." James wanted to scream, *YES! That's absolutely fine!*

Ray turned to make sure Kurt wasn't coming, then lowered his voice. "Just swing it by the shop next week sometime after six o'clock — I'll take care of it." He gave a slight smile, showing a different side to Ray that James had never seen.

"Appreciate it," replied James. He turned and calmly strolled back down the driveway.

Kurt came out of the house in time to see James head back to his side of the hedges. Stepping quickly, he glared at Ray. "What was that? What'd he want?"

There was no way Ray was going to say what happened. "You know that guy is nuts. He came over insisting that I fix his car."

"*Yeah?* And what'd you tell him?"

"I said, sure I'll fix it but it's gonna cost ya'."

"You said that? Man, that's funny. I dent his car and he's gonna pay you to fix it." Kurt smirked and let out a laugh. "He had the nads to come over here and say that to *you?* That *is* crazy."

There was something about the way Ray spoke that sent a different message. He was acting weird, too. He wouldn't face Kurt when he talked.

"I'm tellin' ya' — he's unstable. I'd leave him alone," said Ray with an odd tone.

Kurt fired up his truck and began backing out of his driveway. Sensing his friend's peculiar behavior, he turned his head to see James with ice cream stains running down his arms while he held two teddy bears tight to his chest. James returned a look to Kurt as he passed. At that moment, Kurt realized he had no interest in finding out just how unpredictable his neighbor was.

Tiger had watched the entire incident between the two men. James was clearly an erratic man, and bold, too — standing up to such a large opponent. He would need to be careful when dealing with him. Ballinger was correct; he was dangerous.

James headed into the house and placed the bears on the desk. "I'm going to finish cleaning up that mess — and when I get back — we're going to have a talk," he said rather sternly and went to leave.

Waldo busted. "*What was that?*"

James turned around, surprised that Waldo spoke. "What?"

"That! — *out there*. That big dude!" Waldo had never seen anything like that before, a little guy confronting a big guy. "I heard what you said. You know he could've hurt you — right?"

James gave a grin and stepped back towards the desk. "Yeah. I know. But I also know something that he didn't know — me. People fear the unknown. He doesn't know me. He didn't know what he would be walking into — and without Kurt around — he was on his own. You put most people into that situation and give them an option to back down . . . they will . . . most of the time." James smiled.

"Most of the time? So you really didn't know what he was going to do?"

James rubbed Waldo's head. "I gotta clean up that mess. I'll be back."

After James went outside, Waldo turned to Bobby Bear. "Did you *see that?* That was amazing! What he did! MAN! That was awesome. That big dude didn't know what to do. I gotta remember that one. Two men go in — one man comes out. Who does that?" Waldo noticed that Bobby Bear wasn't even listening. "What's the matter with you?" he belted.

Bobby Bear wouldn't acknowledge him.

Waldo had never seen Bobby Bear mad before and wasn't sure what to do. "Are you upset or something?" he asked tentatively as Bobby Bear stared out the window. "Are you mad?" he asked a little louder and stepped closer. Bobby Bear quickly turned his head when Waldo slid into view. Waldo jumped in front of Bobby Bear. "What's the matter?" he yelped. Bobby Bear only stared at him with no answer.

"*Fine* — be that way," barked Waldo. He jumped down off the desk and ran to the playroom. "What's gotten under his fur?" Waldo mumbled as he went. But then part of Waldo already knew. He was on edge, too, knowing that they might be leaving tonight and may never see Bobbie, James and Debra again. The spring in his step vanished and his shoulders drooped. An emotional wave swept over Waldo. He could have easily burst into tears. The reality of being taken away was sinking in. He walked into the playroom, climbed up on the table in the middle of the room, which had a sketchpad and a box of crayons on it, and began to draw. This was important. There was the possibility that they wouldn't return, and Waldo wanted to leave something with James that would always remind him of them.

James finished cleaning up the car and walked into the office where he saw Bobby Bear sitting in his spot, tapping the pencils in the pencil holder, deep in thought.

"Is Waldo around?"

Bobby Bear shrugged one shoulder. "He ran off, I guess," he answered with a bitter tone.

"What's wrong? You don't seem to be yourself," asked James, pulling out his chair to sit.

"I'm mad, I guess."

"You? — mad?" James quipped as if that were impossible.

"*I can get mad*," he responded curtly.

"Well — yeah. I guess — I just —" He'd never seen this side of Bobby Bear before and knew something had to be very troubling to get him this upset. James had a suspicion of what it might be.

Bobby Bear's emotions came spilling out. "What? I'm supposed to be the good one? I'm supposed to look out for Waldo and make sure he doesn't get into trouble? Yeah, well, look what's happened: he decides he wants milk one day and I try to talk him out of it. The next thing I know is he's using me as a ladder to climb up into the fridge and we get caught. Now, another friend is going to take us away so the Council can punish us for doing something *I didn't want to do. I'd say I'm mad.*" He folded his arms and started breathing faster as the green in his eyes became electric.

"Are you mad at Waldo, or upset that he talked you into something that you knew was wrong? Maybe if you hadn't gone along with Waldo — none of this would have happened. Maybe you're a little mad at yourself," said James.

"I'm not mad at myself!" he bellowed. Bobby Bear was afraid to consider that option. It had to be Waldo's fault. It just had to be.

Ding-dong. The doorbell rang.

Bobby Bear turned blank while James went to the door. He peered out the side window but didn't see anyone. "Hmm, that's odd." He stood there for a moment.

Ding-dong. It rang again.

James opened the door to find Tiffany standing right in front of him. She had her head pressed against the door trying to hear if anyone was home.

Waldo heard the doorbell but didn't pay much attention. He was focused on his drawing. He was also aware that it was too early for school to let out, and who else would come to the playroom? So he kept busy until he heard the one name he won't soon forget.

"Hello, Tiffany," said James, his eyes searched for a parent. "Bobbie's not home right now. She's still at . . ." He then realized whom he was talking to. "Aren't you supposed to be at school?"

"Yeah. I had a dentist appointment."

"Oh. So — what can I do for you?"

"Actually, I'm here to get a necklace that she borrowed from me."

"Hmm, okay. Do you need it right now?"

"Yeah. It's kind of important. I wasn't supposed to have loaned it to her in the first place. I could get in trouble."

"Well, we don't want that. Let me see if I can find it." James turned to go search.

"That's all right. I know where it is. It's in her room," said Tiffany as she let herself in. "Where's her room?" she asked.

"Oh — her room is down the hall on the right. You can't miss it."

Tiffany almost skipped as she went with her backpack bouncing playfully up and down.

James went to the office to work on a few things. Bobby Bear sat motionless, waiting for Tiffany to leave.

The blonde haired girl entered Bobbie's room and stood for a moment gazing at everything as if she were in a museum.

She spied her heart shaped flower pendant resting on the desk and went to pick it up. As she reached for the necklace she noticed Elvis sitting in the Big People's Chair.

"So — can you talk, too?" she asked him, not really knowing what she would do if he answered.

Elvis sat and stared straight ahead, which happened to be directly at her. Their eyes locked. An eerie feeling crept over her as she could almost see the life in his eyes. Without looking, her hand grabbed desperately for the necklace and she hurried for the door. She stopped and turned back to Elvis, who appeared different somehow.

As Tiffany left Bobbie's bedroom she poked her head into the playroom. It was like a magnet pulling at her. Colorful crates full of toys were in each corner. A blue table sat in the middle of the room with several small blue matching chairs scattered about. She walked in and made a large circle, inspecting everything as she passed, scoffing at the picture that sat in the middle of the table with crayons strewn about. There was one box of toys that caught her attention: it had a barnyard set, a few dolls, a large plastic pirate ship and something else that Tiffany was all too familiar with.

"There you are," she said as she plucked it from the box and stuffed it in her backpack. Zipping it tight, she skipped out of the room just as James went to see if she needed help finding her necklace.

James was half way down the hall when she popped out from the playroom. "There you are," he said. "Did you find what you were looking for?"

"Yep," she answered with a smile.

"Good. Now you won't get in trouble," said James and opened the front door. "I'll tell Bobbie you stopped by."

"You don't need to. I'll see her later and tell her myself," she replied.

"Okay, that sounds good. It was nice to see you again. Bye."

"Bye," she called out, skipping off down the sidewalk.

James strolled into the office to see Bobby Bear.

"That was Tiffany at the door," he said and pulled out his chair to sit.

"I know who that was. That was the big Meany," said Bobby Bear in a disgusted tone. "She's not very nice. You know she's a Meany. If she was a teddy — she'd be a *bad bear*."

"Really? I think she's changed quite a bit. She apologized for the past — and she loaned Bobbie her nice necklace, didn't she?"

Bobby Bear thought about it for a moment. "I guess — I don't know. Once a Meany always a Meany, I say."

A scowl was firmly planted on his face because he was still in a mood.

James decided to take this time to write about his day. He opened the drawer where he had placed the stories.

"WHAT?" He put his hand into the drawer to feel around. "THEY'RE GONE!" he said frantically. He searched the top of the desk then pulled open every drawer. "*They're gone!*" He took a step back and stared at the desk as if he would see them from a different angle. His eyes darted across the desktop once again.

Bobby Bear became worried since he'd never seen James panic before.

"W-What? What's gone?" asked Bobby Bear, trying to help.

"The stories! All the stories are gone!" cried James. He stopped to think. His mind sifted through different scenarios of why someone would take them. Between thoughts, he kept reminding himself that this wouldn't be a problem if he had only kept a copy on the computer. *Why didn't I keep a backup?* thought James in frustration. *Who writes on paper any more, anyway?*

From down the hall, in Bobbie's closet, Big Red Fluffy bear could hear James.

The stories are gone? Fluffy bear was elated at the thought. This was the break he was looking for. *If he can't find the stories, then he can't show 'em to anyone. We can leave tonight.* It felt as if the world had just been lifted off his shoulders.

James turned quickly to Bobby Bear with a wild look. "WALDO — where did he go?" he said accusingly.

Bobby Bear didn't have to answer as he already told James that he took off down the hall earlier.

"Why? You don't think . . . NO! He wouldn't do that!" cried Bobby Bear. James dashed out of the room. Bobby Bear jumped down off the desk and ran after him.

"Waldo?" James called out when he entered Bobbie's room. "Waldo!" He didn't see him anywhere. Bobby Bear caught up to him as James was on the floor looking under Bobbie's bed.

"That's not like him. He wouldn't do that," pleaded Bobby Bear.

James wasn't really listening, his mind was clouded. He dashed to the playroom, hoping he was there.

Outside, in the shrubs, Tiger heard the yelling about the missing stories. James was angry, and apparently accused Waldo for stealing them. This was troublesome to Tiger. Things weren't as they appeared. Maybe Waldo stole the stories to protect the STS. Tiger would need to find him to confirm this development.

"Waldo? Waldo!" His head was swiveling left and right. "He's got to be here." Then James noticed the paper on the table. His mood softened a bit while he studied the drawing. "He *was* here. But this isn't right."

"What do you mean?" asked Bobby Bear, now standing next to him. James handed him the paper.

"He was drawing this and I know he wouldn't have left it." He studied the room more closely for any type of clue.

Bobby Bear stared at the picture and became sad. "That's us," he said softly.

James heard him and looked down. "Yeah — and we've got to find him. I'm starting to think you were right," said James and began to think like a detective. "Okay, now — Waldo said Fluffy bear was back and that he was the one taking you away. Where's Fluffy bear? I need to talk to him."

Bobby Bear was in a terrible spot. Being torn between the Code and the love for his family is every teddy's worst nightmare. But he knew this was not going to help anything since Fluffy was not going to move or answer during the day, and especially in front of a human. Fluffy had learned his lesson.

The confused bear glanced up at James and shook his head with futility in his eyes. Without saying a word, James understood what he meant. "Okay — I know — you're right. Let me think for a second."

No longer concerned about his stories (but rather that Waldo was all right) he turned and slowly walked out the door into the hallway. He started running the last few moments through his mind. "Tiffany!" he blurted.

Bobby Bear flinched in surprise. "I told you! I told you she's a Meany, a *big Meany*," he chimed with his eyes shrouded.

"I *thought* she was taking a long time — and I *knew* I saw her coming out of the playroom," said James like a sleuth uncovering the culprit of a crime.

"So now what? We go get Waldo, right?" asked Bobby Bear almost jumping up and down.

"It's not that simple," said James, now having to think of the best way to approach Tiffany and find out if she really did have him.

"We can't just sit here. We've got to do something," asserted Bobby Bear, feeling helpless.

"NO. *I've* got to do something. I'll take care of it. What I want you to do is check with Fluffy bear to find out if he knows anything," commanded James. He turned and headed back to the office to think.

Bobby Bear ran straight to the closet. He dug under the clothes, back in the corner, until he came upon Fluffy bear.

"Did you hear that?" he asked urgently. "Waldo's gone. *He's gone!*" Fluffy didn't move or make a sound. "I know you won't talk to me now, but I don't care. He's my best friend and I'm not leaving without him."

Fluffy remained lifeless. Frustration boiled in Bobby Bear. He turned and scurried out of the closet, running straight to Elvis in the Big People's Chair. "You heard what happened — we need to help him. We know who has him," he begged Elvis, who didn't move. "We need to do something — *it's in the Code.* Tiffany — she's got him and I don't know what she might do." Bobby Bear waited breathlessly for an answer but he wasn't going to get one. This was terrible news for Fluffy. The Council was expecting two bears, not one. Fluffy *did* want to help, he *needed* to help, but now was not the time. They would have to wait for nightfall. Until then, Fluffy wasn't moving.

The sound of the family car pulling into the driveway told him that he had to hurry back to the desk. As fast as he could go, Bobby Bear ran to the office and climbed up over James to his spot.

Bobbie didn't come bounding in as she normally does; she stood outside the office window and beckoned James to join her in the yard. He forced a smile and went to meet her.

She had a grin on her face when James stepped onto the front porch. "Our side won today," she announced cheerfully. "They let us play Tee ball at school. They said they weren't keeping score but I did: ten to seven. It wasn't a real game or anything, they wanted everyone to hit the ball. I like hitting the ball better when you throw it. I don't like that stupid cone thing."

"And, of course, you were the best hitter out there, right?" James crowed proudly.

"Well . . ." she humbly agreed. "Hey, can you throw the ball to me?"

James wanted to tell her what had happened, but he didn't want to say anything about Tiffany — at least, not until he was sure she had Waldo. James would put on his happy face and try to think of a way to find the little white teddy. "Sure, why not."

Bobby Bear found it hard to sit still knowing his best friend was in danger while James was outside playing and having fun.

So, it's up to me now, he thought. He was preparing himself for what he had to do.

A NIGHTMARE BEGINS

One house stood out in the neighborhood where James lives. It's a white two-story, three doors down, on the other side of the street. If a Ken and Barbie doll were actual people this would be their house. The classic white picket fence circled the perfectly manicured lawn with two tall white lamp posts lighting the walkway from the sidewalk. A wrap-around porch with the cutest porch swing sits adjacent to the beautiful stained glass front door. This house was the envy of Glenmore Drive. This was where Tiffany lived.

Tiffany had a lot on her mind as she walked past her mom holding her backpack in such a way so no one would notice. Her mom was chatting on the phone, as she often does, saying, "It happened again, just like when I was little," to an old friend named Jezicca. As Tiffany tried to slip by unobserved, she couldn't seem to remember how to walk normally. Her eyes darted about cautiously and her feet wanted to tiptoe. She glanced at her mom and their eyes met. They both turned away, fearing discovery. Her mom's voice lowered to almost a whisper as she continued talking while Tiffany quickened her step to the privacy of her bedroom.

Closing the door behind her, she gently placed her backpack on the bed. Her heart raced as it never had before. She went to her desk to adjust something that was lying under a shirt that she wore yesterday. She stood in the middle of her princess style bedroom and studied the scene, her eyes shifting from the desk to the play-set table. A chair was pulled out as if waiting for someone. Turning back to the bed, she delicately reached for her backpack and unzipped it slowly, trying not to disturb the contents. The unusual bulge in her pack pushed open the flap as the zipper slid across the top. A white furry ear popped out followed by another. She carefully pulled out Waldo.

"There — are you comfy?" asked Tiffany of the bear who sat stiffly in the play chair.

Comfy? Yeah, as comfy as a bear-napped bear can be, he thought fearfully, unsure of what she had planned.

Tiffany stared at him, thinking of what she could do or say to convince him to talk.

"Look, I know what I saw — and I need to know that I'm not crazy. I'M NOT CRAZY!" she said in a crazy-sounding voice.

Houston, we have a problem, quipped Waldo to himself trying, unsuccessfully, to be brave.

"I'm not a Meany. I'm a good girl and I want to show you that you can trust me," she implored. She then opened a toy chest and reached inside. When she lifted the lid, Waldo saw two teddies stuffed in the box with parts of a tea set and other toys lying on top of the bears. She pulled her arm out of the box, clinching her fist.

"I'm going to tell you something that I haven't told anyone before," she disclosed gently and sat on the floor in front of Waldo. "When I was little my mommy gave me a teddy — Noname. We called him that because I'd change his name, like every day. I thought it was funny, but my mommy kept calling him Noname bear and it sorta stuck."

Tiffany paused a moment and looked at her clinched fist. "One day — I got mad at my mom and ran to my room. I grabbed Noname and hugged him so tight. Then — I did something I wish I could fix. I never told anyone."

She put her closed hand to Waldo's face and opened it. Waldo knew exactly what she was holding.

"They're his eyes," she confessed sadly. "I didn't even remember doing it. I cried for days when I realized what I had done. I put him under my bed and never told my mom because I didn't want her to get mad at me." She was getting upset all over again. "I'm telling you because I needed to tell someone. I didn't mean to hurt him. I don't know how it happened. I would never hurt Noname and I'm not going to hurt you. I just want to know that I'm not crazy. Just talk to me. Just say anything and I'll take you home."

She placed the eyes back in the box and closed the lid.

This did not make Waldo feel any better. In fact, all he could think about was poor Noname bear under the bed.

A knock at the door sent Tiffany into a panic. "Just a second," she called out.

"Tiffany? Can I come in?" her mom asked from outside the door.

Grabbing Waldo, she quickly tossed him under the bed just as her mom let herself in. Tiffany snapped to attention but couldn't hide the guilt on her face.

"What are you doing in here?"

"Just picking up before dinner."

The look on Tiffany's face said something different as her mom studied the room suspiciously.

"It's still pretty messy for picking up." Her mom noticed the chair pulled away from the tea table and the bed skirt lifted.

"I — I just started," explained Tiffany, trying hard to act as normal as possible, but the harder she tried the more guilty she looked.

"Okay, then, dinner is just about ready. Come and wash up."

Her mom slowly left, all the while her watchful eyes surveying the room.

Tiffany followed her to the kitchen while Waldo was lying still under the bed. He could feel something furry at his feet and had a sense of what it was.

"Is that you, Noname?" asked Waldo in the teddy tone. A soft voice came from the darkness.

"Yes. Who are you?"

"I'm Waldo."

"You're Waldo? I've heard of you. She talks about you a lot. Are you here to help me?"

Waldo wished he hadn't asked that question. Part of the Teddy Code says that a teddy should help another whenever possible. Waldo did want to help, but he was a bit more worried about what was going to happen to him, not to mention, he was in enough trouble as it was. How was he going to get himself back to James' house *and* worry about Noname at the same time?

"Um — not really. She just threw me under here," Waldo confessed, wiggling around to get a glimpse. A ray of light where the bed skirt lifted faintly lit Noname's face.

"Whoa!" cried Waldo, startled at the sight of a bear with no eyes. "You're a . . . a . . . Zombie bear."

"Is it that bad?"

Usually, a bear missing body parts turns into a Zombie bear when discarded, but Noname was still with his family.

"No," replied Waldo, sorry he made the comment. "I've just never seen —" Waldo was trying to find a nice way to phrase it.

"That's okay. I'm just glad to have someone to talk to. You sound like a nice bear."

"How long have you been under here?" Waldo asked.

"I don't remember. It's been a long time — so it seems."

Waldo's curiosity got the better of him. "How did it happen?"

"You mean, when I lost my . . . Well, the night she got mad at her mom, she came in crying. We hugged for a long time. She's a good hugger," he added. "She squeezed so tight and my face was pressing against her neck. She was wearing a necklace that somehow got caught. I felt it pulling, but I couldn't do anything. She didn't do it on purpose. It just happened. Now she's too scared to tell anyone. So here I am, stuck, until she says something to her mom — or she wants to see me again."

The two talked for a while until Tiffany returned from dinner. They heard the bedroom door close and her arm reached under the bed, grabbing Waldo. She carefully positioned the tea chair then placed him back in it.

"Do you want to talk to me now?" she asked. "All you have to do is say 'hello' or something like that. That's it, that's all you have to do and I'll take you home." They both sat still just staring at each other.

Back in the office, the mood was tense as James racked his brain for ideas — solutions — anything. It was maddening to just sit and do nothing.

His daughter strolled in looking for the bears but it was only Bobby Bear on the desk.

"Um, Daddy? I think someone's missing."

James turned and stared at the empty space. "Yeah. I know." His voice was somber. It showed on his face. "I'm not really sure where he is," he said in all truthfulness.

"Maybe he just wanted to be alone for a while," she suggested in her soft angelic voice.

As he heard those words from someone so sweet and innocent, he couldn't tell if she really believed in the Secret Teddy Society or she was simply playing along as she normally would. It didn't really matter right then. What mattered was getting Waldo back.

James had to do something and the only thing that came to mind was to confront the problem straight on. "I gotta go do something, Pumpkin — I'll be right back." He grabbed his jacket and went to the door. "I'm going outside for a minute," he called out to Debra.

"All right," she answered from the kitchen.

He walked down the street to the Connors' house. Since James tries to live his life by truth and honesty, he was aware his approach was going to sound extremely foolish. He ran conversations through his head as he knocked on the door:

Excuse me. I hate to bother you but have you seen a small white teddy bear running around your house? He shook his head knowing how ridiculous that was, then tried again. *Hi, your daughter stole my teddy bear and I want him back.* None of them sounded good. Before James could think of a reasonable way to express why he was there, the door opened to find Mrs. Connors a bit distressed.

"Yes?"

"Hi. My name is James. I'm Bobbie's dad. We live right down the street," he said, pointing in the direction of his house. "Your daughter, Tiffany, is in her class."

"Oh, sure. What can I do for you?" she asked in a short tone while her mind was distracted.

"This is where it gets difficult . . ." James began to explain, when he noticed Tiffany's mom was only half listening. "Excuse me, I'm sorry, but did I catch you at a bad time?" he asked, feeling awkward.

"No — not really," replied Mrs. Connors. "I was trying to read something before you arrived and I can't find my glasses." She patted herself down once again. "I was just wearing them a second ago."

James was almost too embarrassed to point out the pair of glasses sitting on her head. "Are those the ones you were looking for?" he asked hesitantly.

She noticed his eyes directed at her hair or so she thought. Suddenly, Mrs. Connors figured out what he was staring at. She placed her hand on her head touching the lost glasses. Her cheeks grew a lovely shade of red. "That's the second time today I've done that. Please excuse me — my mind's not been right since I saw — Oh, never mind, you wouldn't believe me if I told you."

She quickly put the glasses in her pocket and turned her full attention to James. "What can I do for you?" she asked, taking a deep breath with a tired sigh.

"You see, Tiffany came by earlier today, while Bobbie was at school. She said she loaned her a necklace that she wasn't supposed to. I'm not sure how to say this, but — I think when she was in Bobbie's room she may have taken more than just her necklace." He tried to phrase it as politely as one could.

Her appearance went from pleasant to confused.

"You mean she took something that didn't belong to her?" She became indignant at the remark.

"Well, I think so — I'm not really sure," replied James. "That's why I'm here. After she left, I noticed the item was missing. I just can't think of where else to look and I wanted to make sure that your daughter didn't take it. It's kind of important."

"Can you tell me what it is you think she took?" she asked, knowing her daughter would never have done something like that.

He hesitated before answering. "A teddy bear," he said, realizing how that sounded once he said it out loud. "A white teddy bear named Waldo."

Her face changed as she began to understand what was going on.

"I know who you are. You're writing those stories about teddy bears that come to life," she said with a liveliness to her voice. "You know — they're saying that *you* think it's all real." James didn't expect that response. "Can I ask you something? And please answer honestly and not what you think I want to hear."

"Sure, okay."

"Is it real?" She was expecting to hear "no" while hoping to hear a response that would actually comfort her.

He thought for a second and wondered why people keep asking him that. He decided to let her know the truth, since it had been working so far.

"I know how this is going to sound . . . and I don't really know how else to say it —" he started to explain.

Mrs. Connors anticipated what he was about to say.

"I do believe it," she interjected excitedly before he could finish. "This may sound incredible — but, I know. I mean, I saw it. I was positive I saw it. What else could it have been?"

James was a bit confused at this point. "You saw?" he asked.

Her exhilaration was palpable. "I've wanted to say it for a while now but what do you say? Who would believe me? And now you're here — and you were the one that I needed to say it to." She was breathless with excitement.

"Me?" He still wasn't understanding.

"Well — I didn't know it was you until now," she explained. "The other day — on my way home, I stopped at a traffic light. I looked at the car next to me and saw two teddy bears staring out the window. At first, I thought it was some kid holding up some bears to have a little fun, so I stuck my tongue at 'em. Then — the strangest thing happened. One of the furry faces stuck their tongue out. I have to say — I was stunned. I knew what I saw, and yet, still couldn't believe it. The light turned green and they pulled away, but . . . I didn't move. I don't even remember the drive home. I sat in the driveway and kept seeing that face in my head. I couldn't tell anyone — not without sounding loony, anyway. Actually, I did tell a girlfriend of mine. I couldn't stop myself. It just came out. I had to tell someone. She didn't believe me, I don't' think, but I knew *you* would — because you know the truth. It was you in the car next to me, out in front of the fun park. The bear I saw was white — a white teddy bear — and now you're telling me that my daughter might have him?"

James didn't realize that Waldo had done that, but it sure did sound like him.

Mrs. Connors reached out, grabbed his face, and kissed him on the cheek.

"What was that for?" he asked quite surprised.

"That's for letting me know that I'm not crazy." Her relief was obvious. "I'll go have a talk with Tiffany. My name's Kitty, by the way. If she has Waldo I'll make sure he's returned home," she said.

"Thank you, Kitty. I'll wait to hear from you either way. It's good to finally meet you."

"I can't tell you how good it is to meet you," she replied. "You've made my day and a lot more, I should say. Thank you. I'll let you know." She closed the door and went to talk with her daughter.

Kitty almost floated to Tiffany's room, but as she got to her bedroom door she heard talking. It sounded like her daughter was pleading with someone.

"What if I promise to never say anything to anyone?" Kitty heard through the door. "I told you a secret now you tell me one; that's how it works."

Mrs. Connors opened the door to find Tiffany sitting on the floor in front of a small white teddy bear placed in a tea chair. It was the same fuzzy white face that she saw in the car next to her. At that moment her fears came true.

"Tiffany! What are you doing?" Kitty reprimanded, feeling disappointed in her daughter. Tiffany's guilty face said more than she wanted to admit.

"Who is that?" she asked while pointing at Waldo.

"I found him," answered Tiffany. She had a hard time looking at her mother.

"No, Tiffany. I know that's not true." Tiffany blanched and turned white.

"First, you lied to me. And second, you took something that doesn't belong to you."

Water began to well up in Tiffany's eyes. "I had to," she sobbed as tears tumbled off her cheeks.

Her mom had never seen her like this. She pulled her close and hugged her.

"Can you please tell me what's going on?"

Tiffany wiped her tears and caught her breath.

"You won't get mad at me?"

"No. I won't get mad at you. I promise. I just want to know why you did this."

Tiffany pointed to Waldo. "I saw him move. I know you won't believe me but I saw him. I know I saw him. I wanted to tell you but I know you wouldn't believe me. I'm not crazy, Mommy. I thought it was *all* teddies but it's not. It's only him. I can show you if you just watch," she pleaded hysterically through her tears. "Watch — just watch. He talks. I know he does —"

"Sweetie —"

"Just watch —"

"Hey, listen to me. I believe you," her mom said kindly.

Tiffany stopped and stared in disbelief.

"You do?"

"Yes . . . I do. I need to tell you a story and I think you may have a hard time believing *me*," Kitty said then sat on the edge of the bed. "When I was a little girl I had a teddy named Nicholas. We did everything together. I remember, one night, going to bed while chewing bubble gum, which you shouldn't do, by the way. I fell asleep — and when I woke up — my gum was gone. I was still hugging Nicholas when I noticed something. My gum was stuck to his nose. I felt just awful. It wouldn't come off. I cried because I thought he was ruined. I took him to the bathroom to try soap and water but nothing seemed to work. I ran to my bed and cried for a while. Then I saw something that I —"

"What?" interrupted Tiffany, listening intently.

"I looked up from my pillow and could see into the bathroom mirror. I saw Nicholas on the counter, where I left him — but he wasn't sitting still."

"He . . . what?" choked Tiffany as her voice trembled.

Her mom nodded and said, "That's right. I saw him move." She leaned closer. "He was tugging at the gum stuck on his nose. He pulled so hard that he lost his grip and fell off the counter. I watched him fall to the floor."

"Really? What'd you do?"

"I couldn't move. I saw something I wasn't supposed to. I buried my face into the pillow before he noticed. After a while, I looked up and he was back on the counter."

"You never told anyone?" asked Tiffany.

"I only told my best friend, Jezicca, but no one else," she replied. "And you know why — don't you?"

Tiffany nodded. They sat in silence for a moment when Tiffany asked, "Where is Nicholas? How come I haven't seen him?"

"I don't know," her mom answered softly. "About a week or so later — I lost him. He was just gone. I looked everywhere but he was gone. I still don't understand what happened to him. I cried for weeks. My parents got me a new teddy but I didn't want a new one. I wanted Nicholas." Kitty began to get that feeling again.

Tiffany saw the sadness in her mom's eyes.

"It's okay, Mommy. I believe you," she said, patting her arm.

They hugged for a while and began talking. Tiffany told her mom about show and tell and the unbelievable thing she saw. "He stuck out his tongue at me." Tiffany was so glad to tell someone that believed her. This made her mom laugh as she told her daughter about what happened while sitting at a traffic light.

"Wait a minute," snapped Tiffany, "you saw Waldo? He stuck out his tongue at you?" she asked, pointing to the little white bear in disbelief. "Are you sure it was him?"

"Yeah, I'm pretty sure," said Kitty. "A small white bear in the same car that I've seen your friend Bobbie get into. But there was another one with him, it was a brown one."

"So, it's not just Waldo that can move?"

"No. I think all teddies can. I thought about that after I saw Nicholas try to get the gum off his nose. At first, I thought it was only Nicholas but then I wondered: why only him?"

"But if they can all move then why don't we see 'em?" asked Tiffany. "Why don't they tell us?" Tiffany looked hard at Waldo, sitting still in the tea chair, hoping *he* might explain.

"I'm sure they have their reasons," said her mom, "and I'm sure it's a good one. Listen, there's something that I want you to keep in mind; there's always two sides to every story. Don't get too worked up about anything until you know the other side of the story. Remember the other day when you wanted that game at the store? I told you no. Not because I simply wanted to say no, but because I didn't have the money right then."

Tiffany's face softened. "But why didn't you say that?" she asked politely.

"Would it have mattered?" Kitty replied. "I'm never going to say no just because I want to say no. There's a reason. There's always another side — and I'm not always going to tell you, just like teddy bears. There has to be a reason, we just don't know it." Kitty leaned over and wrapped her arms around Tiffany.

Like Tiffany, Waldo also wondered why teddies don't move in front of humans. Nevertheless, after hearing the way her mom explained it, he could only imagine that the Council had a good reason — a really good reason.

It was the best talk and even Waldo was enjoying listening to them. He hadn't realized it was Tiffany's mom at the stoplight. He also felt terrible about what happened to Nicholas.

All he was trying to do was clean his nose, poor guy, he thought.

Waldo really liked Tiffany's mom since she was there to rescue him, after all.

They talked for a while before realizing how late it was.

Kitty's tone turned serious. "So, we'll take Waldo back?"

"Yeah," replied Tiffany. "I'm sorry I took him. He's a great bear. I want one like him."

"You have Noname bear," said Kitty, looking about the room. "Where is he? I haven't seen him for a while."

"He's here somewhere," answered Tiffany, still afraid of telling her what happened.

"Okay, so, in the morning, we'll take Waldo home."

Tiffany nodded and her mom kissed her goodnight. She went to Waldo and stroked his head. "Goodnight, Waldo. You're a good bear," her mom said softly then left the room. Tiffany got ready for bed.

Bobby Bear felt helpless sitting on the desk while his best friend was in danger. He had a plan but needed help before he could start.

James was waiting anxiously to hear from Tiffany's mom first before he did anything.

Did she take him? What if she didn't? Where would he be? Did he run away? James was torturing himself with different thoughts of Waldo. *She has him. She has to have him. I know she has him. She'd better have him. What if she doesn't?*

The only thing James could do to take his mind off worrying was to write about everything that's happened.

In the hedges, outside, under cover, Tiger was listening intently to the voices inside. Three dark figures sneaking along the wall of the house caught his attention. He could tell they were teddies, but what were they up to? Tiger would have to deal with James later. This was most curious.

Debra brought Bobbie into the office to say goodnight.

"Hey, Pumpkin. You ready for bed?" James asked.

"Yep. Are you going to come tuck me in?"

"I sure will. I'll be right there."

James managed a smile as Bobbie skipped off to her room.

"Are you all right?" asked Debra, noticing his unusual demeanor.

"Yeah — sure. I'm fine," he answered, trying to sound convincing.

"I have a busy day tomorrow so I'm going to turn in," said Debra. She gave him a quick peck on the cheek and went to bed.

"Okay, I'll be along in a while," he called out as her footsteps faded in the hall.

James turned back to Bobby Bear. "I had a nice talk with Mrs. Connors and she'll let us know if Tiffany has Waldo or not. She seems like a nice lady and I'm sure Waldo is fine," he said, not sure if he was telling the truth or not. "I'll be back in a bit. I'm going to say goodnight to Bobbie."

Bobby Bear didn't say a word; he remained lifeless as James got up to leave. There was no sense in talking. What could Bobby Bear possibly have said that would make James help rescue Waldo?

The room was quiet after James left, except the tick followed by the tock, incessantly. This annoyed Bobby Bear because it only reminded him of every minute and every second that Waldo was gone.

James walked the long hall to Bobbie's room. When he entered, he found her already in bed. "Well, look at you, all snug as a bug in a rug." The room had a feel of emptiness for some reason, and James couldn't quite figure out why. "Hmm! something's different," he said quietly, not really intending to have said it out loud.

"Like what?" asked Bobbie.

"I don't know." He glanced from side to side. "Hmm, dunno. Did you pick up your room?"

"Yeah, a little, I guess."

"It just feels odd somehow." He couldn't put his finger on it.

"Can you read to me?" she asked, snapping his attention.

"Sure I can. What would you like?"

He stepped towards the bookshelf to find a good bedtime story.

"Not one of those. I want a Bobby Bear and Waldo story," she requested. This reminded him that his stories were missing.

"Hmm — let's see here . . ." He stalled so he could think of the newest adventure he was working on.

Back in the office, Bobby Bear became aware of how much more the ticks annoyed him than the tocks. Suddenly, the clock was out of time. There was a tick, then a tock, followed by a tap. Tick — tock, tap, tap — tick — tock, tap, tap, tap.

That's odd. Out of the corner of his eye he saw a familiar face peering in the window.

"Elvis?" he whispered in surprise.

"Come on, kid — you comin'," bellowed Elvis in the teddy tone, beckoning through the pane.

Tiger stayed tucked in the hedgerow and worked his way down to the sidewalk. He stopped and watched Bobby Bear and Elvis skip across the front lawn and dash down the street. His eyes surveyed the area for cover: Car, garbage cans, hedge, car, garbage cans, hedge. This pattern of cover appeared to repeat itself through the neighborhood. His eyes instinctively searched for humans. All-clear. A white spot on the ground caught his eye. He brushed away the dried leaves, uncovering a baseball at his feet. His mind froze. A memory sparked. His past flickered for the smallest of moments. He saw David, the person that brought him to life. David loved baseball. His Louisville Slugger was always next to the bed, mostly for protection against things in the dark. A slight jingle came from behind. Before Tiger could react, a nose poked through the bushes and large teeth sank into his fur. Rufus heard the rustling leaves and sniffed out the fuzzy shadow in the shrub. Tiger went limp. He was angry with himself. This had never happened before. Tiger was the best, and there was a reason for it — no emotion. Emotion was weakness and Tiger was not weak. Allowing his past to catch up to him was a mistake, one that he will not make again.

Rufus proudly carried Tiger in his mouth to the back yard and straight to the back door where he sat quietly waiting for Kurt to let him in for the night. Tiger was trapped in his slobbery jaws.

James began telling his newest story to Bobbie, which happened to be about Waldo being kidnapped by a mean little girl and rescued by Bobby Bear.

As he told the story, Bobbie felt her eyelids getting heavy. It wasn't long before she was sound asleep. This was good because James didn't have an ending yet, but was sure he would have one soon.

He got up quietly and as he moved towards the door he figured out what it was — why the room felt different. The Big People's Chair was empty. This sent a panic through his body.

Where did he go? he wondered anxiously. He rushed down the hall to ask Bobby Bear. As he entered the office he immediately noticed the emptiness on his desk.

"What's going on here?" he said out loud. "Think — think." He thought of only one thing that would make Bobby Bear risk everything. "Waldo!"

James wanted to act, but he couldn't just run over to the Connors house asking if they've seen a rescue team of teddy bears. He would have to wait and hope to hear from Kitty.

Bobby Bear and Elvis arrived at the Connors house under the cover of darkness. They headed to a shrub at the side of the house where Tiffany's bedroom was. Bobby Bear, already nervous, saw something move up ahead in the shadows and instinctively fell down motionless. A dark figure approached and leaned over.

"Is your scaredicous acting up again?" asked a familiar voice.

Bobby Bear noticed what appeared to be a teddy face as he was lying on the ground.

"Fluffy?" he asked quietly.

"Yeah. Now get up. We can't do this with you just flopping around every time you get scared," jabbed Fluffy with a chuckle.

Bobby Bear felt a little silly lying there but was glad to see him. He got to his feet just in time to see another shadow move. Once again he went limp and fell to the ground.

"What – *are* – you – doing?" scoffed Fluffy bear.

"Is he going to be doing this all night?" asked the mysterious shadow, looking down at the lifeless bear.

"I don't know. Sir Scares-a-lot can't seem to stay on his feet," inserted Fluffy.

Bobby Bear couldn't have felt any sillier. He got up and brushed the dirt from his fur, almost too embarrassed to look, but that voice was familiar. He glanced at the dark stranger and couldn't believe what he saw. "George?" he whispered as quietly as a bear could.

George walked over and threw his arm around his shoulders.

"Yeah, kid. I thought you young guys could use a little experience," he said and squeezed tightly. "Let's go get-cher buddy."

They found Tiffany's window and Elvis called out in the teddy tone, "Waldo! — Hey, Waldo!" A surprised face appeared.

"What are you guys doing here?" he asked from behind the glass.

"We're here for you. Let us in," replied Elvis.

Waldo disappeared for a second then the window slid open. As silent as a breeze, they all climbed into Tiffany's room. He was overwhelmed when he saw who came to rescue him.

George risked breaking the Code for me? he thought. *Why?*

Bobby Bear flung himself onto his best friend. "Are you all right?" he asked worriedly.

Waldo tried to speak but was being squeezed rather tightly. "Yes — I'm fine — But —"

"But what? But what?" Bobby Bear panicked.

"But — you're squeezing too hard," Waldo eked breathlessly.

Bobby Bear didn't realize how firmly he was hugging and let go.

"I'm just glad you weren't hurt by the big Meany," confessed Bobby Bear while he glared at Tiffany sleeping.

Waldo caught his breath. "She didn't hurt me."

"Does anyone else know you're here?" asked Elvis, looking squarely at Waldo.

"Yeah. Her mom knows. She came in and saw me."

"We obviously can't take you with us tonight then — not without breaking the Code," declared Elvis.

"Well, actually —" Waldo started to say.

"We can't just leave him here," explained Fluffy. "I need to take him back *now*."

"Actually —" Waldo tried again.

"You can't expect this to go unnoticed by the humans if we take him," responded Elvis gruffly.

"I'm not leaving here without my best friend," cried Bobby Bear almost breaking the teddy tone.

"Do you want to leave now, Waldo?" Fluffy bear asked.

"Well, actually —" Waldo tried to finish saying what no one would let him say.

"This isn't up to Waldo. This is a teddy thing. This is a Code thing. *Listen*, we can help Waldo — but we stay within the Code. That's not an option —" demanded Elvis.

"Hey! Will you let the kid finish," interrupted George rather strongly. "Go on, kid. What are you trying to say?"

"Actually, they're taking me home tomorrow," Waldo finally revealed.

"How do you know?" asked Fluffy bear with doubt in his voice.

"Tiffany and her mom were talking and I heard them say that they would bring me back in the morning."

"And you believe them?" Elvis asked suspiciously.

"Yes. I do."

"Waldo? Is everything all right out there? What's going on?" came a voice from under the bed.

The room got quiet as everyone was wondering who spoke. Waldo got down on the floor and wiggled under the bed.

Bobby Bear thought something was wrong and lunged after him, grabbing his feet.

"I gotcha, Waldo. Hang on, buddy," he hollered and pulled as hard as he could.

As Bobby Bear dragged Waldo out from under the bed, he was not alone. Another teddy was holding onto his paws when they both came sliding out.

The strange bear slowly stood up and everyone saw a dusty gray teddy with no eyes.

"It's a Zombie bear!" cried Fluffy and then darted for the window. Bobby Bear almost hit the floor again.

"Guys, guys, calm down. This is Noname. He's a friend of mine," proclaimed Waldo. He glared at Fluffy, who was half way out the window. "And he's *not* a Zombie bear."

Fluffy turned back to see a quiet blind teddy standing next to Waldo. He felt foolish and dropped back into the room.

"He had an accident a while back and lost his sight," Waldo continued. "The sad part is — Tiffany stuffed him under the bed and won't tell anyone."

"That's terrible!" said Bobby Bear.

"What *else* is going on here Waldo? Are there any others?" asked Elvis while shifting his eyes back and forth.

George, who had been examining the room, lifted the lid of the toy box. "You might wanna see this," he said, staring into the box.

They all gathered around to see two teddies stuffed inside.

Waldo recognized the toy chest that George opened and said, "This is the box that she keeps Noname's eyes in. She showed me!"

Bobby Bear's lip curled at the thought and he shrieked, "Ewe! She showed you his eyes? How sick is that?" This was the worst thing he had ever heard. "We have to stop her. She's mean — really, really mean."

"Are you guys all right?" Elvis asked the two bears who were tightly squeezed together.

The two small teddies stared up at him but didn't say a word. He pulled them out and set them in the tea chairs.

"Who put you in there?" asked Elvis who already knew the answer.

One of them pointed to Tiffany sleeping. Elvis turned his head.

"I'm telling you, she's mean — really, really mean. We need to do a —"

"Hey! — Bobby Bear! Calm down and let me think," fired Elvis. "What are your names?"

"My name is Slippers," said the small black and white bear with a blue sailors kerchief wrapped around his neck. Bobby Bear chuckled. "*Actually*, my name is Skipper but Tiffany couldn't say it when she was little and kept calling me Slippers. So . . ." He gave Bobby Bear a disgusted scowl. "This is Pinky," he continued. "She doesn't talk much, and after what Tiffany did — who could blame her."

"What'd she do?" asked Elvis.

"After smarty pants, over there, stuck his tongue at her, she came home and tried to get us to do things," explained Slippers. "She tried for days. She would sit in front us and just watch us for hours. Then she started doing things to make us move."

"Like what?" Elvis asked.

"You know — I'm not real comfortable talking about it. Let's just say, that when neither one of us talked, she shoved us in the box," Slippers replied coldly.

"Mean! I said she's mean — mean and rotten. She's a big —"

"Bobby Bear! *We get it*," bellowed Fluffy. "So, what do you want to do?" he asked Elvis.

"It looks like there's only one thing to do," Elvis said as he walked over and watched Tiffany sleep.

In a few moments, the plan was set. A nightmare was about to begin.

The other bears took their spots about the room, hidden from sight. Tiffany was in a deep sleep. It had been decided that Slippers would be the contact bear because he knew her the best. Keeping the subject calm was imperative. They would try to do this while she slept. Create the dream — send the message — wait for the question.

Slippers climbed up next to Tiffany and sat near her head on the pillow. In a soft and extremely subtle tone, he began. "Let's go play."

A questioned look appeared on her sleeping face. With her lids closed, her dreaming eyes moved from side to side, searching for who spoke.

"Do you want to play?" asked Slippers.

Tiffany gently nodded. "Where are you?" her slightly parted lips whispered. A dream was forming in Tiffany's mind as Slippers continued.

"I'm over here next to Waldo. Can you see me?"

Her head barely moved up and down. "Who are you?"

"It's me, Slippers."

The slightest of smiles moved her mouth as she nodded again.

"Do you remember the game we played where you tried to make us talk?" he asked.

Tiffany's brow wrinkled. "That wasn't a game," her breathy voice recalled.

"No — it wasn't. You hurt us. Did you know you hurt us?"

Once again, her head nodded slightly. "Yes," she whispered sadly.

"Why did you want to do that?" asked Slippers. His voice was showing his personal agitation as it became less soft and less subtle.

"Because, I saw Waldo stick out his tongue. I needed to know if it was real. I needed to know that I wasn't crazy," she quietly confessed. Her feet began to fidget. Elvis tried to signal Slippers but he wasn't paying attention.

Elvis spoke in the teddy tone. "Keep it calm. Slow it down. We could lose her."

Slippers heard Elvis but was caught up in the power of the moment. He was upset at Tiffany for the bad things she had done. Being this vulnerable was too tempting to Slippers. "You've treated your own bears very badly. You hurt us and *we don't like you.*"

No one could believe what Slippers just said. He was going too far, too fast. Her legs moved, making Slippers jolt. He realized his mistake and gave a look to Elvis that said so. If she wakes up, in this state, they are all in trouble.

Her face saddened and her voice grew stronger. "You don't like me? I'm sorry."

Slippers calmed down and tried again. "We don't like what you do to us. What you did to Noname."

Her questioned face reappeared. "But that was an accident. I didn't mean to do it. What can I do?"

"Ah — that's the question," replied Slippers, feeling a sense of relief. Seduced by the control of the Nightmare over a human, he was ashamed of himself for jeopardizing the safety of others for his own personal anguish.

There are several purposes of a Teddy Nightmare, and hearing this question was one of them. Slippers took a breath and continued calmly, "Right the wrongs. Take Waldo back to his family. Stop doing horrible things to make us talk, and tell your mother about Noname. Be a good girl. Be a *good* girl."

A solemn look grew on Tiffany's face and her head nodded. "I will. I'll tell my mom. I *am* a good girl. I'll take Waldo home." Tiffany's voice was getting stronger. "I'll tell mom." Her arms flinched pushing Slippers to the floor. Tiffany's eyes opened unexpectedly. She was awake. Everyone froze in their spot. Slippers was the only one out in the open. She blinked and rubbed her tired eyes. Her mind was going over what she just dreamed. "Noname," she said and threw her blankets off. She slipped out of bed and dropped to the floor. Her hand reached for the bear with no eyes. "I'm sorry, Noname. Can you forgive me?" she asked, pulling him close. She then noticed Slippers on the floor. Uncertainty filled her mind. "Uh — how'd you get out of the box?" She spoke out loud. Slippers remained still. "Something's not right." Tiffany began to look about her room. This was disastrous. She can't find strange bears in her house. It would be bad for everyone. If she finds Bobbie's teddy bears in her house — then she has the proof she needed. However, if her mother found someone else's teddy bears in her room then it would be trouble for Tiffany. She would appear as a thief. The bears would be the cause of Tiffany getting in trouble — that can't happen. Sure, she may have taken Waldo but she didn't take Fluffy, George, Elvis and Bobby Bear. There would be too many unanswered questions.

Tiffany was headed towards Elvis' hiding place. Panic flared. He was about to be caught. Suddenly, thoughts appeared in Tiffany's head. *What am I doing? I don't even know what I'm looking for. I'm too tired. Go lay down. Just go to bed. Go back to sleep.*

While Tiffany's thoughts were talking to her, Elvis could see George, from where he was hiding, and noticed his mouth moving. No words were coming out. He wasn't talking in the teddy tone; Elvis would have heard it. *Who was George talking to?* he wondered. His eyes were fixed on Tiffany. She stopped in her tracks. Elvis waited.

With Noname still in her arms, she turned and gazed at her soft mattress. Her fluffy pillow was enticing. She shuffled her feet as she returned to bed. Lying down, she pulled the covers up, batted her eyes a few times before they closed. Soon the sound of sleep filled the room and the other bears came out from hiding.

Elvis quietly approached George. "What were you doing back there? You did something. I've never seen anything like that. Were you actually talking to her?"

"Tell ya' what — if we get out of here in one piece — I'll tell you," George replied.

Noname was quite comfortable in Tiffany's arms. He didn't mind at all.

The bears gathered around Waldo as he sat in the tea chair.

"That was great," said Bobby Bear.

"Guys, we really need to get going," George said, knowing how dangerous this moment was.

Elvis knew George was right and felt the urgency to leave. "Okay, Waldo, we'll see you in the morning, right?" He started for the window.

Fluffy tapped Waldo on the shoulder. "You're a good bear," he said sincerely, "and I'm sorry I'm the one."

Waldo looked at him with the kindest face. "I'm not."

They smiled at each other and said their goodbyes. Bobby Bear had a hard time letting go of his best friend.

"I'll be home tomorrow," squeaked Waldo.

Bobby Bear slowly loosened his grip and backed up to the window, never taking his eyes off him.

"Come on. Let's go!" cried Fluffy.

He stood in the window and took one last look at Waldo. "So . . . in the morning, right?"

"Right," answered Waldo, smiling the sweetest smile.

Bobby Bear turned to jump.

"Hey!" Waldo whispered sharply.

"What?"

Waldo wanted to say so much right then but couldn't. The lump in his throat made it impossible. Besides, this probably wasn't the time. "— Thanks."

Bobby Bear grinned. "You'd have done it for me. I know you would've." He turned and jumped out the window.

Loyalty, friend and family had come to his rescue. Waldo realized what being a teddy was all about as he watched his friends slip into the night. He didn't know what was ahead of him but he did know that he was ready for it.

IT'S TIME TO GO

James couldn't sleep. He kept wondering if Kitty had found Waldo. "I gotta do something. I can't just sit here," he mumbled. "Maybe something to eat." He headed for the kitchen to make a peanut butter and jelly sandwich with a cold glass of milk. Watching the milk pour from the carton made him think of only one thing. "Dang it! That darn bear — he'd better be in trouble, 'cause if he's not, he's gonna be."

James was missing Waldo too much and had a hard time seeing a glass of milk without picturing Waldo with a white foamy mustache.

He finished making his snack and decided to have it in the office. Picking up his sandwich plate and glass of milk, he turned and saw a small figure standing in the kitchen doorway. Startled as he was, he dropped his sandwich and spilled the milk.

Debra rushed out from the bedroom to see what happened. She stopped at the doorway and noticed the mess on the floor. "What happened?"

James could tell she was annoyed. A tickle at her feet caught her attention when she saw Bobby Bear lying flat on his back staring up at her. "And why is there a bear on the floor?"

The truth automatically came out without thinking. "He startled me and I dropped the . . ." James quickly realized that wasn't going to sound good at all — not now at least. She wasn't in the mood.

"Bobby Bear startled you?" she said in a voice that may have sounded friendly but James knew better. As Debra continued, the lighthearted tone evaporated from her voice. "That's what you're telling me; a teddy bear scared you — frightened you so much that you dropped everything?" She glared in silence, either waiting for him to answer or trying to think of what else to add. James stood still not knowing what he could possibly say. "That must have been one scary bear," she said, laced with sarcasm. Her face softened as she remembered the gossip. "What has gotten into you lately? There are all kinds of rumors going around."

"What do you mean, rumors?"

"Mrs. Mallory has seen you talking to those bears."

"Oh, jeeze. Mrs. Mallory is just a —"

"James, no. I've seen you talking to them." She was deeply concerned. "I want to know . . . is it true?"

Something had to be said. But what? How in the world could James possibly explain the unexplainable if he couldn't show her?

"You want to know if I believe my own stories?" Frustrated, James decided to try the only thing he could think of. He picked up the lifeless teddy from the floor.

"Hey, Bobby Bear, I need you to do something right now. You have to tell Debra that you're alive."

James was serious. However, Bobby Bear didn't know that. It wouldn't have mattered anyway. He wasn't going to move. "Come on, buddy, say something." There was nothing.

She watched as James stared intently at Bobby Bear. The awkward tension was building. Unexpectedly, "Hi, Debra," came a squeaky voice as James tried to keep his lips from moving.

It was as if he wasn't taking any of this seriously. "If you don't want to tell me — then fine. Don't tell me. You might think it's funny that people think you're crazy — but I don't." Vexation fumed out of Debra. "I'm going back to bed. I hope you're going to clean up that mess — or maybe Bobby Bear should help since it's his fault."

She marched off to the bedroom and closed the door.

It bothered James that he couldn't tell his own wife about the bears, but he was fairly certain that Bobby Bear wasn't going to expose himself like that. He was acting out of desperation. It was foolish, but it was the only thing he could think of at that moment.

The stories are just stories, as far as people are concerned, but if James were to prove to Debra that it's real — then what? Show Bobbie? Maybe all of her friends? Where would it end? It wouldn't end. James knew that.

He placed the lifeless teddy on the floor next to him and began picking up the mess when he noticed someone peeking around the doorway.

"Ep," he flinched. "Hey, Pumpkin. What are you doing out of bed?" He saw her looking at the mess on the floor. "Oh, right — the noise," he said, answering his own question and went back to cleaning up. "It's all right now. Go back to bed."

She stared innocently and spoke in a soft voice, "Did Bobby Bear really scare you?"

He stopped and realized that she was the only one he could confide in. She believed without seeing, from nothing more than his word. James decided to tell her what's been going on with the bears. He told her everything about the Council and that Bobby Bear and Waldo were to leave soon. She was surprisingly understanding.

Bobby put it in her own childlike way. "So, because they broke the rules — they're being sent to the naughty chair for teddies?"

James chuckled. "Something like that, I suppose. I don't really know what's going to happen to them. We just hope they'll be allowed back," he said hopefully. "You do know how special those bears are, don't you?"

"Daddy, all bears are special," she said as a matter of fact. She leaned over and scooped Bobby Bear off the floor. "Did you find Waldo? I couldn't find him anywhere."

"No. Not yet," answered James. "But I'm sure he'll be back soon."

"Did he run away?"

"*No!*" he snapped. "He would never do that. He's not afraid of anything. Even the Council. He'll be back." James didn't want to admit he had the same thought.

The bright glow from the stove's digital clock caught James' eye. "Hey, Pumpkin, you'd better get back to bed. Bobby Bear and I'll come tuck you in."

He followed her to the bedroom and promptly noticed Elvis sitting back where he belonged. James wanted to say something, but why mention it if she hadn't noticed he was missing.

Elvis and Bobby Bear returning could only mean one thing: that Waldo was probably waiting in the office, sitting in his usual spot.

Bobbie crawled into bed, holding her bear, waiting for her daddy to pull up the covers. He grabbed the top of the blankets and pulled slowly, making a motor sound. Bobbie smiled as the sheets crept up her body. James began to sputter as if the motor was giving out.

"Uh-oh," said James. Bobbie's eyes grew big and her smile even bigger.

"What's happening?" she could hardly say without giggling.

"The Tuck-o-matic 2000 is breaking down." James panicked. "If the covers aren't in place then the Boogie Bears can get in — and it'll be curtains, *curtains I tell ya'*."

"The 2000? Daddy! The 2000 always breaks down, everyone knows that. Why didn't you spend more on the 3000? Aren't I worth it? Don't you love me? Are you trying to kill me, Daddy? What if we can't fix it? How will I get to sleep?"

James sputtered a few more times, each time inching the covers closer and closer, until finally slipping the top of the sheets under her chin.

"Whoa — that was close." James tucked the blankets tightly around her while giving a look of inspection. "I'll call the repair company tomorrow and get someone right on this. I got this thing on sale. I should know better than to try and save a few bucks when people's lives are at stake. We can't have Boogie Bears nibbling on your neck while you sleep. You might just wake up dea —"

"DON'T SAY IT, DADDY!" She was fighting the smile that wanted to burst out.

Two heads were sticking out from under the blankets. Bobby Bear liked being snuggled in bed, especially if there was danger afoot. He was fairly certain that James was joking around, but this was the third time he'd heard about the dreaded Boogie Bears. Apparently, being under the covers was the only place you're safe at night. Just to play it safe, he'd better stay here with Bobbie tonight, although he did miss Waldo.

"Goodnight, Pumpkin."

"Goodnight, Daddy."

Before he could turn the light out, Bobbie pulled her bear out from under the blankets and handed him to James. "Here, Daddy."

"Don't you want to sleep with Bobby Bear tonight?"

"No. I think he would rather be with Waldo."

Bobby Bear thought it was weird how she could tell what he was thinking. He *would* rather be with Waldo, but he wasn't there. Morning couldn't come fast enough.

Down the street, Tiffany sat up in bed. "Mommy?" she cried out. "MOMMY!"

The bedroom door flew open and Kitty flipped on the light. "What's wrong?" Tiffany was sitting up in bed with a sad and frightened face. "Do you feel sick?"

"No," answered Tiffany. "I had a bad dream." She then began frantically searching the bed.

"What are you looking for?"

"Noname, he was right here. I put him right here next to me." The grief stricken little girl lifted the covers then looked over the edge to the floor. Tiffany finally got up and reached under the bed.

CHAPTER ELEVEN

"Honey, what are you doing?"

She pulled out Noname and handed him to her mom.

"Oh, you found him," said Kitty. It was hard not to notice his face. "Sweetie, what happened to his eyes?"

Tiffany began to get upset. "I don't know how it happened. I was hugging him and the next thing I know . . ." She tried to explain, but she couldn't. She didn't understand just how it happened herself. Tears were streaming down her cheeks.

"I think we can fix him. It's not that bad." The reassuring words came as a surprise.

Tiffany was glad to hear that her mom wasn't angry, but she couldn't stop crying.

"It's not that bad. There's no need to be upset. Why don't you climb back into bed and I can read to you."

A sense of urgency consumed Tiffany. "I need to do something and I need to do it now."

"Okay, what is it?"

"We need to take Waldo back."

"We will in the morning."

"No. I need to take him back now!" demanded Tiffany. "Please, can we take him back now?"

"Honey, it's late. We'll take him back first thing tomorrow."

She turned and ran to Waldo, picked him up and headed for the door.

"Tiffany, where do you think you're going?"

She didn't answer. Tiffany walked directly to the front door with Waldo tight to her chest and her mom close behind.

"It's that important to you?"

Tiffany just looked at her as the tears continued.

263

"Okay, let me put my shoes on and we'll go see if they're up."

After tucking Bobbie in, James carried Bobby Bear back towards the office when he noticed movement through the glass at the front door. He threw the porch light switch and heard a little girl's voice. "They are awake. I knew they'd be up."

James opened the door to see Tiffany and her mom standing in their pajamas. "I know it's late but she just had to do this tonight. I hope this isn't a bother," said Kitty, noticing James holding the same brown teddy bear she saw that day at the traffic light.

"No, no. Actually, I'm glad you're here," he said most relieved.

"I don't really know where to begin," said Kitty. "The first thing is to say — we're very sorry; right sweetie?"

Tiffany nodded and slowly held out Waldo. James saw the tears in her eyes as he took Waldo from her, placing him next to Bobby Bear in his arms. It was hard for Bobby Bear to remain still. He wanted to hug his best friend and the urge was almost too strong.

"She had a bad dream and wouldn't go back to bed until she returned him," said Kitty. "We had a long talk, which was really good, because I told her things that I hadn't told anyone before. And she told me why she took Waldo. After the incident at school, she knew that no one would believe her, so —"

James quickly interjected. "And she thought Waldo would have the answers."

"Yes. You must have a hard time keeping all this to yourself. Well — except for your family."

"My wife isn't really a . . . um, she doesn't actually —" James found it difficult to explain why he never told Debra.

Kitty was feeling slightly embarrassed for James. "I'm sorry. I just assumed."

"Most people don't believe me," he explained. "And I'm not going to prove it, so, I just tell the stories and — people believe what they want to believe."

Kitty was curious about one thing. "Do you think there are others that know?"

"I'm sure there are."

Tiffany stood quietly, staring at Waldo while he remained motionless in James' arms. Something happened that night and they both understood without a word being said.

"Well, it's late and we're very sorry for all of this, but I have to say, I'm glad it happened. It was good for both of us," confessed Kitty and reached to stroke her daughter's hair. "Please tell Bobbie that Tiffany didn't mean to —"

"Oh, I haven't mentioned it to her," he said quickly. "I thought it would only complicate things."

Tiffany broke her stare with Waldo to look at James as he continued, "I'm just glad it helped — and I'm sure Waldo had quite the adventure. I hope I'll be seeing you soon — and thanks for bringing him back." He looked straight at Tiffany.

"Goodnight," said Kitty. They turned and headed down the walkway. Tiffany never took her eyes off Waldo as they left.

James watched them step from one street light to the next until they got to their front yard. He went inside and turned out the porch lights.

There was only one thing left to do to make things right: place the bears back in their spot. Going to his office, he set the bears on the desk, plopped down in his chair, took a deep breath and said, "Now that's where you're supposed to be."

Bobby Bear gazed at Waldo for a moment then lunged, wrapping his arms around him. "I thought she was bringing you back tomorrow. What happened?"

Waldo tried to sound tough but it was harder than he thought.

"The Teddy Nightmare worked. She woke up and insisted on taking me home tonight," explained Waldo, trying to hide the shaky in his voice.

"Hey, Waldo, did you know that was Tiffany's mom in the car next to us by the fun park?" James asked.

"No. I really didn't. Weird, huh?" he replied with a crooked smile and a tense laugh.

James leaned back in his chair and watched as Bobby Bear and Waldo talked about their adventure. He found himself suddenly feeling odd about the night's events. "Listen, we'll talk about all of this tomorrow. It's late and I'm simply exhausted. It's good to have you home, Waldo. This is *really* strange for me — teddy rescue teams, teddy nightmares and all." He rubbed their heads then he rubbed his own. "It might seem like a long one, but it sure still feels like a dream. Goodnight, guys." He turned out the lights and left the room.

Bobby Bear had so many questions but they would have to wait until morning because he noticed Waldo's eyes were heavy. He seemed to be falling asleep.

"It's good to have you home," whispered Bobby Bear. Waldo slowly leaned over and rested his head on his friend and replied, "Yeah, it's good . . ." and drifted off.

Bobby Bear wasn't tired; he just sat there feeling as happy as he'd ever been.

A few moments later, there was movement in the doorway of the office. *What was that?* wondered Bobby Bear. He glanced down at Waldo who was sound asleep on his shoulder. Suddenly, a dark shadowy figure climbed up onto the desk. His question was answered.

"Hey — you guys ready?" asked Big Red Fluffy bear, who was now standing in front of them.

Bobby Bear was reluctant to move as nervousness washed over his body. The time had come. Fluffy would be taking them to the Council and he didn't want to go. "Waldo," he said quietly and began tapping his friend's arm.

"Is he asleep?" asked Fluffy bear.

"Waldo, you gotta wake up," Bobby Bear said a little louder, poking his arm harder.

Waldo's eyes came to life and saw Fluffy bear standing in front of him.

"Hey, Fluffy, thanks for everything," Waldo yawned and tried to wipe the sleepy away. "You guys did a great job."

Fluffy wasn't there to chat. "Anytime. Now, come on. It's time to go," he said quickly and stepped towards the window.

Waldo was suddenly wide awake. "Now? You mean, *right now?*"

"Yes, right now. Come on," Fluffy insisted. "Look — you disappeared once already and I can't have you missing again. I'm supposed to have you at the Council *now.*"

Bobby Bear and Waldo looked around the room slowly for the last time. Their eyes landed on each other. They stood up knowing the moment they feared had finally arrived and were as scared as they had ever been, but an unfinished task popped into Waldo's head.

"I forgot something," blurted Waldo. "I'll be right back." Waldo hopped off the desk and disappeared in a flash.

"Hey! Now where's he going?" chimed Fluffy.

"He said he'd be right back," Bobby Bear resounded.

Waldo needed to see the family Network bear, so he ran to Bobbie's room and approached the Big People's Chair.

"Hey, Elvis, can I ask a favor?"

Waldo explained an errand he felt needed to be done and Elvis agreed to help. Waldo wanted to thank him for so many things but didn't know where to start. Elvis sensed what Waldo was trying to say without actually saying anything. They merely smiled at each other and said their goodbyes. Next, he went to the playroom to find the drawing he had started. After looking all over, he couldn't find it anywhere. He thought that maybe someone found it and figured Bobby Bear might know something, so he ran back to the office.

Fluffy bear saw Waldo run into the room and said, "Good, you're back. Let's get going."

His earnestness was obvious when Waldo asked breathlessly, "Hey, did you happen to see a piece of paper in the playroom?"

Bobby Bear pulled out the paper from behind him. "You mean, like this?" He held up the drawing with a smile.

"*Yes!*" chirped Waldo.

Bobby Bear crawled to the edge of the desk and leaned over, holding out the paper. Waldo reached up, snatched it from his paw and darted back down the hall.

Fluffy saw Waldo take off again.

"Hey! *Get back here*," he barked and started after him. Before Fluffy got two steps, a paw grabbed his arm stopping him in his tracks.

"Let him go," ordered Bobby Bear with a bit of a scowl on his brow. "He's got to do whatever it is he's got to do. He'll be back."

An intent glare on Bobby Bear's face was one that Fluffy had never seen before. This was a different face, not the same mild-mannered look he normally wore.

"*Yeah* — How do you know he's not running away?" accused Fluffy bear.

"Because he's not scared of anything — and he's not scared of the Council," he said proudly of his best friend.

"Well — he should be," Fluffy cracked angrily with a snort.

Next door, Rufus was tired of waiting and began to whimper at the backdoor. He couldn't bark with Tiger in his mouth, so he scratched a few times. That got Kurt's attention. The door flung open and Kurt hollered, "What have I told you about scratching?"

Rufus stepped into the doorway. The stuffed bear in his mouth was obvious. "Whoa! Where in the hell did you get this dirty old thing? You're not comin' in here with that." Kurt ripped it out of his mouth to inspect it. "Where'd you get this?" Kurt could only think of one place that Rufus would get a teddy bear. "Have you been out of the yard?" Rufus cowered at his harsh words. Tiger was familiar with those angry tones. He hated bad men, and Kurt was striking a nerve. "If you've been over there so help me I'll . . ." Kurt noticed the small black eyes begin to glow red from the dirty black bear. "What the . . . " Nervously, he flung it over the hedge towards James' house. Tiger flew through the air and fell in the back yard. He no sooner landed when he sprang to his feet and leapt into the bushes.

Kurt slammed the door and locked it. He stood motionless for a moment trying to figure out what he saw. Finally, he gave a half-hearted laugh as he convinced himself it had to be a battery operated bear with electric eyes. Satisfied with his conclusion he turned back to Rufus. "Now, get in here and go lie down!"

Tiger needed to regroup. He was still upset with himself, but he had to focus on the task at hand. What was going on inside the house? Where did those other teddies go? He hoped he hadn't blown the mission. One good thing; James didn't have his stories. The last thing Tiger heard was Waldo had stolen them. All he needed to do now was stop Bobby Bear and Waldo from getting to the Council as Ballinger ordered. But where were they?

Waldo ran back to the playroom to finish the drawing. He didn't have a lot of time. With a couple strokes here, and some touches there, he stopped and gazed at it. The scene was everything he'd always wanted. It wasn't much, just a picture, but to Waldo it was family. It was all that mattered. He drew a picture of happiness, but he couldn't see it until happiness was gone. The more he stared at the picture the more he didn't want to leave. He even thought about running, but he knew that wouldn't fix anything. This was *his* problem and it wasn't going away. Waldo needed James to have something to remember them by in case they never returned. It was, after all, *his* family. — Waldo was ready.

Pushing the door open, to the big bedroom, he walked around to James' side of the bed and climbed up next to him. He watched him sleep, remembering all the fun they've had — then, carefully, he placed the picture next to his head on the pillow. He started to climb down when a voice came from the corner.

"Leaving, kid?" said George, sitting in his nighttime chair.

Sadly, Waldo walked over. "Yeah. I guess I gotta go."

"Hey, it's going to be all right. Just listen to what they tell you. Do what they say — it'll be fine," said George.

"How do you know? How do you know it's going to be fine?"

George looked carefully into his eyes. "I've been there. Trust me. It'll be fine."

Waldo was sure he didn't hear him correctly. "You? What? Wait! But . . . what do you mean?"

"Let's save that for another time," said George. "You're a good kid and they know that. The Council has the oldest and wisest bears and they know what they're doing. It's going to be fine. I'll see you later, kid."

"Really — you will?" asked Waldo, not knowing exactly what he meant but he liked the way it sounded.

George nodded. "Now get going — and remember; you're a good bear."

He never realized how he felt about George until now. He suddenly felt fine with everything. "Thanks, George. I really hope I see you again."

Waldo took one last look at James sleeping then headed back to the office. As Waldo passed Bobbie's bedroom he stopped in the doorway and noticed Bobby Bear standing next to the bed watching her sleep. He walked up to him and stood quietly as they both gazed at their favorite person, the one that brought them to life.

"Are we going to see her again?" Bobby Bear asked hopefully.

"I don't know."

Waldo felt that Fluffy wasn't going to wait much longer.

"Come on, buddy. It's time," he said and threw his arm around Bobby Bear.

The two heavy-hearted teddies entered the office side by side as Fluffy snapped alertly.

"Finally! Can we go now?" he grumbled.

With a somber face, Waldo answered, "Sure — I guess."

Bobby Bear was not in the mood to talk and Fluffy could feel the tension.

"I know it's hard." Fluffy was sympathetic. "And believe me, I didn't want to do this — but I sorta have to."

Bobby Bear and Waldo didn't say anything, they know the power of the Council and didn't blame their friend. They silently headed to the window. Just then, Elvis appeared in the doorway. Since he's the Network bear, he sees after anyone leaving the house.

"It won't be the same around here without you," said Elvis. "I'm going to miss you guys. I hope everything works out."

"Thanks," said Waldo despondently. Remembering his request, he added, "and good luck."

The bears jumped out the window, landed in the yard, and looked up to see Elvis close it behind them. Bobby Bear put his paw in the air to wave goodbye. Elvis returned the gesture.

"Hey, Waldo, why'd you say good luck to Elvis?" asked Bobby Bear.

"I just asked him to do a favor?"

"You asked Elvis to do you a favor — for what?"

"Just something that needs to be done."

"Okay, guys — this is it," said Fluffy seriously. "Stay close 'cause we've got a long way to go. Keep your eyes sharp and no talking."

The night was as dark as Waldo had ever seen before and suddenly nothing seemed familiar. This was not an adventure that Bobbie created. This was no daydream to wake up from. This was real life, and the unknown was waiting for them.

Tucked into the hedges was Tiger and he couldn't believe his luck. The bears he was looking for just ran through the front yard. He was back on target.

THE SCRUFFY MAN

It was late and the house had been quiet for hours when Elvis heard his name.

"Elvis, you there?" called a voice from outside.

He peeked out the window and saw Dakota standing in the yard. "Yeah — what's going on?"

"Open up. We need to talk."

Elvis let him in and they went to the closet to speak privately.

"Where's Fluffy bear?" asked Dakota.

"He left with Waldo and Bobby Bear a while ago," replied Elvis.

"They've left? Oh, that's not good. They're not supposed to leave!" Dakota said in a panic.

"What do you mean; they're not supposed to leave? The Council is waiting for them," insisted Elvis.

"No. That's why I'm here. The Council has learned something that's more important than punishing two young bears . . . The stories."

"The stories? The stories James is writing? What about 'em?"

"They're making a difference to teddies."

"A difference? — How?"

"You know that there haven't been a lot of newborns in recent years and how more and more teddies are being put away?" said Dakota.

"Everyone knows that."

"Yeah, well, this area has jumped in newborns, and elders are back in the open," he said excitedly.

"What are you getting at?"

"His stories — people love 'em — and they're looking at teddies like they used to. He's making people believe again. Don't you see? It's happening right around the school where he's been reading," explained Dakota. "The book at the bookstore is selling. This came from number one, the highest."

"Theodore? You mean Theodore, right? He's the one that's saying it's okay? And this is a Council decision?"

"No. Not exactly. There are some members that don't agree with him."

"So — now what?"

"He not only wants James to keep writing, but he wants Bobby Bear and Waldo to stay, since he's writing about them. He's hoping the stories take off around the country."

"So, now it's okay to let everyone know about our world?" Elvis asked with uncertainty.

"No, of course not — but sometimes telling the truth is more unbelievable. Most people just think these are stories."

"And for the other people?" asked Elvis, still confused.

"They've probably believed all along. And have they said anything? No — Listen, if one person can make a difference in the world then we need to allow it. You remember the other one, don't you?"

"You're not comparing James to him are you?" Elvis scoffed at the implication.

"No," replied Dakota, "of course not — but for now — it's a start."

"So what about Bobby Bear and Waldo? You're telling me that they can do anything they want and forget the Code?" asked Elvis, still not sure he understood.

"No! Here's the thing: they can stay as long as James is the only one that knows. If you find out that they're breaking the Code in view of any other human — you let me know," answered Dakota. Feeling a sense of urgency he continued, "I'm supposed to report that everything is back to normal, but I can't do that when they're missing. I'll put the word out. We'll find 'em. We'll bring 'em home."

Dakota started for the window.

"Wait!" Elvis called out. "I'll go find them if you can do me a favor."

After Elvis explained the details of his request, Dakota thought it would be a good challenge and agreed to help. With no time to waste, and a long journey ahead, they said goodbye and both set off into the night.

Following the route out of the neighborhood and into the city, Bobby Bear and Waldo walked with their heads tilted up at the tall buildings reaching down from the dark sky. Even though Fluffy bear had done this once before, he wasn't used to the sounds in the city. They were different from those of the neighborhood. Danger seemed to be everywhere. Distant hazards bounced off buildings like echoes in a canyon.

Shadows hid some of the most deadly of creatures. It wasn't just human threats such as cars and coyotes and cats and dogs that brought fear to a bear, there were also teddy world creatures that kept their ears pinned.

Zombie bears were as unpredictable as you could get. Rips and stains and missing limbs were the curse of these neglected and abandoned bears. They would do anything to be normal again, to be loved again, and if that something was to take an eye or a nose or even stuffing from a Normal . . . then so be it. However, the most feared yet never talked about creature was the cursed Were-bear. Legend has painted this heartless teddy as a killer. Known to attack humans, these bears are everything wicked in the teddy world. The shadows are the perfect hiding place for any of these nightmarish teddies. Loud noises and people yelling were common outside, just not at James' house. The city was truly a terrifying place for an Insider.

They walked along the dark edge of street lights on the sidewalk until Fluffy stopped just outside an even darker alley. Confusion and uncertainty entered Fluffy's mind as he noticed the mark of the STS etched into a building, about twelve inches off the ground. A three-quarter round crescent with the shape of an ear on the top left was the insignia. Placed just inside the alley, it indicated a safe passageway for teddies. He hadn't noticed it before when he came through. If they used this path, it would save twenty minutes off their travel. Fluffy was leery as he squinted his eyes into the dark but he knew the sooner they got to Brockton Station the better. They entered the alley.

Slowly, Bobby Bear and Waldo found their self-pity and sadness was replaced by fear. Waldo loved a good adventure but this was more than he was ready for. He would never admit to being scared but his chatter gave him away.

"Hey, Bobby Bear, do you think we'll get to meet him? I hope he's nice," Waldo said quietly, his eyes darted from side to side. "We've been walking a long way. How far do you think we've gone? I wonder what time it is. It feels late. Midnight! I'll bet it's midnight. What do you think? Do you think it's that late? I hope we get there soon. It's creepy out here. Hey, I know, let's play a game. You wanna play a game? Let's play I-spy. You wanna play? Okay. I'll go first. I spy with my little eye something creepy, something very creepy."

Bobby Bear wasn't really listening but it was comforting to hear a friendly voice in the dark. Waldo kept prattling on while Fluffy grew increasingly annoyed, in part because he'd reached a point where he started to second guess his decision about entering the alley. He began to feel that saving a few minutes just didn't seem worth it.

"Uh, Fluffy? Where are we?" asked Waldo, still babbling on tensely.

Fluffy didn't know exactly where they were, but he was fairly sure they were still on the route — or so he thought.

"We're on the path," he said sharply, even though doubt had now entered his mind.

"What path?" Waldo asked with his head turning every which way.

"To the station," he answered, knowing full well what Waldo would ask next.

"What station?"

Fluffy bear spun around to snap at him but Waldo was busy gazing up at the buildings. Waldo stepped into Fluffy, which made him fall backwards into Bobby Bear and they both fell down. Fluffy glared at them lying on the ground.

"Guys, I know this is all new for you but let's keep quiet and keep moving. This is a dangerous area," rumbled Fluffy, then suddenly flinched as he heard a noise behind him in the alley. The bears froze as Fluffy stared into the dark. After a moment he slowly turned back to his friends on the ground. "Now, back on your feet and keep a sharp eye," he cautioned seriously.

Bobby Bear and Waldo saw a tall dark shadow growing larger as it approached. They both went limp as Fluffy thought they were kidding around. Unaware of the presence behind him, Fluffy was swept off his feet. Life quickly left his body.

"What do we have here?" said the tall shadow, holding Fluffy bear with both hands.

Bobby Bear and Waldo could only watch helplessly as they saw Fluffy snatched by the tall dark figure.

"You look like a teddy bear." The shadow stepped towards Bobby Bear and Waldo. "Ah, you've got friends, I see. It's good to have friends." He spoke in a gritty voice as he bent over to pick up the teddies off the ground. Holding all three bears side by side, the shadow man walked deeper into the alley where they came to what looked like a big, light brown, cardboard box with a large blue arrow and the words 'This End Up' on the side. The word 'This' was covered with tape leaving the poignant phrase, 'End Up'. A self-described message from the alley bum. The large box was placed against a brick wall with a dim lamp overhead, giving a soft welcoming glow. He pulled open a flap and climbed inside. "It's not much — but it's home," he welcomed the bears and positioned them along an empty side of his cardboard house. He reached over to a small wooden crate and pulled out a bottle. "Do you boys drink?" he asked politely and held out the bottle as if he were waiting for an answer. "It'll grow hair on your chest," he chuckled. "Hair on your chest . . . that's funny because . . . you know . . . you've got . . . hair." The bears remained lifeless. "No? Well, if you change your mind just let me know." He tipped the bottle to his lips and took several swallows then wiped his mouth with his sleeve. "So, where'd you boys come from?" he asked, then paused a moment and stared into the alley as if he were expecting someone. Snapping his attention back to the bears he continued, "I came here by way of Frisco, myself. I know what you're thinking. 'How does a well-educated, handsome guy like yourself end up living in a box in an alley?' That's a good question. I moved here several years ago and got into the repair business. Things were going great. I worked for a good company, had my own truck, even had dental, until one day — Boom! I lost my job and my house, just like that." He tipped the bottle again. "Well, since I was suddenly unemployed and wasn't doing anything, I figured it was a good time to just get out of town for a while. You know, see this wonderful country of ours. I had no money, so I found a cheap way to do it." The shadow man answered a question that no one asked. "No. Well, at first, yeah, I was scared — a little, but after you've jumped your first train — you're hooked. I meet interesting people and travel all over with not a care in the world." He stopped long enough to take another sip. "You sure you boys aren't thirsty?" He held out the bottle again. "There's no need to be frightened." He leaned in closer. "You see — I know all about you bears." He tilted his head towards Fluffy bear. "And you look awfully familiar," he whispered suspiciously. The warm breath of every inebriated word hit Fluffy in the face. The toxic fumes tickled his fur. As quick as a mood can change, he sat up straight and said, "It sure is nice to have company — and you boys are easy to talk to. People just don't listen anymore. Me, me, me, that's all people think about is themselves." He leaned back to make himself comfortable and his words came out a bit slower. "Yep . . . this is the life. Nobody to worry 'bout . . . I used to have somebody to worry 'bout . . . but not . . . any . . . more . . ." he yawned. The large box got quiet as the stranger began deep breathing. Teddies learn this sound early in life.

Fluffy looked at Bobby Bear, gave him a nudge, then swung his head toward the opening.

Bobby Bear didn't understand. Fluffy did it again. The clueless bear shrugged his shoulders not knowing what he was trying to say.

"Let's go," whispered Fluffy, feeling frustrated.

Bobby Bear glanced quickly at the shadowy figure sleeping, then turned back to Fluffy and shook his head fearfully.

"Yes, *come on*," insisted Fluffy urgently, inching toward the opening. "*Come on.*"

The figure wiggled and snorted, freezing Fluffy in his spot. He waited for the breathing.

"Buh, huh . . ." the breathing continued slow and steady. Fluffy inched again.

"*Come on, guys*," he whispered harshly. Sliding his bottom along the ground, Fluffy never took his eyes from the sleeping shadow. Bobby Bear looked at Waldo as they both felt too scared to move. Fluffy got even closer to the opening. "*Are you guys coming?*" he said as loud as he could in the teddy tone. Bobby Bear and Waldo reluctantly started to wiggle their way towards the opening. Fluffy got to the doorway and lunged into the alley, hitting the flap of the box.. Bobby Bear and Waldo kept sliding along the ground when they abruptly felt hands around them.

"Oh, no you don't. You're my bears," the shadow man said in a tired raspy voice. Waldo felt his body being squeezed and lifted from the ground. He and Bobby Bear were placed in the wooden box. Then, something covered the top making it completely black.

"You boys get some rest now. We'll talk more tomorrow," said the stranger. "Now where's the other one?"

The two bears heard rustling outside the box and could only hope that Fluffy bear got away.

The shadow figure crawled out into the alley to look for the missing bear. He had a hard time walking as he stumbled left and right, bumping into garbage cans along the way.

"PIPE DOWN — PEOPLE ARE TRYING TO SLEEP!" a voice shouted from the distance.

Bobby Bear and Waldo heard all the noise and feared the worst. "Hey, Waldo, do you think —"

"DON'T SAY IT," scolded Waldo. "I don't know."

"Waldo . . . are you scared?"

The nervous white bear swallowed hard. "Yeah, but don't worry, 'cause Fluffy's a tough bear. He's fast and quick and is a good hider. He can blend in. He can move like a cat. He can sense danger. He knows when to —"

"Waldo . . . you're doing it again," said Bobby Bear softly.

"Sorry."

They heard rustling and mumbling just outside as it got closer. "It's not safe out there for a teddy bear," they heard the familiar gravelly voice say.

It wasn't long before the sound of heavy breathing filled the box.

"Where's Fluffy?" asked Bobby Bear most concerned as the darkness embraced both bears.

Waldo didn't answer. Bobby Bear felt two arms slowly wrap around him and squeeze. As scared as they were — they had each other.

Elvis walked most of the night searching for Bobby Bear, Waldo and Fluffy until he finally arrived at the transfer station, where they were headed. Rows of large trucks lined the enormous parking lot, waiting to be loaded. A small square glass building sat in the middle of the truck yard where Betty bear sits on the secretary's desk. An adorable pale brown teddy, with a big pink bow atop her head, was in charge of teddy transportation at Brockton Station. This wasn't the largest truck yard but it sure was the busiest in the teddy world.

Elvis made his way to the front door and saw her sitting alone in the dark.

"Betty! Hey, Betty," he called, getting her attention.

She looked up to see a tall handsome bear standing at the glass door. She sprang to her feet and went to greet him.

"Elvis, it's been a long time. How've you been?" she asked, looking through the glass from the inside.

"I'm fine," he answered. "Can you tell me where Fluffy bear is?"

Betty appeared a little confused. "Who?"

"Fluffy bear. He was with two others, Bobby Bear and Waldo."

"I haven't had anyone for days. You know, this is mostly for emergency travel."

"Yes, I know. I thought you knew they were coming," responded Elvis.

Her face changed as she remembered. "Oh, the boys who are in trouble? No — I haven't seen them yet."

Elvis looked around the yard at all the trucks. A thought entered his mind, one that he didn't want to think about — something might have gone wrong.

"I'd better double back. If you see 'em, don't let 'em on a truck. They're to come home. Okay? Tell 'em that they need to come back," instructed Elvis. He turned to leave but noticed a slight glow on the horizon. Dawn was coming and it wouldn't be long before the truck drivers returned.

"Elvis, you can't go now," said Betty. "Come on in and stay till tonight. I'll find a spot for you." She opened a window. Elvis agreed and stepped inside.

They both stood at the window staring at the pastel horizon and he couldn't help but think of his friends, hoping they were all right.

"Fluffy's a good bear. They'll be fine," he said, trying to talk himself into believing it.

In the morning, James woke with something stuck to his face. He peeled it from his cheek and recognized the piece of paper.

"Waldo," he said softly and hurried out of bed. Rushing to the office, he saw his empty desk. "They're gone," he mumbled. He was still holding the paper when he realized that Waldo had finished the drawing. It was remarkable, a true piece of art. The detail, the realism was incredible. But the picture was one that James had seen before, with a slight variation. It was exactly the same as a family photograph that hung in the living room, except Waldo had added Bobby Bear and himself in the drawing. He couldn't help but smile when he looked at it, but the empty desk sent sadness through his body. It seemed no matter where he looked something reminded him of them.

The pencil cup always told him when Waldo was bored. The paper clips they would string together just to see how long they could make it. The sticky note pad Waldo would stick all over Bobby Bear as he slept. All the paper they would waste making pirate hats. James started to get very depressed and plopped down in his chair. He sat wallowing in sadness.

The smell of coffee emanating from the kitchen told him that Debra was up. A voice came from behind, "Your coffee is ready." James didn't move. "Are you awake?" asked Debra. He nodded and slowly got up. "Is something wrong?"

James walked past mumbling something, " . . . gone."

"What? What's gone?"

"The bears — they're gone," he replied softly and kept walking to the kitchen.

Debra looked back at the desk and noticed the empty spot where they sat.

"What do you mean, they're gone?" She didn't understand. "They're probably just in Bobbie's room. Have you checked there?"

"No," he simply answered. He knew they wouldn't be there, anyway.

"I'm sure that's where they are. They're not going to just get up and walk away," quipped Debra. "Do you want some breakfast?"

"No . . . I'm not hungry."

Debra didn't have time to concern herself about the disappearance of the bears; she was running behind schedule. "Can you go wake Bobbie?" Her voice expressed urgency. "Breakfast is almost ready."

James let out a sigh, "Yeah," and dragged his feet to her room.

"Pumpkin . . . Bobbie . . . It's time to get up," James' monotone voice droned.

Bobbie sensed immediately that something was wrong. Her daddy was never like that in the morning. *Where's the song? He's not singing,* she wondered. As groggy as she was, she instantly opened her eyes. "Something's wrong, isn't it?"

James had a hard time saying it. "They're . . . they're . . ." he stuttered a few times.

"They're gone?" Bobbie inserted what he was trying not to say. James could only nod in response. She had never seen him despondent before.

"Daddy, they'll be back. All they need is a time-out. They're not mean bears, they're good bears." James was surprised at how calm she was. Bobbie happened to look over and see that the Big People's Chair was empty.

"*Hey*, where's Elvis?" she said hysterically and sprang out of bed. "*He* didn't do anything wrong. Why's *he* gone too?" She looked desperately to her daddy for an answer. James hadn't realized Elvis was gone. He was there last night. But then again, so were Bobby Bear and Waldo.

They both quickly glanced around the room.

"He's not here," she said in a panic. "He's gone, daddy, he's gone too. Why are all the teddies leaving?"

James dashed to his bedroom to find George sitting on Debra's pillow.

"You're still here. Why is Elvis gone?" he asked in desperation, hoping George would answer — but knowing he wouldn't.

Debra appeared from behind. "Of course he's here. Where else would he be?" she said. "What's all the commotion? And why are you acting so crazy? What *is* going on?"

Bobbie and James looked at each other and felt the truth might not be the best thing right now.

"I was looking for Elvis," said James truthfully. "He must be hiding or something with Bobby Bear and Waldo." James thought that was basically true. He then walked back to the kitchen for his coffee, trying to make it appear that it wasn't a big deal.

Debra was becoming agitated at their little game. The rumors about James from Mrs. Mallory, along with catching him talking to the bears, were taking its toll. Her headaches were feeling worse, which added to the stress. "I don't have time for this right now." Debra went back to finish her breakfast. James felt the silent tension and wanted to explain but feared it would only make matters worse at this point.

Bobbie was ready for school as Debra waited at the front door. She went to the office to say goodbye. She gave him a big hug and stared at the empty spot on the desk. "I miss them, too," she whispered in his ear.

After Debra and Bobbie left, James watched them pull out of the driveway and realized just how quiet the house was.

Mrs. Connors returned home after dropping Tiffany off at school and went about her usual morning routine. First, she ran the vacuum cleaner followed by doing the laundry. Picking up Tiffany's room was always a chore. She grabbed clothes off of her chair and desk, uncovering the family video camera. *That's odd*, she thought. *I didn't know she knew how to use it.* Kitty smiled at the idea of Tiffany being creative and was curious as to what she had recorded. The battery was dead so Kitty found the power cord and plugged it in. Unfamiliar with the camera herself, she hit several buttons before pressing PLAY. The screen lit up with a scene that was slightly troubling. Centered in the frame was Waldo who sat in the tea chair while Tiffany slipped out from her covers and dropped to the floor. *Maybe she's sleep walking*, she wondered. *That has to be it.* She watched Tiffany dig under the bed to retrieve Noname and began talking to him: "I'm sorry, Noname. Can you forgive me?" Kitty felt sad for her little girl and was having a hard time watching this private moment.

Kitty pressed the FAST FORWARD button and stopped it as she saw Tiffany climb back into bed, still holding the blind bear. She watched her little girl close her eyes. Just as she was about to press STOP — something caught her eye. "Oh!" she cried. Her hands began to shake. "No way . . . NO WAY!" Even though Kitty was home alone, she turned her head frantically in hopes that someone else was there to witness. "No way . . . This is incredible . . . What do I do? What do I do?" she screeched excitedly. "It's right there. I mean, it's *right there.*"

It hit her in a flash: "James!" She rushed around in circles searching for her shoes and glasses so she could go out the door. Dimly realizing her shoes were on her feet and her glasses were sitting atop her head, she dashed down the street.

Ding-dong . . . Knock, knock, knock. James jumped from his chair. He had fallen asleep at the desk. Stumbling to the door, James could see through the glass someone pacing back and forth like a racehorse waiting for the gate to spring. He opened the door and saw Mrs. Connors.

"Good morning Ki —"

"Can I come in?" There was distress in her voice while she pushed her way inside. "You won't believe this. I don't believe this. Well, maybe you *will* believe this. Of course, you'll believe it. I *have* to show you something. I didn't know what to do. Then, I thought of you. *You* need to see this,"

"Sure. *Do* come in?" James joked as he closed the door. Kitty held out the camera.

"This — here." She turned it so he could see the small screen and hit PLAY. James saw the reason why she was so excited.

"Where'd you get this?" he asked as he watched Waldo climb down from the tea chair.

"It's incredible, right?" she exclaimed. Her voice trembled and she was having a hard time holding the camera still.

"Yeah — where'd you get this?" he asked again a bit more vehemently.

"Um, Tiffany, I found it in her room," she recalled while her mind was spinning.

His heart sank when she answered. "So — she's seen this?"

"I don't know. I don't think so. She would've mentioned it. She would've shown it to me," she replied. "She probably forgot about it."

James was thinking that this was not good. "And you haven't shown this to anyone else?"

"No. Why?"

"This — isn't what people should see." James was forced into explaining the unexplainable. "Teddies have been around for over a hundred years and if they wanted people to know about their world — they would have done *or* said something by now. I know what this means, and I know how important this is, but there really is only one thing that is more important — *their* code — *their* world. And, as much as I would love to prove that you and I are not crazy — I know we can't." James was extremely sympathetic to her excitement but this was how it had to be.

Kitty could only trust that James knew what he was talking about since he didn't seem fazed by the contents of the video. She, however, could not understand what she witnessed. *Who wouldn't want to see this?* she wondered. Seeing is believing, yet she saw it and still couldn't believe it. That was something that she suddenly thought about. Without the bears actually moving in person, the video they had would merely be criticized as computer animation. It would create controversy rather than proof. She didn't want that. She knew what she saw — but would others? She pressed STOP.

Kitty felt emotionally deflated. "What should we do with this?"

"Can I have it?" he asked kindly.

She ejected the memory card and handed it to him. "So now what?"

"Nothing," said James. "That's it. We do nothing. I'll take care of the card and you have a talk with your daughter to see if she looked at the video." James walked to his desk, pulled open the top drawer and placed the small video card inside.

"Look at me. I'm still shaking," said Kitty, holding out her arm. "I had an experience when I was a little girl with my teddy, but as the years went by I started to doubt what I saw. You know, like it was all a dream." She suddenly thought of Waldo. "Speaking of a dream, is Waldo around? I would love to say hello."

His face dropped in Sadness. "He's gone," said James solemnly. "Actually, they're all gone, except one." James felt that he could tell Kitty what happened without doubt or question, especially now.

As he told the whole story, he began to feel better just letting it out. " . . . and that's why they live by the Code. It's a lot like our Ten Commandments. So, hopefully they'll be able to return the way Fluffy bear did." He took a deep breath and let out a slight smile. "Man, that feels good."

"It sure makes you look at teddies differently now, doesn't it?" confessed Kitty.

"Oh, it sure does."

They stood in silence for a moment before Kitty moved towards the door not knowing what else to say.

"I guess I should get going. I need to keep busy 'cause I can't keep thinking about this. I'll let you know if anything happens with Tiffany, but I'm fairly sure she hadn't watched it," she said.

James opened the door for her.

"Thank you so much for coming over. I really do think this is for the best," he said, trying to convince himself as much as her.

Kitty knew he was right but couldn't stop thinking how fantastic all this was and what it would be like to share this with the world.

"Keep in touch," said Kitty, "and please let me know if your bears come back." She turned and walked back home.

The house returned to silence, which somehow annoyed James. "It's too quiet," he bellowed angrily and went to the living room to turn on the T.V.

The alley, once dark, was filled with daylight. Shadowy figures became colored with life and the unknown was again revealed.

Bobby Bear and Waldo remained in the dark, huddled together, waiting for something, anything.

Unexpectedly, light surrounded them as the lid was opened and a scruffy looking man reached into the small crate for a can that stood next to Waldo.

"What's this? Who are you?" asked the scruffy man. He pulled out the bears and set them on his bed, which was a tattered sleeping bag on the ground, inside the large cardboard box. "How'd *you* get in there?" He studied them closely, picking them up one at a time. "Were you after something to eat?" he asked nicely. "I don't have much — but I'm happy to share." He grabbed the can from out of the crate and placed a metal tool on it and began twisting.

Bobby Bear didn't recognize the face but he's heard that voice, that gravelly voice.

That's the shadow man, he said to himself. Waldo, realizing the same thing, could only wonder what he had done to Big Red Fluffy bear.

"You look familiar. Have we met?" the scruffy man asked. "I'm pretty good with faces and I know I've seen you two somewhere before, but where?" He took the top off the can and dipped a spoon inside. "It'll come to me. Are you hungry? I make a mean can of soup." He put the dripping spoon of soup into his mouth. "Mmm, oh, yeah. Now that's good stuff. You sure you won't have some?" He held out the can.

Waldo could smell something but couldn't decide if it was coming from the can or the scruffy man. Whatever it was — he didn't like it. Bobby Bear now had a face to fill in the shadowy figure and wondered why the scruffy man didn't remember theirs. *How do you forget stuffing someone into a box? That's not something you forget*, he thought. *Maybe he was hit on the head or something.*

"I've got to go out later but you'll be safe here. I won't be long," he said and took another spoonful.

Waldo thought maybe that would be their chance to escape. But it was daylight — and without Fluffy, they didn't know where they were going. The only thing they could do was wait.

ELVIS IS PRESLEY

Elvis quietly waited in a dark cabinet alongside coffee filters, napkins, packets of sugar, paper cups and other items used in the break-room of Brockton Station. His mind wandered to his friends and the possible danger they might be in.

Men came into the break-room for a morning cup of coffee complaining about this and that. Elvis could hear every drop that poured since the coffee maker sat just above his head. Twenty-seven cups were filled, that was a lot of trucks going somewhere far across the country. Elvis liked the idea of traveling far away. He thought dreams of escape would take his mind off things.

He heard one man asking about more cups when the cabinet door suddenly opened. A portly man in a red plaid shirt crouched down to look inside. There was no way he could miss seeing Elvis.

"What are you doing under here?" asked Jarred Baxter, a kindly, overweight truck driver from Wichita, Kansas. He grabbed the large handsome bear and gave him the once over.

Jarred turned and asked several guys standing nearby. "Do you know whose bear this is? I just found him stuffed in the cupboard."

No one answered and went on with their conversation as if Jarred never said a word. He pushed Elvis out at arm's length to get a good look at him. "You're a nice one," he said. Right then, Jarred made a bold decision. He took another quick glance around and saw that no one was paying any attention, so he tucked Elvis under his arm and slinked out the back door of the station.

Jarred has been trucking for fifteen years and recently began talking to himself while he drove to help pass the time. Now he would have someone to talk to who wouldn't fall asleep as he discussed politics and spy novels.

His huge shiny red Kenworth sat parked three rows deep in the dusty parking lot of Brockton Station. He'd never done anything like that before — take something that didn't belong to him. Jarred always tried to do the right thing, but he was terribly lonely on the road and Elvis was just the thing to keep him company. He did feel a little funny walking with a large teddy bear tucked under his arm, but this was going to be his new best friend — and that seemed to justify his thievery.

Climbing up the right side of the cab, Jarred opened the door and gently placed Elvis in the passenger seat. "This is your seat now . . ." Jarred hesitated. " . . .Uh." He wanted to call the big bear by name, but he didn't know it. "What do I call you?" He studied the bears face for a moment. "Buster," he declared with a smile, which quickly faded. "No — you're not a Buster." Jarred turned somber. "I had a younger brother. He was killed in a car crash when he was seventeen. Paul Presley Baxter, Jr. was his name. He was a good kid, great football player, too. We just called him Presley, he hated being called Junior." Jarred reminisced with a tender laugh. His eyes glossed over briefly as he lost himself in the moment.

Snapping out of his fond memory, he said, "I'll call you Presley — if you don't mind." Water sat in the corner of his eyes as he reached up and grabbed the seatbelt and wrapped it around the handsome bear.

Elvis could not believe this was happening. He hoped Betty saw what Jarred had done, but assumed she probably hadn't. When she goes to the cabinet tonight — he wouldn't be there. She'd be worried, but what could he do? His mind ran to Bobby Bear and Waldo. He was supposed to find them and bring them home. The Council and the teddy world were counting on him. But this little snag would put him way behind schedule, maybe even permanently. How would he escape?

Jarred walked around his trailer for one last inspection before hitting the road. While he pulled the straps tighter on his cargo, he felt there was something else he needed to do — but what?

Crystal Johnson, the secretary at Brockton Station, noticed Jarred out the window preparing to leave. She noticed he hadn't filled out his paper work yet so she sent Steve Morris, the maintenance man, to remind him.

"Hey, Jarred!" hollered Steve. "You need to see Crystal before you take off."

The portly truck driver looked up and gave a wave, realizing what he had forgotten. Walking back around to the passenger side, he needed to close the door so no one would see Presley in his truck. He reached up and gave the door a quick flip. Jarred headed for the office and failed to notice that the door didn't latch. His blue, lightweight jacket, thrown loosely on the floor, stuck out enough to stop the door from closing. As Jarred walked off, the cab door slowly swung open.

Elvis saw his opportunity to escape and get back to the cabinet while Jarred was gone, but daytime made things more risky. The Code was in the back of his mind, but he couldn't think about that right now. Breaking the Code was the least of his worries. His eyes changed to a striking steal gray as life filled his body and he began fussing with the seatbelt. A melodic whistling faded into his ear. A happy little tune that grew louder with each note. With the door open, he couldn't be seen moving and went blank. While he sat motionless, the whistling reminded Elvis of James and the silly songs that he'd sing. Home sounded really good right now, but he needed to get out of the truck first.

The whistling was coming from Larry, an on-again off-again yard attendant, who would stroll up and down the rows of trucks trying to appear busy so he didn't have to do any real work.

Approaching the big red Kenworth, Larry noticed the cab door was open. His whistle became a little softer and his eyes shifted about, searching for anyone around. Larry was always looking for things that would make his life easier. Sometimes those things belonged to other people. There's a metaphor about "an open door of opportunity," or something like that. Larry didn't know what a metaphor was. All he knew was this open door was his opportunity. He stepped up to the cab and came face to face with Elvis. Startled at the sight, he flinched and let out a slight chirp.

"Ep," squeaked Larry. "Oh, you're just a teddy bear. You sorta had me there for a second." He laughed, thinking that a stuffed bear got the drop on him. Larry saw the blue jacket on the floor of the cab and thought it would come in handy on the cooler nights and quickly tucked it under his arm. Picking up the jacket revealed a shiny red toolbox. Larry always wanted his own set of tools. He pictured himself walking around with it and people saying; "There goes Larry. He's the best mechanic in the yard." Larry didn't need to convince himself anymore that the small red box was all he needed to make his life better. He threw the jacket over the metal container and held it like a running back busting through a goal line. Both arms tightly wrapped around it to his belly. Again, he darted his eyes left and right to make sure no one saw him and couldn't help but walk suspiciously while he scurried off along the row of trucks.

Jarred was finishing up his paperwork with Crystal when Steel-Joe came out from the break-room asking if there were any more cups.

"They're under the counter to the left," shouted Crystal.

Betty bear was in her spot on Crystal's desk, in between a daily calendar and a picture of Crystal with her sister at the lake, when she heard the response. Betty was afraid that Elvis was about to be discovered. There was nothing she could do while sitting lifelessly on the desk.

"I don't see 'em!" called out Joe from the break-room.

Annoyance flashed in Crystal's eyes. She turned to Jarred and sighed. "Hang on — I'll be right back."

Betty anxiously thought to herself, *They're going to find Elvis. Dingdats, we always have enough cups. Why now? Why today?*

Crystal was gone for only a moment when Jarred looked out the office window, noticing his passenger door was wide open — and someone walking away in a peculiar manner.

Had they been in the cab? he wondered. *Did they find Presley?*

Jarred started getting fidgety, glancing his eyes toward the break-room then back to his truck. The last thing Jarred wanted to be known for was a thief — much less, a thief that steals teddy bears. *'The teddy bear thief', that's what people would call me*, his mind worried.

Crystal rounded the corner mumbling about, "being right in front of you." She plopped down at her desk, let out an exasperated breath and continued stamping Jarred's paperwork.

After Larry slinked away, Elvis felt an urgency. He snapped to life and wiggled out of the seatbelt. From up in the cab, Elvis had a pretty good view of the yard and saw the station house where he needed to go. Elvis looked down from his seat, surprised to be this high. He peeked out the door to make sure the coast was clear. Larry was walking off in the distance and Elvis made his move. He jumped to the ground and rolled under the large truck, hiding behind a tire. The smells were heavy in the air of grease, oil and diesel smoke. Relieved to be out of the truck and free from the bonds of the safety belt, Elvis took the time to smell and listen to the real world. It was very exciting but there was a lot to say about being home.

"That about does it," said Crystal and stapled some papers together. Jarred reached for the paperwork and couldn't get out the office fast enough. Not wanting to be rude or appear suspicious, he calmly said, "Thanks. I'll see you soon," and went for the door. His feet were moving faster than normal and it was hard to tell if he was walking or running, but he managed to get to his truck in time to see the man disappear around a long line of trucks in the distance.

He stood for a moment staring down the aisle where the man went. A sinking feeling hit his stomach. Jarred jumped up on the step-box and instantly saw that Presley was gone. Panic had consumed his mind and didn't even notice his jacket and toolbox were missing when he took off to find whoever that was.

From behind the right front tire, Elvis watched Jarred jump down from the truck and dash off in a hurry. Trucks were moving around the yard causing dust to float like a heavy fog as they passed.

He didn't have far to go to get to the station house, but it might as well have been a mile with all the commotion going on. Daylight brought a whole different kind of problem. Crouched under the truck, Elvis watched the movement of the busy yard and tuned into its rhythm. A man would walk by and a few moments later a truck would pass. This would go on several times before Elvis figured out his next move.

Jarred ran to the end of the row and saw the man heading to an old rusty van in the employee parking lot. He dashed over as Larry was trying to put his key in the door while holding the toolbox at the same time.

"Hey, buddy," called Jarred, slightly out of breath.

Larry turned his head while keeping his body tight to the van so Jarred couldn't see what he was holding. "Oh, hey," he replied innocently, still trying to fit his key in the door-lock.

"I saw you at my truck and I think you've got something of mine," Jarred said plainly.

"Nope. It wasn't me." Larry began working the key more aggressively.

"Yeah, man — it was you," accused Jarred who was growing irritated at the denial.

Larry kept his body turned. "I just found this stuff."

Jarred reached out, grabbed Larry's shoulder and spun him around, revealing the bundle in his arms. He was looking for Presley not his own jacket, which he didn't recognize. Jarred could tell he was hiding something under the jacket and he was sure it was Presley.

Knowing he was caught, Larry began to whimper. "I'm sorry. It was just lying there and I thought people would take me seriously if I had it. No one ever takes me seriously. Real men have their own — but I don't. I'm sorry. Don't hurt me. You can have it back."

Jarred felt sorry for Larry. *Why would anyone steal a teddy bear?* he wondered, then he remembered that he stole Presley first. But this was different; Larry was talking crazy. Jarred realized that maybe Larry needed Presley more than he did. "No . . . That's ok. I want you to keep him."

Larry looked at Jarred in amazement. "What? Really? You really mean that?"

"Yeah."

"You won't tell the yard what I did? I'd lose my job."

"No. I won't tell," replied Jarred kindly. "Just take care of him. His name is Presley."

Larry was a little confused when Jarred referred to a toolbox by name, but he wasn't about to question it.

"Oh, oh, absolutely. Absolutely, I will. I'll take good care of — Presley," gushed Larry, relieved at the generosity of the truck driver.

Jarred smiled and didn't feel like he stole a teddy bear but rather helped someone a bit worse off than himself. He felt good as he walked back to his truck.

Larry kind of liked the idea of a toolbox with a name, but it did make him think oddly towards the strange truck driver.

Elvis was under the big rig waiting for the next man to walk by because that meant a truck would soon be passing. Jarred just happened to be that guy. Returning from his chat with Larry, he climbed up into the cab and started the engine, which was directly over Elvis. Startled as he was, Elvis ran from one tire to the other trying to get away from that sound, but he couldn't leave his hideout — not now. He had a plan and he needed to stay calm.

What do I do? he wondered frantically. *I can't run; I'd never make it.*

While Elvis formulated a new plan, the truck began to roll. He had no choice but to try and keep up. The red Kenworth turned left, away from the station house, which Elvis didn't have time to notice. It was all he could do to stay covered and out of sight as he ran along underneath. Jarred made a large loop around the yard, circling back down the row of trucks, headed towards the glass building and the exit. Once Jarred straightened the wheel the truck began moving faster. Elvis was running as quickly as he could but he couldn't run fast enough. He was no longer under the engine; he was now just beneath the trailer. Dust was thick and Elvis was having a hard time seeing. He could tell by the shadow overhead that he was still somewhere under the truck. That wouldn't last long. He turned his head to see the rear wheels next to him. Unable to move his legs any faster — the tires rolled on by. Soon, Elvis was surrounded by light and dust. The rear of the truck was just in front him and Elvis was out in the open. His feet stopped. Not knowing where he was or what he was going to do next, defeat ran through his body as he watched the big red truck leave the yard. He started to think that he should have simply stayed with Jarred. He wasn't a bad guy, just lonely. Elvis could have easily sat down and cried. As the heavy cloud of dirt, floating in the air, began to settle, Elvis realized where he was. The rear of the station house stood about fifty feet away. With his dust cover fading fast there was only time to do one thing.

Don't look, just run, he told himself while he sprinted for the back door. He got to the rear alcove where a large blue mailbox was placed next to the door. Elvis ran straight for it and squeezed between the blue box and the wall. It wasn't much but it was all he had. You could see Elvis' feet while he stood behind the big postal box, waiting for someone to open the door.

Hoping no one saw him run for the mailbox, he started to reconsider his desire to be a Rough Rider someday. *Excitement is one thing but this is just crazy.*

The natural instinct of a teddy is to remain still around humans. Teddies learn from people, adopting their character and traits, but they know not to move. Elvis was struggling with that very thing. It went against his nature yet the Council needed Bobbie Bear and Waldo back and he was going to do everything he could to make that happen.

It felt like hours before the door opened and out came Crystal for a soda break. She stood in the alcove sipping her diet cola and waving to trucks as they passed. Elvis could only see the corner of her dress while she stood a few feet way. Her cell phone rang and Elvis heard her chatting with her friend Patty. They talked about the weather and movies and a new flavor of ice cream that was "to die for." Elvis hadn't heard of such a thing before, a food that was so good that you actually die. It simply didn't make sense. Crystal said goodbye to Patty and turned to go back inside. She pulled the door open and stepped in as Elvis made his move. He tried to slip in behind her, but he was either too slow or the door closed too fast. Either way, Elvis was stuck in the door. Crystal never looked back and returned to her desk. Out in the open, he could see that no one was in the break-room, which was straight ahead. The main floor was off to the left; and to his surprise, no one in the office even noticed him trapped in the back door. He thought about going limp but he couldn't allow himself to get caught again. The extremely heavy door was squeezing him tighter and tighter. With every push he moved a smidgeon. A sense of panic set in and he gave one huge push, managing to free his body. The door slammed shut. He ran straight to the break-room and the cabinet but couldn't figure out how to open the doors.

Where are the handles? he asked himself. He searched frantically for some type of knob or way to open it. *Are you kidding me? I've come all this way and I can't get into a stupid cabinet?*

The break-room was empty while Elvis was trying desperately to get back to where he belonged, but his luck would soon change when he heard footsteps approaching. Steel-Joe was on his way back for his sixth cup of coffee of the morning. He was still waiting for paperwork that was long overdue. Elvis tried to hide. There was nowhere else to go and all he could do was go blank. He fell to the floor in the spot where people stood to fix their coffee. Joe walked up and about stepped on Elvis as he poured a cup. He leaned over to grab a sugar packet and kicked Elvis by accident.

"What the . . ." complained Joe. "Who put this darn bear on the floor?"

Joe happened to be one of the men standing in the corner when Jarred asked about the lone bear from the cabinet. Remembering the question from earlier, Joe picked up Elvis, opened the cupboard door and threw him in, slamming the door closed.

"What the heck is this?" griped Joe. "You can't get a dang cup a coffee without steppin' on a gal-ding bear." Joe sputtered while he sprinkled sugar in his cup.

Battered and dusty, Elvis was just glad to be back in the cupboard.

It had been hours since Elvis heard the men talking outside the cabinet. The trucks that were busy all day, loading and unloading, now were back in their rows. Elvis waited for Betty to give the all-clear. He played a quiet game guessing the exact moment when Betty would open the cabinet door. "One, two, thee, now!" he whispered. "One, two, thee, *now!* — nnnnnow!" He would do this a hundred more times before he guessed right.

Back in the alley, color faded, as it does every night, into shades of gray and black. Bobby Bear and Waldo watched the scruffy man turn back into a shadow right before their eyes. The sun was gone and the alley was dark.

All day they wondered what happened to Fluffy bear. Night had arrived and the scruffy shadow man was tipping a bottle to his lips, as he had much of the day.

"You boys don't talk much, do you?" His fumed breath grew heavier. "So . . . where you from?"

Bobby Bear and Waldo had heard all this once before, until he said something that caught their attention.

"I've seen one of your kind move before . . . Actually, I chased him into a closet. He wouldn't move when I picked him up . . . but I knew it was real, I knew." The scruffy man took another drink and pulled his arm across his face to wipe the drips from his chin. "I know what I saw. *Don't tell me I didn't see what I saw!*" he roared, glaring at the two bears sitting as still as they've ever sat before. "She told me I was crazy . . . but I knew."

His slurry speech got louder while trying to convince the bears of his story. In fact, he would do this just about every night with or without anyone listening.

"That's how I lost my job. When I wouldn't go back to *that house* to finish the job — he fired me — *he fired me!*" yelled the scruffy man into the alley. His angry words echoed in the distance.

The bears could hear the pain in his voice. Waldo thought about getting up and running after the outburst, while Bobby Bear couldn't have moved if he wanted to.

The fire that was ablaze in the scruffy man's eyes seemed to fade as fast as it flared. He continued in a calm voice. "I told my wife about it and . . . well, let's just say . . . here I am."

Bobby Bear and Waldo had never seen anyone so thirsty as the scruffy man. Sip after sip, he drank from his bottle. He gazed out his doorway into the alley like he was looking at the life he could have had. A quiet moment passed — then he turned back to the bears and began to reminisce.

"I had dreams," he fumed defiantly. "I had good dreams — I wasn't always a repairman, ya' know. Nope. I used to be important. I used to be somebody. I thought I could make a difference — do good things. But some people aren't cut out to be somebody. I didn't have what it takes, I guess." His glassy bloodshot eyes tried to focus as his words grew sharp. "You gotta be mean. You gotta be cruel and heartless. You gotta take what you want and step on those that get in your way." The scruffy man sneered then took a long pull from his bottle. He swallowed hard and caught his breath. "I just wanted to help — but *he* saw to it that I wouldn't help anyone — not there, anyway. He forced me out because I didn't do things his way. I couldn't even get a job pushing a broom in Louisiana. That's when I moved to San Francisco. I lost my flavor for public service and got into the exciting world of repair."

Reality slowly drifted into view. The cardboard walls and the near empty bottle were the only things he had left. Sadness diluted his bitter words as he realized he was trying to convince these poor bears that he was the victim — that none of this was his fault. Tipping the bottle upside down to his mouth, the last drop fell to his tongue. His red eyes fluttered and the space between his words grew longer. "That's when I saw one of you guys move. Boy, try telling someone about that and see where it gets ya'. I'll tell you where it gets ya'. Here! That's where!"

Bobby Bear felt sad for the scruffy man as sorrow filled the large paper box. Out of the corner of his eye, Waldo saw something at the door flap. He watched as the scruffy man blinked more slowly and his voice got softer. Finally, his head fell forward then snapped back. "What'd you say?" he rattled, looking around as if someone spoke. Trying to focus on the bears, sitting against the wall, his lids became too heavy and his eyes closed — one lid at a time.

"Psst," came from outside the box. Bobby Bear was too scared to look but Waldo knew who it was.

"Waldo, Bobby Bear . . . are you two all right?"

Fluffy bear peeked through the opening. Waldo checked back at the scruffy man to make sure he was asleep. Just then the scruffy man moaned and let out a sigh, startling the bears.

Fluffy leaned farther into the doorway and said, "Come on you guys, *now*."

The scruffy man suddenly sat up and reached for Fluffy. "Gotcha!" Fluffy was nabbed. The scruffy man pulled the startled bear up close. The alley light that hung just above the box illuminated their faces. They stared at each other until the memories came flooding back.

"You!" cried the scruffy man.

"*You!*" belted Fluffy, recognizing the face behind the short scruffy beard.

Waldo's mouth popped open. He couldn't believe what he was seeing.

"Do you know what you did to me?" barked the scruffy man.

"Do you know what you did to *me*?" snarled Fluffy bear.

"Well, now — isn't this interesting. Out of all the alleys in all the world, you strolled into mine," said the scruffy man with a vindictive grin. "So, how do you like my home? I have you to thank for this . . . Thank you. *Thanks a lot*," his sarcastic voice echoed in the alley.

"Hey, *I'm sorry!*" Fluffy screamed. "But it hasn't been all butterflies and candy for me either. The teddy thugs came and took me away because of what happened, and now they've turned *me* into a thug. I don't want to be a thug, I love these guys." Fluffy scowled at the alley bum.

Bobby Bear and Waldo were feeling a bit uncomfortable watching a human argue with a teddy.

"Yeah, well, I lost my family," boomed the scruffy man, not even noticing how strange this all was.

"I lost mine, too," hollered Fluffy right back.

They both stared at each other in silence.

A man suddenly appeared at the opening of the big box. He hunched over and poked his head inside. "You okay, Skip? I thought I heard you arguing with someone," said Nate, an alley neighbor that lived part-time in a below-ground stairwell, several steps away. He noticed the scruffy man holding a teddy bear in his hands and two others sitting against the wall. The expression on Nate's face never changed as if he'd seen this before.

"Yeah — yeah. Everything's fine. I was just, umm . . ." the scruffy man searched for words to explain.

"Hey, it's cool," said Nate, "you've got company. I don't mean to intrude." He gave a polite nod to Bobby Bear and Waldo. "I'm making the rounds. Do you and your, um — buddies — wanna come along?" He reached out and scratched Fluffy bear on the head.

"No. I'll catch up with you later," replied the scruffy man, who could only imagine what Nate was thinking.

"Okay, Skip. I'll be right down the alley in case you need to — well — I'll be down there. See ya'." Nate stood up and disappeared from the doorway.

They sat quietly for a moment listening to the sound of trash cans off in the distance.

The Scruffy man thought about everything that happened in his life and came to a sudden realization.

"You know what? It's not your fault," he conceded with a peaceful look about him. Fluffy bear felt confused. "No, I mean really, it's not. Listen, I didn't need to tell anyone. Did I actually think people would believe me?"

Fluffy bear began to understand what he was trying to say.

"Would *I* believe someone if they told me they watched a teddy bear run across the floor? Forget that they were in the refrigerator looking for something. By the way, what were you looking for?" He asked the question that plagued him for the last eight months.

"Uh, the milk," Fluffy answered quickly, not wanting him to lose his place.

"Oh." The scruffy man was a bit surprised that it was a simple answer. "Is that your favorite?"

Fluffy nodded. Bobby Bear and Waldo agreed but remained still.

The scruffy man then said something that Fluffy wasn't expecting. "Every person is responsible for everything they do. We all have choices in life. Actually, that's *all* we have. When it came down to it — I chose to live like this. I could have gotten another job — and I probably could have saved my marriage but — I made a choice, not a good one, but — a choice." There was kindness and honesty in his words. Teddies are very sensitive to tones and they know sincerity most of all.

Even though the scruffy man chose to live like a hobo, Fluffy realized that if he hadn't gone after the milk, that day, that none of this would have happened. They would all be sitting in Bobbie's room right now having tea or something fun. Fluffy did feel responsible for the scruffy man but he was acutely aware that, right now, he had a job to do.

"Listen, Skip," said Fluffy.

"My name's not Skip," snapped the scruffy man quickly. "That's just Nate. He calls everyone Skip or Skipper or some other name. My name's Richard Saint, but my friends call me Rudder."

"Oh, sorry. You seem like a good man, and I'm *very* sorry for what happened. I would love to make it up to you somehow, but I'm in charge of getting these two back to the Council and we *really* need to get going," explained Fluffy bear as gently as he could.

The scruffy man set Fluffy down next to Bobby Bear and Waldo. "I understand. You've got a responsibility and they're counting on you. You gotta go — I get it. If you're ever in the neighborhood, stop by. I could use the company." Rudder got up, gazed at the bears sadly, then disappeared into the dark to join his buddy on the rounds.

Fluffy turned to his friends and quickly said, "Welp, come on. We need to get moving." He stood up to help Bobby Bear and Waldo to their feet.

Waldo was having a very hard time with what he just witnessed and the way Fluffy simply glossed over the whole event.

"Wait a minute!" Waldo chimed. "'Let's get going?' What was all that about? What just happened? You can't just do that! You can't say, 'Let's get going' without saying anything. You're not even gonna —" Fluffy turned, giving a look to Waldo that changed his tone. "I'm just sayin' that was weird — that's all."

Fluffy peered into the alley as Waldo simmered. Bobby Bear had the slightest smile as he watched Waldo stewing over the scruffy man and how they ended up here with him. "I have to say, that was the weirdest thing I've ever seen," Waldo continued. "You mean — that was the repairman that got you in trouble? How weird is that? You can't write this stuff. What are the chances that we run into him after all this time? Here! Ya' know? What are the odds? I mean, really! How can you expect me to believe —"

"Hey, Waldo," interjected Fluffy. "Can we finish this later? We really need to get moving."

Waldo knew he was right and tried to refocus on the moment, but it kept spilling over and made it impossible for him to think.

Fluffy studied their next move from the doorway of the cardboard box, making sure no one was around, and off they went into the alley. As they ran, Waldo's thoughts kept going back.

"Honestly — hey, Fluffy, didn't you think that was weird? I mean, that was weird. Don't you think? Am I the only one that thinks that was weird?" prattled Waldo as they dashed through the dark.

"Waldo?" said Fluffy while trying to keep a sharp eye as they went.

"Yeah?"

"Shut up!"

At Brockton Station, Elvis was still playing his quiet game, when, on the hundredth try: "One, two, three — now!" the cabinet door opened slowly. Elvis remained still until he heard the familiar tone of Betty. "Elvis?" she whispered softly, not expecting to find him in the cabinet.

His bright gray eyes came to life as Betty stared. She didn't understanding how he wasn't discovered by Steel-Joe.

"Yeah," he answered.

Her voice questioned with surprise. "You're here?"

"Yeah." He climbed out and brushed himself off. "What *is* this all over me?"

Betty was still puzzled as she answered, "Well, this is sugar — and this is coffee — and this is . . ." She put her nose to his fur and took a sniff, then quickly sneezed, " . . . pepper." Elvis wiped his face.

"Sorry about that. No one goes in there very often and I thought it would be the most comfortable for you," she said.

"It was perfect. Thanks a bunch," replied Elvis, not really wanting to get into the long story of what happened. "I'm gonna get going. You'll tell Fluffy and the boys to come back if you see 'em, right?"

"I sure will," answered Betty in amazement. "Can I ask you something?"

Elvis could tell what she had on her mind. "I'd rather not go into it right now. It's a long story. Can I come back and tell you about it later?"

Betty smiled and nodded in admiration and hoped she would see the handsome bear again.

They said goodnight and Elvis began searching for his friends by retracing his steps.

TROUBLE WITH ZOMBIE BEARS

Back in the alley, Fluffy cautiously led the way through the dark. As they walked, it was hard to tell where one bear ended and the other began.

"Waldo, will you walk on your own feet, please," scolded Fluffy, pushing Waldo back.

Crash! Bang! A garbage can lid slammed up ahead.

Waldo jumped back on Fluffy's feet. "What was that?" his voice cracked nervously.

"I don't know," snapped Fluffy, "but if I have to run — I know *you* won't have to."

"Me? Why wouldn't I need to run?"

"Because I'd be running for both of us." Fluffy looked down to see Waldo standing on his feet again. "Come on, Waldo, off the feet. When I said 'stay close' I didn't mean *that* close."

Waldo gave a nervous laugh and took a step back.

The mood was tense and Fluffy was feeling the strain. "We need to keep moving."

The bears kept to the sides of the alley, scurrying from one box to the next garbage can. Eerie but strangely familiar sounds echoed off the walls from all directions.

"What *is* that?" asked Bobby Bear with his ears twitching forward and backwards. "Did you hear that? It's like whispering, almost."

Fluffy heard it as well. "I'm not sure."

The anxious teddies stopped in their tracks to listen.

"*There*, there it is again," whispered Bobby Bear. "It's coming from up there."

"No. It's coming from over there," said Fluffy bear, pointing across the alley.

Waldo slowly squeezed in closer to Fluffy bear. His feet were getting that twitch again when he spoke up. "Uh, guys, it sounds like it's behind us."

The shadows around them began moving and the odd tones grew louder.

"Fluffy, what do we do?" asked Waldo fearfully with his foot tapping around, searching for a safer place to stand.

"First, Waldo, get off my feet. Second — I don't know," choked Fluffy as the whispers turned into murmurs.

"Humans?" quivered Bobby Bear, who was ready to fall to the ground.

"No," said Fluffy, listening intently. "It doesn't sound like them. It almost sounds like —"

"ZOMBIE BEARS!" cried Waldo, pointing to a frightful looking creature.

An alley lamp dimly lit the face of a disfigured teddy slowly headed towards them. They came from all directions in search of that one thing they need to be normal again. Without human love, they wander aimlessly trying to understand why they've been discarded.

Bobby Bear saw two coming out from behind a garbage can and a third from a pile of old crates. *"What do we do?"* he screamed.

"Run!" yelled Fluffy and took off down the alley. They rounded a corner only to find a dead end with a stack of crates and wooden pallets.

"We can't stay here," wailed Bobby Bear.

Waldo peeked around the corner and saw the Zombies close behind. "It's too late. They're coming. We gotta hide." They rushed toward the pallets.

"What do they want?" trembled Bobby Bear, catching his breath.

"They take your insides and eat 'em," asserted Waldo while he poked his stomach.

Bobby Bear was hoping someone had a plan. "Fluffy, have you ever seen a Zombie bear?"

"No, but they sure scare the stuffing out of me." He moved back and forth trying to peek through the slats. "Shh, shh — here they come."

One of the mangled bears leaned his head around the corner. "I saw them go down there."

As more and more Zombie bears gathered, one of them called out. "Hey, guys, we know you're here. We're not going to hurt you. Come on out."

Elvis, still retracing his steps, walked past a dark alley and for some reason he stopped. Something caught his eye. Barely visible, as if someone had tried to scratch it out, was the sign of the STS. It was located on the inside corner of a building in the alley. The insignia indicated safe travel for teddies, but this one was different. Elvis knows the mark, and this one had been etched in with something sharp. Official marks are stamped discretely along travel routes in a special ink. Someone wanted them to go this way.

Almost daring himself to enter, Elvis noticed movement up ahead. He hugged the wall and slowly ventured farther. In the distance, he heard a human talking.

"Who would believe me anyway? 'Teddy bears don't walk and talk,' they'd say. 'You drink too much,' they'd tell me." A gravelly voice came from the dark.

Did he just say teddy bears? Elvis asked himself. He continued toward the voice, maneuvering cautiously in the shadows.

"What do we have here? Hmm, looks like you're dead," the gruff voice said as Elvis got close enough to see a tall shadow leaning over a large can.

Dead? thought Elvis. "Who's dead?" he whispered softly. He needed to see what was in that can.

The dark shadow stood up and moved on to the next one. Elvis ran as fast and quietly as he could then jumped, reaching for the brim. He pulled himself up to see inside. "Garbage — it's just — garbage." Discouraged yet relieved, he looked up for the shadow man. Elvis didn't want to lose him in the dark.

"Dum-dee-dum-dum, Dum-dee-do . . ." Elvis heard the shadow figure singing as he stumbled through the alley, stopping at each can on his way. He dashed after the mystery man as this was his only clue to his friends.

"Hey, now, what's this? An overcoat. Very nice," echoed the gravelly voice in the alley.

Elvis circled around but dared not get any closer.

"But do you fit? That's the question." The shadowy figure slid one arm through a sleeve revealing his hand and most of his forearm on the other side. "Too small. You can go in the Maybe pile." He flung it over his arm and continued on.

What's he looking for? Elvis wondered. He followed him until the shadow crawled inside a big box with a blue arrow on the side. An old street lamp, attached to a building, hung over the box, placing a soft glow on the shadowy figure. Elvis saw a scruffy looking man with a pleasant face. He sat among the shadows, outside the box, watching the scruffy looking man to see if he said anything more about his lost friends.

The sound of scuffling feet began bouncing off the buildings. Elvis couldn't tell from which direction they were coming as the steps got closer and louder. Deciding not to take any chances, he went blank, tipping over in his spot, just before he was swept up off the ground.

"Who do we have here?" asked Nate as he inspected the handsome bear.

Elvis could barely make out a thin weathered face that poked through his long black disheveled hair. There was a smell that Elvis couldn't quite figure out, an indescribable pungent odor that seemed to be coming from the stranger. Elvis had been held by many humans before, but none of them smelled like that. He could feel his nose wanting to crinkle.

"I know where you belong," said Nate with a friendly tone. He took a couple of steps toward the cardboard box, and in a second, Elvis found himself thrust face-to-face with the scruffy man.

"Hey, Skip, you left your bear outside." Nate handed Elvis to him. "This isn't a safe place for a teddy bear, ya' know. Especially, one as nice as this."

The scruffy man took one look at the unknown bear and without skipping a beat, he replied, "Oh, thanks, Nate. I thought I was missing one." He pulled Elvis close and studied his face for a moment before turning back to his alley friend who was crouched outside the door flap. Nate happened to notice the other bears were gone. "Where are the others?"

For whatever reason, the scruffy man felt like answering that question a little differently. "I think they stepped out for a bit. They had something to do. They'll be back."

They both stared at each other without saying a word. The silence began to feel a bit uncomfortable.

Nate slapped his thigh and said, "Welp — I'll see ya' round." He stood slowly, because his knees hurt, and backed away, keeping his eyes on Elvis.

"Thanks for the help. I'll see ya'," the scruffy man called out to his slightly confused alley neighbor.

Nate's dimly lit face slowly faded into the dark as he continued on his rounds from can to can. The scruffy man watched his friend disappear before turning to Elvis.

"Hello — the name's Rudder. Who are you?" He set Elvis down in a comfortable position against the cardboard wall. "I haven't seen you before. You must be looking for your friends."

Elvis was in the right place.

They were here. He's seen them, he said to himself. This made Elvis feel much better knowing he was on their trail, but now he was stuck listening to the scruffy man while time was getting short.

"They were here," Rudder explained, "but said they had to go, something about getting to the Council." He leaned forward to say something in confidence. "The fluffy looking one doesn't want to be a thug. He seemed upset about having to take his friends away."

He sat back and grabbed a bottle from the small wooden crate. "Sip?" he asked his new found friend, pushing the bottle towards him. Elvis sat still. "No? All right. I don't want to be a bad host."

Time was wasting and Elvis needed to find the others. Feeling restless, he wanted to leave, but Rudder started talking about the day he caught Fluffy bear in the refrigerator.

As interested as Elvis was in the story, he was too close to catching the others. He couldn't sit any longer.

"Look," blurted Elvis uncontrollably, "I'd love to hear your story but I gotta go." Elvis soon realized what he had done. He'd never broken the Code before. In fact, Elvis was a firm believer in the Code, and everything it stood for, which made his next feeling even worse. He liked it. It wasn't breaking the Code that he liked; it was the adventure. Elvis, for the first time, felt alive — really alive. "I need to catch these guys and bring 'em home," continued Elvis rather boldly.

The scruffy man sat back and sighed. "It seems that everyone's always in a hurry to go somewhere. If you gotta go then you gotta go. I understand. But I thought they were needed at the Council," the scruffy man added. Elvis was caught off guard that a human knew so much about what was going on in the teddy world.

"Yes, but the Council said . . . I'm sorry, but how do you know all this?" asked Elvis, feeling as perplexed as he'd ever been.

"The fluffy one told me," said Rudder. "It turns out we're old acquaintances and we were catching up on old times. Hey, when you see him, tell him to think about what I asked." The scruffy man reached out to grab Elvis by the paw. "I hope you catch up with 'em and everything turns out okay."

Elvis got up and cautiously moved towards the opening while he kept a curious eye on the friendly stranger. "Thanks. I — I mean — thanks." Elvis never had anything like that happen before.

Talking to a human? I gotta report this. But what do I say? What would they say? I need to think about this. Elvis slowly left the box, disappearing into the dark.

As he ran he began to understand what Waldo and Bobby Bear had experienced with James. Interacting with a human was special. It brought emotions and sensations to a new level. This was troubling to Elvis. Why was this wrong? He wondered. Even Elvis didn't truly understand.

He ran for a bit until he heard noises that made him stop. It sounded like a group of bears talking.

"Who are they? What do they want? Do they have any extra stuff?" said a mysterious voice in a tone that Elvis was very familiar.

"I don't know . . . they won't come out," replied a different voice.

"Let's get 'em. We can pull 'em out," yet another voice bellowed defiantly.

Elvis quietly sneaked along the dark side of the alley to get a better view of who was talking.

"COME ON OUT, GUYS, WE JUST WANT TO TALK," called out still another voice.

As Elvis watched from a distance, he could see a number of small shadowy figures moving about. He saw a stack of wooden pallets near a dead end where the figures were all facing. Suddenly, a scared voice cracked from behind the pallets.

"Go away! We don't have anything to say to you."

"Oh, come on, *please!*" said one of the shadowy figures letting out a laugh.

Elvis knows that voice — that scared voice, he's heard it before — *Waldo.*

Just as Elvis wondered what he was seeing, one of the figures passed through a glow of light. His face wrinkled as he saw something more horrifying than he could imagine. *Zombie bears,* his head rattled. *I gotta do something or they're done for — but what?* He could only watch helplessly as his friends were in need of rescue.

"Just leave us alone!" cried Waldo, crouched nervously from behind their barricade.

"We just want to talk," said the closest Zombie bear standing just feet away.

Bobby Bear leaned over and whispered to Fluffy. "What do you think they want to talk about?"

Fluffy gave a strange look back and answered sarcastically, "*I don't know.* Why don't you ask *them?*" He pointed to the alley filled with Zombie bears.

Not sensing the sarcasm, Bobby Bear innocently did as Fluffy suggested. "What do you Zombies want to talk about?" he called out with a quiver in his voice. Fluffy shook his head in disbelief.

The alley fell quiet for a second before a voice replied, "Stuffing!"

Bobby Bear turned to Fluffy with a face of pure innocence. The others knew there was nothing to be discussed. Bobby Bear had no idea what the Zombie bear meant and asked the question that didn't need to be asked. "What about stuffing?" Fluffy dropped his head.

"Do you have any extra?"

"Extra?"

"*Yes*, do you have extra stuffing?" replied the voice with a touch of impatience.

A slight laugh of embarrassment slipped out because Bobby Bear was sure he heard incorrectly. "Uh, could you say that again — 'cause from here it sort of sounded like you said 'extra stuffing.'"

"YES! *Stuffing!* Do you have extra *stuffing*?" The voice became agitated.

Realization and understanding grew in his eyes. "Fluffy, you're right. They want to eat our insides," Bobby Bear whimpered hysterically.

Waldo heard enough. He began looking about frantically as if a way out would magically appear.

"Do you have any extra arms back there?" a Zombie voice inquired. Then more and more voices rang out making their requests.

"How bout eyes — any eyes?"

"I could use a nose. Can I just borrow a nose? I'll give it back, *I promise*."

This made several Zombie bears laugh at the thought.

"Yeah, we'll give 'em back, *we promise*," said other bears, laughing even louder.

The first Zombie voice, which sounded like it was standing right next them, said, "Listen, we just need some things to fix ourselves so we can be normal — like you."

Fluffy thought about what he was hearing. "So, if we give you things to help you — what happens to us?" he asked, waiting anxiously for a good answer — there wasn't one.

"We're not bad bears. We just want to be normal so we can go home. I mean, it's like, one day you're sitting on your favorite pillow and the next thing you know you're sitting in a garbage can in an alley. Why? *WHY*!? *This isn't fair.* We don't belong here. What makes *you* more special than us, huh? What? Because you've got both your eyes? Because you don't have a hole in your side with stuffing falling out? — Or because one day, your person just decides they don't *love you anymore*? WHAT!?" The Zombie bear fumed.

From the shadows, Elvis could hear everything and the situation was growing worse. He needed to help but time was running out. Suddenly, his ears twitched as something crept up from behind. Just as he was about to go limp, a paw slipped over his mouth and he heard a familiar voice.

"Shhh — it's just me," said Dakota softly. He noticed the shadowy figures in the distance. "What's going on?"

Elvis caught his breath and answered, "Zombie bears! They're everywhere." Elvis noticed Dakota wasn't alone. "Who's that with you?"

"This is Lyle. He's an Outsider, too. We thought you might need a hand, and it looks like we're just in time," replied Dakota.

"You sure are. How did you find me?"

"It wasn't hard. You leave a pretty good track. Plus, I saw the fake mark at the alley entrance. I knew something wasn't right." Dakota gave a coy smile.

"So, that's not an official mark? *I knew it.*" Elvis was just glad to have another teddy around, especially a Rough Rider.

He remembered his favor. "So, were you able to find what I asked?"

"All set. Good to go."

"Really, that fast?" Elvis asked, impressed as he could be.

A modest smile slipped out as Dakota asked, "So, what's the plan? What do we do about these guys?"

"I don't know. Have you ever dealt with Zombie bears?" Elvis inquired.

"Yeah, just once. They're kinda tricky."

"What do you mean, tricky?"

"Well, they'll tell you that they just want to talk, but then they try to take your stuffing. You know — tricky," explained Dakota as he watched the disfigured bears wander around the alley.

"Do you know if they're afraid of anything?" asked Elvis.

"I can't think of . . . Well, I guess they're kind of afraid of the same things all teddies are scared of."

As soon as Elvis heard that, he got an idea. "Guys, stay here and keep an eye on things. I'll be right back," he said, then dashed off as quietly as he could.

The nearest Zombie bear tried once more to coax the misguided bears out from their cover. "Look, we've tried being nice, but that, apparently, didn't work, so we're gonna give you one more chance to come out or we're gonna come back there and get you."

Waldo hadn't heard anything more ridiculous. "Nice? NICE!? You call eating my stuffing nice? You're just a big Meany, that's what you are!"

"Whoa, whoa. We're not going to eat your stuffing. Who said anything about eating? Is that what you think we do?" said the Zombie bear.

Waldo felt a slight relief at the reply. "You're not gonna eat us?"

"Noooo, not at all. We just want to borrow some, that's all," the Zombie bear said kindly.

Wanting a little more explanation, Bobby Bear had to ask, "So, how does that work, exactly?"

Fluffy bear and Waldo rolled their eyes, not believing that he didn't get it.

The Zombie bear explained, "You see, we very gently *rip* your sides open and carefully *yank* out your stuffing, easy peasy."

A look of horror filled his face as he turned to Waldo knowing that didn't sound friendly at all. Understanding finally arrived and Bobby Bear was now on board.

Time had run out, along with any hope of escape, and Fluffy could see the closest Zombie moving towards them. He turned to Waldo but there was a contemplative look on the young bear's face. It was not the childlike demeanor he always wore; it was something he'd never seen from the playful little bear. The tip of his tongue was sticking out; he was deep in thought. Something had to be done and it had to be now. Waldo's eidetic memory largely went unrecognized until he searched for answers, and at that moment, that desperate moment, an idea popped into his head, one that he never gave a second thought. Bobby Bear noticed Waldo's protruding tongue. It was a dead give-away. He was up to something. But what? Before he could ask, Waldo stood up and stepped out from behind the crate to confront the menacing Zombie bear. Waldo had a plan, he'd seen it once before.

Fluffy whispered sharply, "Waldo! No!"

Bobby Bear reached for his friend's arm but was too late. They quickly peered through the slats in shock.

"What's this?" scoffed Duke, stopping in his tracks. The tattered dark brown bear was miffed at such a bold move.

Poise was essential. Waldo kept reminding himself to stay calm and be firm. The brave white teddy came to a stop in front of Duke, who appeared intimidating for a normal bear. He stood several inches taller than Waldo, but with one eye missing and a sizable hole in his side it added the frightening features of a Zombie bear.

Nerves wracked Waldo, but he maintained his unyielding appearance. The element of surprise was clearly in Waldo's favor — you could see it on Duke's face.

"So . . . you got something for me?" asked the threatening Zombie bear with a slight laugh. He glanced over his shoulder at his Zombie cohorts and gave an incredulous smirk. But Duke's confidence was questioned. This was not the usual reaction from a Normal. Normals are afraid of Zombies. Why not this one? Maybe this bear's not normal. Duke stood firm but uncertainty had now entered his mind. Waldo's behavior puzzled the now curious Zombies. The alley became still as all eyes were now on Duke. How would he react to an audacious confrontation? Duke was forced into a false bravado. A young small Normal was not going to bully a Zombie bear.

There was calm in Waldo's eyes yet they held an eerily forceful stare. He could feel himself shaking inside and could only hope that Duke didn't notice. "Listen, we clearly have a problem here — but I think I have a solution."

CHAPTER FOURTEEN

Duke couldn't begin to guess what Waldo had up his sleeve. Outweighed and outnumbered his options were extremely limited, but Duke was most interested in his proposal. Teddies aren't violent by nature, even Zombie bears, but desperation makes for unpredictable behavior. Duke was aware of that.

"What's your solution?"

Waldo stepped closer and lowered his voice, his eyes never blinked. "What's your name?"

"Duke. Why?"

"Okay, Duke — let's do this. Just us," said Waldo, remembering what James told him about bullies. "You and me. We go farther into the alley and beat the stuffing out of each other. One winner. One loser. Only one comes out. If it's me — we go free. If it's you — then you get what you're looking for. No other bears. No help — just us." Waldo remained cool and never looked away.

Bobby Bear and Fluffy heard the challenge. What was he doing? Waldo wouldn't stand a chance against a bear like Duke. Bobby Bear suddenly recognized the scene. He knew what Waldo was doing. He only hoped it had the same outcome it did for James.

Waldo gave Duke a choice: Bear-up or shut-up. This was not supposed to happen. Zombie bears aren't scared of Normals. The fearsome Zombie bear studied Waldo's face as he tried to figure out what this courageous or foolhardy bear was up to. Thoughts of a psycho bear trained in the art of Kage slipped into Duke's head. Was this bear capable of defending himself? His attitude showed it, but did he truly want to find out? Was it worth risking further injury or even death? He looked deeper into Waldo's eyes — there was nothing, just an unwavering glare. Duke blinked a few times and slowly dropped his shoulders.

"You know something? —" he began to say softly.

Just then, Fluffy noticed some of the Zombies scurrying off into the shadows. This caught the attention of Duke and Waldo.

"Well, that's funny," said Fluffy.

"You mean, like — ha, ha?" asked Bobby Bear, nervously laughing.

"No. Like — weird."

"Why? What's going on?" Bobby Bear was hoping to hear anything good.

"I think they're — dying," he answered as he watched a few fall lifelessly to the ground.

At the farthest point that he could see, on the opposite side of the alleyway, Waldo noticed two small red dots that appeared to blink then were gone. He paused only for a second but was more interested in what was happening to the Zombie bears.

Duke turned and fled into the darkness as Waldo ran back behind the crates. Watching through the gaps of their cover, they saw the disfigured bears going limp.

"What is it? What's happening?" ask Bobby Bear.

Fluffy began to giggle.

A tall figure made its way through the alley.

"It's a human," said Waldo. "What do we do?" he asked looking at Fluffy bear.

"Stay close and stay low. Maybe he won't even see us back here," answered Fluffy with a slight chuckle.

Waldo gave a concerned look. "Is this funny?"

"No! Why?" Fluffy suddenly realized his nervous tick was flaring again and put his paw over his mouth. Waldo forced a smile and turned back to watch the approaching human.

The tall figure drew closer. Soon all the Zombie bears were lying on the ground or hiding. This would be the perfect time to run — but they couldn't — not with a human so close. As they peered out through the pallets they saw the mysterious person was wearing a long coat. He approached their hiding spot, then abruptly stopped a few steps away.

What's he doing? wondered Fluffy bear.

The bears watched nervously. The long coat opened slightly at the bottom and a small face peered out. Fluffy was confused at what he was seeing. A furry paw slipped through the opening and signaled to them.

"Do you *see* that?" whispered Fluffy bear. Bobby Bear saw the signal and thought it was a trick.

"It's the Zombie bears. They're trying to scare us," said Bobby Bear anxiously.

"You mean, even more than we are?" replied Waldo with a touch of mockery.

Waldo could barely make out a face at the top of the long coat, but this was not a face he expected to see.

"No. It's Elvis," said Waldo, trying to keep his voice low.

"Elvis?" Fluffy started to ask when he saw the top of the coat. It was a handsome teddy face — one that he knows well.

The coat opened a little more and Waldo could see a bear waving them in.

"They've come to rescue us. Come on," Waldo whispered cautiously, hoping the Zombie bears wouldn't hear.

As quickly as they could, they ran to the coat and slipped inside. All three bears huddled together as Dakota pulled it closed behind them.

Waldo, whose nose was sticking in Dakota's chest, happened to notice a set of feet on his shoulders attached to another bear. As Waldo eyes moved upward, he saw yet another set of feet on those shoulders attached to Elvis at the top.

In a lowered voice Waldo said, "Thanks," to a bear he's never seen before. "Who are you?"

"I'll tell you later," replied Dakota quietly. "Let's just get out of here. Now, move to the side and take little steps."

The long coat appeared ghostly as it glided through the bodies of Zombie bears strewn about the alley. Elvis would twist his feet left or right to signal Lyle, who would do the same to Dakota for which way to go.

As they left the Zombie bears behind, no one felt comfortable until they were out of the alley.

Four bears, on the bottom, squeezed tightly together, scuffled along with the feeling that something was right behind them. When Elvis saw the city streets, just up ahead, he gave the all-clear. "Hey, guys — slow down. We're almost there. I can see the street." Elvis had a slight smile on his face feeling like he's just had the adventure of a lifetime. He suddenly heard a shout from behind.

"Gimmie your wallet, man!" demanded a very shaky voice.

Caught in the act of moving, Elvis had little choice but to do what the voice asked.

Down below, inside the coat, the other bears didn't know what was happening.

CHAPTER FOURTEEN

"What's going on up there?" asked Dakota with two bears standing on his shoulders. "Who's out there?"

"It's a human — and he wants a wallet — do we have one?" Elvis looked down inside the coat.

"WHO ARE YOU TALKING TO?" shouted the shaky voice from behind.

"I was asking about the wallet you wanted. I don't know if we have one," replied Elvis.

"PUT YOUR HANDS UP!"

Elvis threw his paws in the air but the long sleeves just flopped to his sides.

"I SAID PUT YOUR HANDS UP!"

"They are up," insisted Elvis.

"ARE YOU BEING FUNNY? ARE YOU SOME SORT OF COMEDIAN? YOU THINK I'M KIDDING AROUND?" the shaky voice yelled.

Waldo, Bobby Bear, Fluffy and Dakota were looking all around for a wallet.

"What's a wallet?" Bobby Bear asked Waldo.

"I don't know, but it must be important or this guy wouldn't be this upset. Maybe if we knew what it looked like."

"Hey, Elvis," called out Fluffy bear. "Ask him what it looks like."

Before he could ask the question, the man with the shaky voice walked around to face Elvis. The loom from a distant street lamp illuminated Elvis' face.

"*What the* —" cracked the shaky voice, as he saw a small furry face atop the long overcoat. "What's goin' on here? Who — who are you?" he shuttered.

It didn't seem possible for a voice to get any shakier. A mature slender face, cloaked in a dark hooded sweatshirt, stared at Elvis as he stared back.

"What's it look like?" asked Elvis, trying to stay calm.

"WHAT? WHAT ARE YOU TALKIN' ABOUT? DON'T MOVE! PUT YOUR HANDS UP! WHO ARE YOU?"

Dakota shouted up to Elvis, "There's nothing down here. Tell him we don't have any wallet."

Dakota was starting to get very tired of having two bears standing on his shoulders.

The shaky man jumped back as he heard voices coming from the coat. Elvis relayed the message from below. "It doesn't look like we have a wallet. Sorry. You really need one bad, huh? Is that why you're so shaky?"

Dakota couldn't take it anymore and poked his head out from the overcoat. "Elvis, you guys are getting too heavy. Can you get down now?"

The shaky man saw a second face sticking out from the coat.

"IS THIS SOME SORT OF TRICK?" he shouted, quickly reaching out and pulling open the coat.

There, stood three bears, one on top of the other, while three more huddled around the bottom bear.

Startled at the sight, he tripped and fell backwards to the ground. He struggled to get to his feet and crawled like a frightened crab until he bumped into a street lamp. Grabbing the pole like a life preserver, he pulled himself up and ran off into the night.

"I don't think he was feeling well," said Elvis and climbed down from Lyle, who then climbed down from Dakota.

Bobby Bear had genuine concern for the nervous man. "He really needed a wallet. I wish we had one for him, poor guy."

"He was so shaky that he didn't realize he dropped this," discovered Elvis, and bent over to pick up a folded sleeve of leather off the ground.

"What is it?" asked Lyle.

Elvis studied it, turning it over several times. "Hmm, don't know."

"Should we just leave it here?" asked Waldo.

"What — for someone else to come along and find it?" scoffed Fluffy bear. "No. We'll take it with us. It's because of us that he dropped it, so we'll return it somehow."

Feeling the danger was behind them, Bobby Bear and Waldo suddenly realized that Elvis was standing in front of them.

"Elvis, what are you doing here, and how did you know we were in trouble?" asked Bobby Bear with delight glowing from his face.

"I didn't. I was out looking for you," he replied.

"Looking for us? Why?" asked Fluffy bear.

"Because — you're not supposed to go. The word was given to bring you back home. You guys get to stay."

The troubled bears looked at each other, not fully understanding. Waldo asked the one question before Fluffy and Bobby Bear. "But — why?"

"Because of the stories," explained Elvis. "They're making a difference to teddies. They want James to keep writing, *and* since he writes about you guys, they want you to stay."

Bobby Bear wanted to make sure he heard correctly. "So — we can go home?"

"Yeah!" said Elvis.

"Like, right now?"

"Yes. Right now."

Bobby Bear threw himself at Waldo. "I told you everything would be all right. I told you," he said, squeezing tightly and began to cry.

"Umm . . . you never said that," Waldo inserted politely as he hugged his friend back.

"No, but I knew it. I just knew it," replied Bobby Bear hugging tighter.

"Actually, you said they were going to throw us into a dungeon and lock us away," recalled Waldo, not intending to ruin the mood.

"*You know what?* You're such a fun bum," Bobby Bear snapped and pushed away.

"*Fun bum?*" cried Waldo. "*You're* calling *me* a fun bum? Oh, that's right — THAT'S RIGHT!"

"HEY GUYS? Can we stop arguing and get going home?" barked Elvis.

"What? With this guy?" cracked Waldo, looking at his former best friend crossly.

"This guy?!" snipped Bobby Bear. "What does that mean?"

Elvis rolled his eyes and they headed for home. Bobby Bear and Waldo bickered along the way while a smile filled Fluffy bear's face.

CHOMPERS

The long trip home began. It was hard for Bobby Bear to walk without singing a happy song. One of James' silly made up songs kept bouncing around in his head. Bobby Bear was happy. Life seemed to make sense again. He wasn't going to the Council. He wasn't going to be punished. Things were right with the world once more and he started to remember how much he loved being a teddy.

Waldo couldn't keep his eyes off Dakota, wondering just who he was and how Elvis knew him. Dakota, who was leading the way, could feel the stare from behind and it was starting to bother him.

"*What?*" chimed Dakota, glaring at Waldo. "Why are you looking at me like that?"

"Nothing . . . Nothing, Jeeze Louise." Waldo was embarrassed.

Fluffy bear chuckled then leaned over. "He's an Outsider," he said softly as they walked.

Waldo's eyes flared. "He's a Rough Rider?" Fluffy bear nodded. "I *knew* there was something about him. His whole life is adventure," said Waldo looking up to admire Dakota. "I'll bet he's got some stories."

Bringing up the rear was Lyle, who overheard Waldo. "He sure does," he interjected. Lyle spoke softly so Dakota wouldn't hear. "He was on the first division."

Waldo's mouth popped open in awe. "So, he's met . . . *him?*"

"He was one of the best," said Lyle.

"But why is he way out here? Is he on some secret mission or something?"

"Not exactly, he was . . . reassigned," said Lyle, putting it mildly.

This caught Fluffy bear's attention. "Something happened, didn't it? He did something." There had to be more to the story, Fluffy could sense it.

Lyle suddenly felt uncomfortable talking about it, but he didn't want them to have the wrong impression. "Yes, but it wasn't like that. It's . . . complicated," he said. His eyes cautiously turned to Dakota who was still leading the way home. Lyle lowered his voice and started to explain. "He found out, through the network, that teddies were being destroyed, a lot of teddies, and some very important ones. The Council tried to keep it quiet. But, when one of his friends went missing, he kind of went over the edge." Lyle was only half-whispering.

Fluffy recalled hearing the rumors a while back. "I remember that."

Lyle continued, "He started digging around and found out that a human was suspected of these atrocities. Dakota was devastated. So, he went to Bullock bear himself and told him of his suspicions."

"Wait a minute. You mean Chief . . . Chief Marshall? So, Dakota's a hero," said Waldo most impressed.

"Well, not exactly. Bullock told him to keep out of it. He said that it was a Council matter and he shouldn't be involved," Lyle said.

"What? Keep out of it? Why? That's what he does, right?" argued Fluffy bear, not understanding why the Council would say something like that.

A mischievous smile emerged on Waldo's face. "He didn't keep out of it, did he?"

Lyle leaned closer. "No, he didn't," he whispered with a slight grin and a wink. "He gathered up a couple of his closest friends and secretly did a Nightmare."

As they walked, Bobby Bear and Elvis followed closely behind Dakota, while Waldo and Fluffy were hanging on every word that Lyle spoke.

"So, did it work?" asked Fluffy bear curiously.

"Yes — but it revealed something he wasn't expecting, something that the Council wouldn't like," he answered.

Fluffy and Waldo had never heard anything more intriguing.

"The human said a name that changed everything," said Lyle, then glanced up at Dakota, "the name of a Council teddy."

Lyle was finding it difficult to keep his voice down.

Waldo's mouth dropped open once again. His breath became short. "W-What? — Who? Who was it?"

Fluffy bear was in a trance as he focused on Lyle's mouth and waited for the answer.

Quickly looking around, Lyle whispered, "Ballinger."

It was as if the whole world stopped. Neither Fluffy nor Waldo could believe what they heard. They had to believe it. However, both bears were thinking the same thing.

"But he's . . . he's a Council bear," stuttered Fluffy as Waldo shifted his eyes back to Lyle.

"So, that means he's a — a bad bear," hissed Waldo. Disbelief permeated his body at the thought of a Council bear being such a thing.

Lyle continued to explain: "Dakota thinks that Ballinger has learned how to use the Sublimitone. It's a tone that humans can hear in their head. It's like it's their own thought."

"The what?" asked Fluffy.

"It's a secret tone that takes years to learn how to do, and most teddies don't even know about it. It's not a good thing for a teddy to know because of its power."

Waldo was stunned. "You mean . . . he can make a human think whatever he wants?"

"Yes — just about anything," replied Lyle. "Ballinger was making this human think that certain teddies were bad, and that he was doing a good thing by getting rid of them. But really, they were bears that knew what Ballinger was up to, that he was trying to take over the Council. And, before any of them could tell Bulloch or Theodore — they were — you know." Lyle noticed Elvis taking an interest in what was going on.

This was almost more than Fluffy could stand to hear.

"And the Council . . . did he tell the Council?" asked Fluffy, not even aware they were still walking.

Waldo needed to know more. "Yeah, so, what happened?"

Lyle stopped talking when Elvis scolded, "Keep it down back there."

Waldo, Fluffy and Lyle walked in silence, trying to look innocent, but they were not very convincing. When Elvis looked away, Lyle finished saying, "He did. He went straight to Bulloch and even Theodore himself and explained what was going on."

Waldo had never heard anything like this before. *Mystery, intrigue, and an evil villain — it has everything a great adventure should — and it goes all the way to the top.*

Lyle looked around quickly before he continued, "It turns out Theodore was aware of something going on. He didn't know what — and he didn't know who — but he had his suspicions."

Waldo shook his head in confusion. "So why didn't he do anything?"

Lyle was at a loss for words. He was trying his best to explain but it was too technical, too complicated. "Because he couldn't prove it," he answered bluntly.

Dismay and frustration slapped Waldo's face. "What?" he said rather loudly.

Dakota and Elvis stared back at Waldo.

"Is everything all right back there?" Elvis called out.

Waldo gave a silly smile and nodded. "Yeah, fine," he answered sheepishly. Elvis turned away and Waldo looked back to Lyle and asked, "Why is Dakota way out here?"

That was the difficult question. Lyle didn't want to say why. It was a disgrace. It was embarrassing to admit, but he relented. "For doing the Nightmare without consent."

It was hard for Waldo to keep his cool when he heard Lyle's answer. "You're kidding me. He discovered the truth — and *he's* the one that gets punished?"

Lyle had to agree that it didn't make sense.

"But, how do *you* know all this?" asked Fluffy.

"I used to belong to that human . . . Louis Longley. That's how I met Dakota. I left because of him. If he hadn't done the Nightmare, I might still be there, stuck in that smelly chest. He gave me the courage to leave. I shouldn't be telling you this, but I get worked up about it sometimes. Dakota's the best — and what happened to him was wrong."

Right when the story couldn't have gotten more interesting, Fluffy bear and Waldo realized what Lyle had done. He went against his person. That is the toughest decision for a bear to make. Lyle chose between good and evil and that is the most difficult thing to do.

Fluffy heard something that had never crossed his mind. "So you just left?" Fluffy didn't understand how a teddy could leave its family, because Fluffy didn't have a family like Louis Longley and Ballinger — he had James, Debra and Bobbie.

Dakota did tell Lyle about his talk with Bullock and Theodore, but he didn't mention the real reason why they were sent away. He wanted to — but he couldn't, and for the same reason Theodore couldn't tell Bullock to which outpost he sent D.

Waldo asked the most obvious question that had been overlooked by Fluffy.

"What happened to Ballinger?"

Lyle was just about to answer when Dakota's voice rang out. "Keep it down back there. We need to stay quiet."

They had just turned into another dark alley to stay off the streets.

"Another alley?" asked Fluffy bear, looking about nervously.

"Yes," said Elvis. "We'll be fine."

Elvis thought it would be true. In fact, he liked being outside. He was thinking more and more that he wanted to become a Rough Rider. For most teddies, there comes a day when they are no longer needed. They're put away. Different fates await each bear in time. Elvis didn't want to sit around and do nothing when his time came, so he put his name on the list to become a Rough Rider. Having this adventure made him feel alive and he was beginning to like it.

Dakota was on alert, noticing everything, as he led the way. It was difficult to stay out of sight with so many following. He couldn't use his normal stealth techniques. He needed to improvise and rely on his training as a Rough Rider. With his ears twitching and his head shifting left and right, he felt danger everywhere as they kept to the shadows. He's done this many times before but not with four Insiders slowing him down. They walked through the dark dirty alley when a particular noise caught his attention. He stopped in his tracks and gave the signal to Lyle to hold up. Before anyone could ask what was wrong, Dakota hissed, "No one make a sound."

He stared off into the distance with his ears perched forward listening intently to what he hoped he hadn't heard.

Elvis was trying to listen as well but didn't know what he was listening for. Everything was new to him. Out here, Elvis didn't really know what danger sounded like. He was used to indoor sounds. The city had noises of its own and they were coming from all directions.

Urgency consumed Dakota and he quickly turned to say, "We gotta move. Now! You two with me," he pointed to Elvis and Bobby Bear.

His eyes shifted to Lyle and shouted, "You take those two. — Dog!"

Dakota took off farther into the alley with Elvis and Bobby Bear following close behind. Waldo tried to follow but Lyle reached for his arm and said, "No! You come with me."

The grave look on Lyle's face told Fluffy something serious was happening. "Just do as I do. Stay close and don't make a sound." Lyle took off in the opposite direction with Waldo and Fluffy trying to keep up. They didn't know what they were running from but they did sense their lives were at stake. Waldo believed one thing: when an Outsider tells you to do something, you do it.

This was not the same large dark alley where the scruffy man lived. This was long and narrow with nowhere to turn. All Waldo could do was follow Lyle and trust he knew what he was doing. Watching Bobby Bear run in the opposite direction was hard, but he didn't have time to think.

A dog was headed their way. The name on the collar read "Bogart". However, no teddy had gotten close enough to read it — not one that survived. They called him Chompers, for what would be obvious reasons. His jaws were immense. Though Dakota was relatively new to the area, he did know about the vicious canine. He was also aware that this was not his neighborhood. Chompers was blocks away from his normal territory. This alley was supposed to have bypassed his street.

Dakota led his team to the closest object — a large garbage dumpster standing close to a brick wall. They managed to squeeze into the small space behind it but Dakota knew they were far from safe.

"We need to get inside and we need to do it fast," said Dakota, keeping a watch out knowing that real danger was closing in.

"Why are we running?" asked Elvis with fear slipping into his words.

"You need to get in there and you need to do it now!" replied Dakota. There was no time to explain.

Elvis didn't have to ask again, for his question was just about to be answered. He could hear a faint jingle in the distance, a similar sound he's heard many times at home from Rufus, the neighbor's dog. His collar had the same jingle when he played between the houses.

"Is that a dog?" asked Elvis, feeling this was all unnecessary. That's because Elvis knew about dogs; well, he knew about Rufus. Rufus liked to lick things. He liked to play and have fun. He was a friendly dog. Elvis was about to find out that this was *not* Rufus.

"It shouldn't be. There are no dogs on this street — not out at night, anyway." The sound of the collar was familiar but Dakota refused to believe that Chompers would be this far away from home. The dog was moving slowly for some reason. Why? One good thing was, it hadn't noticed them yet.

Dakota firmly grabbed Bobby Bear from behind and pushed him up the backside of the dumpster.

"Now get up there and get inside," ordered Dakota.

Wrangling his way to the top, Bobby Bear found two big black plastic lids covering the large metal box.

"It's closed!" whispered Bobby Bear urgently while leaning over and looking down at his friends. "I can't get in."

"Uh! It figures," sighed Dakota. "You go!" he told Elvis and pushed him up the same way.

Pulling himself to the top of the dumpster, Elvis saw what Bobby Bear meant. He turned and peered into the alley. From that vantage point he could see something — a large shadowy figure slowly headed their way. The jingle was getting louder.

Elvis lifted a corner of one of the large plastic lids and Bobby Bear curiously peeked inside.

"Get in," directed Elvis, holding the top open.

It was too dark to see but his nose told him all he needed to know.

"You want me to go in there?" asked Bobby Bear, squinting intensely, trying to see just what he would be jumping into.

"Yes. Now go on."

With no time to hesitate, Elvis released one of his paws from the lid and gave him a little push. Bobby Bear was not expecting the assistance and tumbled into the can. His landing was soft and a bit squishy.

"Hey, it's not bad," said Bobby Bear having no idea what he was sitting in.

Elvis released the lid, hurried to the back of the dumpster and dropped to his stomach to reach down for Dakota. Elvis watched as Dakota put one paw on the wall and one paw on the large bin then shimmied up like a spider. Before Elvis could get to his feet Dakota was standing next to him. Elvis was very impressed but thought Dakota was just showing off.

"Okay, now you. Get in," said Dakota and pulled the plastic lid open just enough for the handsome bear. Elvis stared into the smelly darkness and reluctantly threw himself into the garbage. He landed next to Bobby Bear who said, "See, it's not that bad." Elvis didn't respond.

Dakota stood atop the dumpster looking off into the alley and saw the dog moving in. That's his jingle — there was no denying it. "He's not supposed to be here. Something's not right." Dakota caught a glimpse of movement out of the corner of his eye. Chompers was focused on something else — not on them. The ferocious animal had been lured into the alley by a rodent, a cat or something. Dakota strained his eyes to see what it was but it was too dark. What was Chompers so interested in? What would tempt the dog enough to leaving his block? Maybe he was chasing nothing more than a shadow. He couldn't wait any longer; he had to hide.

Dakota turned and looked behind him for any sign of Lyle, Fluffy bear and Waldo. He felt better knowing they were out of sight. He lifted the lid, slipped inside and fell next to Elvis.

"The good thing is he hasn't seen us," said Dakota softly. "So keep quiet. Don't move — and don't speak."

Elvis still didn't understand why all the fuss over a harmless, licky, dog. But he wasn't about to say anything to Dakota after being warned. Outside the dumpster, the jingle grew louder and they could now hear the sound of panting. There was a slight scratching that went up the side of the bin to the top. Bobby Bear's eye's followed the subtle noise to the lid of the waste bin, and he was now looking straight up.

Something's up there, thought Bobby Bear nervously. He turned to look at Dakota but the darkness was too thick. He couldn't see his own paws.

The bears sat, nestled in the garbage, listening to the dog circling just outside. The panting was replaced by a strong sniffing sound that was focused in the same area in which they climbed. Bobby Bear remembered hearing that same sound from Rufus who would do the same thing from the other side of the hedge. Since Bobby Bear doesn't know any other dogs, he just assumed it was Rufus.

Knowing what Dakota said about keeping quiet, Bobby Bear thought he'd use the teddy tone, since only teddies can hear it. "Hey, that sounds like Rufus."

The panting and sniffing stopped. It was dead quiet. Bobby Bear waited for a reply which didn't come from a teddy. It came from outside. That's when the growling started. Bobby Bear hadn't heard anything like that before from Rufus and something told him that it wasn't friendly.

"I told you to keep quiet!" whispered Dakota harshly.

"But I used the teddy tone," said Bobby Bear not understanding what he did wrong.

"Dogs can hear the teddy tone," scolded Dakota.

This was news to both Bobby Bear and Elvis. They thought only teddies could hear such a high tone.

The growling escalated into a nasty snarl, which grew to a loud angry bark that echoed in the large metal bin.

Bobby Bear threw his paws over his ears to block the sound. They only muffled it slightly.

The beast tried desperately to dig his way into the dumpster. The sound of his claws striking the metallic can rang in their ears like a butcher sharpening his knife.

"I'm sorry! I'm sorry!" cried Bobby Bear frantically. "What do we do? What do we do?"

Lyle had taken his team back to the entrance of the alley where a car was parked in the street. They crawled underneath and huddled close together behind the front wheel. Waldo could hear the barking and snarling in the distance. He turned to Lyle and asked, "What is that? What's going on?"

Lyle could only stare into the darkness and hope their friends were safe. "That's a dog," he replied in as serious a tone as Waldo has heard.

"A dog? You mean like Rufus? *That's* not a dog. They're not like that. Not like *that*!" Waldo was baffled with Lyle's response.

"I don't know Rufus," said Lyle, "but I do know about alley dogs, and I know this dog. His name is Chompers. You don't want any part of that dog. He can shred a teddy to pieces in seconds." Lyle was as confused as Dakota. "But this isn't his alley. He shouldn't be here."

There wasn't any part of that sentence that Waldo found comforting. In fact, it brought instant concern for his best friend.

"Why is he so angry?" asked Waldo. "What if they're in trouble? What if they need our help? What do we do?" There was sincere worry in his eyes. He stared into the dark alley trying to see something — anything. There were so many shadows and shapes that it was hard for Waldo to tell what he was looking at. This made things worse for some reason. The dark was hiding the danger and that's where his friends were.

"We stay put, we stay quiet, and we stay alive," answered Lyle, keeping his eyes trained on the alley.

Waldo couldn't sit still while his best friend was in trouble. Since Lyle wasn't going to help then he would have to do it on his own.

There was a little ball of energy building inside of Waldo as he sat under the car. Fear and loyalty, courage and friendship brewed into something that would push Waldo to do something even he didn't know he was capable of doing. The small tip of his tongue slipped out of his mouth as a bold plan popped into his head and he never thought twice. *Distract the dog so they can get away.* Not knowing just how he would accomplish his mission, he rolled out from under the car as Fluffy yelled, "What are you doing? Get back here!"

Watching Waldo take off into the alley, Lyle yelled, "You don't know what you're doing! Wait! Come back!" He quickly lost sight of the small heroic white bear.

Lyle turned to Fluffy bear, who was mortified at what he witnessed, and said, "We gotta go after him. He can't be harmed. We have to protect him."

Lyle started to wiggle out from under the car when Fluffy stopped him.

"If you go out there and get killed then what about Dakota and the others? What about me? *What happens to me?*" whimpered Fluffy bear.

Lyle didn't like seeing this side of Fluffy and knew it was just the fear talking, but he did make sense. Lyle couldn't risk everything for one bear. This was a difficult decision and Lyle didn't know what to do. None of it felt right. Going after Waldo was foolhardy but staying was cowardly. Then Lyle remembered that Waldo *was* the mission, he was the reason they were all here.

He gently reached for Fluffy's paw and gave a caring stare.

"I've got to go after him," said Lyle kindly, knowing that Fluffy was too scared to move. "You stay here in case he comes back. You need to stay here and keep a lookout. Okay?"

Fluffy bear looked deep into Lyle's eyes as they both sensed what was really going on but kept the façade — it was for the best.

"Just stay behind the tire and you'll be fine," said Lyle. Fluffy nodded slowly, not saying a word. There was a distance in Fluffy's eyes as if he were somewhere else.

Lyle slipped out from under the car and started for the alley when he heard voices coming from down the sidewalk. He ran towards a shadow on the alley wall, becoming an obscure small lump that could be easily mistaken as a wad of newspaper.

Meanwhile, two teenage kids, out for a bit of mischief, were looking for any opportunity to make the other do something stupid.

"I'll bet you can't take out that street light with a rock," said Tommy Plevin, a seventeen-year-old, blondish haired boy. He was a ruggedly handsome, stocky kid that was well-known by the neighborhood police.

"What . . . from here?" replied Mike Piccato, his sixteen-year-old, dark haired friend. "That's easy. I'll bet *you* can't break that car window." He was pointing to the very car that Fluffy was hiding under.

Mike had a reputation for helping certain struggling business owners with insurance claims. Some involved fire, and some involved theft, but Mike was always involved. He allowed the owners to have a solid alibi as nefarious "accidents" took place. There was always a fee but it was not the type of assistance Mike could advertise in the paper.

Tommy was the best at finding trouble. He was so good that trouble simply stopped hiding. He could walk into any room and spot it instantly. Trouble would try disguising itself in clever ways, but it never seemed to matter, he would find it. Tonight he found trouble conveniently parked on the side of the street in front of a dark alley in the shape of a 1988 blue Ford Mustang.

Lyle could still hear Waldo running off into the distance but he couldn't leave Fluffy bear without making sure he was safe. Hiding in the shadows, he watched the boys walk towards the car. Fluffy was frozen with fear and decided to go blank. His eyes turned to small black marbles and his body became limp. Teddies are vulnerable in this state but their bodies don't feel things the same way as when they're awake. It's a bit like being numb.

Tommy found a beer bottle in the gutter. He walked around to the driver's side, and threw it at the window, smashing it to pieces. He reached in, unlocked the car and opened the door. Tommy slid into the front seat and began tampering with some wires under the steering wheel to see if he could start it.

Just as Mike was about to hop into the passenger side he noticed a furry lump under the right front tire.

"Hey, what's this?" he said and bent down to look. "It's a teddy bear. Someone lost their bear. Aw, I'll bet some little girl is crying right now. Wah, wah." He pulled the fluffy red bear from under the car and turned to Tommy. "Hey! You know what we should do?" he asked with a stupid smile.

Tommy shook his head and continued to hotwire the car.

"Flatten it. Let's see how flat we can make it. Yeah. This'll be like our lucky bear. Every time we steal a car we'll squish the bear for luck." Mike began laughing at the thought. Tommy, however, thought it was a stupid idea and quietly rolled his eyes.

From the shadows, Lyle heard Mike's voice bouncing off the building walls and it turned his stomach. He had to do something. What could he possibly do? The Code gets a little fuzzy when it comes to helping others. If you're caught moving while trying to save a life, does that violate the Code? Lyle didn't know the answer, but he had a feeling he might find out.

As Lyle's mind raced, he heard the car engine suddenly roar as Tommy hollered, "Yeah, now that's what I'm talkin' 'bout!" He stepped on the gas pedal a couple times, revving the engine with a devious smirk. "Come on, man, get in," shouted Tommy. Mike opened the door to climb in and stopped.

"Wait a second. I wanna do somethin'." That stupid grin of his slipped out. "We gotta squish the bear." Mike started to giggle as he went to the back of the car and placed Big Red Fluffy bear behind the rear wheel.

Lyle's mind went completely blank and his body lost all feeling. Uncontrollable fury flashed through him like lightning as he bolted from the shadows. Those two were bad humans. He wasn't going to sit and watch them kill Fluffy bear.

Mike stood up and said, "Okay, man. Do it!"

Out of the corner of his eye Mike saw a fuzzy blur speeding towards him. Whatever it was, it wasn't slowing down. He instinctively stepped backwards, tripped off the curb, and fell to the ground. Lying flat on his back, Mike could feel something standing on him. He lifted his head slowly to see a teddy bear on his chest.

"You're a te —" Mike sputtered in surprise.

Lyle wasted no time and kicked him square in the nose before he could say another word. Mike's head snapped back and struck the pavement, knocking him out.

Tommy threw the car in reverse and was about to step on the gas when he saw his friend tumble, disappearing behind the car. Thinking Mike had merely tripped and fallen, Tommy jumped out of the car laughing and went to check. When he got to the back of the car he saw a furry creature standing on his unconscious friend. There was a look on Lyle's face that could only be described as pure rage. Tommy couldn't move. His mind told him one thing yet common sense said another. It appeared to be a teddy bear, but teddies don't move. So that meant — that wasn't a teddy bear. He glanced at Mike's seemingly lifeless body. For all Tommy knew, that angry looking bear-like thing had just killed his best friend. The two stared at each other in a frozen moment then Lyle reached out and grabbed Fluffy by the arm and dragged him off into the alley.

Just as Lyle and Fluffy disappeared into the dark, a neighborhood patrol car happened by. They spotted Tommy standing behind a car, next to, what looked like — a dead body in the street.

Tommy was actually glad to see the officers arrive, but what would he say? He didn't have time to think of anything. It wouldn't have mattered anyway since he wasn't that smart.

Officers John Blake and Kevin Drake approached Tommy while he stood perfectly motionless.

"Hey, Tommy. What's going on here?" asked Officer Blake as he cautiously placed his hand on the butt of his pistol.

Tommy noticed both officers stepping slowly with their hands on their weapons.

"Whoa, whoa, whoa!" he cried, realizing what they must be thinking. "I can explain! It's not what it looks like. We were attacked!"

The two officers looked at each other and allowed Tommy the opportunity to tell what happened.

"Attacked? Who attacked you?" asked Officer Drake and waited to see what lies would spew from his mouth. It was always somewhat entertaining to hear what Mike or Tommy would say in the most precarious situations.

"I don't know who attacked us," confessed Tommy. "I couldn't really see, but I think Mike is dead." He stared at his friend motionless in the street.

Officer Blake hurried over to Mike and reached for his throat, trying to find a pulse.

"He's alive," he said.

John called his name a couple of times. "Mike — hey, Mike — can you hear me?"

A moan came from the dazed teen and his eyes fluttered open. "What happened?" asked Mike, not knowing where he was. Tommy let out a relieved sigh and went to his friend to help him to the curb. Mike reached for the pain on the back of his head and felt a lump the size of a plum. His head was tucked to his knees when he noticed the feet of two other people standing next to Tommy.

Officer Drake knelt down in front of him and asked, "What happened here, Mike? Who attacked you?"

The fog was lifting in Mike's head and the scene came flooding back. He had to say something but he couldn't say what really happened. What then? What would he say? That face was burned into his mind. It was a teddy bear — he was sure of it — but everything he knows about stuffed bears tells him that it was impossible. He needed to say something fast. The officers were waiting.

"Uh, we saw this guy trying to break into this car so we told him to scram, you see?" Mike was doing the best he could to think of a reasonable story, but his head was hurting and his mind was stalling, as it usually does, and that angry furry face was still stuck in his head.

John and Kevin looked suspiciously at Mike as he told his tale when Officer Drake spoke up. "So, you're telling me that you guys were trying to stop someone from stealing this car?"

"Hey, we're just tryin' to do the right thing, officer," said Mike with a false sincerity. He winced in pain every time he rubbed his head for a more dramatic effect.

"So if we dust the car for prints — we won't find yours or Tommy's inside, right?" asked Officer Drake.

Mike hadn't thought that far ahead, but then again, he never did. His face went blank as he tried to come up with something that could possibly explain what happened.

Officer Blake spoke up first. "Mike, if you don't tell me the truth, you guys are going to jail — not to Juvie."

Even though Mike was quite familiar with juvenile jail, he didn't like the idea of being locked up with hardened criminals. It was as if the Navy had fired a shot across his bow. This was getting serious, fast. He decided to change his story.

"It was Tommy. He's the one that broke into the car. It's his fault, not mine," squealed Mike. Tommy's face turned pale as his best friend ratted him out to the cops.

Feeling they were in the safety of the shadows, Lyle placed Fluffy bear down against the wall and spoke in a gentle voice. "Hey, Fluffy, it's me. We're safe. You can wake up now."

Fluffy's eyes changed back to his normal soft powdery blue as he gazed at Lyle kneeling next to him.

"You saved me," said Fluffy bear softly. "That was the bravest thing I've ever seen. That was incredible — what you did — I mean — wow. No one's ever done anything like that for me."

CHAPTER FIFTEEN

Lyle put his paw on Fluffy's shoulder tenderly and asked, "Are you all right?"

Fluffy thought for a second and checked his body over. "Yeah, I think so. They were gonna flatten me. Did you see that? They were gonna run me over with that car. Just run me over. I was done for, and you — you saved me. You —"

Lyle was glad Fluffy bear was feeling better but they needed to go find Waldo.

"Hey, Fluffy," interjected Lyle. "We need to help Waldo now. Okay? Can you do that with me?"

A new sense of courage emerged deep inside Fluffy. Watching Lyle take down a human all by himself gave him the bravery that he'd always wanted. Apparently, it was always there, it just took Lyle to bring it out of him. Fluffy gave a confident stare and replied strongly, "Yes, I can help you. Let's go get the others."

They both got to their feet and ran deeper into the alley.

Waldo was running as fast as he could toward danger. He never gave a second thought about what he was doing but he did start thinking about what he would do when he got there.

He could hear the growling and scratching just ahead. Still, no plan formed in his mind. He couldn't think of a thing. As he got closer he could see the dog snapping his jaws with every vicious bark at the dumpster. His friends had to be in there. All they needed was a little time to escape. Waldo would give them that time.

He didn't slow down. Waldo ran by the large garbage bin and yelled, "Hey, you big Meany — why don't you try to catch me!" Waldo noticed a dark figure on top of the metal box with small glowing red eyes that seemed to follow him as he ran. *There it is again. What is that*, he wondered? But there was no stopping now.

From inside the garbage bin, Bobby Bear heard his best friend holler to the angry dog as he passed.

"Waldo?" cried Bobby Bear, sitting in the dark.

Chompers looked up in time to see a small furry white bear streak through the alley. He didn't need anything else to convince him that he was wasting his time clawing at a metal box when a perfectly good victim happens along. Chompers took off after Waldo.

Already a bit winded from trying to get the three bears out of the dumpster, Chompers wasn't able to run as fast as he normally could. Waldo had a good head start but that angry and winded dog was gaining ground.

Waldo began talking to himself as he ran. "What am I going to do when he catches up to me?" said Waldo in a rhythmic breathy voice that went with each step.

"When he catches up to me!? — He's going to catch me! — What happens then?"

Real worry set in as Waldo's two little legs were no match for Chomper's four. He had never run that fast before. Then again, he'd never run for his life before, either. Waldo could see the city lights at the end of the alley. He needed to get to the street if he were going to have any chance at all. Waldo could only hope his friends were using this opportunity to escape.

It was too quiet outside as Elvis, Bobby Bear and Dakota sat in silence not knowing what happened to Chompers.

"Did anyone else hear that?" asked Bobby Bear.

"I don't hear anything," Elvis answered.

"No!" snapped Bobby Bear, growing frustrated. "Waldo! Did anyone else hear Waldo outside? Just then — it was him."

Dakota jumped up and pushed open the large plastic lid. He climbed out and stood attentively, looking and listening into the dark. The others followed him out of the garbage can and stood next to him trying to do the same. Bobby Bear leaned forward, thinking that he could hear better if he were that much closer. The faint jingle of a collar rattled off in the distance. Chompers was running away, in a hurry.

"He's gone," said Dakota and turned to climb down off the dumpster.

"You mean, Waldo?" asked Bobby Bear worriedly.

"No! Chompers," said Dakota before crawling over the edge and dropping to the ground. "We don't know if that was Waldo."

"That *was*! I know his voice," argued Bobby Bear. "He got rid of Chompers for us so we could escape."

It was hard for Dakota to believe that anyone was that brave or that stupid to try to outrun a mean dog. "You think your friend risked his own life to save ours?" asked Dakota.

"Yes," replied Bobby Bear quickly, not needing to think twice about it. Before Elvis and Dakota could react, they saw Lyle and Fluffy bear run from the shadows.

"I'm glad to see you guys are safe," said Lyle, then looked at each bear and counted heads. "I'm not seeing Waldo. He's here, right?"

"He's not with you?" asked Dakota in a surprised voice.

"No. He ran off to help you guys. He heard the dog and just took off."

"That *was* him. I told you so," said Bobby Bear proudly. "He distracted Chompers for us so we could — wait a minute — that means he'll be . . ."

Bobby Bear realized the deadly trouble that his best friend was in and took off after him. The others shouted at Bobby Bear as he left when Dakota turned to Lyle and said, "You lead them out of here and continue on home. I'll catch Bobby Bear and we'll meet you there."

"But what about Waldo?" asked Fluffy bear with deep concern.

"I'll do the best I can," replied Dakota, then hurried off.

The piercing sound of dog nails striking the pavement close behind forced Waldo's ears back. He could feel puffs of hot breath on his fur as he ran for the end of the alley. The street was close and Waldo was literally running out of time. He found himself thinking about everything that culminated to this moment and oddly didn't have any remorse. His short life flashed before his eyes: Fluffy teaching them about being a teddy, James catching them in the refrigerator, Bobbie's laugh every time she asked about their day. Everything. It all seemed worth it. If he didn't make it, he only hoped his friends did. The alley dumped into the street and Waldo kept running with Chompers on his heels.

Across the street was a city playground with swings and slides and cement tunnels. *I can make it,* Waldo told himself. He sailed across the sidewalk and flew into the road, heading for the playground when two headlights lit up the street like the sun. It was too late. A car was on top of him as he crashed to the ground, rolling and tumbling underneath. Chompers didn't have time to stop, and ran straight into the side of the car with his head, denting the driver's door like a tin can.

The car slammed on the brakes and skidded down the dark street. Bumping and bouncing under the car, Waldo couldn't tell which way was up. Tires skidded across the pavement as the car came to a screeching halt. The large sedan came to rest almost sideways in the street, the motor still running.

Chompers lay motionless several feet away from the car.

The Pattersons were driving home from a late night dinner party when they saw a small white flash disappear under their headlights. Thinking they just ran over someone's kitty, Peter Patterson quickly applied the brakes, locking his wheels, only to have something very large crash into his door. The car slid to an abrupt halt. Peter immediately turned to his wife and asked, "Are you all right, Abby?"

She slowly opened her eyes and realized she was unharmed. "Yes — I think so," she answered quietly.

Peter pulled the lever on his door but it didn't open. Leaning with his shoulder, he pushed the door, creaking and crumpling as it opened. The seatbelt, still attached, choked him as he tried to exit the vehicle. Frustrated, Peter unfastened his belt and threw it off. He stepped out of the car, his heart pounding and his head was spinning with worry about what he would find in the road.

A large dark lump lay behind the car. His wobbly legs stepped cautiously as he approached. He saw a black dog with big white paws and a silver chain around its neck, barely breathing.

From inside the car Abby could see her husband standing next to the dark mass in the street. "What is it?" she called out.

"It's a dog," he replied.

Assuming that any dog that ran into the side of a moving car wouldn't still be alive, Abby was afraid to ask the question. "Is it . . . ?"

"No. He's still breathing."

"He was chasing a cat," said Abby. "I saw something run in front of us. Do you see a kitty anywhere?" Her eyes were wide with shock. She didn't want to get out of the car.

Peter crouched down to check under the car but didn't see anything. Waldo was lying on the other side of the rear tire, which was blocking Peter's view, making it impossible to see the dazed bear.

"I don't see it. I think it ran off," said Peter. He turned back to the injured mutt and had to act swiftly. "This guy needs attention. We've got to take him to a doctor." Peter knelt down to pick him up and read his dog tag. "Bogart" was engraved on the metal tab attached to his chain.

"It's okay, Bogie," said Peter softly. "We're going to take care of you." He gently picked up the big black dog, cradled it in his arms and walked back to the car. He finagled the rear door open and placed him carefully in the back seat.

While he was lying on the seat, Abby stared at his stomach to make sure Bogart was breathing. She had trouble catching her own breath, as her heart pounded in her chest. Peter closed the back door and jumped into the car and sped away.

Waldo was alone in the middle of the street when Bobby Bear reached the sidewalk at the end of the alley. He stayed huddled close to a shadow at the entrance peering from the dark, looking for any sign of Waldo and Chompers. He looked left and right then saw something moving in the road. Waldo sat up slowly as Bobby Bear ran to his side.

"Waldo! Are you okay?" he asked worriedly. Waldo stared at him for a moment then squinted his eyes and saw his best friend.

"Oh, hey. Yeah. I'm fine — I think," said Waldo with his head swimming and a buzzing in his ears. "What happened?"

"I was just gonna ask you the same question," said Bobby Bear. "Where's Chompers?"

"Who?"

"You know — the big dog that was chasing you? Chompers — where'd he go?"

"Oh — I don't know. I'm not real sure." Waldo took a slow look around. "He was right behind me, and then . . ." Waldo tried to recall. He began rubbing and squeezing his head as if he could somehow grab the lost memory. All it seemed to do was make the spinning worse.

"Then *what*?" asked Bobby Bear, waiting to hear how he miraculously escaped the most vicious alley dog in town.

"Then . . . Then . . ." As Waldo tried to remember, he noticed the playground on the other side of the road. He dropped his head sadly and softly uttered, "I didn't make it."

Bobby Bear was a bit confused. "What are you talking about? You *did* make it. You did it! You're alive. A little banged up — but you did it."

Bobby Bear bent over and hugged Waldo then tried to help him to his feet.

Dakota reached the sidewalk in time to find the two bears hobbling to the shelter of the shadows. He instantly rushed over and threw his arm around the other side of Waldo and helped them settle into the dark of the alley entrance. Dakota kept a sharp look out for danger.

Waldo was starting to feel better with every minute but the memory was still lost. Dakota was extremely impressed with the brave little bear that somehow saved everyone from a ravenous dog. He quietly whispered, "You'll make a great Outsider one day."

Bobby Bear, Waldo and Dakota sat silently waiting for the others to catch up. It wasn't long before they saw Lyle and the rest slinking along the wall.

Fluffy bear was the first to speak to Waldo. "You're alive!" he cried happily. They stared at each other without a word. Waldo couldn't talk anyway. There was a large lump in his throat that made it impossible to speak and even harder to breath.

Lyle was stunned and overjoyed to see Waldo alive and well. "I can't believe what you did," his voice cracked. "The way you disappeared, I thought you were done for. What happened?"

Waldo looked at Dakota and smiled. The others smiled as well, not really knowing what they were smiling about, but they were all together again, and that was enough.

Dakota spoke up, "Waldo got rid of Chompers . . . and that's all we can tell you for now. The rest is classified." Dakota slipped Waldo a wink.

Hearing Dakota say that, along with a good knock on the head, gave Waldo a different perspective to the Code; that it wasn't just about living strictly by the rules. The fact that the Council was allowing them to return home was proof of that. It was about doing what was right — even if it was wrong. The Code was there to protect teddies and humans, but sometimes — sometimes — you have to go outside the Code to do what's best for both worlds.

CHAPTER FIFTEEN

No one said another word as they continued home.

Tiger crept to the edge of the shadow at the end of the small alleyway and watched the weary band of teddies walking in the opposite direction. They were headed home. Since no one was to know about his covert mission, Tiger could not receive any word from Ballinger. Why were they going back?

The lone Kage Kuma had watched Waldo stand up to an alley full of Zombie bears and live. He saw self-sacrifice as he used himself to lure away a vicious alley dog to save his friends — and live. There was something special about this intrepid little white bear. Tiger saw it. His mission was to see that they never made it back to the Council. Tiger understood exactly what Ballinger meant by his words, but even the ruthless Kage Kuma didn't want to hurt another teddy. He had kept his word; they weren't going back to the Council. What about the stories? Tiger heard that Waldo had taken them — to protect the teddy world, perhaps. The stories were gone, as far as Tiger was concerned. Either way, his job was over. He would return to Ballinger with his report.

THE RETURN

Walking through Glenmore Park was almost like being home for Waldo. It wasn't far now. They could see the house from here. Waldo's mind flickered with thoughts of Zeek, wondering if he were still loose in the park. George never did tell him that it was just a bad dream. It was so real that Waldo wouldn't have believed him anyway.

They arrived home and stood in the yard just outside Bobbie's room.

"Okay, we're here, boys," said Dakota,

Elvis called out to George who quickly appeared with a pleasant smile from behind the window.

"Safe and sound, back home again," said Dakota. "I can't say it hasn't been fun. And Elvis, using the long coat was pure genius. You'll make a great Outsider when your time comes. Hey, Bobby Bear, Waldo, you are two *very* lucky bears. You not only have a good family, but you have great friends." He looked directly at Fluffy bear and Elvis. "And now this guy's gonna write stories about you? You know, everyone's gonna know your name." Waldo hadn't really thought about that.

Dakota smiled and said, "It's been quite an adventure. You boys be good. I'll see you around." Dakota rubbed Waldo's head and turned to leave. "You comin', Lyle?"

Not knowing when or if he'd ever see Lyle again, Waldo remembered his question about Ballinger. He wanted to ask Lyle but he needed to do it privately. Waldo quickly said, "Hey, Lyle, um . . . can I ask you something?"

Lyle paused and turned to Dakota to say, "I'll be right behind you."

Dakota gave Waldo a wink and strolled off into the night. Lyle turned to Waldo and asked, "What is it?"

Waldo took a few steps away from the others to whisper, "So, what happened to . . . you know — the bad one?"

It took Lyle only a second to get what he meant.

"Oh," he replied, glancing around quickly and lowering his voice. "Nothing — nothing happened. He's still there." Waldo was dumbstruck.

"He what?" Waldo gasped. "He's still a Council bear?"

Lyle could only nod. He then reached out and put his paw on Waldo's shoulder. "You're a good bear. We'll talk again. I have a feeling we'll be seeing a lot more of you." Lyle then waved to Fluffy bear and gave a sweet smile to Waldo before turning and walking away.

Waldo watched until long after the little figures disappeared into the dark. Elvis broke the silence. "We'd better get inside."

George opened the window and one by one, they climbed up. Bobby Bear was the first one in and couldn't believe he was home. He walked over and stood next to Bobbie's bed just to watch her sleep. Waldo climbed up and turned to help the next one in. He watched as Fluffy bear gave Elvis a hug.

That's nice, he thought.

Fluffy took a step back and looked up at Waldo standing at the window. He raised his paw and waved slowly. Waldo had no idea why Fluffy was waving until he saw him turn to leave.

"Where's he going?" Waldo mouthed silently to Elvis. Waldo looked back to Fluffy but he was gone. He wanted to cry out but couldn't. He stared at Elvis as he climbed in the window.

"Where's he . . . What's the . . . Why?" The words stumbled out of Waldo's mouth.

Elvis put his arm around him. "He had something he had to do and asked me to say goodbye for him," said Elvis sadly. "He really loves you guys but he needed to go."

"But he'll be back, right?" asked Waldo hopefully.

Elvis patted his shoulder. "I don't know. I really don't know."

They stood at the window and stared into the night for a moment until Elvis realized it was time to get to their spots before the sun came up. However, Elvis had one more thing to do.

Waldo joined Bobby Bear at his side and they both watched Bobbie resting.

"It's nice to be home," said Bobby Bear softly.

Waldo watched Elvis leave the room as Bobby Bear noticed someone was missing.

"Where's Fluffy?" he asked.

Waldo didn't really know how to answer since he didn't understand it himself.

"He left," answered Waldo. "He just — left. He told Elvis there was something he had to do."

"You mean — he's gone? Like, he's never coming back?" He stared with those big sad eyes.

"I guess so. I don't really know for sure."

Elvis came back in the room and stood behind Waldo and Bobby Bear. "You guys ought to get to the desk and get some rest; it's been a long night," said Elvis and gave a pat on the back of both of them, then climbed up into the Big People's Chair.

Bobby Bear walked over to Elvis and said as sincerely as one could, "Thank you. Thank you for saving us from the Zombie bears and bringing us home safely."

Feeling a lump in his throat, Elvis could only nod to say you're welcome. Waldo headed back to the desk with his best friend by his side.

Climbing up to their spots, they gave each other a look that didn't need any words: just a slight smile that said everything was as it should be.

The adventure was over, but Waldo knows there's another one lurking just around the corner as he drifted off to sleep.

"Goodnight, Bobby Bear."

"Goodnight, Waldo . . . Lully."

James was restless, kicking and squirming, tossing and turning. "It's getting late. Are we gonna make it in time?" He was frantically trying to make the car go faster. His passenger said nothing.

Street lights flickered past the window, faster and faster, as the sporty red Camaro traveled at a dangerous speed.

"It's all my fault, isn't it? I know it is. *Dang it!* Why did I have to do it?" James chastised himself while driving recklessly through town. A piece of the car flew past the window. Not thinking anything about it, he was only hoping to get there in time.

"Turn up here!" said the passenger. James couldn't recognize his face but he knew they were friends. Of that he was certain.

James glanced over. "*Are you sure?*"

"Yes! TURN!"

He spun the wheel hard and the car glided around the corner, as if on a rail. They raced down a dark street lined with old abandoned warehouses as far as the eye could see. Each warehouse was identical to the next.

"Where are they? How much farther?" he asked, pressing the gas pedal to the floor.

"They're in one of these buildings," said the passenger.

"What? One of these?" cried James. "They're all the same." The row of buildings continued out of sight. "Which one?"

He could only keep driving and hope he saw anything that told him when to stop. Something caught his eye in a flash. "What was that? Did you see that?" he asked his friend, who didn't answer.

"*There!* There's another one. Did you see *that?*" asked James, noticing what looked like a large ice cream cone lying in the street. More and more ice cream cones dotted the road. "It's a trail," hollered James excitedly. "They left us a trail."

He followed the cones until they came to an end.

"STOP!" yelled the passenger.

James didn't even hit the brakes when the car came to a halt in front of a small colorful building wedged in amongst the warehouses.

He recognized this building. "Sir-Licks-A-Lot?"

"There's a light on. This is it," the passenger said and jumped out of the car. They both raced to the front door and James put his hand on the doorknob.

"On three," said James. "One — two — three!" He opened the door and ran inside. Tied to two chairs, in the middle of a large empty room, sat Bobby Bear and Waldo.

"You guys okay?" he called out. They didn't answer. "Something's wrong."

James walked toward them. He wasn't getting any closer. He started to run, but the bears seemed farther still. The faster he ran the farther away they got, and soon he couldn't see them at all. James stopped and turned to his friend who was standing next to two empty chairs. A piece of paper was all that remained. Picking it up, he saw a drawing of their house circled with a heart.

"That was them — and they're gone," said James. His heart sank. "They're gone."

The face of his friend was different. He suddenly found himself standing next to George, his wife's teddy bear. To him it was the same face from the beginning. George looked at James and put his arm around his shoulders. "They're fine. Everything's fine," said George.

"You don't *know* that. They're in trouble," James insisted, feeling helpless.

"No — they're not. They're fine. They're where they're supposed to be. You're happy and they're happy," said George in a calm and soothing voice. "Let's go get a cup of coffee, a *good* cup of coffee."

James felt the weight of the world lift from his body, tension melted like snow on a warm spring day. He couldn't help but feel completely at ease when George simply smiled and said, "Breakfast is ready."

James opened his eyes to find Debra holding his favorite mug.

"Good morning. I brought you some coffee," she said. James lifted his head from the pillow and glanced about the room, seeing George in his nighttime chair. "That must have been some dream you had. You were kicking like crazy and talking in your sleep."

He sat up and somehow felt a sense of calm as he reached for the cup.

"You said, 'They're gone,' and that someone's in trouble. — Who's in trouble?" asked Debra.

"Oh, nothing. It was a silly dream," replied James, not ready to explain his concern about the bears.

Debra gave a worried look. "Are you okay?"

His eyes melted and a smile formed. "Yes. I am now . . . Hey, I want to say — I'm sorry for acting a little weird the last couple weeks."

His words could not have come at a better time. "I'm glad to hear you say that, 'cause if I have to hear one more thing from that nosy Mrs. Mallory." She grinned and let out a relieved breath. "Well, hurry up, your breakfast is on the table." She turned and went back to the kitchen.

James put both hands on his mug and pulled it closer to smell the aroma. He let out a relaxing breath and gave George a smile.

"That was you, wasn't it?" he said and took a sip of coffee. "Mm, that is good coffee . . . Thank you. I know they'll be fine. I just hope they're not scared or anything," James continued talking as George just listened. "You're like the dad of the house, aren't you? I can see that. — A handsome old bear like you. Whatever you did — it sure helped." He placed his mug on the nightstand and got out of bed. "I feel much better." James reached over and rubbed George on his head.

On his way to the kitchen, James peeked in Bobbie's room and noticed the Big People's Chair was occupied.

"Elvis," he whispered happily. "Boy, am I glad to see you. I thought you left us, too." James stepped to Bobbie's bed and thought up just the right song to wake her with a smile.

> "*Surprises come in many ways,*
> *Like rain drops falling on a sunny day.*
> *I sing this song 'cause I'm trying to say,*
> *Elvis came back and he's over there.*"

Bobbie quickly rolled over. "Daddy, that doesn't even rhyme," she said, beaming from ear to ear. She sat up and gazed at Elvis in his chair. "Where do you think he went, Daddy?"

"I don't know. Maybe he helped Bobby Bear and Waldo somehow."

Debra poked her head in the room. "Are you two going to come and get your breakfast?" Bobbie jumped out of bed, grabbed Elvis, and raced to the kitchen.

After breakfast, Bobbie went to her room to get ready for school while James remained at the kitchen table to read the morning paper, which happened to be at the front door, and have another cup of coffee. Elvis, seated in the chair next to him, was glad to be home but wanted to rest.

After collecting her books and her backpack, Bobbie went to say goodbye. "Bye, Daddy," she said, giving him a hug and a kiss then turned to Elvis and gave him a kiss on his face. "Bye, Elvis. Thanks for coming home."

"Goodbye, Pumpkin. Have a great day," said James.

Debra and Bobbie walked to the front door when James heard his daughter call out, "Daddy!"

Looking up from the paper, he answered, "Yeah?"

"Someone's here to see you!"

James thought it was somewhat early for company. He put down the paper and headed down the hall.

Bobbie was standing at the doorway to his office just smiling. This, of course, made James smile without even knowing why.

"Someone's here? Who's here?" he asked with a big grin.

Bobbie glanced back into the office and James did the same.

"What? — How? — Why?" he asked, confused and excited. Bobbie joined him as they both hurried to the desk and picked up Waldo and Bobby Bear, who were back in their original places.

Debra stood there not understanding what the fuss was about. Still thinking this was a game they'd been playing, "Hide the bears" or something, she thought they were just acting silly, as they often do.

"Bobbie, we need to get going," said Debra, touching her wrist.

Bobbie looked at her daddy and put Bobby Bear back on the desk. They didn't need to say a word. They both smiled and felt the same thing. She went to the front door then turned, giving the sweetest look. Debra opened the door to leave and noticed a package sitting just outside on the Welcome mat. Written in black ink on the box was one word, "James."

"Were you expecting something?" asked Debra. She bent down, picked it up and handed it to him.

"No," he replied. "Hmm. No address on it either. Maybe a neighbor dropped it off."

Urgency tugged at Debra as time was growing short. "We really need to get going. I'll see you later. Come on, Pumpkin," she said, then walked briskly to the car with Bobbie close behind.

James stood in the doorway and waved goodbye as they backed out into the street and drove off.

Stepping back inside, his attention turned to the unknown box with his name on it. He went to the office, sat down in his chair, and began to open the package. Waldo's eyes came to life. Bobby Bear noticed Waldo crawling to the edge of the desk and did the same. As James pulled open the box flaps, he found a piece of paper resting on a blue satchel stuffed inside the package. It read:

Please help him. Don't say anything to anyone. Tell no teddies.

James was now officially curious. He pulled the satchel out of the box and cautiously peeked. He couldn't quite make out what was inside. Bobby Bear and Waldo leaned closer to look; however, James remembered the note's request. Rocking back in his office chair, the bears stared at him strangely as to why he wouldn't share the mystery. James didn't really know why he was keeping it a secret either, but the note knew about teddies and James wasn't about to take any more chances with the bears. He pulled the mouth of the satchel open farther and saw what appeared to be a teddy arm lying on some white fluffy material. The more James dug into the satchel, the more pieces of a teddy bear he found. Bobby Bear stood up on the desk and got a good look into the bag that James was holding on his lap. He was horrified at what he saw. "WHAT IS THAT?" he cried, catching a glimpse of a severed arm.

James couldn't speak. He looked at Bobby Bear's face and didn't know what to say. Waldo immediately jumped up and tried to see inside but James had collapsed the bag closed with his hand.

"WHAT IS THAT?" repeated Bobby Bear with eyes that screamed in pain. Waldo had no idea what could have possibly gotten Bobby Bear that upset, but it sent Waldo into his own panic.

"WHAT IS THAT?" Waldo screeched, feeding off Bobby Bear's hysteria.

"I DON'T KNOW!" hollered James. "*I don't know.* I think it's a — I think it's a teddy. I'm not sure. Just calm down and let me look."

"Well — is he all right? — 'Cause that's not normal," said Bobby Bear, referring to the arm not attached to anything.

James was no longer concerned with keeping it a secret from Bobby Bear and Waldo. His focus was on why someone would send him a mangled teddy bear.

He opened the satchel again and pawed through stuffing and teddy parts until he found a head. To prevent Bobby Bear and Waldo from seeing the ravaged bear, James quickly closed the satchel and sat back in his chair, not knowing how to say what he didn't want to say.

Two bears sat anxiously on the desk watching every move that James made with sincere concern.

What do I do? The look on their faces tugged at James and he knew he should just tell the truth.

"I'm going to tell you something . . . and I want you to know that I'm going to do everything I can to help. Someone sent a teddy bear that's in pretty bad shape. I don't know who, and I don't know why — but there was a note that asked for my help and I'm *going* to help."

James was angry that someone could do such a thing to an innocent teddy bear. To everybody else a stuffed bear is just a stuffed bear, but James knows differently. Since catching Bobby Bear and Waldo in the refrigerator, everything James knew about teddy bears was wrong. They are smart, funny, loving, caring and learn everything from us, which gives them all different personalities. They are real and, unfortunately, he was one of the few that knew it.

The bears stared at the blue bag sitting in James' lap and the tension was thick with unanswered questions. Who was the teddy in the blue satchel, and why would someone do this? The first place to start was to help the unknown teddy.

Waldo got the nerve to ask, "Who is it? Is it someone we know?" His eyes never left the satchel.

"I've never seen him before," answered James.

"What do we do?" asked Bobby Bear calmly, feeling glad to have James to turn to in this terrible time.

"The note said, 'Tell no teddies,'" replied James. "So, I think who ever sent him needs this to be a secret. I say we keep this to ourselves until we find out more. Agreed?"

Bobby Bear and Waldo agreed and gave a slight smile knowing that James would do his best to help a teddy in need.

He cinched the bag closed and placed it back in the box. James placed the box under his desk and looked at the two alarmed bears.

"I'll figure out how to fix him and we'll find out who did it. We'll get to the bottom of this," said James confidently.

Bobby Bear gazed at James and said the word that Bobbie made special when she was learning to talk, "Lully."

James couldn't explain the happiness he was feeling right then when he heard that.

"I lully you too — both of you," he replied, then paused a moment to think of something else that begun nagging at him.

"*Butterflies* — that's what that is," said James, trying to describe the feeling in the pit of his stomach. "But these are good butterflies, I think."

Bobby Bear had heard him say that before.

"I want butterflies," said Bobby Bear in a most serious voice.

James picked him up and gave him a big bear hug.

"You do? What would you do with them?" James asked in a playful way.

Bobby Bear continued with all the possibilities of Butterfly uses while James could only smile.

The city had been awake for hours when one of the residents woke to the sound of the garbage men doing their job.

"I guess it's that time," he mumbled aloud to no one in particular. As the blur cleared from his eyes, he saw a small reddish object sitting against the cardboard wall.

"What's this? I know you," said the scruffy man. "Yes, I know you. It's very good to see you, old friend. I hoped I would see you again. Can you stay a while?" he asked.

That tingly feeling began fluttering in his stomach. Big Red Fluffy bear was glad to see him, too.

"Are you hungry? Let's go get some breakfast. What would you like to do today?" asked Rudder. "Never mind, I'll pick it. Let's start with some food — then I can show you around," he said with excitement. He picked up the fluffy red bear and headed out into the alley. "Then I'll introduce you to some of the guys. Watch out for Rusty though, he's a bit — unpredictable. After that, I'll take you over the bridge to the park. Do you like the park? — Of course you like the park, who doesn't like the park . . ."

The scruffy man did all the talking and Big Red Fluffy bear loved hearing the happy in his voice while they strolled deep into the city.

Down the street from James, Tiffany was getting ready for school when she noticed something different about Noname bear.

"MOMMY!" she cried out.

Her mom walked into the room and saw Tiffany holding her bear.

"He can see again," said Tiffany. "His eyes — he can see." She was almost crying as she held out her old friend.

"I told you we could fix him," her mom replied.

Tiffany looked shocked. "You mean they didn't?" she started to ask. Tiffany was hoping to hear that the other teddies helped fix him.

"No, sweetie. I had to operate. And, I must say, he was a *very* good patient," said her mom and reached out to take him from her. "Now, he's going to be a little sore, and his vision will be a little blurry for a few days, but he'll recover and be back to his old self."

Tiffany was only sad that she hadn't told her mom earlier so this never would have happened.

Kitty placed Noname comfortably on the bed. "What he needs now is rest, and *we* need to get you to school."

Tiffany stood on the front porch, while her mom locked the house, and noticed something sitting on the porch swing. "What's that?" asked Tiffany curiously.

Her mom turned to look and became quiet. She stared for a moment then started to mumble nervously. Tiffany was becoming upset at the sight of her mother's odd behavior.

"Mommy?" she asked worriedly. "Is something wrong? It only looks like a teddy."

Kitty walked slowly to the swing, staring intently on what appeared to be an old familiar face.

"It can't be. There's no way," said Kitty, who began looking around to see who could have put it there. She reached down and picked up a dark brown, tattered, teddy bear.

Her voice shook as she said, "Nicholas?"

She studied him closely when she saw the proof of who it was stuck to his nose. Her eyes filled with water and could hardly see as she pulled him close.

"Oh, my God," Kitty whispered. She thought she could feel him hug back as she buried her face into his fur and took a deep breath. The smell was the same as when she was a little girl snuggling her best friend.

Tiffany stood back as her mom rocked back and forth hugging her bear. "It's you. It's really you!"

Tiffany became sad at the sight of tears falling to the ground. It was impossible for her to tell whose tears were falling since her mommy's face was pushed into Nicholas'. "Mommy?" she asked softly.

"It's him," her mom said sweetly. "It's my bear. I thought he was gone. It's really him."

For a moment she had forgotten where she was, completely lost in the moment and time. Tiffany joined the hug as the morning sun reminded Mrs. Connors they were going to be late for school.

The obvious question was never asked: How did this happen? So many things happened lately that they couldn't explain. This was just one more.

Smiles replaced the tears and Tiffany asked her mom, "Can Nicholas ride to school with us?"

Kitty quietly nodded and walked to the car. She held her bear with both arms crossed over him, tight to her chest, the way she did when she was scared or upset. But she was neither. This time she was happy.

Tiffany climbed in and buckled up when her mom handed Nicholas to her. "Hold him tight; it makes him feel safe," she whispered. The feeling was in her stomach — one she hadn't felt since she was little when her mommy would take her and Nicholas for ice cream.

Hidden in the bushes, Dakota watched as their car pulled away. He was glad he could reunite two old friends and bring the family back together. That's what being a Rough Ride was about: helping teddies and keeping them safe. Waldo was the one that requested his return. After he heard Kitty tell the story in Tiffany's bedroom, he felt there was an injustice done. Nicholas should be returned home. Waldo had run to Elvis and asked for one last favor before he left. Elvis heard the story and agreed to help. Nicholas had been an Outsider in a nearby neighborhood for the last several years. He would often visit the house and watch Kitty from a distance. He didn't know if he would ever get to be back with his family again. So much time had passed. However, nothing is more important than family, and Nicholas was home because of a courageous little white bear.

While Kitty drove Tiffany to school, James was busy at home listening to Bobby Bear and Waldo tell their adventurous tale.

Waldo explained that the Council allowed them back.

"So, the stories are a good thing?" asked James, trying to make sense of what he heard. "Is that what you're telling me?"

Waldo nodded and smacked his lips. "You know, a glass of milk would really help me remember things," he said.

Bobby Bear's eyes lit up. "Boy, it sure would," he piped in.

Both bears were smacking their lips in a playful manner.

"Help you think better? *Please.* Don't you have that memory thing? You know, how you remember *everything?*"

Waldo rolled his eyes. "It still helps me think!"

"Okay, Okay, milk it is." James went to the kitchen. He could hear the bears giggling as he left.

"How 'bout some tastysquishes, too?" called out Waldo, feeling like a new day had come. James had no idea what that was but he poured three glasses of milk and went back to the office.

Seeing the look on their faces was the best thing he could imagine. He had to start writing all this down. While the bears started to drink, James opened the top drawer to get some paper and immediately saw something he was not expecting.

"Hey — you gave them back," he said in a thankful voice.

Bobby Bear and Waldo had no idea what he was talking about.

He pulled out the stack of papers with all of his stories and notes.

Waldo stared at him with the usual milk mustache. "Huh?"

"The stories — thanks for putting them back."

"Uh, we didn't take 'em," said Waldo, turning to his best friend. "Did you take 'em?" he asked his buddy.

Bobby Bear wiped his mouth and swallowed hard. "Nope — I didn't," he replied.

James rifled through the pages with delight when Waldo remembered Elvis leaving the room when they got back. He could only smile and take another sip of milk.

"This is fantastic!" said James. He pulled out a new piece of paper and a pen. "Okay, start at the beginning and don't leave out anything."

As Waldo started the adventure, James was trying to keep up with every detail. Page after page, he wrote as fast as he could. Waldo would only stop from time to time to take another sip of milk and give Bobby Bear a chance to tell his side of the story. There was so much to write. This was everything he needed to finish his first book.

***

Two weeks later, James finished reading his last chapter aloud and gave a satisfied sigh. "So, I know it was a little long and I may have elaborated on a few things but all in all, what do you think?" James asked two stuffed bears sitting very still and very quiet on his desk.

Then a voice from behind said, "I liked it a lot, Daddy." James turned to see Bobbie standing behind him.

"Thank you, Pumpkin. I was just wondering if they liked it."

"*Daddy* — of course they did. It's about them," she said knowingly. She walked up to the desk to pat Bobby Bear on his head. "Goodnight, Bobby Bear." Looking Waldo square in the eyes, she added, "and you be good." She scratched behind his ears then leaned over to give her daddy a big hug. "I love the stories, Daddy."

"Goodnight, Pumpkin. And thank you."

"Goodnight, Daddy." She smiled politely and skipped off to bed.

He turned to the motionless bears. "Well, I hope *you* liked it," he said out loud. They didn't say a word. He tucked the pages into his desk and closed the drawer.

"Goodnight," said James and turned out the light.

The bears remained still, in the dark. After everything that's happened he couldn't help but feel this was all a dream as he went off to bed.

The room was quiet except the footsteps fading down the hall.

"I thought it was pretty good, didn't you?" said Bobby Bear suddenly.

"He made you sound taller," replied Waldo.

"What — like I'm shorter than you?"

"Well, you're no giant."

"Yeah? Well, you're a fun bum."

"What? You're calling *me* a fun bum?"

"Yep — fun bum. That's you."

"Oh, Yeah? You're just a —"

"La la la la la la la, I can't hear you . . ."

They bickered into the night, unaware of the next adventure looming just outside.

Secret Teddy Society